High Intensity

High Intensity

Belle Reilly

QuestBooks
a Division of
RENAISSANCE ALLIANCE PUBLISHING, INC.
Nederland, Texas

ISBN 1-930928-33-5

First Printing 2002

9 8 7 6 5 4 3 2 1

Cover design by LJ Maas

Published by:

Renaissance Alliance Publishing, Inc.
PMB 238, 8691 9th Avenue
Port Arthur, Texas 77642-8025

Find us on the World Wide Web at
http://www.rapbooks.biz

Printed in the United States of America

For my sister, "Ko," who shares my passion for the heights and lets me walk among the clouds, while keeping my feet planted firmly upon this earth.

"There is no wind here and things look hopeful."
> George Leigh Mallory
> Mount Everest Camp V, 6 June, 1924

"But now that I was finally here, actually standing on the summit of Mount Everest, I just couldn't summon the energy to care."
> Jon Krakauer
> Summit of Everest, 10 May, 1996

"It's not making it to the top that's most important. It's living long enough to get down to tell about it."
> Veronique Bouchard
> Everest Base Camp, 10 April, 2001

Chapter
One

Step. Breathe.

She stopped there for a moment, perched as she was on the roof of the world, suspended above the clouds on the final ridge leading to the summit. There, on that last narrow track of snow-covered rock and ice, the earth seemed to fall away from the sky. Far below to her right was Tibet; to her left, Nepal slumbered peacefully in a blanket of mist.

Got to keep moving.

Step...breathe.

She could see the summit from here. It was so damn close, it hurt. And these last few steps were the easiest of the climb, after all. No rappelling. No working with her ice ax. But God, it was so cold. And the wind! Squinting bloodshot eyes towards the summit, she thought she caught sight of a flash of color. The Buddhist prayer flags? Yes...and though she had to have been too far away, she fancied she could hear them, snapping in the Jet Stream winds that raged over the icy fingertip of the mountain.

Step...breathe. Step...breathe.

She chanted it silently like a mantra as she pushed herself forward, shoving back against a weight that pressed down upon her like the burden of Atlas, threatening to crush her here in this cold, desolate world.

Step. Breathe. And breathe again..

It was getting harder now, harder than she'd thought it could ever be, and she stood hunched over, gasping for air through her oxygen mask like a poor fish tossed onto the bottom of a rowboat.

It was a beautiful day, really, if one thought about it. The sharp, high altitude sunlight bounced its glare cheerily off the snowy ridge, here in this rarefied air higher than many jetliners flew. And the sky...so striking that she wanted to remember it in her soul forever. It was shockingly, breathtakingly blue, like a robin's egg on a spring day. So lovely it would've brought tears to her eyes, had she the fluid left in her body to form them.

Step. Breathe. Can't stop now.

She put her head down against the wind, her ears deafened by the hum of the Jet Stream, blowing, threatening to carry her off the edge of the earth into oblivion.

Step.

She drew in another labored breath, pulling weakly on the useless oxygen, the dry air burning against the rawness of her throat. So tired. How many hours...days had it been, since she'd last had any sleep? She couldn't feel her hands, and her feet—it was as if they were someone else's that she was directing through the snow. A dangerous thought at this altitude, she knew, fully aware that this sort of lethargic complacency had cost many climbers their lives.

Step. Breathe.

No one in front of her. No one behind her. She was all on her own. And that was how she'd wanted it to be anyway, right?

Many things could cause death on a high peak. A great gust of wind at an inopportune moment. An ice screw that loosened its hold on the mountain. Lack of skill or preparation. An error in judgment. Inattentiveness...taking the mountain for granted.

But most of all, it was the cold.

It wore you out, the mind-numbing, bone chilling blasts. The kind of cold that made you just want to lie down and rest—if only for a moment. That sort of trick-of-the-mind happened to you up in the high altitudes, where the thin air could quickly turn even the best of climbers hypoxic. Where the lack of oxygen basically starved your body, causing delusions, lassitude, even death. But that wouldn't happen to her, Veronique Bouchard. For she was one of the best.

Step. Breathe.

So tired. Unable to take another step, she felt the knees that were no longer hers, buckle. And then she was down in the snow, curling up in a bulky, frostbitten ball. For just a moment she would rest here, she told herself, as she struggled to force air into her tortured lungs. Hearing nothing now but the sound of her own rasping inhales and exhales, she gazed calmly up at the brilliant blue sky. Perhaps she would breathe more easily if she removed the cumbersome oxygen mask that kept the pure, pristine natural air from her lungs?

A weary tug, and the mask was free. She smiled and closed her eyes, feeling better already, tucked into her snowy feather bed—so toasty warm, so peaceful.

She had plenty of time to make the summit, she considered, as she drifted off into a forever sleep.

All the time in the world.

No!

Veronique Bouchard jolted awake, gasping, her hands pawing at her face and one booted foot kicking the seat back in front of her.

Merde!

Eyes now opened wide and alert, she breathed in deeply of the stale airplane air, quickly gathering herself and sparing a quick glance around the interior of the plane to make sure no one had noticed her embarrassing little display. Fortunately, her fellow passengers had better things to do than take notice of the tall, quiet woman sitting in the rear of the plane. Their eyes were glued to the windows, drinking in the majestic scenery passing below as the engines of the Thai Airlines ART 72 hummed towards Kathmandu.

She stretched, feeling the pull of the strong muscles in her arms and back, and fought to slow the still-rapid firing of her heart. *Snap out of it, Ricky,* she chided herself. *It was only a dream!*

But one whose basic facts rang all too true in her spooked belly. She knew well enough how quickly a mountain could turn on you, how in the foggy world of a hypoxic cloud your brain forgot everything it ever knew about safe mountaineering, betraying your better judgment, until finally you betrayed yourself.

Sighing, she ran a hand through the long, dark hair that tumbled to her shoulders, and reached into the empty seat next to her for a folder bearing the label: *Peak Performance Adventure Company.*

Her employer.

For perhaps the thousandth time in the past three months, she wondered whether she'd gone too far and broken her own personal climbing code. What would Jean-Pierre, her former climbing partner, think of her now? Had she sold out?

No...not really.

But $30,000 was a lot of money, more than she'd ever had at one time before, all in U.S. dollars, thank you very much. It was the fee she would receive from her boss and team leader, Jim Harris, for acting as a professional guide on Peak Performance's latest expedition to Mount Everest.

Ricky flipped open the manila folder, revealing notes and color photocopies of passport photos of the Peak Performance team and guest clients who would comprise the climbing group. She and Jim Harris, along with another guide, Paul Andersen, would be responsible for getting a total of six clients, all with varying degrees of mountaineering experience, to the top of Everest.

Past performance no guarantee of future results, of course.

But she was confident.

Hell, for herself this would be her third Everest ascent, providing these clients didn't hold her back.

Looking over the profiles of the team members reminded her of what she already knew: Jim Harris and Paul Andersen were experienced high altitude climbers. If they hadn't been, she wouldn't have signed on with Peak Performance Adventure Company in the first place, no matter how much money they offered her. Jim Harris, a big bear of a man with movie-star cheekbones, had summitted Everest once before, two years earlier, his first success after an attempt the year prior. And though fellow guide, Paul Andersen, hadn't yet reached the top of the world's biggest mountain, the tall, fair-haired man from Minnesota knew his way around quite a few 8000-meter peaks.

As for the clients, that was another story. Skeptically, she began to review the notes.

Kevin MacBride and Phil Christy were a couple of thirty-something, rock-hound climbing buddies from Boulder, Colorado. Much of their experience had been accumulated in just the past three or four years or so, mostly in the US and Europe. While they were clearly new to the sport, they'd built up their

resumes rapidly, and both had climbed the 7000-meter Aconcagua in Argentina, the year before. As long as their gung-ho
testosterone levels remained in check, they would probably make
out okay.

On the next page, two smiling faces grinned up at her—
Mike and Patsy Donaldson, a husband and wife duo from Dallas,
Texas. Both were 42, and though they'd been climbing for over
20 years, Mike had clearly undertaken the more challenging
climbs, although nothing on the order of Everest. They both
would bear watching.

Lou Silvers, an attorney from Los Angeles, looked to be in
excellent shape for a 45 year old, and he had the climbing credentials to match his compact, well-toned physical appearance,
including an ascent of the 8000-meter-plus Broad Peak, in Pakistan. But that had been over ten years ago. She would have to
keep an eye on him to make sure he didn't overdo it, pushing
himself beyond his limits. Whether you were young or old,
Everest treated you all the same. But how you responded to it,
depending on your age and expertise, was another matter
entirely.

And then there was Allison Peabody. Some hoity-toity New
York stockbroker by way of Boston, Massachusetts. By far, she
had the least climbing experience of any in the group. Ricky's
gaze fixed on the wide-eyed young blonde staring out of the page
at her. *Great. She looks like some perky little thing out of* The
Mickey Mouse Club. At age 27, Allison Peabody looked to be in
excellent physical shape, at least. That would help. As long as
you were in top condition, with some high altitude experience—
and Peabody had at least climbed the 6000-meter Mount McKinley—then Peak Performance would take you on.

As long as you paid your expedition fees, of course.

Because, after all, this sort of climbing was a business.
When, down to her last $200, Ricky Bouchard had first met with
the burly Jim Harris in Peak Performance's Denver offices, he'd
made that point eminently clear to her. At a cost of over
$100,000 for Peak Performance's Nepal climbing permit alone,
there was no room for fooling around, for free climbing off on
her own. If she took the job, she'd have to live by the rule: the
client is king.

Slipping the folder back into her travel bag, she marveled at
the idea that the clients along on this expedition had paid
$70,000 each—not including airfare and personal equipment—

for the privilege of risking their lives on the world's highest peak.

Mount Everest.

Or Chomolungma, as the Tibetans called it: Mother Goddess of the Earth.

The aircraft rattled closer towards its destination, and Ricky noticed that the level of excitement towards the front of the cabin had increased. The people were craning their necks, searching for that first glimpse of Everest. No doubt, some of her clients were among the passengers in the half-filled 60-seater. In fact, she was certain she'd spotted the Donaldson couple, and perhaps the two men sitting across from them were Kevin MacBride and Phil Christy. But she hadn't bothered to make herself known to them. She wasn't on the clock yet. And there would be time for that soon enough over the next two months, when she'd have to formally tolerate their company. Then, she would be a professional and do her job. No more, no less.

"Hey! I think I can see Everest!"

That had to be Patsy Donaldson's squeal of delight. Immediately, the attention of the entire plane shifted towards the port side of the cabin.

Ricky glanced out her window, spying the peak that was eliciting the "oohs" and "ahs" from the passengers. Great. These idiots couldn't even tell Everest from what was obviously Annapurna, sitting regally in the snowy distance. Everest was out there, sure enough, but on this particular afternoon it was obscured by swirling clouds and mist.

Ah, hell! The mountaineer swallowed hard, doing her best to ignore the sudden tightness in her chest. *What am I doing here?* After all she had been through, after all she had witnessed, hadn't she learned her lesson? *No,* she admitted, knowing after all that the lure of a mountain, the indescribable rush she experienced each time she challenged the forces of nature—and herself—and won, was an elixir she was addicted to. She could never give that up, never. It defined her. Made her what she was, and who she hoped to be.

So she would take the money Jim Harris offered her, and run. That was all there was to it. Do the job, get it over with, and then her fee would give her the freedom to do her own brand of climbing for at least the next six months—maybe a year, if she parceled it out right.

Fair enough.

And maybe she would eventually get around to writing that article for *Intrepid Magazine* that its chief editor, her friend Ty Halsey, had been begging her to do. It would pay a few more bills.

"Christ Ricky, you're one of the best high-altitude climbers Canada has ever produced. Hell—one of the best in the world, as a matter of fact! No other woman has climbed more 8000-meter peaks than you. But dammit, you're also one of the world's best-kept secrets! How the hell do you expect to get the big corporate sponsorship and endorsement deals without getting yourself a little publicity?"

Publicity.

Attention.

Scrutiny.

Not for her. No way. She simply wanted to be left alone. Was that too much to ask for?

Veronique Bouchard, world-class mountaineer-turned-babysitter, groaned and leaned back in her cramped seat. She closed her eyes, blotting out the Himalayan range from her sight, but the image stubbornly burned its way into her mind's eye, insistently holding her captive in its gleaming white spotlight.

❀♦❀♦❀♦❀

Kathmandu has stood as the exotic gateway from the western world to Everest for over the past 70 years. A generation earlier, would-be climbers had had to slog every bit of the way to Everest from Kathmandu on foot, horse, or horrid-smelling yak train. Now, transportation to the base of Everest was slightly more civilized, though not by much. In two day's time, an old Russian-made Mi-17 helicopter would transport the expedition to Lukla, a village at the foot of the Himalayas in the Khumbu region. From there, they would be begin a leisurely trek up the Namche Trail, each at their own daily pace, eventually arriving at the foot of the Khumbu Icefall.

And Base Camp.

But for the next two days, "home" would be Kathmandu. Jim Harris had booked the Peak Performance Adventure Company into the old Hotel Garuda, located in the heart of Kathmandu's bustling Thamel tourist district. The Garuda had long been a traditional jumping off point for both the casual trekker exploring the Himalayan region and the serious mountaineer tackling Everest. Faded, tattered photos and newer, overexposed Polaroids of climbers past and present adorned its aged walls, and many of the snapshots bore autographs.

A part of Veronique Bouchard was dismayed at the changes she'd seen in Kathmandu in just the past ten years or so, all in the name of "progress." Here, the tourist dollar, American dollars in particular, pumped the economy full of cheap knock-offs of anything Everest-related. Miniatures of the mountain were everywhere, as well as woodcarvings, prayer flags, even the occasional "medicinal" cigarette to soothe one's jangled nerves. Still, Nepal was such a poor country, Ricky could hardly begrudge the one chance that any of the locals had to make a better living for themselves in the name of tourism.

Back at the airport, when it had become apparent that they were all trying to get to the same place, she'd grudgingly introduced herself to the Donaldsons and to Kevin MacBride and Phil Christy. After a hair-raising cab ride through a chaotic warren of streets to the Garuda, she had withheld a grin when she'd heard Patsy Donaldson expressing her dismay over the "deplorable" condition of the old hotel. A five star accommodation, it was not. But it would be the last hot shower Patsy would be likely to get for weeks, and the mountaineer bit her tongue to keep from telling her so.

Quickly, she'd separated herself from the group and retreated to the small but clean room she'd been assigned. Dimly lit, it smelled of freshly laundered cotton sheets and old musty wood. The mountaineer tossed her travel bag onto the bed and strode over to the window, pushing open the pine shutters. She was immediately hit once again by the blast of heat rising up from the dirty streets; by the smells of a city she felt she barely knew anymore. She gazed out over the crazy quilt of souvenir shops, teahouses and bars, to the snow-capped range beyond.

Her goal.

She could feel the excitement hit her blood, and her pulse quickened as that old familiar sense of the chase kicked in. It would be different this time, guiding an expedition-for-profit with strangers, instead of climbing a mountain alone or with Jean-Pierre simply for the sheer, unadulterated joy of it.

Well.

She closed the window against the sights and sounds of the boisterous city, resolving to make the best of it. To find a place somewhere between those two extremes, where she could make a peace of sorts between herself and the mountain.

Glancing at her watch, she sighed. She was due to meet Jim Harris and Paul Andersen in half an hour. A quick shower and a change into a pair of khaki colored shorts and a T-shirt later, the tall woman took the stairs down three flights to the hotel bar. Stepping into the darkened room, it was easy to locate Jim Harris. Not only because of his large size—the man was a good 6'3 and 220 pounds—but also because of his rumbling belly-laugh. The man clearly lived life to the fullest, enjoying every minute of it. Ricky had been impressed with him: an expert alpinist, who clearly possessed more business acumen than she'd ever had the desire to acquire. His mission was simple: to open the high peaks of the world to climbers who might never have an opportunity to conquer them otherwise—whether due to logistics or technical climbing skills—and to make money doing it. So far, in this, his sixth mounted expedition to an 8000-meter peak and his third to Everest, he'd been successful.

Hesitantly, Ricky made her way towards the table where Harris sat along with the sandy haired Paul Andersen. Not quite as tall as Harris, or as big, Andersen had the classic lean, broad-shouldered physique of a traditional climber. The two men sat side-by-side, nursing beers, while being loudly entertained by the Donaldsons.

"Well, you should have seen Patsy, trying to load all her climbing gear into that ricksha!" Donaldson laughed, slapping a meaty hand down on the coarse table. "Why, I thought the poor driver was going to keel over on the spot!"

"Oh, you know me, Mike!" Patsy blushed, giggling, and rested a heavily jeweled hand on her husband's arm. "I wanted to go native!"

"Wait until we get up the trail a little bit." Harris took a healthy slurp of his beer. "There'll be plenty of time for that!"

"So I hear," Patsy replied, and then she winked, whispering, "I brought the toilet paper."

The table erupted into laughter.

Catching the lanky mountaineer's eye, Harris called, "Hey, Ricky, over here!" He rose to his feet. "Have a seat. You know Paul. And I believe you've already met the Donaldsons?"

"Yes," she said, nodding. "Mr. Donaldson. Mrs. Donaldson." There was just the faintest trace of a French accent in her alto tones.

"Oh, pooh-pooh on that! We're Mike and Patsy, please! That's what all our friends call us!" Patsy Donaldson smiled sweetly, her rounded, pale face framed by a mop of red curls.

"Sure...Mike...Patsy." Ricky smiled painfully, knowing that in the lower-tax-bracket circles in which she traveled, the Donaldsons would be the last type of people that she might ever encounter, much less call "friends."

"Well, if you folks don't mind," Jim Harris cleared his throat, "Ricky, Paul and I have a little business to take care of. We'll catch up to you later, all right?"

"Terrific." Mike Donaldson grinned, wrapping an arm around his wife who stood at least two heads shorter than he. "Let's go look at more of those pictures, shall we, dear?"

"And maybe some shopping, too?"

Mike ushered Patsy towards the exit. "Whatever your little heart desires, cupcake!"

"Nice people," Jim commented, looking after them as Ricky took her seat. Prudently, she decided to withhold her opinion on that matter for the time being.

"So, Mademoiselle," Jim motioned for a beer for Ricky, "how was your trip?"

"Fine," she smiled faintly. "All my gear's been stowed and is ready to go."

"Super. We're all just about here. Besides the Donald-sons—"

"Those two guys arrived from Colorado," Paul interrupted, a flat Midwestern twang in his voice. "You know—the ones who have some pretty good climbing experience."

"Yeah." Ricky took a sip of the bitter-tasting beer, welcoming its coolness against her throat. "They were on my plane."

"Those guys are hard-core," Jim said, flipping open a Peak Performance folder similar to the one Ricky had been issued.

"But not a lot of total years climbing," Ricky said evenly.

"Well, as good as they appear to be," Harris shuffled his papers, "they won't be your concern anyway. I'll be climbing with them."

Ricky remained silent. Although she had more high altitude experience than both Jim Harris and Paul Andersen combined, she knew she was along on this expedition as a junior guide only. Jim was team leader, and Paul, due to his prior experience guiding clients and working with Peak Performance, would be senior guide. Paul seemed nice enough, but it grated on Ricky a bit, knowing she could eat his mountaineering boots for breakfast. As it was, the junior guide nearly always ended up climbing with the least experienced members of the team. Which in this case meant the Donaldsons or, worse, that Allison Peepers...Peabody...whatever.

Ugh.

"Regardless of anybody's experience level, yourself included, Ricky," Harris turned his deep brown eyes to her, "I want to take it nice and slow going up the Namche Trail. Between Lukla and Base Camp, I've scheduled in a week for the trek. That should give everyone plenty of time to start the acclimatization process. It's important that we do everything we can to make sure our clients adapt to the altitude as comfortably as possible."

Ricky silently nodded, and took another sip of her beer. Harris was right. Altitude sickness was potentially the biggest problem for newcomers to the mountain. A pounding headache, lightheadedness, nausea, these were the warning signs. Some people acclimatized quickly, some only after a few minor bouts of sickness, and some never adapted at all and had to leave the mountain before a more serious edema condition took hold. Ricky had seen it happen before, to everyone from novice climbers to experts.

She had never had a problem with altitude herself. Her body adapted amazingly well in an environment where there was a paucity of air; she was renowned in climbing circles for her ability to function without bottled oxygen in elevations of 25,000 feet or more, a frigid, Godless place otherwise known as the "death zone."

In that environment, atmospheric oxygen is only 1/3 of that found at sea level. The body begins to starve itself, to shut down, and hypoxia sets in. But Ricky's previous three summits of Everest had been without the assistance of bottled gas, and she would've had every intention of doing the same thing this time, were it not for the fact that Harris insisted his guides use supplemental oxygen on the final ascent. This, he believed, would help keep Paul and Ricky in better overall physical condition so they could readily help the clients if they ran into trouble.

"Sandy Ortiz is already at base camp with half the Sherpa team," Harris continued, "and things are setting up nicely."

Sandra Ortiz, a physician friend of Harris' from Tacoma,

Washington, was a weekend climber who had been recruited to serve as the Peak Performance team's Base Camp manager and physician.

"And boy, did we get a good location!" Harris' eyes twinkled.

"Yeah, I've heard how competitive it can be for the prime camping spots," Paul said, shaking his head. "There's what—six or seven other teams heading up?"

"At least," Harris answered him. "But don't worry. I've already got our Sherpas staking out the best campsites at the higher elevations, too. We've got it made!" He pushed back in his chair, looking quite satisfied with himself.

"I hate crowds," Ricky mumbled, her mind flashing to Everest bottlenecks of years past. Suddenly uncomfortable, her blue eyes flickered around the bar as though the walls were closing in.

"Anyway..." Harris consulted his papers again, "Lou Silvers is arriving later tonight."

"I'll swing by the airport and pick him up," Paul volunteered, rubbing a hand on the wispy, fair beard that was already sprouting on his chin.

"And Ricky," Jim Harris kept his eyes on his paperwork, "Allison Peabody lands tomorrow at 10 a.m. I faxed her that you'd be meeting her at the airport."

A moment's pause.

"Fine," Ricky replied, swallowing the initial flair of anger she felt. This was her boss talking. From here on in, she was on the job.

Let the baby-sitting begin.

Chapter
Two

Where was a nice hot towel when you needed one? Or maybe a cherry-topped ice cream sundae? Fat luck getting her hands on either of those first class luxuries on this flight. Allison Peabody rubbed at her dry, burning eyes. She was hungry, tired, and cranky, in that order. The plane would be on the ground in Kathmandu within the next 20 minutes, thank God. Or at least, that's what she'd *thought* the captain had announced. His English had left much to be desired.

It had been one hell of a series of flights to Kathmandu: from New York through Los Angeles, and then on to Hong Kong and Bangkok. Now, all she wanted to do was get to the hotel and relax a bit. She hadn't relished the thought of sorting her way through customs and the streets of a third world capital to find the damned place, and so for $70,000 she'd insisted that Jim Harris have one of his staff meet her at the airport.

Some guy, a Ricky Bouchard, was supposed to do just that. He was one of the guides, or so she'd been told. Well, she hoped he had a good strong pair of arms and shoulders, because she sure had a lot of baggage. It had been difficult, trying to figure out what to pack, even though Peak Performance had sent her suggested equipment checklists. After all, this was the biggest climb of her entire life, and it was best to be prepared, right?

It was hard to believe that she was actually here, after all those months of planning. The faxes, the phone calls, the working out, the packing. And then, finally, those last few frazzled days at the office before she was able to get away. Fine time for the financial services sector to go bullish, just as she had to take off. It had taken every ounce of inner strength she'd had, to leave her laptop behind. Besides, she understood that there would be a satellite phone, fax and Internet connection at Base Camp, anyway. The usage fee would certainly not be a problem. She could check in with Marcie back at the firm and see how the indices were doing, or log on to the JKJ portfolio database...

God, Allie! Knock it off! You're on vacation, for heaven's sake!

Some vacation. Climbing Mount Everest. Staring out at the snow-capped Himalayan range, Allison could not prevent a smile from slowly creeping across her face at the memory of how her boss had reacted.

"What the hell, Allie! You're telling me I've got to do without the second highest revenue producing personal securities broker in JKJ for two whole months? And I thought it was bad enough that you needed a month last year!"

"Everest is different than McKinley, John," she replied, grinning. *"And I promise you, when I get back, I'll make it to number one, on at least twice the volume of your number two. I guarantee it."*

John Redshaw, Executive Vice President of Sales at Johnson-Kitteridge-Johnson, one of Wall Street's hottest brokerage firms, would not go down without a fight. Allison Peabody was one of his best. It was hard to let her go. But he knew he would have to, if he wanted to keep her. Another firm would snap her up in a New York minute, if she became disgruntled. "Well...if this is the last of your crazy adventures."

"C'mon, John." Allison handed him a pen to sign her leave request. *"National Geographic 101. Everest is the highest. That'll be it for me. So think about it. Number one in sales. At twice the volume. When have you ever known me to tank on a deal?"*

The answer was—never. John Redshaw had signed, and here she was, 30,000 feet over Nepal. Knowing that in just a few weeks time, she would be taking a stab at getting to the top of something only a few hundred feet short of that mark.

But would even that accomplishment be enough?

All her life, Allison Peabody had played by the rules. The

only daughter of the right family. Had the right friends. Went to the right schools, right up through getting her Harvard MBA. From there she had proceeded to the right job in the right city, and spent her weekends dodging advances from the right boyfriend that her Boston Brahmin parents were convinced would make the perfect husband. By whom she would bear the perfect children, of course. God...it was all so damned perfect and right, that she felt she might choke on it.

Her only release, her escape, more like it, was in taking on new and difficult challenges. Ones that in turn thrilled her and scared her half to death, and were sure to mortify her parents. Part of that was accomplished through her work. In just a few short years, she'd risen to the top of her profession, defying her parents' assumption that she would simply "put in her time" at JKJ, and not get her pretty little hands too dirty.

Another part, a much larger part, was accomplished by how she played. From bungee jumping to parachuting. From white water rafting, to swimming with the sharks in the Caribbean. Extreme sports. Adventure tourism. She eagerly chased after whatever was the thrill seeker's flavor of the month. As long as it stirred that part of her soul that was slowly dying, and dismayed her parents in the bargain, then that activity was for her.

She was never one to stay involved in any one sport for too long, for that would be too painful. She would learn it, do it, and then move on. In that way, she avoided becoming deeply connected with another thing or a person, and so was able to deny to herself the knowledge that there were possibilities of another life out there to be lived, one more intensely satisfying than the shallow life she'd allowed to be fashioned for her. Otherwise, the truth of it simply hurt too much.

In fact, this mountaineering kick was the longest she'd ever stayed focused on any one of them; "Allie's little hobbies," as her mother referred to her hair-raising activities. She'd caught the climbing bug a couple of years ago when she'd recalled with some fondness her post-grad photo safari tour through Africa. The best part of the whole darned thing for her hadn't been the magnificent culture, or the joy of seeing wild animals in their own native habitat instead of behind a steel cage.

No, for her, it had been the climb up Mount Kilimanjaro.

The roof of Africa, rising up over 19,000 feet above the plains of Tanzania.

She'd given her parents a snapshot of herself standing at the top—on Uhuru Peak. She remembered how she'd felt when the guide had taken her picture, like she'd finally found a place where she belonged. And the expression on her face in that photo...so connected, so alive...was one that she rarely recalled seeing on herself any time she looked in a mirror. Her parents had smiled, told her how adorable she looked, and promptly filed it away in a drawer. But Allison had never forgotten how good she'd felt, making that summit, when other, more experience trekkers had been forced to turn back on the final push in the pre-dawn cold.

In her orderly, perfect little life, she desperately wanted that feeling back. And so, she'd hit the gym. Biking and running. The Stairmaster and the rock climbing wall. Then she'd taken it outside, joined a club, and began to take on increasingly difficult climbs, including those giving her high altitude and snow experience. She pushed herself, summitting Mount Rainier after just a year's time training. Then, last year, Mount McKinley.

If she were brutally honest with herself, she supposed that she'd known all along where she was going with this. Why do it at all, if you didn't want to go all the way? It was a buddy in her climbing club who had told her about the Peak Performance Adventure Company.

And in a twinkling, the far-away vision she'd always harbored had suddenly appeared in close-up. The Peak Performance brochure had listed the recommended mountaineering credentials for climbing Everest, and she was surprised to see that she more than met them. In a phone conversation with Jim Harris, he'd told her that being in top shape and having overnight, ice-climbing experience like she'd had with McKinley, was all she needed. Having a positive, "take the mountain" attitude was just as important as any technical climbing resume. If she promised to go for it, then he and his world-class climbing guides would do their best to get her to the top.

Allison Peabody couldn't sign on the dotted line fast enough. She blurred through the "waiver of responsibility" and "recommended independent emergency evacuation procedures" forms, and express-mailed the contracts and her check back to Peak Performance.

Her parents had been flummoxed.

Her boyfriend, Lionel Kitteridge—God, did he *have* to be the grandson of one of JKJ's founders?—had been outraged. Forbidden it. And then, he had laughed at her. Told her she was crazy, that she'd never be able to do it.

For one brief, terrifying moment, she'd feared he was right.

Then, she'd recovered. Told him what he could do with himself, and then walked out. So maybe she wasn't the best technical climber in the world—so what? She was strong, and she wanted this for herself. Now, more than ever. She would do it. She would show them. And then she would see what was what.

Now...if only that useless flight attendant could get her a champagne and orange juice!

❊ ✦ ❊ ✦ ❊ ✦ ❊

Veronique Bouchard stood inside the building that Kathmandu generously called its International Terminal, and watched as a line of tired but exuberant passengers walked from the airplane, across the tarmac, and through customs. Shifting her weight from one foot to the other, she lifted her sunglasses and took one last look at the passport photo in her folder. What if she missed her target in the crowd of trekkers and travelers streaming past, blowing her first Peak Performance assignment?

She closed the folder and turned her eye once again towards the arriving passengers. Students in jeans and T-shirts. Climbers and hikers in boots and trail gear. Leather and denim. Khaki and...silk?

Ricky groaned inwardly. This had to be the one and only Miss Peabody. Short, feathered blonde hair and green eyes, just like the recent passport photo indicated. Plus, a knee-length, flowered cotton skirt, a crème colored sleeveless silk blouse, and matching chunk-heeled sandals. And she was hauling two carry-on bags whose weight threatened to bend her in two.

Ricky stepped forward. "Miss Peabody?"

"Why...uh, yes."

"I'm from Peak Performance. Welcome to Nepal." She thrust out her hand, feeling awkward already at this "meeting and greeting" thing.

Allison's two bags *thunked* to the ground. "Pleased to meet you—"

"Veronique Bouchard."

"Ricky?" Allison said, looking at her strangely.

"Yes, many people call me that."

"I thought...well..." Allison raked a hand through her hair.

"Never mind. I've got these two bags, plus a bunch more coming through over here." She snapped her fingers towards where passengers were already crowding around huge carts full of luggage and climbing gear. "I'm beat, I'm starving, and I could use a shower. Let's go."

The stockbroker turned on her heel and headed towards the carts.

Simmering, Ricky effortlessly picked up the two carry-ons, and flagged down a porter. It took some time for Allison to point out all her bags, and the porter's cart was groaning under the weight of them all when they finally edged their way out of the milling crowd and headed towards the exit.

Just like I thought—over-packed and under-experienced, Ricky thought, coming to the porter's aid as a boot bag tumbled from the top of the luggage mound.

"The Garuda hotel, right?" Allison inquired, watching the next taxi move up in line.

"Yeah," Ricky grunted, feeling the perspiration break out on her back as she began to help the porter unload.

"Well, listen. I've got to lie down before I fall down. Take care of getting all my gear stowed for me, would you?" Allison grabbed one of her carry-on bags and stepped into the cab. "And be a sweetheart and give him a tip for me." She motioned towards the porter. "Whatever you think is best, okay? Catch you later!"

And with that, the taxi took off in a cloud of dust.

The next taxi moved up, and the confused porter looked up questioningly at the mountaineer. "You go now, me'm?"

"Yes, *fine.* I go now," she forced out between clenched teeth. *"Be a sweetheart,"* she mimicked under her breath. *Lady,* she straightened to her full height and looked after the departing taxi, *you have no idea what I think is best. Not yet.* She grinned evilly. *But you will.*

Chapter
Three

After two chaotic days in Kathmandu finalizing last-minute preparations, the Peak Performance expedition team climbed aboard an aged, severely overloaded plane for the short, 100-mile hop to Lukla. Standing at the foot of the Himalayas at an elevation of 9,200 feet, the little village and airstrip served as the informal entrance to Nepal's Sagarmatha National Park. International trekkers used Lukla as a starting point for their sojourns through the lower regions of the Himalayas, and serious climbers choosing Everest's Southern Route started the upward push from the village towards the higher elevations, and Base Camp.

The expedition members had been kept too busy in Kathmandu to spend much time bonding, but Jim Harris wanted to make sure that on this, their last night before setting out on the trek to Base Camp, the team had a full understanding of what lay in store. And a boisterous evening in the tiny hotel bar in Lukla, drinking Nepalese beer and telling tales, would do wonders for the group in terms of getting to know one another, he decided.

Ricky Bouchard stood tall and dark in the entrance to the bar, her blue eyes piercing the room like a beacon. Many of the climbers had already begun assembling, including the Donaldsons and Allison Peabody. She'd studiously avoided any encounter with the stockbroker since the airport episode, worry-

ing that she might say something that would get herself fired
before the expedition had even begun.

The spoiled brat. Treating her as if she were a servant girl!

Now, gazing at the long wooden table where the team was
gathering, she knew there was no avoiding her. She braced herself, steeling her mind and her attitude against the mindless
small talk that she knew would follow, content in the knowledge
that soon the time for all this forced socialization would be past.
Soon, she would be on the mountain. Where the ice-covered
rocks and snowy peaks didn't talk back.

Barely noticed, she quietly slid into a seat next to Lou Silvers.

"Nice to meet you at last, Ricky," the attorney said, taking
up the mountaineer's hand in a firm greeting. "I want you to
know," his pale eyes sparkled, "that when I found out you were
going to be one of the guides on this trip, it was then I decided I
had to be here."

"Really?" Ricky's eyes widened in surprise, taken aback as
she was by the attorney's words.

"Yeah," he softly replied. "I really respect the work you've
done. And obviously Jim must too, or he wouldn't have asked
you to come on board." He hesitated for a moment, before leaning his compact, gymnast's body forward. "I used to consider
myself quite the climber, until work got in the way these past
few years." He grinned wryly. "Making partner takes time. You
know how it is."

"Sure," Ricky said agreeably, although she really had no
idea at all what he meant, and didn't much care to. Now, if the
topic were the degree of difficulty in climbing the Eiger in the
sharp freeze that follows a dry, windy *foehnsturm,* well, then
they could talk.

"But listen to me, talking about work. Like any of that crap
matters here, right? Anyway," he blushed slightly before he continued, "any tips you can offer me, I sure would appreciate it. I
really want to get to the top, you know. It's been a dream of
mine for so long. And boy, I can't wait to see the looks on my
partners' faces when I tell 'em. The couch potatoes!"

He chuckled, and Ricky could not help but join in. She
liked this older man with his silver-threaded dark hair, and easy,
down-to-earth manner. "You've got some solid, high-altitude
experience on difficult terrain," she told him, recalling the notes
on his Broad Peak climb. "Just stay within yourself, listen to

your body, and you'll do fine."

"Thanks, Ricky." His voice was low, earnest. "I appreciate your confidence in me."

My confidence in him? Well, well. It was something that Ricky hadn't thought about to that point, the idea that people might actually be looking to her for advice or inspiration. Oh, sure, she would be there to help them from a climbing perspective, that was her job. But otherwise...what the hell. All she knew how to be was herself. Let people take from that what they wanted to.

They always had.

Quickly, the small bar filled with the rest of the team, and as the beer flowed and laughter grew more raucous, Ricky found herself quietly withdrawing into the background, content to nurse a single beer while listening and observing. The time would come soon enough when she'd be able to look at all the clients in action, gauging their "hands-on" skill levels and how well they handled themselves at altitude, under pressure. In the meantime, she silently bore witness to the excessive self-disclosure that she'd seen occur time and time again in the past, when groups of people were thrown suddenly together and felt the need to, too quickly, share the most intimate details of their lives with complete strangers. All in the name of attention and entertainment.

Allison Peabody had already volunteered to handle Mike and Patsy Donaldson's personal investment portfolio, once she returned to New York. And Ricky decided she'd heard quite enough about Phil Christy's amateur day-trading exploits, not to mention Kevin MacBride's boy-hero days playing football at the University of Colorado. Additionally, it was apparent to her that the two buddies had taken quite the interest in the young blonde stockbroker, and Allison reveled in their attention, at times being flirtatious, and then alternately playing the shy naif.

It turned out that MacBride and Christy were both project engineers for a national construction firm based in Boulder. The two men had taken up an interest in climbing just four years ago, but were quick to point out to the other team members how rapidly they'd advanced in terms of their difficulty rating. It turned out that they'd done their best in recent years to get themselves posted on jobs that sent them to prime climbing locales in the US and Canada. The Rockies. The Cascades. And then there was their big summit of Aconcagua the year before.

The two men were brash, bold, and willing to take chances, that was obvious, with MacBride being the more outspoken leader of the two. They were out to impress themselves with their own prowess, as much as the friends they kept back home, confirming Ricky's initial assessment that the two men would have to be watched to prevent them from pushing too far, too fast, and getting into trouble.

The liquor flowed and spirits were high as the night wore on, and Ricky Bouchard felt more out of place than ever. Just when she thought she couldn't bear it any more, Jim Harris pushed his beer away and held up a silencing hand.

"Before we head out tomorrow, I'd like to go over the game plan one last time with you good people."

"Make it to the top!" Kevin MacBride proclaimed, raising his glass.

"And get back down," his buddy Phil added, drawing laughter from the group.

"Well, that's not far from the truth." In the darkened lamplight of the bar, Jim Harris' smile flashed white against his tan skin. "It is the Peak Performance Adventure Company's policy that getting up the mountain is voluntary." He swept his eyes over the climbers. "But getting down is mandatory. And we all need to support each other to make sure that happens."

"What are our chances, Jim?" Lou Silvers asked quietly. "Really."

Harris rubbed a beefy hand against the back of his neck. "If the weather holds, and if everyone handles the altitude well, I don't see why, on summit day, we can't all make it."

Ricky's brow creased as she listened to Jim's claim, concerned at his confident statement. So many things could and did go wrong up there. There was no way to predict from one minute to the next what would happen. An avalanche in the Icefall. An unexpected injury. A sudden storm blowing in from Tibet. But Jim's words appeared to be just the thing that the clients wanted...needed to hear. Their faces lit up.

"We're counting on it," Mike Donaldson grinned. "Especially with you guys...and gal," he acknowledged Ricky with a nod, "showing us the way." Like many of the men in the group, he'd already started the beginnings of a beard, wanting to look the part of a mountain man. And it did make sense, after all. Everest was no place to take time for a shave in the morning. "I know Jim's summitted before," he continued, his eyes resting on

Paul Andersen, "but have you?"

Paul shook his sandy haired head "no." "Not yet. However I'm planning on it," he said, his blue eyes shining, "real soon. But I've left my lucky silver dollar on the top of K2," he told them, naming the second-highest peak in the world.

"How about you, Ricky dear?" Patsy Donaldson, with just a hint of condescension in her voice, turned her attention to the silent mountaineer. "Will this be your first time, too?"

Ricky looked startled, like a deer caught in the headlights. "Uh...actually, it'll be my third time," she replied, acutely aware of the sudden quiet that had fallen over the table. "My second time on this route. My first time to the summit was by way of the North Col."

The treacherous North Face route to Everest's summit was deathly steep and rocky, and hadn't been climbed at all until a group of wild Australians did the deed in 1984. For Ricky Bouchard's first Everest ascent to have been by way of the Northern route, was nothing short of amazing.

"Yeah," Jim jumped into the awkward silence, "Ricky knows the neighborhood, that's for sure. Anyway," he continued, "here's the plan we'll be following for the next few weeks." He placed his Peak Performance folder on the table, but left it unopened. This part, the climber knew by heart.

"We'll all leave here tomorrow morning for the trek to Base Camp. Each of you will set your own pace, and we'll meet there in a week's time. A strong, fully acclimatized climber could make it in two to three days, but I want you all to take it easy. Enjoy the views. Get comfortable with your bodies at altitude."

"What about the rest of our gear?" Allison Peabody spoke up, looking worriedly to the rest of the group for support. "How will we carry it all? Surely, you don't expect us to."

Ricky slouched in her seat. *Don't look at me.*

"The rest of our Sherpa porters will take the heavy stuff, our climbing gear, directly to Base Camp," Jim calmly explained. "Separate out of your gear what you anticipate you'll need for the week's trek, and the porters will make sure it gets to each night's stop. During the day, just carry in your backpacks what you'll need: water, a jacket, your camera, snacks and the like. Don't overload.

"You're on your own during the trek," Jim continued, "but feel free to see me, Paul, or Ricky if you have questions or run into a problem. But you're pretty much free to do as you please.

However," his voice grew serious, "once we get to Base Camp, things change. My word on the mountain is law. It's essential for our success that you listen to what I say, and do what I say to do, when I say to do it. Particularly when we move to the higher camps."

Kevin MacBride, still looking the part of the rough and tumble starting half-back he'd been, frowned. "How much freedom will the stronger climbers have to climb?"

"What do you mean?" Harris asked slowly, knowing full well where this was going.

"What if the stronger climbers want break away from the pack, if things start to slow down during the push?" MacBride gazed around at the group. "I mean...we wouldn't want to blow everybody's chances, would we?"

Ricky couldn't help herself. "So, you wouldn't mind if we had to leave you behind, right?" She lifted a questioning eyebrow.

"Wha—that's not—"

"We stick to the plan." Jim Harris' eyes grew hard. "What you've brought up Kevin, is a situation I'll assess at the time, if need be. We're a team, and we stay together. That's our best chance for success."

"Everest is an endurance sport," Ricky softly added. "It's not about power."

"Well, that makes me feel better." Allison Peabody regarded the mountaineer with some relief. "I've been doing a lot of long-distance running."

"Nobody's run up Everest yet, Allie," Kevin morosely took a swig of his beer, clearly not liking the response Harris had given him, "but you're welcome to try."

"Running is a good way to stay in shape," Ricky's eyes bored into the stockbroker, "but it can't replace the experience you get from actually climbing, developing your technical skills."

"Back to the route," Jim interjected, trying to regain control of the conversation. "As you know, we're taking the South Col route to the summit, which some say is the easiest climb on Everest." He looked at them evenly. "Let me tell you, there is no such thing. The route is treacherous, and even though the stormy season won't kick in for another couple of months, a localized weather disturbance could crop up at any time, causing white-out conditions."

"What happens then?" Mike Donaldson wanted to know. "We wait it out?"

"Exactly. Whether you're at Base Camp, or Camp IV, you stay put. In the past, climbers blinded by storms on the mountain have walked right off the edge of a cornice. It's 7,000 feet straight down the Kangshung Face into Tibet." He paused. "But we'll be relying on a top weather broadcasting service from London to let us know when we've got a good window. That'll be a big advantage."

Patsy Donaldson shivered involuntarily. "Good. I'd hate to be caught up there in a storm. I've had nightmares about that."

"The other issue we'll have to deal with, is how each of you handles the altitude. I've seen novices do wonderfully, and experienced climbers—with no prior history of altitude sickness—go down. There's no rhyme or reason to it. But I can tell you that if you keep eating, drinking, and drink, drink, drink some more—"

"Got you covered, dude!" Phil Christy hoisted his beer, and the table broke out in nervous laughter.

"Then that's your best defense. We're going to use a strategy to acclimatize that has worked for plenty of expeditions before. You really aggressively take on the mountain." He smacked a fist into his hand for emphasis. "We'll progressively be moving to the higher camps, and then returning back to the 'thick air' to recover. Until finally, we push up from Base Camp for the summit."

"What does that look like, in terms of days?" Kevin MacBride caught his friend Phil's eyes as he posed the question.

"Base Camp is at 17,600 feet. Taking the week to get there will be a great start, altitude-wise. We've already established a camp location there, and the remainder of the Sherpas with our supplies will be arriving, too. We'll take another week then at Base Camp, setting up our own individual tent sites, checking our equipment, and getting acclimated on short hikes. Then, weather permitting, we'll run our first sortie to Camp I. At 19,500 feet, it'll be just above the Khumbu Icefall."

"I'm not scared or anything," Allison Peabody said, her green eyes wide and dark, "but I've heard that's the worse part of the climb." She swallowed hard. "You know, avalanches and all."

The Khumbu Glacier hugged the lower half of Everest like a white muffler, a frozen river of ice groaning and creaking its way down the mountain until it ended in the tumbled, frozen rapids of the Icefall. There, great chunks of frozen rock and snow called "seracs," could detach without a moment's notice, starting an avalanche and crushing any hapless climber who stood in its path. Worse, the tentative footing of the Icefall was further compromised by a minefield of icy crevasses; many were invisible to the naked eye until a climber's boot stepped through a thin covering of snow, plunging him or her into a black, bottomless tomb.

"You're not scared of the Icefall?" Ricky spoke up again. These idiots would end up killing themselves if they didn't have a little more respect for the mountain. "Well, I am. It scares the shit out of me." She forced a smile to soften her words, knowing her boss was looking on. "You just need to know what to look out for, and stay alert."

"The Icefall is tough," Jim patted Allison's arm reassuringly, "but don't worry. We'll only be on it early in the morning, before the direct light of the sun hits it. It's the heat of day and the melting that cause most of the problem. Anyway," he cleared his throat, "we'll climb to Camp I twice, and on our second trip, we'll actually camp there overnight. We'll stay two nights, in fact. And then, weather permitting—"

"And health permitting," Paul Andersen pointed out. "If you're going to have a problem with the altitude, you'll really start to feel it here."

"—we'll move up to Camp II, which we also call ABC— Advance Base Camp. Sort of our home away from home, higher up in the Western Cwm, at 21,300 feet."

"What does 'Cwm' mean?" Patsy giggled, pronouncing it "koom" as Jim had. "Sounds so funny!"

"It's a Welsh word, meaning 'valley.'" Lou Silvers filled in. "The glacier flows right through it."

"And some valley it is," Jim exclaimed. "Beautiful. Just beautiful. With the walls of Everest on your left and Nuptse standing to the right, it's a gorgeous sight."

"And it can be tricky to climb, too," Ricky added, wanting to make sure these people knew what they were in for. "It's a glacier, don't forget, so we'll still have to keep alert for the crevasses. And the ice...one false step, and you can slide all the way down the Cwm. Also, I've seen climbers get dizzy from the radiant heat in there, once the sun hits it. So make sure you dress accordingly. Removable layers. Polypropylene. No cotton, unless you have a death wish. Cotton's fine at sea level, but at altitude it keeps moisture in, heating you up when you're hot, and cooling you down when you're cold."

Kevin MacBride smirked at the mountaineer. "No T-shirts, huh?"

"No T-shirts." Ricky's eyes glittered.

Jim continued to outline the plan. "So...we'll stay three nights at ABC, before heading back all the way down to Base Camp. We'll recover there for three to four days, and then in a single day make the climb from Base to Camp II. We'll acclimatize there for two nights, and then the next morning, *early*," he emphasized, "we climb to Camp III, halfway up the Lhotse Face."

Allison scrunched her nose distastefully. "How early?" She definitely was not an early-bird. Getting up before dawn was the part she'd disliked the most about her Rainier and McKinley ascents.

"4 a.m.," Jim replied, not batting an eye. "We'll spend the night there, at 24,000 feet. Now, there'll be a bit of technical climbing on this leg," he allowed. "We'll have to get over the *Bergschrund*—the ice wall where the Lhotse Face meets the Khumbu Glacier."

"Piece of cake," Kevin MacBride said. "Plant a few ice screws, fix some rope, and you're there."

Ricky sighed. These gung-ho guys were more clueless than she'd thought. "Try doing it at ten degrees below zero, in the dark, when you're hypoxic," she told him, not fighting too hard to keep the sarcasm out of her voice.

"As Ricky points out," Jim shot the mountaineer a warning glare, "it's important not to underestimate the mountain at this stage. The climb from Camp II to Camp III has the highest dropout rate during every expedition. If you don't have a problem with altitude already at that point, you may, if you don't stay warm and hydrated. I don't want to mislead you—Camp III is rough. And we won't have our climbing Sherpas there overnight, because the ice ledge where we'll be staked out is so small. We'll be on our own."

"The Sherpas will be coming to the top with us, won't they?" A look of concern flashed across Allison's pale face. "I mean, they'll be the ones fixing the ropes and stocking the high camps, right?"

"You bet," Jim said, smiling. "You good people won't have

to lift a finger in that regard. That's what the Sherpas are paid for. Your job is to get used to the altitude, and save your energies for the summit push."

"The Sherpas will be working harder than any of us," Ricky told them. "It's important to respect that. They get paid very little and take all the risks."

"Hey—it's their job," Kevin MacBride snorted.

The mountaineer bit her tongue. She had a deep, abiding respect for the Sherpas and their way of life. Even the best climbing "sirdars" or head Sherpas, barely made more than $1,000 for their season on Everest. There was a fierce sense of pride among the Sherpa community who lived and worked in the Mother Goddess' shadow, and just as many Sherpas as westerners had lost their lives on the slopes of Everest. Life for the Sherpas was hard, and Ricky Bouchard did not like to see them belittled.

"Anyway," Jim continued, "after staying overnight at Camp III, we'll move back to Camp II—and stay there overnight. Finally, we'll descend all the way back to Base Camp. Camp IV, at 26,000 feet on the South Col, you won't actually see until you're heading to the top. It's the last stop before the summit. We'll rest down at Base Camp, breathing that lovely thick air for another five or six days, and then," a broad smile spread across his face, "weather permitting, the summit push!"

"YES!" Kevin MacBride high-fived Phil Christy, spilling some of his dark beer onto the rough-hewn wooden tabletop.

"Ditto, that!" Harris gave MacBride a healthy slap on the back. "See you on the trail, bright and early, people." With that, the big man stood. The rest of the climbers did the same, conversing excitedly amongst themselves as the group broke up.

Ricky Bouchard, however, bolted from the bar as though it were in flames.

"God, what is her problem?" Allison Peabody muttered to no one in particular after Ricky had pushed by her.

"She's on the quiet side, but don't let that bother you." Lou Silvers drew up to Allison, watching the tall, dark figure of the mountaineer disappear into the murky hotel. "She's good."

"You mean, she's got an attitude," Allison corrected him. She was cross at Ricky Bouchard. Ever since the airport, the guide had dodged her whenever she saw her coming, thinking she hadn't noticed it. And tonight, she certainly didn't appreciate the way the woman had spoken to her and everyone else in the group.

"No offense, Allison," Lou smiled at the small blonde not unkindly, "but when the chips are down, there's no one else on this team I'd rather be sharing my rope with, than her. She's one of the best. In spite of all the shit she's been through...I know she lost her climbing partner a couple of years back in an ava- lanche on Dhaulagiri. That had to have been rough."

"Oh." Allison lowered her eyes and shrugged. "Yeah, that's too bad. But...oh, well, I guess I'll just try and stay out of her way."

"No, don't do that," Lou told her, walking her to the corri- dor leading to the guest rooms. "That's not the point. Just...let her have her space, that's all. A woman like that...she needs it."

"I'll see what I can do." Allison placed her hands on her hips, the beginnings of a plan gelling in her mind's eye. "But if she's as good as you say she is, and I want to get to the top, then I'm going to stick to her like glue." She paused, biting her lip. "Whether Miss Ricky Bouchard likes it or not. After all, I *am* the client!"

※ ♦ ※ ♦ ※ ♦ ※

The trek from Lukla to Mount Everest began early the next morning. All the expedition members were anxious to get started, and a hike earlier in the day was infinitely preferable to the sweaty prospect of trekking in the afternoon, once the tropi- cal intensity of the sun kicked in. Regardless of whatever force of God or nature had thrust the Everest massif and its Himalayan brethren to their dizzying heights, Everest itself lay at only 28 degrees north in latitude relative to the equator. As a result, the lower regions of Nepal and its sister, Chinese Tibet, were cov- ered in jungle-like vegetation, thickly carpeting the ground in a rich, green growth of leaves, vines, and impossibly huge rhodo- dendron.

They set out from Lukla, winding their way through the gorge of the Dudh Kosi, an icy-cold glacial river strewn haphaz- ardly with great rocks and boulders, as though some ancient giant hand had tossed them about at play. The first night the full group stopped in Phakding, a settlement of just a few homes and lodges, mostly catering to the tourist trade. Buddhist prayer flags hung on ropes strung together from building to building, creating a riot of colors seeming to link the structures together against the blue sky background. Dinner was tea, beer, a yak meat stew and, unbelievably, tacos. Nepal was not necessarily known for its cuisine, existing as it did on sparse natural resources. As a result, many lodge-owners did what they could to emulate western-style dishes, the better to attract the trekker crowd.

By the morning of the second day, the usual informal partnerships and strategic alliances had begun to form within the party. Kevin MacBride and Phil Christy had made a show of walking with Allison Peabody when the group had started out on the first morning. But soon, they'd taken off at a brisk pace, in a hurry to get to Everest. Looking forward to getting to Base Camp himself and continuing the expedition preparations, Jim Harris stayed close to the two men, trading jokes along the trail as they went.

Lou Silvers had walked with Allison for a time, before taking a detour off the trail to check out an unusual wall of carved *mani* stones he'd heard about in a nearby village. Mani stones were small, flat rocks carved with sanskrit symbols and were sacred to the Sherpas, and Lou explained he had a particular interest in learning more about the Sherpas and their traditions.

Hiking at a moderate pace, Mike and Patsy Donaldson had struck up an easy conversation with Paul Andersen, and Mike had taken it upon himself to counsel the young guide on just what tools he'd need to enter the business world after his climbing days were finished.

Paul had laughed, shaking his head in protest. "But I don't intend to ever stop climbing!"

"That's what you say now, Paul," Mike had warned him. "But someday, you'll want to have a wife. Buy a home. Support a family. What then?"

"Look at you two," Paul had protested. "You're together, you have a family, a business. And you're here on this expedition!"

Mike had hooked his thumbs into the straps of his backpack. "That's my point *exactly*!"

"You should listen to him, dear," Patsy had given Paul a motherly smile, and then the three had wandered off up the trail.

Leaving Allison Peabody, and Ricky Bouchard, behind.

Jim Harris had already requested that Ricky run sweep at the back of the trek, just in case anyone ran into problems. "After all, you've got the most experience in these parts with the locals," he'd said, studiously ignoring the frown that skipped across her face as he hurried to catch up with MacBride and Christy.

If he wants me to be last, I'll be last, all right. And so she lagged behind on the trail, *way* behind, in fact, concentrating on her breathing, and on the sights, sounds, and smells of the lush forest around her.

Alone with her thoughts.

Or at times, when the memories got too painful—simply alone.

❀ ♦ ❀ ♦ ❀ ♦ ❀

Allison Peabody didn't understand it. Both yesterday and today, when she'd slowed down on the trail so that Ricky Bouchard would catch up to her, it hadn't happened. Rather, the tall, silent guide had fallen even farther behind, at times barely visible amongst the trees, like some woodland sylph. In any case, as it was, it wasn't as though Allison thought she could go much slower without coming to a complete halt.

Although...she had over-stuffed her backpack both yesterday and today, and the load was really starting to wear her down, though normally it shouldn't have been a problem for her. She had listened to Jim Harris' "travel light" instructions, but still! How could she be expected to leave her Walkman and CDs behind? Or the extra pair of boots in case hers got wet? And then there was her change of clothes. The additional lenses and spare batteries in her camera bag. The latest book by her favorite author. Too bad it hadn't come out in paperback yet. And of course there was the pouch full of remedies for every possible traveler's ailment. Just in case.

Speaking of which...she hadn't been feeling too well since leaving the village in the morning. She felt hot, too hot even to attribute to her tropical surroundings. And then there were the ominous grumbles from her stomach. Not hunger pangs, certainly. The oatmeal mush she'd had for breakfast should have taken care of that. Perhaps the wobbliness was from that last bridge she'd crossed over.

She glanced casually over one shoulder, wiping the sweat off her brow, and glimpsed the angular form of the mountaineer just coming into view around a bend in the trail. Well, she certainly had the look of a climber about her, Allison thought. Her knee-length khaki trekking shorts did nothing to hide a pair of strong, well-muscled calves and thighs.   Her shoulders, and God...those arms!   Had the woman free-climbed the North Face, or what?   And then there was her face.   All shadowed and tanned, framed by hair as dark as midnight, and eyes that...*Christ, Allie! Are you getting feverish, or what?*

Allison continued to push her way up the trail, trying to shove any thought of Ricky Bouchard from her head.   She had greater worries now, right?   Like, what seemed to be going on in her stomach, and in regions even farther south.   This was no time to be focusing on a loner with one hell of an ego, apparently. Really!   All she'd wanted to do was talk to her a bit.   See if she could pick up some climbing tips.   Obviously, the woman knew her way around Everest.   And from what Lou Silvers had indi- cated, she was one hell of a climber, to boot.

Allison had no illusions about her own climbing abilities. She hadn't been at this as long as everybody else on the expedi- tion had, that was true.   Her other two high-altitude climbs had been with friends she'd met through her climbing group, and she'd been the most inexperienced there, as well.   But they had welcomed her with open arms, and taken their time with her, and she had lucked into good weather on both of those summits. Things could just as easily have turned out differently.   She'd heard the stories.

But with *this* expedition, well, for 70 grand, she wanted her money's worth!   And she was scared to death of the mountain, she could admit that to herself, at least.   But she was frightened even more of walking away without having given it her best shot.   As though that would mean she were giving up on every- thing else in her life too, waking up one morning to find herself living the life her parents had led.   A life that, smothered with the best of their intentions, they so desired for her, too.

No way.

This was the time.   This was her moment.   She was drown- ing.   And the icy white summit of Mount Everest was her life preserver.

Now, if she could only get one taciturn guide to open up a bit.   She couldn't quite put her finger on what it was about Vero- nique Bouchard, but she felt certain that if the mountaineer were somehow convinced of the notion that she, Allison Peabody, could summit Everest, well, then it would be so.

It was just that now, here in the jungle midlands of Nepal,

the mountain seemed so very far away. And the damned pack on
her back was so heavy! Not to mention the heat.

Maybe she should rest?

No.

How embarrassing would it be to have Ricky finally catch
up to her because she'd stopped from exhaustion? That would
never do. She'd heard "Miss Climbing Thing's" comments in the
bar at Lukla. Her words had been few, but loaded with meaning.
And Allison had gotten the message loud and clear. Hell, if she
couldn't negotiate the Namche Trail on her own, how could she
possibly handle Everest? The last thing she wanted was the
climber having to come to her rescue now.

"Ungh!"

Allison bent slightly forward, hoping to curb the pain in her
cramping gut. *Maybe I should stop and put my pack down. But
if I do, I don't know if I'll ever be able to pick it up again!*

Slowing, she turned to look down the jumbled trail behind
her. Ricky Bouchard was gaining on her.

Damn!

❀ ✦ ❀ ✦ ❀ ✦ ❀

Veronique Bouchard passed over another 15-foot long sus-
pension bridge, one of at least 10 they'd see on today's trek. Her
feet slapped against wooden foot-beams that were roped together
with thick, moisture-slickened rope. Best to take it easy on a
footbridge like this. Some, like this one, spanned particularly
rocky areas of the path, while others afforded hikers passage
over frigid, glacial run-offs. Even on a hot day such as today,
those cold waters would make even her think twice before plunging in.

Well.

Other than the mind-numbingly slow pace she'd been forced
to take to evade Allison Peabody while still doing her "sweep"
job, it had been a good trek so far. The scenery was breath taking; there was no doubt of that. She never tired of it. Around
each curve on the trail was another post-card view of plunging
river valleys and roiling rapids. Or tiny villages cut into hills
above the river, their postage-stamped-sized terraced farms,
growing potatoes and barley, clinging precariously to the sloped
earth.

A simple life.

One she so craved for herself. If only she could find that sort of peace.

There were a good number of other people on the trail today too, many who'd passed her by with a smile and a wave. Climbers heading for the other Himalayan expeditions that were on the mountains. Day-hikers, seeing the sights. And then there were the Sherpa porters lining the rocky trail, bearing baskets and packs crammed with foodstuffs and climbing gear, occasionally leading a string of yaks along to the next village, or beyond, to Everest.

Everest.

How far she'd come from the days of her youth, growing up in the raw, uncluttered Laurentians region of Québec. Born in the village of Val-David, a sort of heaven on earth for wandering artists, rock-climbing hounds, and nature lovers. Her mother, Marie Bouchard, was an artist of some local note, and displayed her works in a little gallery on the main street of the town. Her father, Andre, had known that if he were to keep the woman he married, he would have to return with her to her hometown from Montreal, where the young couple had met and fallen in love at McGill University. After all, even petite Val-David could use a good dentist, *non*?

As an only child, young Veronique had reveled in her parents' attentions, and loved the free, fresh-air environment of Val-David. Never knowing, or caring with her child's mind, whether there was anything else in life. Until that day when, barely old enough to walk, or so her mama still swore, she'd climbed the great oak tree that stood in front of their home. She'd simply wanted to see what it was like at the top, and it was that simple explanation she'd hiccuped to her father afterwards through the tears of the spanking she'd earned. The pain of that indignity soon faded, but the memory of the brilliant view from the top of the heavy oaken limbs, the rich, moist scent of the leaves, and the wonder of it all—did not.

Soon, she had a partner in crime. The little boy next door, Jean-Pierre Valmont. With his dark hair and blue eyes, he was the brother she never had. She led the way and he gladly, earnestly followed, content to stay in her shadow as the two friends grew, and the climbs became more challenging. By their teen years they had mastered the Passe-Montagne, a jagged edifice in their own back yard of Val-David. From there they sought out whatever other rock and ice-bound climbs they could find in the remainder of the Laurentians; and then they moved on to Charlevoix, taking whatever jobs here and there they could to finance their next adventure.

By the spring of her 18th year, when her father lay awake at night praying she would go to university, and her mother ground her teeth to the nubs struggling to keep an open artist's mind to it all, she and Jean-Pierre had headed west, to the Canadian Rockies.

And never looked back.

That was then. This was now. Now she looked back plenty, especially to that deceptively beautiful day on Dhaulagiri. The sky had been clear and there were no storms on the horizon when Jean-Pierre set off with the rest of the group. She should have been climbing with him, instead of sitting on her butt in camp with a sprained knee.

"I can stay here with you, Ricky, if you like," he'd offered, the corners of his bearded mouth turning up in a smile, his eyes hidden from view by his sunglasses.

"No, go on," she'd waved him away. "I'll join you tomorrow. Be safe, eh?" And then she'd returned his smile, knowing that, like her, there was only one place for him to be: on the mountain.

Later, she and the others in camp had heard the great boom that sounded like cannon fire. And then the deep, groaning rumble that made the earth move beneath her feet.

If only she'd been there. She could have done...something: seen the signs in time to warn Jean-Pierre and the other two climbers of the wave of white death sweeping their way. Instead, she'd ended up losing the best friend she'd ever had.

The only friend.

She'd searched for days, long after the others had given up. Never feeling the throbbing of her swollen knee, or the beginnings of frostbite in her hands and feet. But there was nothing. Not a trace. Whatever remained of Jean-Pierre and the others was buried under tons of snow and ice, somewhere between Camp I and Camp II on Mount Dhaulagiri.

C'est la vie, right? That was life and death on the mountain. Acceptable risk. They all had known about the possibilities. The dangers. The rewards. So then why did it hurt so much, even after all this time? Glimpses of the "why" came to her at night, in the dark, in her dreams. It was because she'd been meant to die that day too, and hadn't. So if not then, when?

Ricky's response to that question had been to lose herself in her climbing. To push herself to her vertical limit, and beyond. So that when the day came, at least she would know it. Feel it. Live it. She would not be taken by surprise as Jean-Pierre had. She would be ready.

But for now, for today, the challenge was Miss Allison Peabody. Whose energy reserves were clearly flagging.

Ricky had had every intention of giving the young woman a hard time...at least when she wasn't avoiding her entirely. After all, one had to have respect for the mountain...and for one's self; and they were both areas where, in her mind, Allison Peabody was clearly lacking. Still...it wouldn't be as enjoyable making the girl jump through hoops if she weren't feeling up to par. That went against Ricky's instincts of fair play.

The blonde was laboring, moving slow, slower than her snail's pace of yesterday when it had been obvious to Ricky that Allison had wanted her to catch up with her. But she would have none of it.

Today, however, the girl had been sluggish from the get-go. So much so, that despite Ricky's best laggardly efforts, she was actually gaining on her. Part of the problem was the heavy load Allison was carrying. Hadn't she listened to a word Jim said about traveling light as they moved towards higher elevations? She was going to burn herself out.

And now, as she caught sight of the girl's face when she turned around, Ricky noticed that she looked flushed. And she had stumbled once or twice.

Ricky angrily kicked a stone in front of her as she moved up the trail. Her job was to run sweep. That was it. Stick to the bare essentials, right? What would it matter if she let the spoiled brat flounder for a bit on her own? No real harm done; and it would serve her right.

Merde!

Gritting her teeth, Ricky found herself quickening her pace up the trail. *She's the client...she's the client...*

"You know," she easily caught up to the girl, "you'd conserve your strength better if you lightened your load."

"Well, it's a little late for me to do something about it now, isn't it?"

Under the high flush of Allison's cheeks, Ricky could now see the pallid cast of her skin.

"I could carry something for you." She heard the words

tumble unbidden from her mouth. God, what was she thinking? No wonder Allison Peabody thought she was her own personal porter!

"No thanks. I'll be fine," Allison replied through a clenched jaw.

"Are you sure?"

Ricky heard a low groan come from Allison's mouth as the smaller woman pulled off her backpack and dropped it to the ground.

"Yes. I just have to re-arrange a few things in my pack and...and—"

Allison's face twisted into a mask of pain and dread, colored with the most interesting shade of green that Ricky had ever seen. Clutching at her stomach, she staggered into a stand of nearby bushes off the trail.

"Uh...ah, are you okay?" Trying to be polite, Ricky posed the question over the most ungodly of noises coming from the position where she guessed Allison must be. A quick glance up and down the trail showed the two of them to be alone for now, so Ricky supposed the girl should be grateful for small favors. Although one's modesty was usually the first baggage to be jettisoned during an extended climb.

After several long moments, Allison's head popped up over the bushes, and she walked slowly, deliberately, back to the path. "I...I'm fine," she panted, though Ricky noticed her eyes were now glassy and a thin sheen of perspiration dotted her brow. She ran a hand through her limp hair. "Just a little stomach complaint."

From where she was standing, even Ricky could hear the ominous, loose rumblings from the girl's rebelling digestive system.

"Well," panic skipped across Allison's face at the thought of another round, "maybe not so little." She charged back into the bushes.

Uh-oh. She's in for it now. Ricky had seen this before. More times than she cared to count.

Delhi-belly.

It happened even to the most seasoned of travelers in these parts. It was luck really, whether you picked it up or not. One time, on their way to Annapurna, Jean-Pierre had come down with a dose of it. And if that weren't bad enough, it had come on him just when he was in the middle of an impromptu romantic evening with that blonde trekker from Sweden. He'd been able to laugh about it later, when the trekker indiscreetly spread the word. He never let things get him down for long. That was his way.

Ricky smiled at the memory.

One of the good ones.

Allison was gone for a protracted period of time, and just when Ricky was debating going in after her, she reappeared from the thick jungle vegetation. Looking even the worse for the wear.

"Listen." Ricky stepped close to her, ignoring the vaguely unpleasant odor rising from the girl. "You're sick. You've got a fever and a stomach bug. When you...when we," she amended, knowing she was taking a step towards where she'd sworn she wouldn't go, "get to the next village, you should stop there. Take it easy. I know something you can take for this." It was only right. She couldn't abandon a client now.

"N-no." Allison held up a trembling hand. "You go on. I'll be fine. I've got some stuff in my pack I can take."

Was this girl suicidal? If she didn't take care of herself and instead got dehydrated at these elevations, she was asking for trouble. "At least let me carry your pack." Ricky reached for it, growing more exasperated by the minute.

"No."

"Please—"

"I said *no*!" Allison's voice was cracked and hoarse as she grabbed for her backpack. "I may not have as much experience as you," she cried, tears of embarrassment and frustration pooling in her eyes, "but I can pull my own weight."

Okaaay. Ricky thought about that for a moment, before deciding there was no better time than the present to broach the next item in a long line of distasteful conversational topics she seemed to be having with Miss Allison Peabody. "Then in that case," she said slowly, carefully, "you won't have any problem pulling those leeches off your legs."

"*What?*" Allison's shriek echoed up and down the trail, bouncing off the rocks and trees of the river gorge. Desperately, she began to paw at several of the dark, sticky, creatures that had attached themselves to her legs.

Leeches were everywhere on the jungly hillsides, clinging to the moist vegetation as they waited for the next warm meal to pass them by. Ricky was surprised they hadn't seen more of them before now. She had known leeches to drop onto a victim, attach themselves with their prong-like fangs, have a good long drink, and then drop off without even raising a tickle of a pinprick.

They weren't dangerous, they didn't hurt or itch, and oftentimes the only way you knew they'd paid you a visit, was by a thin trace of blood on your leg, arm, or...wherever, thanks to an anti-coagulant they injected in you while dining. The problem, really, as Allison was finding out before her very eyes, was that they were just so damn...disgusting!

Like slimy little vampires, once they attached to you, they were reluctant to let go until they'd had their fill. In pulling them off, their skin would stretch like rubber, until with a sucking *pop!* you found they were now stuck to your hands, instead.

"Oh God...Fuck-fuck-fuck!" Allison did a strange jerky dance, unlike anything Ricky was sure this forest had ever seen. The mountaineer stood back, unsure whether to offer her assistance or to give the agitated stockbroker a wide berth. Best to wait until the client told her what she wanted. And anyway, it looked like she was doing a pretty good job of de-leeching on her own.

"Oh...oh..." Allison's sharp cries turned into weak mewlings as she finally flicked the last of the worm-like creatures from her hand. Her feverish green eyes stayed locked on her palm. She swallowed hard, focusing on the splotches of bright red blood she found there.

Her blood.

She blanched, blinked several times in rapid succession, and let her gaze track up to Ricky. "Oh, *shit.*" With those words, Allison pitched face-forward towards the ground.

Already on the move, Ricky barely caught her in time. *You could say that again.*

Chapter
Four

Am I dead?

In a foggy, dream-like state, Allison Peabody ran a thickened tongue over dry, chapped lips. *Or, is it more a case that something else died—in my mouth?* Involuntarily, her gag reflex kicked in, and it all came flooding back to her in a rush. How ill she'd felt, back there on the trail.

The heat.

The leeches.

And God, the humiliation of it all, putting her shortcomings on full, flagrant display in front of Ricky Bouchard! And then...what?

Eyes still closed, Allison's brow furrowed, and she released a groan that seemed to sound so far away. *What happened?* Try as she might, she could not put the fragmented pieces together.

"Sssh...it's okay. You're gonna be fine."

She felt a cool trickle of water on her forehead, and then the light weight of a—something. A compress? The palm of a hand? She had to find out. One green eye plunked open. And then another.

"Allison?"

She forced her senses to do their work. Felt the coarse cloth covering her, some sort of thin sheet or blanket. Heard the faraway sounds of muted conversation and booted footsteps on wooden floorboards, and beyond that, the delicate tinkling of yak-bells. Detected the light scent of a wood-fire, and cooking smells. Saw the blurred whiteness of a plaster ceiling and wooden beams.

She redirected her gaze, just in time to see a hand draw away from her face. And saw two piercing blue eyes raking over her, clouded with worry, before they visibly relaxed and assumed the blank, indifferent look she'd become accustomed to over the past few days.

"Where am I? What happened?" Her voice crackled, and she was uncertain whether it was from the soreness in her throat or the dryness of her mouth.

"You're in the Khumbu Lodge in Namche Bazar. You passed out on the trail." Ricky Bouchard placed a damp cloth next to a small bowl resting on a nearby table, trading it for a container of bottled water. "Think you can drink some of this?" Her face was impassive. "The doctor says you should. The sooner you do, the sooner you'll be back on your feet."

Allison's eyes fell upon a small Band-Aid on the back of her hand. "Doctor..." She edged herself up onto her elbows, the confusion plain on her face. God...her entire body felt as though it had been run over, and run over again, and there was Ricky Bouchard, sitting there looking so cool, calm, and collected.

"Yeah. Jonathan Simons, the doc for the British expedition. He happened to be heading out of Namche when we arrived. Let's see," Ricky began counting off her fingers, "a shot of an antibiotic and an anti-nausea med, a quick hit of intravenous fluids, and he was outta here. But he left this behind for you." She lifted a little brown plastic bottle and shook it. "You take these pills until they're finished. Got it?"

"Got it," Allison replied, her voice a hoarse whisper. Gratefully, she accepted the water from Ricky, and took a couple of swallows.

And waited.

"Well, that's progress," Allison sighed, preparing to take another drink. "At least it's staying down."

Ricky folded her arms. "Your fever's come down, too. You'd be surprised, once you get the proper treatment, how quickly you bounce back. Of course, it's a different story, if it happens in the higher elevations."

"We're high enough." Allison put the bottle down on the table, and let her head fall back on the pillow. She was exhausted to the bone, her head ached, and all she wanted to do was sleep. But it was true, in spite of that, she felt measurably better than she had back on the trail.

The trail.

"Hey—how did I get here, anyway. I mean—we were—"

"It wasn't any problem. I enlisted the assistance of a Sherpa and his yak who were passing by."

"A yak," Allison repeated flatly.

"Sure. He was on his way to Namche Bazar anyway, and I finally persuaded him, with the help of a few rupees, that you were at least as valuable a cargo as the crate of chickens he was hauling."

"Chickens."

"Yep. There was just enough room for me to tie you across the yak's back like a sack of oats, and here we are."

Allison's mouth opened in outrage. "You did *what?*" This Ricky Bouchard had some nerve! My God, as if she hadn't been humiliated enough today!

"Now if you find a stray chicken feather or two somewhere on your...person, don't blame me," Ricky continued, blithely ignoring Allison's agitated state. "The poor Sherpa simply would not leave those hens behind."

"Oh..." Allison flung an arm over her eyes, desperately attempting to blot out from her mind's eye the image of what must have been her grand entrance into the village: her beleaguered backside pointing skyward while her head hung over some yak's nether regions. And then there were the chickens. Good God. Perhaps she might die of this ailment after all.

"You only slid off once."

"*What?*" she cried out, and it was then that she finally caught the twinkle in the blue eyes fixed upon her, saw the smile tugging at the corner of a mouth.

"You're yanking my chain, aren't you?"

"Yanking your chain? Nah," the mountaineer replied, a full grin over-spreading her features. "Now 'yakking' your chain? Absolutely."

"Ha-ha. Very funny." Allison pursed her lips and tried to stay angry, but found it quite impossible to do so. This whole...thing was just so ridiculous, after all. Plus, it probably wouldn't do her innards any good if she persisted in stressing herself. And so she returned the smile. "Try it again. The truth, this time."

"There was a yak," Ricky grudgingly admitted. "And chickens. The Sherpa was kind enough to let his yak carry our gear, while I carried you."

"You...carried *me*?"

"Sure. It wasn't that far." Ricky's eyes dropped to examine a spot on the floor before she continued. "I couldn't exactly leave you there. It seemed the best thing to do at the time. Anyway," she lifted her gaze to Allison, "you felt lighter than a 40 pound pack at 21,000 feet. I figured it was a good workout."

"Well." Allison suddenly found herself reddening in the presence of the taller woman. She'd been lucky that Ricky had been there today, and she knew it. "I—I'm sorry. That sort of thing has—has never happened to me before."

"Hey—don't worry about it. It was the bug from whatever you ate."

"Those damn tacos," Allison muttered.

"Add to that the heat, and the fact that you were dehydrated—"

"Don't forget the leeches." Allison shivered at the memory.

"And a sudden shock," Ricky corrected her. "It's understandable."

"Well, on the mountain it'll be a different story." Allison forced a bravado she did not feel into her voice. "You'll see."

"Yeah, well...you'll be fine in a couple of days." The mountaineer pointedly did not address Allison's words. "Jim recommends that all the clients stay here acclimatizing for a couple of days anyway, before moving on. So you'll be right on schedule."

A yawn caught Allison by surprise, and with some bit of regret, she watched Ricky push herself to her feet.

"I'll leave you to get some rest for now. Later, I'll have some tea and soup sent up." She paused. "Anything else I can get you?" Ricky told herself she was only doing the right thing for a sick client. And even though the small blonde was feeling better now, she certainly hadn't looked too well when she'd passed out on the trail.

Ricky had been relieved beyond measure to find that the British doctor had been in Namche Bazar. Odds were that Allison would have bounced back just fine, given proper rest and fluids. But still...once in a while the bug got out of control, with devastating results. And her charge had been so pale and still on the way up to Namche. Ricky barely had any memory at all of the ground they'd covered, so quickly had she moved, leaving the yak herder far behind in her dust.

"No, I'm fine." Allison pulled the thin, white blanket up under her chin.

Ricky silently nodded, and headed for the door.

The voice was so soft, so quiet, she barely heard it.

"Thank you."

Ricky stopped in the doorway, imagining she should say something, but not knowing quite what. So instead, she simply drew closed the blanket that served as a door.

And walked away.

❀ ♦ ❀ ♦ ❀

What a difference two days made.

Just as Ricky Bouchard had predicted, in two days time, after plenty of soup, tea, and antibiotics, the intestinal bug that had laid Allison lower than low left her for greener pastures. Straight into Kevin MacBride and Mike Donaldson, from what the stockbroker had heard, although the two men had toughed it out and left Namche Bazar after only one day's stay. From the sour look on Ricky's face and the tense set of her mouth, Allison knew that the mountaineer disagreed with their decision to move on so quickly, but she had little say in the matter.

Already, there seemed to be a bit of macho posturing going on, with an unspoken competition underway to see who could make it to Base Camp first. MacBride and Phil Christy, with Jim Harris at their side, appeared intent on claiming the honor. But it turned out Mike Donaldson was focused on giving the younger men a run for their money, pushing his discomfort aside and dragging a huffing and puffing Patsy along with him for the high-altitude ride. Paul Andersen simply shook his head, smiled, and struck out after them. Only Lou Silvers seemed content to undertake the journey as the leisurely, acclimatizing, sightseeing trek it was intended to be.

Allison might have been willing to give it a go, keeping up with the head of the pack, if only to show Ricky that she could. But where her spirit was willing, her body, in no uncertain terms, told her it was not.

"Take it slow and easy," Ricky had told her when they'd left Namche Bazar in the morning. "The mountain isn't going anywhere."

And so Allison had swallowed her pride, for the time being anyway, and contented herself with moving along at a pace, under the watchful eye of Veronique Bouchard, that her recovering body did not find objectionable.

Lou Silvers had decided to trek with them this day, and Allison privately welcomed the older man's company. He had poked his head in on her a number of times while they were in Namche Bazar, checking on whether she needed anything, and sharing some quiet conversation. She enjoyed his friendly, easy manner, and found she could talk to him in a way that she'd always wished she could with her own father. And from what she could tell, Ricky seemed to enjoy his company as well, and that had to be a rare enough occurrence. In addition, Lou's presence served to lessen the awkwardness she might otherwise have felt in the presence of the tall, quiet mountaineer.

For although Ricky's distant, icy exterior had seemed to thaw a bit in those first few moments after Allison had regained consciousness back in the lodge, her mask had quickly been put back into place. Oh, Ricky had been appropriately concerned for her welfare, been solicitous of her needs like a good guide should be, but that was it. In fact, over the past two days while she was recovering, Ricky had had very little to say about anything—period—despite Allison's best efforts to draw her into conversation.

Now, she, Ricky, and Lou Silvers walked side-by-side on a widened section of the trail outside of Namche. Taking it easy, just as the mountaineer had recommended. Allison's backpack was lighter by far than it had been, and that was a help. She'd gone through it the night before with Ricky's assistance, deciding on what items could be safely relegated to the Sherpa porters. The dark haired woman had relented when it had come to the camera, water, Walkman and a couple of CDs, but the changes of clothing, the hard-back book, and the extra pair of boots were whisked away to the porters' care.

Glad to be moving again after her days of inactivity, Allison took a deep breath of the fresh, clean air, and sighed. "God, what a gorgeous day!" The weather on the trail was bright and clear, but in the distance she could see the wispy mist of clouds that obscured their ultimate goal: Everest.

"I wish we could bottle some of it for when we're summit bound," Lou said. He turned to Ricky. "What do you think the weather will be like up there?"

"On a day like today, for example?" Ricky squinted towards the distant peaks. "Hard to tell, from here, but any day with clouds up high isn't a good one. And when we're actually going for the top—it's a crapshoot, really. All you can do is hope for a four-day break in the weather, if you're starting out from Base Camp. 36 hours, tops, if you're already starting out from a higher camp and you want to make sure of getting up and down again."

"Getting down being the ultimate objective," Lou grinned, his pale eyes sparkling warmly.

"What about this weather service Jim talked about?" Allison pointed out. "That should be a help, right?"

"Sure...I suppose," Ricky answered her. "But even the best weather service can't predict the localized storms that can suddenly appear out of nowhere. One minute it's a sunny day, and the next, you're in white-out conditions."

Catching something in the tone of her voice, Lou carefully regarded the mountaineer. "Has that ever happened to you...up there?"

Ricky hesitated a moment before answering him, her blue eyes clouding over. "Yeah," she softly admitted. "My first time up, on the North side. The funny thing is," she let loose a low, bitter laugh, "we weren't even heading for the summit that day. We were still acclimatizing. Our high camp—Camp IV—had to be stocked, and our expedition then didn't have the use of as many Sherpas as the big commercial ones do now. So—"

"So you volunteered."

"Sort of." She smiled wryly at the attorney. "The truth was, I was willing to grab any chance I could to work my way up high. I was the new kid on the block, and I figured I'd need whatever edge I could to stay one step ahead of the other climbers. To make sure I got my fair shot at getting picked for the top. Taking some canisters of O2 up there, along with some food packets and fuel—I grabbed at the chance. It would mean that except for our Sherpas who'd set up the tent two days before, I would've been higher than any of the other...men on the expedition."

Allison lifted her head at that comment, and took in the serious, tanned face of the climber. Women on Everest were commonplace now, but when Ricky had been a part of her first North Face expedition, it would still have been very much a male dominated mountaineering world.

With all the baggage that went with it.

No doubt, a young Veronique Bouchard had had much to prove.

Allison slowed her pace, listening to Ricky's tale, and noticed that Lou Silvers had done the same.

"Anyway," Ricky continued, a distant look in her eye, "my climbing partner was against the idea. Said we should wait...that the plume off the summit just didn't look right. But the weather reports gave the all clear for the next 36 hours. Plenty of time for us to get to Camp IV, above 26,000 feet. We could spend the night, acclimatize, and then head down the next day. If we waited for the Sherpas, that would put us another couple of days behind schedule. And...I was afraid. Afraid I'd lose my shot."

"So you started climbing." Allison's voice was a breathless whisper.

"I did. And Jean-Pierre came with me after all. I think he just couldn't tolerate the thought of being left behind." She grinned at the memory of her doggedly determined partner. "It was tough going. Our Sherpas had fixed the ropes when they'd gone up to establish the camp, but it had snowed since then, and we had to break new trail. We both were climbing without oxygen. For me, if I pace myself, I have no problem. But Jean-Pierre..." She shook her head, and fell silent for a moment. "It took longer to get to the high camp than we thought. By that time, it was late afternoon. The winds were simply unbelievable...ripping everything to shreds. And the cold..." she squeezed her eyes shut for an instant. "Well, by that time, it was obvious that a storm was moving in."

"The North Col is no place to be in bad weather," Lou said, shuddering at the thought despite the warmness of the air around them. "What did you do?"

"We could have stayed there," Ricky allowed, "taken our chances. But on the mountain, it's hard to tell if a storm will last for five hours or five days. Jean-Pierre wanted to stay...to wait it out. And more than anything...I wanted to stay, too. That way, Jean-Pierre and I would be at the front of the line. But the way this storm was coming in... It seemed to be shrieking, cursing at us for our folly...and I knew we had to get out of there." She pushed a loose strand of dark hair behind her ear, remembering. "It was already snowing by the time we began our descent."

"Oh, God," Allison groaned, "what a nightmare."

"*Non*," Ricky said quietly, her booted feet moving lightly along the gravelly trail. "Worse. We'd grabbed a couple of headlamps from the Camp IV supplies before we left, so we had them. But they don't do much good when the snow is blowing so hard that you can't see a foot in front of you. Literally. Jean-Pierre and I clipped onto the lines and roped ourselves together, too. We were going by sense of feel, more than anything. But when you're frozen solid and your hands and feet are numb, you're not sure whether your next step brings you that much closer to your camp, or right off the edge of a sheer face."

"Wow."

"If Jean-Pierre hadn't been there...if we hadn't been there for each other," Ricky said, her eyes locking on Allison, "I'm not sure we would have made it. It would have been so easy to just sit down...and that would have been that."

"But you made it," Lou said hesitantly, "right?"

"We made it. We got back to Camp III shortly after 1 a.m. We were too exhausted to even melt snow for tea. We simply collapsed into our sleeping bags—frozen, exhausted, and probably hypoxic. But at least we were alive. It wasn't until the storm broke three days later, that we found out that two climbers on the South Col had been lost in the storm."

"Well, you made the right decision," Lou assured her, "in coming back down. You never would have been able to survive three nights at that altitude, in that kind of weather."

"The right decision to come down...yes." Ricky's lean face was set in a grim line. "But we never should have gone up in the first place." She paused. "I was wrong."

"You live, you learn, I guess," Allison said, taking a gulp of bottled water.

"And sometimes you die learning," Ricky said sharply, her eyes flashing. "It's a fine line. I *tell* you this story," she ground out, "because it's important that you never underestimate the mountain. Or worse, overestimate yourself."

The three trekkers walked on for a time, in silence. A light breeze had picked up, gently swaying the lush, green branches draped over the trail. Though the summit of Everest was still distant, the air was gradually beginning to change, to cool.

"You know," Ricky finally spoke, her voice low, "Jean-Pierre and I had stopped at a monastery on the Tibet side on our way up to Base Camp that year. It's a tradition of sorts, with some of the climbers, to make an offering and seek out the blessings of the *Rimpoche*, the head lama, for the success of one's journey. We went through the ceremony, and as we were leaving, one of the monks tried to give me...this." Her fingers went to a knotted red braid she wore about her neck. "It's a 'protection cord.' It's supposed to ensure your safe passage on Everest."

"It's beautiful," Allison said. She'd noticed the unique braided necklace around the mountaineer's neck before, but had been hesitant to ask her about it.

"Jean-Pierre accepted his, but I wouldn't take mine from the monk," Ricky chuckled. "Not then. I told him I'd pick it up on the way back down, after I'd assured my own success. And so I did. Can you imagine...the arrogance!"

Allison kept her mouth shut. It was true that she thought Ricky Bouchard hefted around one rather large ego. But at the same time, the young blonde was beginning to detect that there was something else at play here, and she suspected there was more to the mountaineer than the frosty veneer she'd been exposed to thus far. And, God knew, Ricky had every right to think the same of her, as well. She knew she hadn't been able to impress the tall woman so far, other than perhaps by the fact that she'd been able to afford her expedition fees. Some accomplishment.

"There's a monastery further along this trail, isn't there?" Lou gazed evenly at Ricky.

"Yes, at Thyangboche."

"I'd love to stop there. I've heard the blessing ceremonies are quite something."

"Well, we'll have the traditional *puja* at Base Camp," Ricky countered.

"That's where the Sherpas build a shrine at your camp, right?" Lou scratched at his head. "They get a local lama to come out and bless your ice ax and stuff, right?"

"Yeah," Ricky replied. "So you could do that, instead." She looked to the sky, checking the sun's position. "At this rate, we wouldn't get to the monastery until late afternoon, and the ceremony takes some time. Maybe you'd rather keep moving—"

"I'd like to go, too," Allison interjected. Her eyes flickered to the rocky ground and then back to Ricky again. "That is...if we wouldn't be intruding."

Ricky looked into Lou and Allison's hopeful faces. Lou Silvers was certainly a decent guy. Ricky had already noticed the interest he'd taken in experiencing the local culture, and the respect he had for it. She was glad to have his company along for this particular expedition. Although his career had kept him from doing much technical climbing recently, he was clearly a man who had enjoyed the time he'd spent years before in the vertical life. And who knew? If he had decided to chase 8000-meter peaks instead of a law firm partnership, he might have ended up just as hard-core as she was.

The jury was still out on Allison Peabody, however. True, since she'd gotten ill she had lost a bit of her "high and mighty" attitude. Perhaps the bug had helped to dislodge whatever blessedly undefined large object she'd had stuck up her rear end. And the fact that even now she'd expressed an interest in a monastery visit, when just a few days ago Ricky knew that the young blonde would've done anything to keep up with the "Hardy Boys," Kevin and Phil; well, maybe there was hope.

"Okay." Ricky gave in. "We'll stop." The trio was just rounding a bend in the trail, coming upon a breathtaking overlook. "After all," a small smile played at her lips, "we should try to keep the 'Mother Goddess' appeased." And with that, she flung out an arm towards the mountains. The mists had cleared, and in the distance above them, stood the pearly-white pinnacle of Ama Dablam. Beyond, pushing up towards the sky like a rough-hewn rocky blade, was the icy summit of Everest itself. The jet stream winds blew a plume of white from the top, a snowy, crystallized pennant flying in the breeze. Far below them, the deep gorge of the Dudh Kosi wound its way down towards the valley, carving a path through the underbelly of the Himalayas.

"Oh my God." Allison's voice was hushed, overwhelmed as she was at the raw, powerful vision assaulting her senses. "It's beautiful."

Ricky Bouchard fixed two blue ice chips on the summit. On the Mother Goddess. She from whom all life was given.

Or was coldly taken.

"It is."

❋ ◆ ❋ ◆ ❋ ◆ ❋

The warm rays of the late afternoon sun angled their way through the trees, casting gentle beams of light upon the forest floor. The monastery itself stood at the head of a hot, dusty trail, detouring through the forest from the main path. It had been a good day's trek, overall, and the altitude they'd covered made the soaring peaks above them loom closer, heavier. They could all feel it, the icy weight of the massifs bearing down upon them.

Thyangboche was tucked into the side of a hill, at the edge of a rock-strewn glacial moraine. The stark, whitewashed building had been battered over the years by both the elements and earthquakes, but the spirit of the devout monks who inhabited it, endured.

A young monk welcomed them at the door, bowing a greeting, ushering them into what appeared to be a main gathering room. The aged walls were decorated with textile hangings and art, and the scores of candles burning in yak butter did little to ward off the cool chill of the stone interior. Wordlessly, the monk beckoned them to sit down on a set of floor cushions facing a raised platform and altar.

"What happens now?" Allison whispered, speaking in low, church-like tones. The sense of holiness of place was strong, vibrating through the air and working its way into them, like a tide that could not be turned away.

"Just follow my lead," the mountaineer replied, crossing her legs. "And whatever you do, don't insult them," she warned. "This ceremony has great religious significance for them." She eyed Allison carefully. "You take what is offered, with a 'thank you' and a smile."

The hall began to fill with at least a dozen other monks, all featuring shaved heads and wearing the rich, maroon robes of office. Ricky gazed at the altar, which was laden with prayer scarves, offerings, tattered bits of paper scribbled with prayer requests, and pictures of the Dalai Lama. The air they breathed was thick with the mingling odors of incense and age, of the damp mustiness of ancient carpets, and the sour scent of the yak butter.

Ricky knew that for both the monks and the Sherpas, yak butter represented a scarce resource, a great gift from God to be valued and treasured. The monks put it in everything, including their tea, as Allison and Lou were about to find out.

The original young monk who had greeted them slipped back into the room, bearing a large kettle of the dark brew. This was an important part of the ritual, the drinking of the tea, heavily flavored with salt and yak butter, while negotiating a fee for the blessing and *khatas*—white silk scarves—that were to be presented.

Ricky did the talking, settling with the English-speaking monk on an "offering" price of 200 Nepalese rupees.

Almost indiscernibly, the monks began to softly chant. Then, gradually, the chanting began to build in volume. As if by hidden signal, from a side entrance near the altar the aged *Rimpoche* entered, and took his seat on a large brocade pillow atop the raised platform.

The tea was poured and consumed: three separate ritual sips were required by tradition, with the monk refilling their cups each time. The mountaineer could not resist sparing a sidelong glance towards Lou and Allison. The attorney seemed to be doing all right, but it was obvious that Allison Peabody was struggling.

Even on a good day, the monks' tea was a difficult swallow. For the Nepalese, the drink provided the nutrients essential to life in the higher elevations: a stimulant, fats, and salt. But to the western palate, the taste could be somewhat...off-putting. Ricky hid a smile behind another sip of the tea. Allison was turning quite a peculiar shade of green; this was apparent even in the darkened interior of the hall. Still, she had to give her credit. The girl offered a tight smile and held out her cup for more, and the monk cheerfully complied.

The chanting continued, filling the hall with deep, comforting sounds: "*Om mani padme hum*"—"Hail to the jewel in the heart of the lotus." Soon, the voices were joined by the reverberating tones of two long brass horns, over six feet in length, reminding Ricky for all the world of the great alpenhorns she'd seen in Austria. Other smaller instruments joined in, accompanied by the mesmerizing beat of cymbals and drums.

Ricky found herself swept up in it all as she always did: the heady effect of the tea; the thick, heavy incense swirling around her; the intense devotion of these monks to their God as a living, breathing thing. She lost herself in the magic of it all and, for a brief moment, allowed her soul to be touched by the inner peace that so eluded her.

Suddenly, the instruments stopped, and a delicate, jingling bell quieted the chanting of the monks. Then the Lama spoke in halting, quaking tones, giving them his blessing to aid their journey through the mountains. With the help of two monks, he came down from the platform, bearing three of the white silk *khatas.* He shuffled over to the three climbers and draped the

scarves around their shoulders, anointing them with a vial of
blessed water.

"Wear these to the top of the Mother Goddess," he said, the
skin on his face as wrinkled and thin as old parchment. "It will
please God, and keep you safe from harm."

After gracing them with one last blessing, his face lit up in a
beatific smile, and he took his leave. Together with his atten-
dants, the old Lama retreated from the hall using his private
doorway.

The ceremony was concluded.

"Well, that was something," Lou Silvers said, shouldering
his rucksack as the inlaid monastery doors swung shut behind
them. Departing from the dark, mysterious coolness back into
the warm light of day. Stepping back across the threshold from a
journey to a place frozen in the rituals of times past, returning to
the immediacy of the present.

Allison Peabody gratefully let the sun hit her in the face and
warm her arms, breathing in deeply, ridding her lungs of all
traces of the incense and dank mustiness. She could not help but
feel the lingering sense that she'd left something behind in the
old monastery. And perhaps taken away something, too. She
lightly fingered her silk scarf as they made their way back to the
trail. "No protection cord, eh?" The scarf was beautiful, but she
had been looking forward to acquiring neckwear similar to the
piece Ricky wore. It didn't make her too nervous in terms of
their safety; they'd been given the scarves, after all. And of
more immediate concern to her was getting a good gulp of clear
water to quell the worrisome lurching of her yak-buttered stomach.

Still lost in her thoughts, Ricky smiled faintly and lifted her
eyes to the mountains towering above them. "No, no protection
cords. Guess on this trip, we're on our own."

Chapter
Five

The remainder of the trek passed uneventfully. They climbed higher and higher into the mountains, past forests of . juniper and blue pine, eventually leaving the green, verdant valleys of the lower elevations behind. The villages along the way became smaller too, and the lodges where they stayed, more crowded and very basic, in terms of amenities. Young trekkers and climbers jammed into tiny bunkhouse accommodations, replete with hard dirt floors and food that proved to be highly suspect.

When they'd passed the tree line, things became particularly grim. The air turned cold and bitter, especially at night, and in the tiny Sherpa villages where they stopped, the locals burned dung for fuel, as opposed to the more costly, rare wood.

The stench was unbelievable.

"Oh God, there is *no* way," Allison declared, gazing at the filthy, fumes-infested lodge where they were supposed to spend their last night prior to reaching Base Camp. "Can't we camp outside or something?" The stockbroker had felt herself returning to full strength over the past few days, and feared that a night spent in the local so-called "guest house" might leave her with a raging cough, at the minimum. Or worse. *Been there. Done that.*

Ricky had to admit it—Allison had a point. The young

woman and Lou had done well over the past several days, moving at a steady, healthy pace. But now that they were higher up
in the mountains, it didn't take much for the altitude to begin to
affect one's constitution. A smoky fire could lead to a nagging
cough, which could lead to separated or broken ribs.

Meaning the end of a climb.

She had seen it happen before.

"Okay...let me see if I can find a couple of our Sherpas."

She did, and in quick order she'd grabbed some camping
supplies from them. By the time darkness fell, a tent had been
set up behind the lodge, strategically placed in-between two glacial boulders.

"But this only fits two people," Lou puffed and grunted on
his hands and knees as he unfolded a sleeping bag.

"It was all our Sherpas had. I'll be fine out here," the
mountaineer replied, setting up her kit adjacent to the tent.

"You'll...you'll freeze!" Allison's eyes flew open wide. As
she spoke, plumes of white vapor billowed from her mouth.
"Maybe..." She gazed at the inside of the tent, as though willing
it to magically increase in size. "If you—"

"I'll be fine," Ricky assured them, busying herself with preparing her little camp. "Besides," she smirked, "I'm hot-
blooded."

"Are you sure, Ricky?" Lou Silvers was doubtful. "I suppose I could do the gentlemanly thing and switch with you—"

"No!" Ricky surprised herself with the quickness of her
response. There was no way she'd allow a client to sleep out-of-
doors while there was a warm tent nearby. Not to mention the
fact that she found the thought of being in such close quarters
with Allison Peabody slightly...unsettling. And why did the girl
care anyway whether she was comfortable or not? Why wouldn't
she just leave her be?

"I love sleeping under the stars," Ricky haltingly explained.
"I do it all the time. It reminds me..." she paused, "of when I
was a kid."

"Well, okay, kiddo." Lou shook his head as he unzipped his
jacket. "I'm too tired to argue." He crawled inside the tent and
with an exhausted groan, cocooned himself in his sleeping bag.

Allison simply stayed on her knees in front of the tent,
watching the dark haired woman arrange her sleeping pad and
bag on the rocky ground. It was obvious that Ricky knew what
she was doing, and indeed she had appeared to actually relish the

thought of sleeping outside, unprotected. Alone.

Still.

Ricky felt a pair of eyes upon her. "What?"

"Nothing. I'll...I'll be right back." Allison pushed herself to her feet, breathing hard. She was beginning to feel the effects herself of all this exertion at a higher elevation. They all were, but Ricky had told them that it was to be expected.

"Whatever." Ricky shrugged, returning to her work.

In a few more moments, Ricky had completed setting up her campsite. She leaned against a cold, gray boulder and removed her hiking boots. Her toes—all ten of them—crackled as she flexed them. Her feet had served her well over the past few years, and had never let her down. Other mountaineers, she knew, were not so fortunate when climbing.

Brutal cold, snow, or moisture would penetrate your gaiters, and next thing you knew, frostbite would set in.

Good-bye toes.

She stretched her arms out above her head, admiring the brilliant, cloudless night sky. The stars twinkled like gemstones against the velvety darkness. And Everest...the behemoth stood silently, majestically under a half-moon light. A three-sided pyramid, seeming to emit an icy glow from within, shadowed by glittering, rocky onyx. She could feel its pull, now, stronger than ever. Urging her forward, and up, up, until she no longer knew nor cared about the who and the why of it; there was just herself, and the mountain, and they were one.

"I'm back."

Shit. In a jarring instant, Ricky felt herself sucked back into reality, a disembodied dreamer, awakening.

Allison Peabody.

"So you are," Ricky snapped, slightly annoyed that her solitude had been interrupted. "Well...goodnight, then."

"Um, listen—would you like some of this?" A flash of white teeth in the dark.

It was then that the mountaineer saw that the small blonde was carrying two cups of steaming hot Sherpa tea. "Well—"

"C'mon—it's all about hydration, right?" Allison stepped closer, her boots crunching on the uneven ground.

Ricky realized it would be silly to refuse the girl's offering just...because. And anyway, the sooner she accepted, the sooner Allison would be gone. "Okay...sure."

"Here ya go."

To the mountaineer's consternation, Allison settled herself down next to her.

"Uh...thanks," Ricky mumbled. She cupped the warm beverage in the palms of her hands, breathing in its slightly bitter scent.

"I took it easy on the yak butter," Allison said wryly, and Ricky could not help but chuckle at that.

"Yeah, well, you do have to acquire a taste for it, that's for sure." She blew at the edge of the cup before taking a sip, allowing a silence to fall.

Hmnn.

Here they were, just the two of them. The thing she'd been trying most to avoid. Ah, well. She supposed she'd better get used to it, since they were bound to be in close quarters on the mountain anyway. Maybe they had gotten off on the wrong foot back in Kathmandu. And the girl had certainly shown some spunk, hitting the trail so strongly after her bad dose of Delhibelly.

They sat quietly, side-by-side, drinking their tea, enjoying the night. Ricky soon found her attention drawn back to the mountain and, glancing sidelong at Allison, saw that she, too, had fallen under its spell. The mountaineer waited, betting that the stockbroker would soon feel the need to fill the night air with idle prattle or conjecture about the climb: was the route through the Khumbu Icefall fixed yet? How had the other Peak Performance members fared on the trek to Base Camp? What were the other expeditions on the hill up to?

Instead, there was nothing.

Just two people, united in their deep, abiding admiration for the great, hulking beauty hovering above them. Drawing them in. In the face of it all, Ricky had to admit that words seemed somehow...superfluous.

After a time, Allison tossed her tealeaves out onto the dirt, and stood. "Goodnight, Ricky," she said softly. "Sleep well."

"Thanks, uh...again." Tongue-tied, Ricky watched the blonde walk away and duck into her tent. Well, that was different. God, why was it so difficult for her to string a few words together? Why did this...person, throw her off balance so?

Ricky took a deep breath of the brisk night air, catching on the wind the invigorating scent of ice and snow. She returned her gaze to the mountain, pushing away all thoughts of everything and everyone else, and immediately she found her center again. This was what she knew best, what she could count on above all else.

For in the timeless embrace of the Mother Goddess, she was at home.

❋ ◆ ❋ ◆ ❋ ◆ ❋

The next day dawned cold and raw, with clouds beginning to move in over the mountains. They started off early, anxious to make Base Camp by midday. This last bit of the trek was over rough ground, a trail of barren rock and ice, silent reminders of the great Khumbu glacier slumbering nearby.

They followed the glacier's path, and as the going became more difficult, they fell into single file. Ricky took the lead, followed by Allison and Lou Silvers. The mountaineer carefully picked her way over the unsettled ground, conscious of the huffing and puffing going on behind her. Conversation was little more than "yes" or "no" grunts, as they attempted to keep their footing on the ash and gravel that had been haphazardly tossed on the ice to afford a better traverse.

The climbers concentrated on simply putting one foot in front of the other; dodging the streams of melt-water that, with one misstep, threatened to douse their boots. No one would voluntarily live in this desolate, dead area, and so even the little trailside huts eventually disappeared.

But Allison noticed that as they got closer to the base of Everest, a collection of stone monuments sprang up, lining the path. They were randomly constructed and of varying sizes, made mostly with stones and boulders that would have been found in the immediate vicinity.

"Wha-what are they?" Allison gasped, as another of the strange cairns came into view.

Lou came up behind her. As fit as the compact attorney was, he'd definitely been feeling the effects of the altitude over the past few days. And had one hell of a headache, due to the altitude no doubt.

"The Sherpas...put them up," he explained, his normally ruddy face pale in the late morning sun. "To honor those who've died on Everest. See." He reached out a gloved hand towards markings on the stone. "This one is for a...a Sherpa. And here," he sniffled in the cold, "the year that he died. 1982, it looks like."

"Oh," Allison gulped and started to move off again, feeling guiltily as though she'd trodden on someone's grave. She noticed that Ricky hadn't bothered to stop at the cairn. Of course, she had to have known what the monuments symbolized, and just hadn't bothered to say.

The mountaineer had been very quiet this day, that was true. But Allison decided to take no offense at that. Hell, they all had been saving their breath. The fact that they were on the final approach to the 17,600-foot elevation of Base Camp was at last taking its toll. Her throat was dry and sore, her feet hurt, and despite the large quantities of water she'd been forcing herself to drink, her head was buzzing as though she'd just left a front row seat at a rock concert.

Still, she felt better about things than she had in days. She felt ready, somehow, to take on the mountain, and part of that had to do with the truce that had evolved of its own accord between herself and Veronique Bouchard. At least, she felt as though the mountaineer no longer desired to toss her off the nearest cornice every time she looked at her. And as for herself, well, she still thought that Ricky was her best ticket to getting to the top of the hill. But it wasn't just that. There was a quiet confidence about the tall woman, an inner strength and a force of will that Allison...envied, in a way. Plagued as she was with her own self-doubt and uncertainty, she craved the focus and self-reliance that seemed to effortlessly flourish in the spirit of the mountaineer. Maybe, just maybe, she could learn from her, and take away a bit of that for herself. Reflecting back on the capricious void that was her life to date, she felt sure that with just such a psychic push, it might make all the difference.

Everest. They were nearly there.

As the sun burned off the low-hanging clouds, the free-standing ice pinnacles of "Phantom Alley" stood out in sharp relief against the glittering blue ice of the glacier. Looking for all the world like tumbled stalagmites, the sightless monoliths lined the final approach path to Base Camp.

"Okay, this is it!" Ricky tossed back over her shoulder, the first real words she'd spoken in hours.

They turned a corner, tramping along the crest of a slope towards the base of the glacial moraine. And there, spread out among a rocky lunar landscape, was a tent city of several hundred nylon domes. Crawling with Sherpas, yaks, shrieking birds, and the multitude of climbers who made up the expeditions staging for the southern route to the summit.

It was all Allison could do to breathlessly take it in, and then—shouts.

And suddenly a group of people pelting down the trail towards them. Allison could not identify them as members of the Peak Performance expedition, but it was hard to tell, bundled as they were against the elements. There were Sherpas among them, and several "western" looking climbers as well, wearing their sunglasses, brightly colored jackets, and wind pants.

Exhausted, struggling for every breath, Allison tried to sort it out. A welcoming committee, perhaps?

But as they drew closer, she could see she was mistaken. They were gesturing. Shouting in several languages that she didn't understand. And between them, they carried a stretcher.

Oh, God!

Arms waving, it became apparent they wanted them to move out of the way. They hurtled down the trail, oblivious to the jostling the body on the stretcher was receiving. Allison did her best to step aside and give them clear passage. Behind her, she heard Lou Silvers breathlessly scrambling to do the same.

The party was starting to push past them now, and Allison stood there, frozen, unable to pull her eyes away from the unfortunate soul on the litter. He was a Sherpa, she could tell that much. His eyes were glassy, unresponsive. An oxygen mask had been clamped onto his face, but in spite of that she could see the pale, pink froth seeping from the sides of his mouth, trickling down his cheeks. His hands and legs weakly convulsed of their own accord, no longer in the control of their owner. Several of his fellow Sherpas trailed along next to him, chattering away, encouraging him, but Allison doubted that the poor man could hear.

Suddenly, Veronique Bouchard stood in front of them, blocking their path. *"Arrêtez!"*

Uh-oh.

A violent argument ensued, confusion and fear tracking across the faces of the Sherpas as their two western masters went toe-to-toe with Ricky. They weren't American or English, Allison surmised, and from the sound of their accents, she doubted they were even French. Their faces flushed as their words became more heated. Ricky was livid, angrily pointing at the man on the stretcher. Allison feared the quarrel was about to come to blows when Ricky finally gave in, and stepped aside.

Quickly, the little caravan tumbled off down the trail.

"Idiots!" Ricky spat out a few more epithets in French, not caring whether they heard her or not.

"What...the *hell* was that all about?" Allison tried her best to keep her voice calm and even, but truth be known, she was feeling a little ill.

"That man shouldn't be moved." Ricky stomped back up the path, her face stormy. "Or at least they should have stabilized and 'bagged' him first," she said, referring to a pressurized "Gamow" bag, common to many expeditions' medical equipment. The bag was a portable hyperbaric chamber frequently used to treat severe conditions of high altitude pulmonary and/or cerebral edema. "He's got a dose of HAPE."

Lou coughed nervously. "That's...that's high altitude pulmonary edema, right?"

"Yeah." Ricky looked after the departing group with disgust. "They're with an international expedition. Russians, Uzbekistanis, and who the hell knows who else. Seems like their Sherpas were trying to lay claim to the better spots for the higher camps. Hell!" Ricky swore, her blue eyes flashing. "The route can't even have been fixed yet! These guys think they can race up there, drop a tent, pound a few ice stakes into the ground, and it's all theirs." She angrily shook her head. "He went up too far, too fast."

"Where are they taking him?" Allison asked weakly. Her knees were wobbly, and her heart was pounding, struggling to pump blood through her system at altitude. She felt like she wanted to sit down right now, but if she did, she wasn't sure she'd have the energy to get going again.

And if only her stomach would stop doing flip-flops, she might be able to think more clearly. She swallowed, hard. *God, that poor man!* She tried to blink the disturbing image out of her sight.

"They're heading down to the clinic at Pheriche," Ricky replied, the muscles bunching in her jaw. "But he'll never make it that far."

Pheriche was at the lower end of the Khumbu, at an elevation of about 16,000 feet. A small medical facility had been established there a few years before, staffed by several western doctors. Climbers who were ill or injured were typically taken there for treatment first and evacuated from there, if necessary, by helicopter. As an added benefit, the small clinic provided services year round to the local Sherpa community as well.

"He...he'll be okay, won't he?" The buzz in Allison's head was getting louder, and shapes began to swim before her eyes, but there was no way she was going to faint again. No way. She labored as she forced herself to breathe, her lungs struggling to pull in oxygen from the thin air.

Ricky turned to Allison, her eyes narrowing. "He's a dead man." Her lips formed a thin, tight line. "Welcome to Mount Everest."

Chapter Six

"Good mooooorning, Miss Allison!"

Ugh. She burrowed into her sleeping bag. *Just another five minutes.*

It seemed as though barely a minute had passed by, since the moment when she'd secured her tent and zippered herself up in her sleeping bag for a good night's sleep. Well, a night's sleep, anyway, as there was nothing "good" about the restless tossing and turning that newly acclimatizing climbers were prone to at Base Camp.

"Miss Allison, wakey-wakey!"

"All *right,* Lopsang!"

Groaning, Allison pushed her tousled blonde head to the surface. She took her time, edging herself into a sitting position, expecting to be hit with the shortness of breath, heart palpitations and nail-driving headache that had greeted her each of the previous three dawns. But this day, amazingly, blissfully, there was nothing. Not a trace of the high-altitude symptoms that had been plaguing her.

"And how are you, this fine day?" The brown, smiling face of Lopsang Chiri appeared in Allison's tent flap. The head Sherpa cook bore a steaming hot mug of tea.

"Pretty good, Lopsang," Allison replied, and she meant it. God, could this be the day that her body at last arrived at an equilibrium of sorts with the mountain? She hoped so. Over the previous three days, she'd done little more than languish in her tent, leaving it only for the rocky walk to the dining tent for meals and the odd stroll or two around the Peak Performance encampment, getting the lay of the land. Her every excursion had left her gasping for air and exhausted, and she took little comfort in the fact that she was not alone. They all were feeling it to varying degrees.

She'd seen very little of Lou Silvers since they'd staggered into camp, and she understood that the Donaldsons had been hit particularly hard. Mike was still feeling the effects of his digestive woes, and Patsy had received a house call in her tent from Sandra Ortiz, the team's Base Camp manager and physician. The petite redhead had been treated with an injection of dexamethasone or "dex," to help alleviate the rather severe symptoms of altitude sickness she'd been experiencing. Allison could not help but wonder whether Mike and Patsy's ailments had anything to do with the way they had insisted on chasing the younger Kevin MacBride and Phil Christy up the trail.

The gung-ho men had followed Jim Harris right into Base Camp, the first of the Peak Performance clients to arrive. MacBride had appeared to be completely recovered from his brush with Delhi-belly, and the two friends had spent the last few days exchanging stories with Harris and Paul Andersen and visiting other expedition camps in the vicinity. And as for Ricky Bouchard, well, Allison hadn't seen much of her, really, other than at mealtimes. Then, she'd seen her eating and laughing with the Sherpas outside the cooking tent. She found them better company, apparently.

"Breakfast ready soon!" Lopsang cheerily handed her the tea, as he had every morning since her arrival. It provided some small measure of comfort; a piping hot beverage delivered to all the climbers each day before they had even left their sleeping bags.

"Thanks, Lopsang." She smiled gratefully. "See you in a few."

Anxious to check out her environment with a clear head, for once, she quickly gulped down the tea, zipped on a powder blue jacket, and jammed a matching knit cap on her head. Pushing open her tent, she stepped out into a snow-capped, glittering dawn. Base Camp rested a safe distance away from the Khumbu Icefall, and in the early morning light, the chunky, groaning blocks of ice shone with myriad shades of refracted blue. She could just make out the tiny shapes of Sherpas, clambering over the ice and readying the path for the climbers that would follow. Allison had overheard the grumblings between Jim Harris and Paul Andersen, at how not all the expeditions on the mountain had been willing to chip in with Sherpas and resources towards the effort to fix lines and break trail. Particularly, the financially strapped "international" expedition.

Stuffing her hands into her jacket pockets, Allison's mind turned back to her arrival at Base Camp, and the shocking scene that had greeted her.

The international team's Sherpa had died.

Ricky had been correct in her assessment: the poor fellow, stricken with high altitude pulmonary edema, had expired without ever reaching the clinic at Pheriche. The internationals were an expedition on a shoestring, it seemed, lacking even a team physician. A dangerous way to take on the mountain. Worse, they'd suspiciously refused the aid of the docs from other groups, preferring to handle the medical emergency in their own way. And it had cost the Sherpa his life. A chill skipped through Allison as she returned her gaze to the mountain. Everest had claimed its first victim of the season. Would it be the last?

Drawing in a deep, high altitude breath, she began to pick her way towards the dining tent, taking note of the activity as Base Camp stirred. The Peak Performance encampment was not unlike others at the rocky foot of the Icefall. Climbers slept in their personal dome-shaped tents that had been set up in advance by the Sherpas; there seemed to be as many colors of tents as there were climbers. Adding to the rainbow effect, were the streams of prayer flags that the devout Sherpas had strung up on poles, fluttering away in the breeze.

Centrally located were larger tents holding the communications center and dining facility. A separate cook tent was built of glacial stone, with a tarp pulled across the top to serve as a roof. A smaller tent held Sandy Ortiz' Peak Performance medical facility. Smaller still, was a bathing tent. It was complete with a makeshift hot water shower, supplied by melt water heated by the Sherpas in the cook tent. Finally, adjacent to the shower, stood the expedition's much-used privy.

This particular morning appeared no different than the others Allison had experienced since her arrival, save for the fact that she felt better than she had in days. The Sherpa climbers she'd seen in the Icefall would have gotten off early, fixing ropes and ladders across the unstable glacier crevasses. She could see other expedition members from various teams emerging from their tents: some energized and breathing normally; others were pasty white, taking in the new day through bloodshot eyes. When it came to acclimatization, the mountain played no favorites.

Approaching the cook tent, Allison's mouth watered at the breakfast smells wafting through the thin air, taking satisfaction in the fact that her normal, healthy appetite seemed to have returned. For the past three days, she'd been able to tolerate little more than tea, oatmeal, and soup.

"Hi, Lopsang!" Allison poked her head into the cook tent, offering a wave to the Sherpa and his two assistants. A series of kerosene-fired stoves were blazing away, with a variety of foods in various states of preparedness. "What's for breakfast?"

"Bacon, ham, pancake, cheese omelet, juice, tea, coffee..." The Sherpa wiped a kerchief over his face. "You want something special, Miss Allison, I fix it right up. Oatmeal?"

"No, Lopsang, an omelet and ham will be fine." She'd had enough of the bland oatmeal; that was for certain. Time for some real food. "And how about you add a couple of pancakes to that, too?"

"No problem. Coming right up!" He bowed his head and smiled.

The normal Base Camp menu was full of artery-clogging selections that might never have appeared on her plate at sea level. She tried to eat right...most of the time, anyway. But here on the mountain, it was important to load up on as many proteins and carbohydrates as possible, since extended exposure to the cold and altitude sapped both your strength and appetite. Allison had read that it was not unusual for some climbers to lose twenty or more pounds during summit bids.

"Thanks, Lopsang." She continued on into the adjacent dining tent, her stomach growling happily in anticipation. The Peak Performance management had done their best to re-create home-style comforts in what normally became the informal hub of expedition operations. Meetings would be held here in the dining tent, plans made, alliances formed and dissolved. Plastic tablecloths lined a long slab table, and pink wildflowers in tiny vases stood among the place settings. A smaller side table held tea, coffee, bottled water, and a selection of juices and snacks. Soft music emanated from a stereo system, and solar powered lights brightly lit the interior.

"'Morning, Lou!"

Sitting alone inside the tent, was a rather bedraggled look-ing Lou Silvers. The attorney's salt-and pepper hair stuck out at odd angles from his head, and his face was drawn and pale. He appeared to have finished eating, and sat nursing a steaming hot cup of Sherpa tea.

"Allison!" He smiled faintly. "How ya feelin'?"

"Actually...pretty good," she replied, hardly believing it herself. "I think I've finally gotten my 'thin air' legs." She grabbed a clean mug and poured herself some tea from a simmer-ing brass kettle on the side table. "You?"

"Getting there, but I'm still not 100%." He tiredly rubbed at his face. "Unlike Kevin and Phil. They took off for the Ice-fall this morning, with Jim and the climbing Sherpas."

"You're joking." Allison took a seat across from Lou. "I thought we don't go up there for another couple of days?"

"That's what I thought." Lou shook his head. "But Jim wanted to check on how the route was shaping up, and those two begged to go along. He finally gave in, after they promised they wouldn't venture too far up."

"Geez." Allison shivered, thinking of the creaking, groan-ing seracs, ready to break off and avalanche downward without a breath of a notice. "We'll have to get through the Icefall soon enough. I can wait on that." She took a sip of her tea.

"Yeah, well, I just hope I'm ready for it." Lou paused, as a spasm of coughing rattled his chest. "You know, I thought I was in the best shape of my life before I got here. Better even, than when I did all that high-altitude climbing years ago. But this place has knocked me flat on my butt."

"You'll do fine," Allison assured him, as one of Lopsang's assistants bustled in with her platter of food. "Just give it some time."

"Here's hoping." He lifted his mug to her in an impromptu toast. "At least I'm doing better than poor Patsy Donaldson. Mike was in here earlier, getting some juice for her. I under-stand if she doesn't come around soon, there's talk of taking her back down to Pheriche. Poor thing."

"That's a shame," Allison agreed, knowing in her heart that Patsy's condition might've been her fate as well, if she had been of mind and body to attempt to keep up with Kevin and Phil in their rush up the Namche Trail. Thank God for that bug, after all. Still, if one had to come down with a dose of altitude sickness, better to be hit with it at Base Camp rather than at the higher elevations. The headaches, nausea, and shortness of breath could be devastating to a climber going for the summit, and Allison had heard stories of mountaineers who had fallen victim to it without warning. All it took was pushing the body too high, too fast. Or else there were the more subtle catalysts, such as forgetting to stay hydrated, or the bright sunlight burning into a climber's corneas for just those few moments when he or she had tucked their glacier sunglasses into a pocket.

Sometimes, all that was required for recovery was a quick shot of "dex," breathing in some pure O's, and a rapid descent. Other times, the body never bounced back, and the climber had to forego his or her shot at Everest. Allison sincerely hoped that would not be the case for Patsy Donaldson.

"God, real food for a change!" Allison tucked into her plate with gusto. "Oh," she said between mouthfuls, "sorry, Lou!"

"Nah, enjoy it while you can," he chuckled. "Believe me, if the sight of it still bothered me, I'd be halfway to the latrine by now. Anyway, you'll be dining on freeze-dried, reconstituted, dehydrated...whatever, soon enough."

"Shit."

Lou snickered. "You said it, not me."

"Well, as long as they don't run out of chocolate bars up there," Allison grinned, "I'll be fine."

"I found a Milky Way wrapper on the summit of Everest, once." A large shadow darkened the tent doorway.

"You're joking!" Lou Silvers' voice crackled as he fought back another bout of coughing.

"Am I?" the figure replied, removing its sunglasses and lifting an eyebrow.

Ricky Bouchard.

"I...I've heard that there's a lot of trash on the mountain," Allison sputtered, taking in the form of the tall mountaineer. Ricky wore a black fleece jacket with red piping, black climbing pants, and boots. Her dark hair was pulled back in a hair clip, and she wore a red baseball style cap with the Peak Performance Adventure Company logo emblazoned above the brim: a scripted "PPAC" superimposed over the profile of Everest.

"You should've seen Base Camp a few years ago," Ricky

said, remembering. "Garbage everywhere. People just...just destroying the site. But since then, there've been quite a few clean-up campaigns." She stepped into the tent, her sharp blue eyes falling on her clients. "It's a lot better now, but there is still much to be done. What you bring on the mountain, you take with you when you leave, eh?"

"Oh, yeah," Lou rapidly agreed. "We wouldn't want to make the Mother Goddess angry."

"No, that would not be a good thing," the mountaineer said firmly, pushing up the brim of her cap.

Allison remained silent, mentally swearing to herself that no matter what, she would not let a single candy wrapper go astray. Particularly, if Ricky Bouchard were nearby.

An awkward silence descended on the group as Ricky stood there, staring at them. The climber shifted her weight from one foot to the other, looking decidedly uncomfortable, as though she'd rather be anywhere else than in the Peak Performance dining tent.

"Where...where's Paul?" Allison said at last, daubing at her mouth with a paper napkin. "Has anyone seen him today?"

"Yes," Ricky replied, relief flooding her face. "He's off talking to some of the other expedition leaders, trying to work out who's going to fix the ropes up high."

"No one wants to go first, I'll bet."

"You're right," Ricky told the attorney. "Not with the deep snow we've heard is up there. A small group, going it alone, will burn out. Anyway, speaking of climbing, that's actually why I'm here." She took a deep breath before continuing. "Jim said I should take a group out on an acclimatization hike today."

"Not to the Icefall!" Allison panicked. God, not yet! She wasn't ready for it—not today! Let Kevin and Phil crawl all over the Icefall if they wanted to. Hell, she hadn't even had her crampons on once since she'd arrived.

"No-no-no!" Ricky held up her hand, the displeasure plain on her face. Obviously she disproved of the two men's early outing to the Icefall with the Peak Performance team leader. "It's too soon to head up there...at least, I think so. I thought we'd head up and over to Pumori," she said, naming one of Everest's sister mountains. "No crowds. Nice view. We'd be back in time for the group meeting before dinner."

"Meeting?" Allison looked from Ricky to Lou, confused.

"Yeah." The older man gestured towards a small sign she

hadn't noticed, hanging on the far tent post. "Jim wants everybody to get together with Doctor Ortiz to go over a few things,
and roll out the schedule for the next few days."

"Sounds good." Allison had felt out of the loop since she'd
arrived, and looked forward to getting together again with her
fellow expedition members. And this hike sounded good, too.
An opportunity to strap on her boots and get out there, doing
what she'd come here to Everest to do. And the fact that one of
the best mountaineers in the world was making that offer, well,
what was there not to like?

"Of course, if you're still feeling the altitude," Ricky
quickly continued, her sun and wind burnished skin growing
oddly flushed, "that's okay. You can take another rest day and—
"

"I'd love to go." Allison pushed away her plate. "Count me
in. Lou?"

"Nah...it's not happening." The exhausted attorney waved
them off. "At least, not for today. I'll take a rain check."

Ricky looked disappointed. "I saw Mike Donaldson on my
way over here. He's decided to stay put with Patsy." The mountaineer let her eyes rest on the young blonde. "So...I suppose
it's just you and me." She put her sunglasses back on. "Grab
your pack and be ready to go in 15 minutes." She turned on her
heel and left the tent, her footsteps crunching on the rocky
ground.

"*Shit!*" Allison bolted to her feet, and grabbed an armful of
bottled water and packaged snacks from the side table.

"Have fun, you two!" Lou grinned as the younger woman
bolted from the tent.

Allison Peabody and Veronique Bouchard.

The attorney poured himself another mug of hot tea and
shook his head. Those two women were so different, and yet
they were both good people. Perhaps they could learn from one
another. He took a swallow of his tea. Ah, well. Stranger things
had happened, here on the Mother Goddess.

❀ ♦ ❀ ♦ ❀

Allison swore she was hotter here in the shadow of Everest,
than she'd been at any time earlier, hiking on the Namche Trail.
It was amazing, the strength of the brilliant sunlight at the higher
elevations. As long as there was no snow or wind sweeping

down from above, then a near cloudless sky such as today, coupled with powerful, midday rays, made for beach-like weather.

Ricky Bouchard was moving strongly in front of her, and Allison was pleased beyond measure to note that she'd had little trouble keeping up with the mountaineer. God, what a wonderful day it was to be alive! She was breathing easily, even at these slightly higher elevations, noting how the sun-warmed air still smelled of snow, rock, and ice. The ground was loose stone, mostly, with a bit of ice cover mingled in. Like Ricky, Allison had left her crampons behind, unnecessary as they were for this hike. But she had brought along her climbing poles, just in case. And she had used them as they'd pushed higher towards Pumori. Been happy to have them along, in fact, stabbing them into the earth periodically for leverage and balance.

But Ricky Bouchard...even here, on this relatively easy sortie, Allison was beginning to get a glimpse of just what kind of a climber the woman was. No poles for her, not on this trip, anyway. Her bare arms swung freely at her sides, and her strong legs powered her forward steadily, surely. No missteps for her. The tall mountaineer had tied her jacket about her waist and stripped down to a white T-shirt. Despite the heat and all her exertion, she barely seemed to have broken a sweat.

Hmnn.

Well. At least she'd acquitted herself respectably, Allison considered. Ricky Bouchard would have nothing to complain about, as far as her performance was concerned. From the moment they'd started out from Base Camp, they'd both swung into a comfortable rhythm, talking little, simply enjoying the day and the scenery. Plenty of time to think, or else just let your mind drift aimlessly, openly, freed from the constraints of order, of convention.

How far away Wall Street and Johnson-Kitteridge-Johnson seemed! And how...small, and meaningless, too. That life. *Her* life, the one she'd made for herself.

The next deal.

"Finish up with this crazy 'Everest' nonsense if you must, Allie," her boss told her. *"And when you finally come to your senses and get back here, if you play your cards right, you'll be first in line for my job once I move onto the board. 'Allison Peabody, Executive Vice-President of Sales.' How does that sound?"*

The next date.

"Allison, dearest, you make me the laughing stock of our friends when you take off like this! Whatever will people think?"

"Our friends? They're your friends, not mine, Lionel. And what gave you the idea that I give a damn about what people think?"

The next dinner with her parents, where the three of them would all behave quite civilly, making polite conversation about the news, the weather, the tenderness of the meat. As though they were strangers, meeting for the very first time.

Strangers.

Allison swallowed hard, and stopped, telling herself it was because she'd finally decided to take off her jacket. She lifted her face to the sun, welcoming the heat of it, rationalizing that it was the sharp brightness of it, of course, that had caused the tear to leak from her eye. It was all so much simpler here, where all that mattered was the placement of your next step or enjoying a drink of cool water while sitting on glacial rocks, aged older than time.

"You okay?"

Ricky had stopped on the path above her and had half-turned, facing her.

"Fine," Allison quickly replied. "Just a little warm."

The mountaineer glanced back towards Pumori, and then returned her gaze to Allison. "There's a good spot up ahead where we can break and have lunch. How does that sound?"

Allison tied off her jacket at her waist, re-shouldered her pack, and grabbed her poles.

The simple life.

While she was here, by God, she would enjoy it. She smiled brightly at the mountaineer, chasing away the shadows of her own making.

"Lead on."

❈ ◆ ❈ ◆ ❈ ◆ ❈

It was one hell of a view, Ricky Bouchard had to admit to herself. Sitting here, perched at the foot of Pumori, with Everest, Nuptse, and the Khumbu Icefall shimmering in the afternoon sun like some heavenly, snow-drifted mirage. It was the uncluttered beauty of it all, the pureness of it, that drew her back time and time again.

That drove her to take calculated risks, to push herself

beyond what even she suspected she was capable of, in order to seize a moment such as this for herself. It fueled her blood and nourished her spirit, and was the only religion she cared to know. It made all the other...bullshit, worth it.

Take today, for instance. Jim Harris was her boss, and so she'd had little to say about it when he'd told her to take a group out on an acclimatization hike. Truth be known, she would have preferred to go into the Icefall to help fix the route, along with Jangbu Nuru, the expedition's climbing sirdar, and the rest of the climbing Sherpas. Driving in ice screws, securing lines, and laying down ladders across gaping crevasses would've not only provided her with welcome physical activity, it also would've made her feel useful, that she was a more valuable member of the team.

After all, she'd been used to doing much of the labor on her previous expeditions. But here, on this "deluxe" guided tour, it was not meant to be. Instead, Jim Harris relegated her once again to the role of chief Peak Performance baby-sitter. Still, it could have been worse. Jim could've opted to send her around to the other camps, trying to drum up support for a collective effort to break trail and fix ropes up high. Paul Andersen had been given that responsibility, while Jim himself had headed up to the Icefall; and it was just as well. She'd never been much good at politicking and negotiation, preferring instead to let her deeds to the talking. Screw 'em if they didn't want to help out in the higher elevations; she'd do it herself. She had before.

And the hike hadn't turned out too badly, after all. The Donaldsons had been too under the weather to go, and Lou Silvers still seemed to be suffering from the effects of altitude. Ricky's gut told her that unlike Patsy Donaldson, however, the older attorney would find a way to turn it all around and get back onto his feet soon. She liked the man, and hoped that he'd get his chance at the top.

As for Kevin MacBride and Phil Christy, Ricky certainly hadn't approved of Jim Harris taking the younger men to the Icefall. The less time spent there, the better, particularly if you were unfamiliar with the way the beautiful, surrealistic landscape could suddenly turn deadly. On the Icefall, more so than anywhere else on the hill, a lack of experience or, worse—just plain bad luck—could get you killed. In letting the two men join him, the expedition leader was establishing a bad precedent. And as much as the Peak Performance expedition members were called a "team," it was becoming painfully apparent to Ricky that they were far from it.

"Thanks for this."

Ricky returned her attention to her companion, Allison Peabody. The young stockbroker waved a hand at the view she'd been admiring, and at the tiny, colorful tents dotting the slope far below: the Everest Base Camp.

"And thanks for this, too!" Allison held up the last bit of a ham and cheese sandwich, one of several that Ricky had produced from her backpack.

"No problem," the mountaineer replied. "Once Lopsang found out we were going off on a hike, it was all I could do to keep him from coming with us and preparing something *al fresco*. So I made him settle for giving us a pack lunch."

"Well, it sure hit the spot," Allison said, swallowing her last bite and chasing it down with a swig of bottled water.

"And, an acclimatization hike like this is always a good idea," Ricky continued, "especially if you've been inactive for a few days. Up here, it's a struggle to hold onto whatever sort of muscle tone you've got."

"Well, I'm feeling those muscles today," Allison chuckled, reaching to massage her calves, "but in a good way, I mean."

"Mnnn."

Ricky leaned back against a large rock. The area in the hillside where they sat formed a natural concave shelter from the winds, while at the same time it absorbed the radiant heat from the sun. The two women were both down to T-shirts now and had removed their climbing boots. Allison also had doffed her knit cap and had applied a layer of sunscreen to her arms and face. Sitting here in the shadow of Mount Everest, with the distinctive scent of cocoa butter in the air, Ricky found herself very easily imagining that this Allison Peabody would no doubt be very much at home on some high-class tropical island resort, or an exotic cruise. That sort of vacation, with all the expensive trappings and golden spoon service, seemed more her style, or so she thought.

But here on Everest...taking a month or two out of your life, giving up room service and central heat just so you could eat freeze-dried casseroles and feel so dirty that you were ready to crawl out of your own skin, not to mention literally risking life and limb...it just didn't add up. Could it be Allison was completely clueless about the whole thing, as she had first suspected?

Ricky was beginning to think not.

Allison had done well today on an uphill hike over uneven ground that would've been a cakewalk at sea level. But at 18,000 feet, it was a whole new ball game, and the smaller woman had kept up with her, stride for stride.

Although the stockbroker's first few days at altitude had been rough, that was fairly common. Today, she seemed to have definitely turned the corner. She was in shape, that was for certain; the mountaineer could not help but notice that the younger woman, though slightly built, was compact and muscular. Maybe there was something to be said for those Stairmasters, after all.

So, Allison Peabody was in good enough physical condition to attempt the climb. And though her technical skills weren't at a level Ricky would have liked to have seen, at least she had more experience than, say, a Patsy Donaldson. The only real technical area of the Everest push anyway, would be at the Hillary Step. The Step was named after New Zealander Edmund Hillary, who, along with Sherpa Tenzing Norgay in 1953, were the first men to successfully summit Everest. It was a near-vertical pitch of 50-foot high rock and snow, but getting over the impasse could be easily done by technical climbers.

As long as said climbers weren't hypoxic, and their hands and feet were still functioning normally. Not a given, at nearly 29,000 feet. Could Allison handle it? If she couldn't, she had no place on the mountain.

"Wow, look at that plume!" Allison pointed towards the familiar white cloud lengthening from the summit of Everest. "It must be getting windier up there, blowing off all that snow."

Ricky followed Allison's gaze towards the plume. Climbers often used its length and intensity as an informal means of forecasting the weather on the summit. "It's not snow, actually," Ricky said, feeling Allison's eyes turn towards her.

"But it's white and sparkly, and it's blowing..."

"A lot of people make that mistake," Ricky tucked a water bottle back into her pack, "because of just the reasons you've said. But really," she faced Allison, "it's because of the heat."

"The heat?" Allison shook her head. "I don't understand."

"On a clear day like today, when the sun hits the Kangshung Face of Everest, it heats up the whole area, evaporating the moisture from the snow. Think of it like steam rising after a summer rain storm," Ricky explained, holding out her hands to illustrate her point. "The steam rises on the eastern side, until it hits the summit and gets slammed by the colder, western winds blowing over the top."

"So when the hot and cold air masses collide—"

"The moisture condenses again, creating the plume."

"And the longer the plume, the stronger the winds."

"Right," Ricky confirmed. "I've seen beautiful, windless days like today, where the weather at Base Camp is perfect. But with one look at the plume, you can tell it's bad news, up high."

"I'll keep that in mind," Allison said, regarding the mountain thoughtfully. She pulled her knees up to her chest and rested her chin on them, falling silent for a time. And then, quietly, "Do you think I can make it?"

The mountaineer knew right away what the younger woman meant. God, had she been reading her mind earlier, or what? Now, here she was, asking her a question that Ricky had no ready answer for.

"That depends on you," Ricky began slowly, gathering her thoughts. "And on a lot of other factors, some that you simply can't control. The weather, your health, other people...crowds, even, trying to summit on the same day as you, just because that's the only weather window there is." She sighed. "It's more crowded this year than I've ever seen it before. Too damn many people who don't know what they're doing."

Realizing how that must have sounded to her companion, Ricky turned to her, fumbling. "Not...not that you—"

"No, you're right," Allison said, reddening. "I'm not as good as you...or Jim, or Lou." She took her sunglasses off and leveled her eyes at Ricky. "But I'm here. And I'm gonna do what it takes to get to the top. I have to make it. I *have* to," she said more softly. "Or else, what's the point?"

They both were sitting too close to each other for Ricky not to notice the tears forming in the younger woman's green eyes, to see the pain storming there. Okay. So she had the fire in her belly. Ricky above all could understand that. But was it for the right reason?

"You...you'd better get those glasses back on," Ricky said lamely, not knowing how else to respond. "It's awfully bright out."

"You think I don't belong here, right?" Allison's features stiffened as she replaced her sunglasses. "Don't bother denying it. You haven't tried very hard to hide it."

Shit. Now it was Ricky's turn to feel uncomfortable. *She's the client. She's the client.* A score of responses sprang to mind, any one of which might have served to mollify the woman somewhat, to soothe her ego, or alleviate her concerns. But it was the truth that finally fought its way to the surface and found its way to her tongue.

"No, you don't."

Allison thrust her jaw out in the face of the stinging comment, defiant, but Ricky could see how her lower lip trembled slightly.

"You don't belong here," the mountaineer said quickly, passionately, "but I don't either. *None* of us do, Allison. Not really. Our bodies weren't built to withstand this sort of punishment, this...this trial by fire and ice. We put ourselves on this mountain...constantly battling to get enough to eat and drink, to stay warm, to have just one night where we sleep through and not wake up from a nightmare that we're suffocating. And so we sit. And wait for that perfect moment when the skies clear, when we're fully acclimatized and ready to go. But by that time, our bodies have already begun to waste away." She laughed bitterly. "So what? We don't care. Because getting to the top is the only thing we can think about. And so we don't give a damn about the nasty weather.

"Or the death of a teammate.

"Or the fluid building up in our lungs that's choking us.

"We push past the altitude sickness and climb, passing by the bodies of climbers who've died on past expeditions. Maybe you knew them, maybe you didn't. Maybe they could *be* you, if your numb hands haven't been able to fasten your harness properly, or if your oxygen starved brain thinks you've already clipped onto the rope when you haven't."

Ricky paused, worried that perhaps she'd gone too far, but there was no turning back now. Allison Peabody had asked her a question. She deserved an answer.

"And then," she said quietly, "when your body has reached its limit, when you're literally falling apart, you have to call upon yourself to execute one of the most physically demanding things you've ever done—the final push to the summit. And you have to ask yourself: is it worth it? Do I have what it takes? Or not?"

"I'm not afraid."

"Well, you should be!" Ricky declared. "You should be scared shitless!"

"I have what it takes," Allison said fiercely, swallowing hard. "Maybe...maybe I didn't come here for the right reasons, not at first. I was wrong. I can see that now. For me...it's about doing something for myself. Proving that I can for me—no one else. Everything at home, my life there, it pales in comparison to this! *This* is what has value...has worth." She bit her lip. "If you knew...knew what kind of crap—"

"We all have our baggage," Ricky interrupted her, knowing she herself carried more than her share. God knew that with every step she took on this mountain, *every* step, Jean-Pierre was there, right alongside her. "The question is, how do we deal with it? Do we let it weigh us down, killing us, or instead, do we open it up and take a look at what's inside, and find some way to use it to our advantage?" *Hmmn,* Ricky considered, *that sounded pretty good. I'll have to try it sometime, myself.*

Allison was silent, absorbing the mountaineer's words. She sat there, gazing up at Pumori for a time, and then gathered herself. "Geez, listen to me!" Allison rubbed a fist to her nose, sniffling. "I—why am I telling you all this?"

I have no idea. "Everest does that," Ricky replied, not unkindly. "It brings out the best in us...and the worst. I think...understanding why you're here...getting in touch with that, is a good thing."

"Well," Allison released a sharp burst of air, "I know there are no guarantees in this life. But I want to get to the top, and I'm going to give it everything I've got." She smiled faintly. "Heck, it'll probably be the most pure, honest thing I've ever done in my life. The first thing that's not a lie."

In a visceral, immediate response, the mountaineer was surprised to find her hand reaching out, giving Allison Peabody's shoulder an awkward pat. The younger woman's words had struck a familiar, resonant chord in Ricky's soul.

"I'll tell you what: you do your best to climb this mountain, Allison, and I'll do my best to make sure you get to the top." Her tanned face creased into a smile. "And down. Deal?"

Allison grinned and stuck out her hand. "Deal."

Chapter
Seven

"Okay...okay! The sooner we get started, the sooner we'll be finished, and Lopsang and his people can get dinner in here!" His hulking form filling the front of the tent, Jim Harris played high-altitude traffic cop, ushering everyone to benches and plastic chairs. The dining tent was filled to bursting with all the Peak Performance guides and clients, as well as several Sherpas, including Jangbu Nuru, the head climbing Sherpa.

Ricky slipped into the tent and made her way to stand by the back wall, trying to look as inconspicuous as possible. This was Jim's show; let him run it. She was just a hired hand, and a junior one, at that. She caught sight of Allison Peabody, seated at the main table between Lou Silvers and a rather pale looking Patsy Donaldson. Allison waved a "hello," and Ricky nodded in return. Allison's face was flushed and healthy looking, as were the faces of all of the climbers who'd been spending time out-of-doors. Jim Harris, wearing bright red Patagonia bibs and a thick black turtleneck, looked as though he were physically able to climb Everest single-handed. Strong, dynamic, good-looking, Ricky considered the fact that he was probably better suited than any of them to the job of team leader, a position that required being equal parts businessman, climber, and customer service guru. At best, Ricky knew that she herself was only one out of the three. But she was proud of that fact, being a mountaineer.

No one could take that away from her. No one.

Kevin MacBride and Phil Christy shouldered their way into the tent, their eyes bright and excited; both men had clearly been energized by their morning in the Icefall with Jim and the Sherpas.

Paul Andersen was last to arrive, and found a position next to Jim. The tall, lean guide looked a bit weary from his day of negotiating, but otherwise in good health. Mike Donaldson and Lou Silvers, however, appeared as though they had both just rolled out of their sleeping bags, and Ricky suspected that perhaps that was not far from the truth.

And as for Patsy Donaldson...clearly the woman was still feeling the effects of the altitude, although she was bravely trying to tough it out for the meeting. The food cooking next-door couldn't have smelled too appealing to her in her condition, and she'd jammed a multi-colored knit cap down onto her head, covering her ears and compressing the whorling curls of her red hair. The woman looked to be barely able to make her way back to her tent under her own power, let alone climb the world's highest mountain.

"All right, everybody," Jim waved the expedition members down into their seats, "what I'd like to do tonight is go over the schedule for the next couple of days, and let you know what we're going to be doing. This is crunch time, kids, so everyone's got to be up to speed and with the program. Your safety, and that of your fellow team members, could depend upon it." Jim gestured towards a petite, dark skinned, 30-ish woman sitting on the side table. "Speaking of safety, for those of you who haven't met her yet, this is Doctor Sandra Ortiz, our expedition physician and Base Camp Manager." He gave a courtly bow in her direction. "Sandy."

Led by Kevin and Phil, the tent erupted in applause and cheers. "Thanks," the doctor said, blushing. She pushed herself off the table and stood, taking a moment to adjust the small-framed wire glasses on her face. "Jim and I have known each other for years," she said, running a hand through her short, brunette hair, "and I look forward to getting to know all of you over the next few weeks."

"I hope you mean personally, and not professionally," Kevin MacBride said, and everyone laughed.

"Well, if this is anything like the other expeditions Jim has talked me into," the physician flashed a gleaming smile, "it'll probably be a mixture of both. Which brings me to my little two-minute public service announcement here tonight." Pausing, she cast a sidelong glance at Jim Harris, who bade her continue. "It's about staying safe and healthy while you're here on the mountain. As healthy as you all may think you are down in the thick air, it's a different story up here. The medical tent is open for business 24/7," she said firmly, "and you'll be seeing me for things like blisters, headaches, muscle aches, or coughs. And that's not all." She started counting off on her fingers, "You'll have confusion, trouble sleeping, lack of coordination, nausea, dehydration, diarrhea, dizziness—"

"Please!" Patsy Donaldson held up a hand and smiled weakly. "And I was just feeling better, too!"

The majority of the crowd laughed nervously, but Ricky Bouchard did not. Privately, she worried that if the ill woman pushed herself up the mountain in her condition, there would be nothing but trouble ahead. And it didn't help matters any that she'd heard Mike Donaldson state more than once that he was determined that he and Patsy would be the first American couple to successfully summit Everest.

"Sorry." The doctor's voice was sympathetic. "I know some of you've already had first hand experience with what I'm talking about. The point is," she regarded them seriously, "I don't want any of you playing doctor on your own. You don't feel good—you come to me. You think somebody else doesn't look good—you send them to me. Because *they* may be the last to know they're in trouble." She folded her arms. "Up here, ignoring something doesn't make it go away. It makes it get worse. I guarantee it."

Jim Harris began to move towards Dr. Ortiz, carrying a small duffel bag. "The big things we all have to worry about, are hypoxia - altitude sickness, or worse, high altitude pulmonary edema or cerebral edema." He placed the duffel bag on the table next to the physician.

"Or, HACE and HAPE, as they're better known," Sandy added. "We've already had one fatal case on the mountain this season."

Ricky shifted uncomfortably in her place at the back of the tent. Yes, it had been a fatal case. One that never should have happened.

"That's why we want you all to have these." Jim opened the duffel, and the doctor withdrew several small containers that looked like toothbrush travel holders. "We'll go over the usage of these, but for now, know that each one of you will be given these pre-loaded syringes of dexamethasone. It's a steroid used to treat severe cases of hypoxia, HACE, and even HAPE. Carry them inside your climbing suits next to your skin to keep them warm. Use it if you have to, on yourself or someone else. But hopefully," she replaced the syringes in the bag, "you'll never need it."

"We'll also be issuing you with these." Jim Harris took out a small radio kit, with an earpiece and lapel mic. "Everybody who goes up the hill, whether guide, client, or Sherpa, will be issued one of these." His voice grew somber. "I think lack of communication...knowing where people are on the mountain, has caused many of the tragic problems that have occurred here in the past. With this," he held up the unit for all to see, "we can stay in constant contact with Base Camp, and with each other."

Ricky had to admit it; she was impressed. She'd worked only infrequently with radio comm before, mostly because it was an added cost that the expeditions she'd been on before simply couldn't afford. Only the team leader might have been issued one or, if it was just herself and Jean-Pierre, it hadn't been necessary.

"The next thing," Jim continued, "is oxygen. Now...I know some of you haven't used supplemental O2 before, or at least aren't familiar with it. "From Camp III on up, I want everybody breathing gas." The big man reached into the duffel, and took out a large, orange, steel and Kevlar canister, along with a regulator, rubber hose, and mask. "It'll help you keep your strength, and keep your head, up there in the thin air." He held up the dark oxygen mask, a big, bulky contraption not unlike those worn by fighter pilots. "We'll show you over the next few days how to use them."

"That's right," the doctor said, picking up the regulator. "Figuring out how to change bottles of O2, and adjusting and regulating the flow of the gas, is a lot easier here at Base Camp than it is at the South Summit. You've got to know what you're doing. If you're up high and start to go hypoxic...well, I've heard of some climbers who got into trouble because they'd inadvertently turned the flow *off,* instead of on."

"Whoa," Mike Donaldson said, the solar-powered lights in the tent shining on his balding head. "A bad thing to have happen, in thin air."

"That's actually a misnomer," the physician said, putting the regulator down. "'Thin air,' I mean. There's a normal amount of oxygen in the air at the summit. The problem is, you can't get it into your lungs due to the reduction in atmospheric pressure. For example," she explained, "a barometer reading at sea level would register 2/3 less at the top of Everest. For those of you who've been there, it feels as though only part of your lungs is working. You've got to work extra hard to catch your breath, and you end up nearly hyperventilating."

"In other words, up top," Jim said, "you've got to breathe three times as fast to get the same amount of oxygen you'd get at sea level. Unless," he lifted the orange bottle, "you're on this."

"Some climbers are better able to handle the high conditions than others," the doctor continued. "Their physiology makes them better suited to process the oxygen in their lungs, and get it into their bloodstream and vital organs where it's needed."

Jim Harris looked Ricky's way. "For example, our own Ricky Bouchard, here, didn't use gas on her previous Everest summits, right, Ricky?"

"Umn...yes, that is true," the mountaineer replied, feeling slightly uncomfortable at being pointed out.

"But she will this time, as your guide. Staying strong, breathing gas, is the key."

Ricky nodded her head "yes," a tense smile finding its way to her lips. She was strong enough to get to the top of the highest peaks in the world *without* using the cumbersome oxygen, thank you very much. She hated the damn things, the extra weight they added, they way they were always breaking down. And the feel of it on her face, choking her, smothering her, and cutting off her field of vision. In all the climbing nightmares that plagued her while she slept, she was always wearing one.

"It looks awfully cumbersome," Allison Peabody said, voicing Ricky's thoughts. "What if we run into some difficulty up high?" From where Ricky stood, she could see the frown on the younger woman's face.

"No problem," Jim assured her. "A guide will always be nearby, or you could radio for help. Don't worry, Allie, we'll make sure you can work these things in your sleep, before we send you off. Which brings me to the last item I'm sure you've been waiting for." He let his eyes sweep the room. "The way through the Icefall is nearly fixed. Two days from now, we'll head up through the Khumbu, touch Camp I, and come back.

We'll be under way!"

"*Yes!*" Kevin MacBride gave his buddy's back a slap. "Let me at it!"

"We'll leave early, about 5 a.m., to get a jump start on the other teams. That way, too, we'll be sure to be up and back before the heat of the day hits the ice...or else we could run into some problems."

"Yeah...like...look out below—*boom!*" MacBride laughed at his own joke.

"We'll talk about how to get through the Icefall *safely*, Kevin." Jim smiled and shook his head. "And, we'll practice here at camp, walking back and forth on top of a horizontal ladder, while wearing full gear and crampons."

"I don't want to be seeing you guys for twisted knees, or worse," Sandy said, flexing her knees slightly. "It's important that you try to find the sweet spot, taking it one step at a time, and saddle it where your spikes are on either side of the rung. It's about balance and coordination."

"And no look down!" Jangbu Nuru, the climbing sirdar, spoke up at last. His dark eyes sparkled, and his weathered, tanned face was illuminated by a bright smile. "You follow Jangbu, you be a-okay!" He gave a thumbs up, and they all laughed, Ricky included. She knew Jangbu well. They'd worked together on her previous south-side foray, and it was on that expedition that he'd earned her great respect. He was one of the best sirdars in all of Nepal and Tibet, and she trusted him with her life.

"Well," Jim chuckled, scratching the growing beard on his face, "on that note, who's hungry?"

❋ ✦ ❋ ✦ ❋ ✦ ❋

"Okay," Allison Peabody muttered softly to herself, "one more time...let's make sure. Backpack," she touched the dark blue frame, "ice ax, harness, carabiners, jumars, helmet, crampons..." She'd laid out her gear at least four or five times over the past several days, making sure everything was in order: dry, functional, and ready to take on the mountain. This absolutely would be the last time she'd have a chance to do it, for tomorrow, early, they would be off for the Icefall.

Time to shut up and put up, Allison. She crawled to the edge of her tent and edged out of it, lifting her eyes towards the Khumbu. It was lit nearly bright as day by the full moon overhead, all the peaks surrounding them were, shimmering and glistening in the rarefied air. Her pulse quickened and her stomach fluttered as she took it in, absorbed it, memorized its details.

Was she ready?

God, she hoped so. She'd had no problem negotiating the practice ladders; she'd always been nimble and blessed with good balance. Ricky had been pleased with her performance on them, she could tell. And as for the oxygen rigs, at this point she was sure she would be able to build one from scratch, if need be.

Allison had been a patient student during the little "seminars" Sandy, Jim, and the guides had put on. But it was apparent that others, Kevin and Phil, in particular, thought they were a waste of time for individuals of their level of climbing experience. Jim Harris had looked the other way when the two men walked out of the radio "lesson." "Ah, I'll catch up with them later on this," Jim had said. "And anyway, I think they're pretty familiar with this stuff."

And Mike Donaldson had seemed to have a hard time understanding why he and Patsy would have to be responsible for carrying their own second 15-pound bottles of oxygen with them on the final summit push, and not the Sherpas. "You definitely need two bottles to get up and down," Sandy had explained. "Maybe even more, if you run into trouble. The Sherpas will be carrying the extras, just in case."

"Well, it just doesn't seem right," Mike had stubbornly declared, clearly put out. Patsy's green eyes had merely widened, and her face blanched.

But Allison had listened, and nodded, and drilled, soaking up every word of it, driven by the words of Ricky Bouchard that kept echoing in her mind: *"You don't belong here."*

Okay.

Since that was a given, it was up to her to do everything possible to mitigate the risk, to tip the scales in her balance, to seal the deal. And with Ricky's help, she just might make it.

Restless, Allison crawled the rest of the way out of her tent, and propped herself down on a flattened rock. In the distance, she could hear the boisterous laughter and music coming from the dining tent. It was the rest of the team and the Sherpas, celebrating the night before heading up the mountain. Normally, the old Allison Peabody would've been right there along with them. But now she had a new focus, a new purpose.

She hadn't had an opportunity to talk with Ricky Bouchard

since they'd returned from their hike, not really. They'd both been so busy, and Allison had to admit that she was surprised at the calm patience the mountaineer had shown while instructing them on the ladders and with the other equipment. For some reason, she'd thought the tall woman might have been inclined to lose her temper...but no. She'd done her job. In fact, Allison had preferred to take Ricky's instruction over Jim's or Paul's. Listening to the mountaineer's low, alto tones, explaining to Patsy Donaldson for the third time how to find the Base Camp frequency on the radio, gave her confidence, somehow.

And in a sense, certainty; in herself, most of all.

Allison sighed, bundling her jacket tightly against the chilled night air. How gorgeous Everest looked in the night sky! How fortunate she was, to be in a place like this! And how lucky she was, too, to have someone like Ricky Bouchard on their team. She could see that, now. Lou knew it too, but she wondered if the others did. Or even cared. There was something about Ricky...a sort of magic. She was beautiful, yes, one couldn't help but notice that; but there's something else, too, something Allison just couldn't put her finger on yet. And so she planned to stay as close to the mountaineer as possible, until she had it all figured out.

"Bon soir."

Allison almost fell off her rock. "Oh, hi! I...I didn't know—"

Blue eyes flashed in the moonlight. "Sorry. Did I startle you?"

"No...I uh, well, yeah you did, but—"

"See you tomorrow, then." The mountaineer turned to walk away.

"No, wait!" Allison's voice croaked. "I was just going over my gear. Have...have a seat."

Wordlessly, Ricky settled down on an adjacent rock. With the onset of darkness the winds had stilled, and though the temperature was dropping and their breath formed puffs of white mist in the air, it was still relatively comfortable.

"I saw you leave the dining tent early," Ricky began. "I wondered if you were feeling okay." She stole a sidelong glance at Allison.

"Oh, I'm fine. I just...just wanted to get out of there and check on things."

"Things?" Ricky arched an eyebrow. "If you mean your

gear, I've seen you pack and repack it three or four times, at least."

"Yeah, well," Allison blushed in the dark, "I can't help it. It's...it's almost like it's Christmas Eve, and I can't wait until morning comes so I can open up my presents. Only this time," she lifted her eyes to the mountaineer, "I'm getting something I really want." She paused for a moment. "How about you—why did you leave, really?" There was no way the tall woman would've left just to check up on her, right?

Ricky was quiet for a moment, and then released a sharp burst of air. "I guess getting drunk on *chang* isn't my idea of a good time," she replied. "Altitude and alcohol—they do not mix." A pause. "I'll never forget the first time Jean-Pierre made me try it." She shook her head. "He told me it was a Himalayan version of soda pop. And I drank it like it was, too. The next day..." she chuckled, "I would've killed him, if only I'd been able to get out of bed!" Ricky's laughter died away. "Now...I'd drink all the *chang* he wanted me to if only..."

"You...you miss, him, don't you?" Allison could not help but ask the question, knowing she was treading onto dangerous, personal ground.

"Yes," Ricky said slowly, "I do. He should be alive. Married by now, bouncing babies on his knee, teaching them to climb." She fell silent.

Allison could see the mountaineer struggling with her emotions, fighting to conceal inside the hurt and sense of loss she dared not show. Best to change the subject. "Thanks for talking to me the other day, out there on the hike."

Ricky shrugged. "It was nothing."

"Yeah, well, I appreciated it."

An awkward silence hung in the air.

Damn! Allison thought. *Why is holding a conversation with this woman so difficult?* "Just look at that," she finally said, nodding towards Everest. "Tomorrow we'll be on it. All 29,028 feet of it."

"Actually," Allison could see Ricky's white teeth flash in a grin, "it's 29,035 feet now. A GPS satellite re-calibrated its height a couple of years ago."

"Great," the young blonde groaned. "That means I've got farther to climb."

"Then about time we get started, eh?" And with that, Ricky Bouchard stood. "See you tomorrow, Allison." With a small wave, she headed towards her tent.

Watching her depart, Allison could see her heading towards the small yellow tent she'd set up on the periphery of the encampment. Still a part of the group, and yet...distant. She marveled at how little sound the tall woman made as she traveled over the rocky ground.

"Until tomorrow," she said softly, watching the dark figure disappear. Sighing, she glanced at her watch and grunted. *The hell with tomorrow. It's today already.* Her eyes tracked upwards to Mount Everest. *Allison Peabody, this is your wake-up call.*

Chapter
Eight

On the initial approach to what was, ultimately, the highest point on planet Earth, there was a traffic jam.

Unbelievable.

Allison breathed in deeply, slapping her gloved hands against her arms, stomping her boots, trying to stay warm.

This is worse than mid-town Manhattan at rush hour.

Except that here, rush hour was at 5 a.m. and 17,700 feet.

Allison's heart had been pounding in her chest from the moment she'd jolted awake in the pre-dawn darkness, alert and ready to go. This, in spite of the fact that she'd barely slept over the few hours that had elapsed since she'd crawled into her sleeping bag. She'd slipped in and out of a doze, visions of the Icefall playing through her mind. In the murky interior of her tent she'd unzipped from her sleeping bag and quickly donned her layered climbing clothes, then gathered her equipment and hustled to the dining tent. Inside, where the spitting gas-fired heaters labored to ward off the chill, she'd inhaled a breakfast of scrambled eggs and fried potatoes, and "brewed up" on all the hot tea she could swallow.

It had been strange in the cold tent, as members of the Peak Performance expedition came and went. Glances were averted, voices hushed, with everyone absorbing the weighty implication that this was the day, at last. The beginning of the siege.

Everyone wanted to make to it the top. And they all knew that, inevitably, very few of the total number of climbers on the hill, would. It was a long, tortuous road to the top, and plenty could go wrong. Along the way there would be individuals jockeying for position, partnerships formed, resources used—and exhausted. Or else a climber could get sick, and no one wanted to be the one left behind, or forced to turn back.

Survival of the fittest.

Sure, the Peak Performance people were a team, but it was becoming apparent to Allison that that was in name only.

When she'd arrived at the dining tent, Jim Harris had already left for the Icefall with MacBride and Christy. "Jim wanted to get a head start; make sure that Camp I was in good shape," Paul Andersen had informed her. "You'll be climbing with Ricky and Lou today, okay? I think I saw Ricky already heading up there. Now...let me go and find out what's up with Mike and Patsy," the young guide had said, and then he was off.

With Ricky and Lou Silvers nowhere in sight, Allison had made her way across the rocky moraine towards the base of the Khumbu. She fell in with climbers and Sherpas from other expeditions, until she had arrived at her destination.

"Wow." Her breath formed a billowing cloud in the cold air.

There were crowds, all right. A number of teams had already started up the Icefall, brightly colored blobs against the blue-white ice. The sun was just beginning to creep above the peaks, but it lent no warmth to those cooling their heels in the six degrees Fahrenheit air. The atmosphere was charged with voices murmuring, the jingle of equipment, and the crunching of boots on the ice and stone. One after another, the climbers hooked onto the line to begin the traverse, anxious to be well under way before the heat of the day set in.

Allison got down on one knee and began to strap on her crampons, keeping one eye on the Icefall. Even at this early hour, the glacier spoke in a voice all its own—creaking, popping, sounding an ominous warning. They could hear it day and night, even back at Base Camp, knowing that the deep grumbling was merely an indication that they were perched on the edge of a vast, frozen river, one that was moving forward at a rate of about three feet per day. The signs were small enough in camp that you could ignore them: the awkward pitch to the bathing tent that had not existed the day before, a miniature lake that formed overnight in the middle of the cook-tent.

But here, at the foot of the Icefall, it was easy to see the violent force and primal strength of the mighty Khumbu. It was an ice-bound, roiling mass of frothy river, driving along before it gigantic blocks of ice the size of houses, landing them in delicate, nonsensical, gravity-defying patterns. It was these seracs that tended to give way under the weight of a midday sun bearing down. Sections broke away from their brethren, catalyzing the dangerous, unpredictable avalanches that stalked every climber who made the traverse.

It had been easy for Allison to keep her mind busy as she'd made her way over the rocky scree, pushing aside the apprehension she felt at this—the most dangerous part of the Everest climb, or so she'd been told. But now, cooling her heels and nervously clicking her climbing poles together, a sliver of apprehension wormed its way into her gut, twisting and jabbing at her, telling her to get the hell out while she still could.

Great, Allison. You're gonna wash out before you even get started? You fraud.

"You won't have any problem with this part of the climb."

Allison almost shot out of her boots at the sound of the deep burr behind her. That Ricky Bouchard certainly had a habit of appearing out of nowhere.

"Oh, hi," she said, trying to keep the chattering nervousness out of her voice, and hoping if a bit of it did creep into her tones, that the tall mountaineer would simply chalk it up to the cold.

"You did fine on the practice ladders," Ricky continued, planting one of her climbing poles into the ground as she spoke. "The rest of it is just clipping and unclipping, and moving your way up the ropes. You're in good shape." Her eyes acknowledged the blonde's compact, muscular form. "You can handle it. Just keep moving. Don't let yourself get stuck. The idea is to spend as little time in the Icefall as possible."

"I agree with you there," Allison replied, hating herself for the shudder that crept into her voice.

"Let's get going," Ricky said with a hint of a smile. "We're up." She led the way to the base of the Icefall, where the first of the fixed lines were in place. Lou Silvers was already there, geared up and ready to go, along with one of the Peak Performance climbing Sherpas, Pemba.

"How are you feeling today, Lou?" Allison could not help but notice how sallow the attorney's skin was, and how he'd lost weight in the week since they'd arrived at Base Camp. Still, his pale eyes sparkled.

"Ready to rock and roll, Allie!" he grinned and lifted a climbing pole towards the Khumbu. "I've been waiting for this moment all my life."

"Then let's not make you wait any longer," Ricky replied. She did a quick visual check of her companions' equipment and harnesses, satisfied with what she saw. "I'll take the lead. Follow me; step where I step. If you run into problems, stay calm and call for help. We'll be keeping about 20-30 yards space between us on the lines. Pemba will be anchoring us." The mountaineer expertly clipped herself into the line and gave it an experimental pull. "Any questions?"

Without waiting for any response, Ricky was off, making her way up the Icefall.

Acutely aware of the crowd of climbers building behind them, Allison realized that this was her moment of truth. She swallowed, hard, gazing up at the glittering blue massifs of ice.

A soft laugh behind her. "Ladies first."

Allison felt a prodding nudge in her back, and shot Lou Silvers a withering glare. She was ready to do this. *Right? Or what if... Aw, hell!* Just what was her problem, anyway? How many people were as lucky as she was, to be here at this moment, with this kind of a chance? Let alone, to have one of the best mountaineers in the world showing her the way! And so she dug down deep within herself, tapping into the dogged tenacity that had made her one of the best brokers on the Street. Dammit, if she had survived the annual meeting of Johnson-Kitteridge-Johnson's shareholders, she could more than handle this. With a firm hand and a steady heart, she clipped onto the line and looked up towards the sleek, black and red figure moving easily, effortlessly, along the Icefall: Ricky Bouchard.

"Eat my ice cubes, Silvers," she said, and then she was climbing.

❋ ♦ ❋ ♦ ❋ ♦ ❋

Tibet or Nepal.

The North Face or the South Col.

For decades, mountaineers had debated the pros and cons of each route to the summit of Everest, arguing the logistics, assessing the technical merits of each. Certainly, the North route was the more difficult climb of the two. It required solid mountaineering skills to get past the First and Second Summit Steps, before you finally tackled the North Summit Ridge.

In the early 1920's, British mountaineer George Mallory led a series of expeditions to the Mother Goddess, anxious to claim the pinnacle of the world for himself and the British Empire. One look at the steep, broken river of the Khumbu convinced him that if the summit was to be attained, it would be by the Northern route.

Even with the appallingly primitive climbing equipment of the day: woolen jackets and gloves, military provisions, and a nascent version of today's oxygen apparatus, Mallory and his team made a serious run at it. And despite the tragedy and hardships they faced along the way: Sherpas killed in an avalanche, bitter cold conditions, frostbite, and snow blindness, they were able to climb to elevations of over 28,000 feet. Little more than 1000 feet below their goal.

It appeared as though the summit was in reach after all, right up until that early June day in 1924, when George Mallory and his climbing partner, the young, inexperienced Sandy Irvine, disappeared into the mists below the Northern Ridge's Second Step.

Everest was not ready to be conquered, not yet, and it would be many years before the Kangshung Face gave up its secrets as to what misfortune had befallen Mallory and Irvine, the Ghosts of Everest.

The North-South debate was idled in the middle of the century when the Chinese closed the borders of Tibet. Mountaineers, by logistical necessity, were forced to revisit the southern approach. With the aid of more sophisticated climbing equipment, it seemed the mighty Khumbu was not insurmountable after all, if you took care and had a bit of luck in your pocket when making the traverse. It was relatively easy technical climbing once a climber was through the Icefall, although at altitude nothing was taken for granted. The Southern Route was prone to deep, paralyzing snowfalls—monsoon storms blowing in from the Bay of Bengal—which could founder an expedition below the Camp III or 24,000 foot level. Ironically, those same deep snows could help secure footing up high over the rocky, loose limestone scree of the Yellow Band.

It was Edmund Hillary and his hardy Sherpa companion, Tenzing Norgay, who at last stood on the top of the world in 1953, courtesy of the Southern Route. Since then, ascents from both the north and south had been completed, and there had even been the rare, tortuous attempt or two from the wild, deadly, western side.

North, South, West—Ricky Bouchard didn't give a damn, actually. A mountain was a mountain. Some were bigger than others; Everest most of all. But that didn't mean you ignored the good sense you'd been born with when making a push. You planned the best you could, and hoped like hell the weather and other more earthly foibles didn't shred that plan to pieces. You signed on with a good team, partners you could count on...trust. And when you climbed, you climbed safe. Smart. You didn't take any unnecessary risks.

Ricky's blood was pumping, and her breathing, while slightly labored, was well within her comfort zone. She was finally climbing, and her soul sang with the sheer joy of it. Feeling her muscles work over the Icefall, calling on them to perform and taking satisfaction in their prompt, solid response, helped her to get rid of some of the tension, the stress, that had been building up within her since the last time she'd been on a mountain.

Switzerland.

The Eiger.

Over 6,000 feet of pure icy hell.

Mountaineering friends of hers—they had been Jean-Pierre's friends, too—had invited her along on the trip. They planned to climb the dangerous, thrilling North Face of the foreboding massif—the *Norwand*. She hadn't seen the friends in quite a while...hadn't seen anyone, really.

"Join us, Veronique," they'd said. "What have you got to lose?"

Nothing.

And so she'd gone. It was like the old days; crampons, ice screws, boots and bodies all jammed into a little chalet—shack, more like it—in Scheidegg. The climb would take two days, maybe three, if the weather held.

But it hadn't.

The *foehn* winds had swept down from the summit, brutally strong blows that threatened to rip your eyeballs from their sockets and tear the clothes from your back. The impassive face of the Eiger would melt and refreeze, avalanching; and the shitty black ice and brittle limestone rock offered footing that was tenuous at best; nonexistent at worse. Climbing on it had reminded

Ricky of how, as a child back in Val-David, she'd always been willing during the spring thaw to take Jean-Pierre up on a dare, and to cross over the frozen pond that was behind their homes.

Knowing that the ice could give way at any moment under her feet. Feeling it undulate and hearing it crackle, seeing the telltale spider-veins racing out from the pressure of her footsteps towards the oh-so far-away shore.

But she'd never mis-stepped, and she'd never turned back.

Some years before, she and Jean-Pierre had attempted the Eiger. They'd had their fun in Scheidegg, socializing with the other climbers, not really caring whether the weather would comply with their plans, as long as the beer flowed. They lasted until their time and money had run out, which was long before the *foehnsturm* stopped blowing.

This time, the bad weather was along for the ride once more, and one by one the climbers dropped out or turned back after half-hearted attempts. Not Ricky Bouchard. She was determined that this time, the Eiger would be hers.

And so in the pre-dawn darkness after another howling night, she and a remaining group of three climbers had set out. The weather forecasts from Geneva predicted conditions only slightly less horrendous than those they'd been experiencing, but Ricky figured that the colder temperatures forecasted would at least help to firm up the rotting, icy face of the *Norwand.*

Things had gone well, at first. They'd each taken turns leading the pitches up the near-vertical slope. But as a gray dawn appeared, they'd begun to be peppered with falling rock and black ice from above, and Giselle had turned back.

Before they'd reached the first night's bivouac site, Marcus had had enough, as well. "You've got to be insane to keep trying in these conditions," he'd said over the howling *foehn*, his lips blue from the cold.

On a ledge barely wider than the width of their bodies, Ricky and Gerard had spent a sleepless night, being buffeted and clawed at by the brutal winds. Ricky had remained awake, watching, waiting, anxious to be under way again. This mountain would not beat her, not this time. She would make her way across the pond...there was no turning back.

The next morning, a bleary-eyed, clearly rattled Gerard, begged her to go down. "It's impossible, Ricky," he'd pleaded as the winds screamed around them. "You're going to get blown off this bastard, straight back down into Scheidegg!"

Ricky Bouchard had considered the risk. Considered what she was capable of, and what her objectives were. She wanted to bag the Eiger, for both herself and for Jean-Pierre. For most people, making the attempt under these conditions would be out of the question. Gerard was right. But then again, she was not most people. Growing up a solitary child in Val-David, with only the little boy next door to call a friend, she'd known it even then.

So she'd flashed a frozen half-smile at Gerard. "Just make sure you have a beer waiting for me when I get there," she'd said. And, after adjusting her glacier glasses and checking her harness one last time, she'd struck out for the summit.

Solo.

It was fitting somehow, she'd thought, that she should find herself alone in this place, with only the spirit of Jean-Pierre to keep her company.

"This is crazy," he would have said, but he would have cheerfully continued the climb along with her, knowing it would make for one more entertaining story later around the fireplace.

She remembered little about the remainder of the ascent, other than the fact that she'd been able to count on one hand the total number of secure anchors she'd been able to drive into the unforgiving *Norwand*. It was simply a matter of keeping moving, of not getting stuck.

Of weighing each foot placement as best as you could, your toe kicking out a bit of a ledge in the ice, hoping it would be enough to get you up and over into the next pitch. Towards the end, when the gray skies parted and allowed a trickle of sunlight to shimmer through, for all intents and purposes, she'd been free-climbing. The anchors had turned out to be as worthless as thumbtacks in a peg-board.

But...she'd made it across the pond.

Later, when she'd strolled into the chalet as though she'd just returned from a walk in the park, the other climbers had looked at her as though she were a ghost. Well, with the phantom of Jean-Pierre beside her, maybe so.

That was then, when she'd been responsible for no one but herself.

Now, as a guide with Peak Performance, she had others to worry about. Today, as they made their way up to Camp I, that meant Lou Silvers, Allison Peabody, and even the climbing Sherpa, Pemba.

Ricky stopped, and gazed back down the Icefall at the black form that was Lou Silvers. She had been a little concerned at how he would do, knowing the he'd been quite ill during the week. But the climb seemed to energize him, and he was moving along nicely.

Below the attorney, Pemba was clearly a pro, and was having no trouble negotiating the lines and ladders.

And as for Allison Peabody...Ricky was pleased as she regarded the powder-blue figure immediately below her, working steadily over a crevasse. The mountaineer had been a bit concerned for the smaller woman, sensing her fear in the early dawn over the dangers of the Icefall. But once they'd gotten under way, Allison had kept up, and had not had to pull over for any prolonged rest along the way. It was just a 2000-foot difference between Base Camp and Camp I, but one easily felt by climbers still in the throes of acclimatization.

Ricky had only seen the girl waver once, when a Sherpa from another team had unclipped and pushed past her on a particularly dicey pitch. It was bound to happen, as Sherpas loaded with supplies for the higher camps rushed to be the first to claim the best locations. But still...it was dangerous, if not done prudently, and Ricky had given the Sherpa an earful when he'd passed her, head down, boring full speed ahead. Whether he'd understood her or not, she didn't care. Speaking her mind had made her feel better. And there was no way she was going to let anything happen to anyone on her team. All part of the job, of course.

Ricky took in a deep breath of the cold, bracing air, and clamped her jumar into the next line.

Time to move up.

❉ ◆ ❉ ◆ ❉ ◆ ❉

"Hey, Allison! Welcome to Camp I!" The booming voice of Kevin MacBride echoed over the cluster of tents belonging to the Peak Performance Adventure Company, situated a safe distance from the gap-toothed edge of the Khumbu Icefall. The muscular climber approached her, bearing a mug of hot tea, his eyes obscured by a pair of dark blue glacier glasses.

Allison had looked for Ricky as soon as she'd surmounted the last vertical ladder section leading into the Western Cwm, but the mountaineer was already busy sorting and stowing equipment, as well as checking on the progress of the remaining climbers in their group. Ricky had barely given her a nod when she'd hauled herself over the final lip of the Khumbu.

"C'mon." Kevin tugged at her sleeve, and Allison allowed herself to be drawn towards the others. "Get something hot to drink. Jim, Phil, and I already hiked up the Cwm a bit, checking it out. It's freaking amazing," he crowed, the excitement plain in his voice.

Camp I would be the most temporary of all their camps. In the early days of the climb before they headed for the higher elevations on the mountain, it would serve as an acclimatization device only. Later, theoretically in better condition to handle the altitude, they would make the trek from Base Camp to Camp II at the end of the Western Cwm, non-stop. In rare instances, a climber on the descent might arrive at the head of the Icefall too late in the day to safely make it down, whether due to heat or darkness, and they would hole up in Camp I until the cold, more stable dawn.

In the tiny camp, which was no more than five or six colorful tents, Jim Harris was engaged in animated conversation with the sirdar, Jangbu, and several other climbing Sherpas. He broke off his conversation as Allison approached. "Welcome!" he greeted her, flashing an engaging smile. "We've got water, tea brewing, tomato soup, energy bars, chocolate bars—"

"Say no more." Allison held up a hand. "Chocolates for me, and keep 'em coming," she grinned, "along with some tea."

Jim laughed and ushered her to a seat on top of a pack. "How was the hike, darlin'?"

"Not too bad, after all," Allison told him, and she meant it. Once she'd gotten under way and found her rhythm, she'd focused solely on the climb, on keeping moving, as Ricky had told her to. She'd been able to shut out the ominous warnings sounding from the Khumbu, the crackles, thumps and groans that protested her presence like a balky hotel ice machine. Some of the crevasse ladders had been more wobbly than others, and her heart had been in her mouth when that Sherpa had clambered past her with nothing more than a grunt of a warning. But she hadn't let him throw her off her stride, and she'd had to smile to herself when over the sounds of the Icefall and her own heavy breathing, she'd heard Ricky Bouchard bawling him out. All in all, the three and a half hour climb had flown by quickly, uneventfully—just how Allison preferred it to be.

"Did Kevin tell you how he puked his guts up halfway up the Icefall?" Phil Christy appeared, adjusting a baseball cap on his dark, sweaty hair. "It was...like...look out, below." He gave his friend a playful nudge in the stomach.

"Are you okay?" Allison asked, worried, remembering how Dr. Ortiz had said that nausea could be a sign of altitude sickness.

"Never better," MacBride gruffly assured her. "I think I just had too many bottles of *chang* last night. That last one was a bitch." He swatted Christy on the back of his head. "Remind me to thank you later for making me look good in front of the ladies."

"Any time, buddy," Phil chuckled, and headed off for more tea. "Any time."

One by one, additional climbers appeared over the edge of the Icefall. Lou Silvers and Pemba trekked into camp, and climbers from other expeditions, too, were making their way to their respective encampments.

"We can relax for about an hour, people," Jim told them, looking every inch the mountain man in his climbing gear, "and then we'll be heading back down. Don't worry," he said over their collective moans, "it's a quicker trip on the return, as usual. Give it an hour, and you'll be warming your toes at BC."

Allison swung her gaze around the camp. "Where are Paul and the Donaldsons?" She hadn't seen them arrive, and the hour was growing late.

"They radioed in that they turned around," Jim explained. "They did pretty good, made it about two thirds of the way up, but they were moving slow. And with the time of day—"

"Best that they turned around," Lou Silvers finished for him. "Poor Patsy...I'm surprised she was even able to get her boots on, today, after what she's been through."

"Yeah," Jim agreed. "She's a tough lady. She sure gutted it out."

"No pun intended," Kevin MacBride snorted.

"Speaking of which," Jim Harris eyed Kevin carefully, "make sure you keep pushing the fluids, bro. Last thing you want is to get all dehydrated up here at altitude."

"Got it covered," the ex-footballer replied, hoisting his water bottle.

The climbers settled down. Some, like Lou Silvers, contented themselves with a mug of hot tea and a light doze in the warming, high-altitude rays. Others ate, drank, and relaxed, discussing the morning's adventure and what the return trip might hold. Allison watched as Jim Harris passed a few words with Ricky, who was just finishing her work on the equipment. She saw the mountaineer nod, giving a final tug on the rope she was working with, and then Jim left her, heading inside a nearby red and yellow dome tent.

Ricky sat down at last, kicking her long legs out in front of her. She leaned back and stared up at the mountain, her face unreadable behind her dark-framed glasses.

The mountaineer was alone and, making up her mind, Allison got more tea for herself, a second mug for Ricky, and picked a path across the ice and rock.

"How 'bout something hot?" She held out the tea.

For a moment, Allison thought she detected the beginnings of a frown making its way across Ricky's features, and she hesitated while the expression slowly gave way to bemusement, and then an easy grin.

"You always seem to be serving me tea."

Allison smiled, remembering their cold night along the Namche Trail, and another time, after they'd been training in Base Camp on the ladders. "Well, it's a sure ice-breaker."

"Thanks." Lifting an eyebrow, Ricky reached out an ungloved hand to take the tea. "I think."

Unbidden, Allison sat down next to the mountaineer. By God, she'd just climbed the damned Khumbu Icefall, and she wanted to talk about it with someone! Well, not just with any someone.

"You're welcome." She hesitated. "But I *have* noticed that if you're not busy working, then you're usually just...just staring up at that mountain." Allison threw a hand towards the summit of Everest, its very tip-top visible now, here in the low end of the valley of the Western Cwm. From Base Camp, while the plume was in plain sight, the actual summit itself was obscured. "Somebody's gotta snap you out of it."

"I–I..." At first, Ricky gave half a thought towards denying the blonde's playful accusation, but then thought the better of it. "I just like to stay focused on what I'm moving towards," she said simply, and it was true. She was always thinking, analyzing, planning. Considering choices. Consequences.

Take Allison Peabody, for instance. It was plain to her that the girl had taken something of a shine to her. She'd caught the stockbroker frequently eyeing her when she thought she wasn't looking. And Allison had gone out of her way this past week to work with her in the training groups at Base Camp. Or else, she was paying her little visits like this.

At first, Ricky had been perplexed. They'd certainly gotten off on the wrong foot, and why would someone like Miss Allison Peabody, of the Boston Peabodys, want to spend time with her, anyway? Everyone on the expedition already liked her...particularly Lou, Kevin, and Phil. Hell, back home she must have all the friends she could possibly need and then some, living the kind of life she led.

Or...maybe not, based on some of the comments the girl had let slip. Still, Ricky herself wasn't looking to make any friends, or form any attachments.

She was a solo climber all the way now.

It would have been easy enough to scare Allison off, in a way that would not have angered Jim Harris.

Cold. Distant. Professional.

A schtick she had down pat. Heck, she'd done quite a good job of it during the first few days of the expedition, hadn't she? But strangely, she found she didn't want to turn Allison away. Not yet, at least. There were consequences to that action, or lack of it. It was bound to come back and bite her in the ass like a poorly slammed piton, if she didn't deal with it soon.

Well, she would.

Later.

"Talk about focus, well, I'm focused on moving up the Cwm," Allison said, her eyes regarding the vast quiet valley, floored with snow and ice, sweeping up before them. The "Valley of Silence," as climbers over the years had come to call it. The sun was already reflecting off the whiteness of the Cwm, famous for its intense heat, and it was growing warmer; Allison wasn't cold at all now. Blips of varying sizes were moving up the valley—Sherpas, fixing lines and ferrying supplies to Camp II and beyond. In the distance, at the base of the Lhotse Face, were tiny splashes of color that marked the beginnings of Camp II.

A deep, rumbling laugh sounded from Ricky Bouchard's chest. "First things first. You've got to get back down the Icefall, you know."

"How could I forget," Allison said, pausing to munch on a mouthful of chocolate. "But you know...it wasn't as bad as I thought it would be. I mean...it was," she corrected herself, "but I did what you said. I just kept moving, watched your place-ments...it was kind of...beautiful down there, in a way. I know that sounds silly," she blushed, "but—"

"No." Ricky's head dipped down, and her voice grew soft. "I know what you mean. Sometimes, when the sunlight hits it in a certain way, it just comes alive with color, the blues, the greens, so vivid you think you've never seen colors so true. And the way it all plays out in front of you...like some giant threw down fistfuls of sparkling, sunlit crystals and jewels, laying down a blanket so warm and inviting, you could lose yourself in it." She paused, remembering. "And all along the way are those crevasses so deep and dark that you wonder whether if you fell into one, would you just keep going and going...forever. And you think that that's not a bad thing, really, because isn't 'for-ever' what it's all about?" The mountaineer fell silent, and now it was her turn to feel the flush in her cheeks. She cleared her throat. "Or something like that, anyway."

"Uh...yeah." Allison found herself taken aback at the way Ricky had spoken, letting the door to her soul ease open just an inch or two. She cleared her throat. "What you said."

A smile split Ricky's face. "You did good this morning, you know. I was watching...everybody."

"Thanks." Allison basked in the mountaineer's praise. "It was some climb, for sure."

"It'll get easier each time you go through it," Ricky told her. "You'll get familiar with it, like an old friend. You'll mem-orize its twists and turns, which ladders are shakier than others, which seracs look ready to go—"

"Please!" Allison held up a hand. "I don't want to get that familiar with the seracs."

"But you will," Ricky quietly assured her. "You will." She took another swallow of her tea, and poked at a loose chip of ice with the toe of her boot. "How are you doing with the altitude?"

"Okay. As long as you *know* it's gonna take a while to catch your breath, I'm all right with it. You just pace yourself accord-ingly," Allison said, proud of the way she and the altitude seemed to be getting along over the past few days. "I know Lou said he was feeling a little pooped. And as for Mike and Patsy..."

"Yeah," Ricky said, the muscles in her jaw tightening. "Jim just said that Paul radioed up that they made it back to Camp okay. But.they were really feeling it."

"I hope they'll be able to move up in a couple of days." Allison thought of their next sortie, which would have them climbing through the Icefall, spending a couple of nights at Camp I, and then advancing up the Cwm to Camp II for an additional three night stay. "For that matter, I hope I am, too."

Ricky did not answer her right away. Instead, she turned her sun-burnished face back to the mountain, boring her eyes into it, as though she were searching for answers to the mysteries of the universe. And at that moment, Allison considered that if anyone could find those answers up there and wrest them from Everest's icy grip, it would be Ricky Bouchard.

"You're in top condition, Allison. You've got good basic mountaineering skills, and you've got the desire." She paused. "Are you wearing your prayer scarf?"

Allison's hands fluttered to her neck, feeling the slight bulge of the white scarf under her Polartec top. "Wouldn't leave camp without it."

"Good." Ricky turned to her, the corner of her mouth quirking in a small smile. "Then you've done all you can. As for the rest," she gestured towards the Everest massif, "you'll have to see her."

Chapter
Nine

Climbing back through the Icefall, Allison Peabody wryly thought that once again, Ricky Bouchard was right.

The temptation was to rush yourself down through the frozen river, to get the hell out of it as quickly as you could. And while that strategy was sound to a certain extent, it was important not to let that haste lure you into making a mistake. You had to be careful, taking your time on the ladders and ropes; and Allison was discovering already that on this, her first descent, many of the landmarks were familiar to her.

Just as Ricky told her they would be. Although their appearance was slightly different, their images more sharply defined by the brilliance of the mid-morning light.

There was the aluminum ladder over the crevasse just after the spot where that hurrying Sherpa had pushed past her. And there was that groaning, crackling tower of dark and light ice, over ten times her own insignificant height, shaking a fist at her as she clambered by. The great serac didn't frighten her, not really. It was as though, by virtue of her successful traverse of the glacier earlier in the day, she had a right to be there. *Just passing through,* she told herself. *I won't bother you, if you don't bother me.*

She was moving well, her air was good, and there was still a lot of gas in her legs. All-in-all, a pretty good morning. There were a number of climbers on the Icefall now, all making their way back to Base Camp and a much deserved rest. Allison was conscious of Lou Silvers and Pemba behind her, and she was grateful for that—felt more secure. But her real strength and confidence came from diligently following the black and red clad figure in front of her; up and down, over and under the threatening blocks of ice, like two fighter planes flying in formation among the clouds.

Wherever Ricky led, she would follow.

Something she never could have predicted a couple of weeks ago when she'd first arrived in Kathmandu. Then, she'd had a different agenda, and Ricky Bouchard was supposed to merely serve as a cog in the wheel of her plan. It was simply to be another death-defying adventure, bought and paid for. Another colorful "vacation" story, one that she could scandalize her family and friends with, not to mention her colleagues at work...and Lionel.

Mr. and Mrs. Lionel Kitteridge, III.

God...just the idea of it now made her skin crawl. It was amazing to her how little she'd missed her would-be fiancé over the past few weeks, or even thought about him at all. Perhaps that wasn't too surprising, considering the shambles she'd left their relationship in.

Everything in her life was changing, she knew that now. Things that had been important: rebelling against her parents, taking no prisoners at the office, and doing the right thing...eventually, with Lionel, seemed be receding gently into the background of Everest, like snow melt disappearing into the stony ground.

It was as though she just didn't give a damn any more, about those "proper" things, anyway. What the hell was wrong with her? Was this what a nervous breakdown was like? Allison thought about that for a moment, as she worked her way horizontally across a crevasse. She took one step at a time on the ladder, just as Ricky had taught her, gingerly seeking out the sweet spots on the rungs, confidently balancing herself with the aid of her climbing poles.

She was breathing heavily by the time she made it across, but it was a good feeling. She felt energized. Alive. No, this was no breakdown. It was more like daring to take a step off the edge of a precipice, into a new life. It was both electrifying and terrifying at the same time, but she was already on her way.

There would be no going back.

And if she were honest with herself, she'd admit that a certain Veronique Bouchard was a big part of the fear and the thrills she'd been experiencing. Getting to know the woman better had been a frustrating exercise in stubbornness and endless silences, but Allison was determined to see the "project" through. She'd initially told herself that finding a way to break through the mountaineer's icy veneer was simply a way to stick close to her, of bettering her chances of getting to the top.

But now...God, her face heated with embarrassment as she thought of some of the ridiculous ruses she'd undertaken to draw the woman out, to engage her in conversation. Not caring that she risked rejection and humiliation at every turn, particularly if Ricky caught on to her. So, why was she doing it?

The old Allison Peabody, of the Boston Peabodys, would have found a thousand rational, logical reasons for why her behavior made perfect sense. But the new Allison, she who was being reborn here on the unforgiving slopes of Everest, now understood things differently. And so she was able to push past all the bullshit in her heart that she'd so adroitly cultivated over the years, and admit to herself the naked, unexpected truth: she liked Ricky Bouchard.

A lot.

Was drawn to her in a way that she'd never been to any woman, or any man for that matter. It was all so...so confusing. There were still so many things she had to work through, to figure out. But here on Everest, where all you did was eat, climb, and sleep, she had plenty of time. And in the meantime, no matter what, she was determined that Ricky Bouchard would stay none the wiser.

God, she'd be mortified if she let herself slip! In more ways than one, Allison thought, as she saw the marker flag ahead signaling another crevasse.

Before she arrived at the ladder, she heard the crunching and jangling of another climber coming up close behind her. Turning, she saw that it was a Sherpa, one she didn't recognize. He could've belonged to any one of the thirty-odd expeditions on the hill. He wasn't carrying much of a load, and Allison guessed that he'd already been to the higher camps this day or the day before, stocking them.

Jim Harris had told them over the break at Camp I that their climbing sirdar, Jangbu, and a small group of Peak Performance

Sherpas, would be off to finish stocking Camp II that afternoon. There were at least a dozen Sherpas working for PPAC, Allison knew, and eight of them were climbing Sherpas. The best among them, like Jangbu and Pemba, would assist the clients on the final Summit push. Others were mainly responsible for ferrying supplies up and down the mountain; burying their food, fuel, and equipment under tarps and rocks, and marking the sites with small locator flags. Later, when the time came for the higher camps to go "live," the tents and supplies were already there, ready to be assembled, and the better camping locations were secured.

The life of a Sherpa was not an easy one, and Allison had been impressed with the solicitous, respectful way Ricky treated them. Some Sherpas, like Jangbu Nuru, were friends to her from previous expeditions. Others, whether the mountaineer knew them or not, she worked with as equals, as the expert high-altitude alpinists most of them were. And so Allison had found herself attempting to do the same.

The Sherpa was coming on her fast. With his orange jacket, dark climbing pants, and floppy Sherpa hat, he was like a bullet on the descent, rocketing by with a smile splitting his darkly tanned face.

Allison stayed where she was to let him pass, and gave him a wave. "Hi."

"Hello, lady!" he greeted her, as he unclipped to get around her.

Well, he seemed nice enough. Maybe Ricky wouldn't take this one's head off.

It happened before Allison was even able to answer him.

She felt it at first, the vibration beneath her feet, and then she heard it, the explosive crack as tons of ice and snow loosed itself from the mountain. Allison turned disbelieving eyes towards a great white wave sweeping towards her, with an impenetrable cloud of vapor and ice particles flying above it like the mists above an ocean breaker.

She might have screamed; she couldn't tell, as a sickening shock of understanding jolted through her system: she was falling, and there was nothing she could do to stop it. The avalanche would bury her or, worse, take out the line she was on and carry her broken body all the way to the bottom of the Khumbu.

She felt the first wash of spindrift hit her face, choking her. Instinctively, she held her breath, knowing that you could smother simply by inhaling the thick cloud as surely as though you'd been entombed under a blanket of white. She skidded down the Icefall, deaf but for the thunderous roar of the avalanche, waiting for the brutal pummeling that was sure to follow.

Feebly, her arms and legs swam; she tried to arrest herself, to get her feet pointed downhill, wherever down was. An agonizing pain shot up her back, as the rope to which she was still attached grew taut, fighting against the surging wave for possession of her body. She felt herself pivoting, and then she was slammed face-first into something hard and cold, expelling the breath from her lungs in one crushing impact, and sending stars into her whiteout field of vision.

And as suddenly as it had started, it was over.

She lay there, her chest heaving, oblivious to the glacial coldness beneath her body, listening to the sound of the avalanche bleeding away. Everything was so bright, so sparkly, and it was then that Allison realized she'd lost her sunglasses. And by the feel of it, her hat was gone, too. *If that's all you've lost, this is your lucky day, Allison-girl.* Groaning, she pushed herself onto her elbows and reached for her ice ax, digging it into the mountain to secure her position.

"Allison! Allison!" A distant, frantic voice. "Are you okay?"

Fuzzily, her mind began to put together the jumbled pieces of the last 20 seconds. She wasn't dead. The line had held, at least part of it anyway, and stopped her fall. And the voice belonged to Ricky Bouchard, who was calling her name.

"I'm okay!" she called out shakily. "At least I think so," she muttered softly, blinking her eyes clear of snow particles and raising her body up to have a look around. The landscape had changed, been washed clean by the cascading avalanche. She was at least 30 to 35 feet away from where she'd last stood, and indeed, the ice screws had held, or at least one of them had, stopping her from breaking totally free of the line and tumbling down the mountain along with the cresting wave. She could see Lou Silvers standing well back, and Pemba behind him; obviously they'd been well clear of the danger.

And Ricky?

She turned an aching head downhill, or rather across the hill, over the rocky, choppy blocks of the Icefall, for now she was almost parallel to the mountaineer's position. Ricky was making her way towards her, a grim expression on her face. The ladder over the crevasse was gone, but Ricky chanced a snow bridge that had formed below it, and quickly made her way to Allison's side.

"What happened?" Allison sputtered as the mountaineer drew near.

"Avalanche," Ricky replied, stating the obvious. "Right when it was about to hit you, it caught up on that rise there." She gestured towards a low, narrow wall of ice just above Allison's original position. "It sort of skipped over you...passed you by."

"Is everybody else okay?"

"I think so," Ricky told her. "It kinda ran out of steam down below, and petered out." Carefully, Ricky helped her to her feet. "Take it easy, now. You did get taken for a bit of a ride," she said, her voice hoarse from calling out, no doubt. "You sure you're all right?"

"Yeah, just a little rattled, that's all," Allison said, brushing the snow and ice off of her clothes. "But..." her green eyes flew open wide, "Ricky," she said, alarm bells going off as the memory came flooding back to her, "there was a Sherpa! He'd just passed me," she pointed, "heading towards the ladder. I don't know whether he had time to clip back on yet or—"

Cursing, Ricky was already on her way to the lip of the crevasse. "I can see him!" Allison followed her, moving cautiously over the newly churned terrain. Ricky shucked off her pack and began shouting down into the crevasse.

No response.

By the time Allison caught up to the mountaineer, Ricky was already on the radio, calling Base Camp.

"Everyone in my group is okay, but we've got an unknown Sherpa part-way down a crevasse," she said tightly. "Looks like he's fading in and out of consciousness. We're going to need some help here getting him out."

"Roger, that," Dr. Sandra Ortiz' voice crackled over the handset. *"We've got Pemba heading your way now, Ricky. Jangbu's started down, and I'll alert the other expeditions as well. Hang in there until then, okay?"*

"Right." Ricky violently toggled the radio, the frustration plain on her face.

Just as Allison dropped to her knees next to the mountaineer, an ominous, chattering sound came from within the crevasse, and Ricky's head whipped around.

"What was that?" Allison wanted to know. Gazing down into the jagged opening, she couldn't see the bottom. But she could see the injured Sherpa. He had luckily landed on an ice ledge jutting out about 20 feet below the top of the dark blue ice wall. Allison felt her stomach somersault as she detected a trailing spatter of blood marking the Sherpa's descent down the side of the crevasse. He weakly moved an arm, as though trying to grab onto the wall, but that was the sum of his efforts to help himself. It was clear that he was in bad condition. Worse, the ledge, that had given him a temporary reprieve from certain death, didn't appear at all stable.

Quickly, Ricky sprang into action, driving a snow picket into the ice at the top of the crevasse. "It's the ledge he's on," she explained. "It's giving way." She clipped a carabiner to the anchor and looped a length of rope through it. "It's not going to hold until a rescue team gets here. And the way he's fading in and out of it," she spared a quick glance over the side, "he's liable to roll right the hell off."

Frowning, Ricky leaned over the edge of the crevasse. "Stay still!" she shouted to the injured man. "It's gonna be okay. We're gonna get you out of there!" She placed her pack on the edge of the hole and anchored it, so that the rope going over the side would not dig into the ice and snow under her weight.

"Hold it—where are you going?" Allison shoved herself to her feet, dismayed by the dawning realization of what the mountaineer was about to do.

Ricky did not look at her while she continued to work. "I'm going down there and getting him out."

"That's crazy. The ice here is crap." Allison pointed to the ragged, crumbling wall. "That anchor will never hold you. You've got to wait until help gets here!" Her eyes raked the glacier frantically. She could see Pemba moving slowly towards them, with Lou Silvers close on his boot heels. Other climbers were cautiously making their way to the crevasse from below, but they had to fix new ropes to replace the ones the avalanche had swept away.

"No time for that." Ricky's mouth was set in a tense line. "If I don't secure him, we'll lose him." She took a step towards the edge of the crevasse. "When the others get here, have them rig a pulley and a sling. We can get him out that way."

Allison regarded the makeshift anchor gouged deeply into the dubious looking ice, and then lifted her green eyes to the mountaineer. There was no way that anchor would hold if it were forced to bear the full weight of the dark haired woman, let alone if she had a grip on the Sherpa. Ricky had to know that, didn't she? What kind of a foolish chance was she taking?

"Ricky, wait." Allison grabbed at a red sleeve. "You can't do this thing. You can't!" She tried to keep the panic from her voice. "That anchor won't hold you for long, and you know it! At least, let me belay you, instead."

Allison couldn't see Ricky's eyes, hidden behind her dark glacier glasses, but she could readily imagine the fury in them at being physically restrained. It was plain enough in her voice.

"Let go of me." Ricky roughly pulled her arm free. "Step away from this edge, and let me do my job."

"No, goddammit!" Allison threw all sense of self-preservation to the wind. "Are you suicidal or something? How can you ask me to stand here and watch you peel off the side of this crevasse?"

Another crack sounded from the bowels of the fissure, and Ricky turned her attention to the mission at hand, resolutely ignoring Allison's desperate pleas.

Think, woman! Think! The young blonde watched Ricky give the line one last, tentative tug. *Use your head. Do what you know! You're supposed to be the hottest thing Wall Street has to offer, right?* She mused, considering her deal-making expertise. Surely, she could summon up some of those skills now, right?

"Fine," Allison said sharply. "If you won't let me belay you, then I'm going down there with you." And with that, she drove her ice ax deep into the snow and began to fish for a carabiner on her harness.

Ricky stopped dead in her tracks. "No," she said, anger darkening her face. "You can't. The ground is still too unstable—"

"Screw, you, Ricky Bouchard." Now it was Allison's turn to rage. "You either let me belay you," she fought to struggle out of her backpack, "or else I'm going down there with you. You can't stop me, you know." She grabbed at a length of rope, passed it around her hips, and then through the carabiner on her seat harness. She threw the rope towards Ricky's ice anchor, defiance snapping in her eyes. "So. What'll it be?"

The mountaineer stood stock still, clearly unaccustomed to being challenged on the mountain. Especially by one so young and so relatively inexperienced. "We don't have time for this bullshit," she grumbled at last and rapidly began to switch lines. "Make sure your brake hand never leaves the rope, and—"

"I *know* how to belay, Bouchard," Allison said, trying to hold back a hint of a smile at her small victory. They were far from home yet. Bracing herself, she nodded towards the crevasse. "Get going."

In a blur of red and black, Ricky Bouchard swung herself over the side.

And then Allison was alone.

Okaaay, just what have you gotten yourself into here, Allison? It would be impossible to hear any of Ricky's belay commands from the depth of the crevasse, so she'd just have to try and gauge by the mountaineer's pace when she needed more slack or when to pull in. She could feel the taller woman's weight on the rope, and began to wonder just who the crazy person was. Belaying Ricky certainly gave her a better chance, but if the guide's weight fell upon the rope at the same time the shaky anchor gave way, then Allison's sole remaining tether would be to the ice picket on the fixed rope that had saved her during the avalanche. And how could she possibly hope to hold onto Ricky, at the same time everything else gave way?

Even now, Allison could detect movement in the anchor behind her. "C'mon...c'mon," she muttered beneath her breath, willing the rescuers to her side. Then Ricky's need for slack stopped, and Allison guessed that she'd made it to the ice ledge. There she would ditch the Sherpa's pack and find some way to secure him. That would mean either a temporary hitch to the rope or reliance on a freshly driven ice screw. Both would be equally unreliable at this point, given the conditions inside the crevasse. Everything now depended on Pemba and the others getting there, and setting the rescue pulley and anchors.

But could she wait that long? She was pushing herself to her physical limit, in an operation that would have been hard enough 10,000 feet below. And suddenly, the exertions of the day, the tumble she'd taken during the avalanche, and the altitude conspired together to wear her down.

Fuck!

A shuddering started in her legs, "sewing machine legs" climbers called it, working its way through her torso to her arms. Her laboring breaths had to be coming at least five times as fast as normal, but still she just couldn't seem to get enough air into her beleaguered lungs.

She heard voices behind her, Pemba, and the others, but she didn't dare turn around. Her world tunneled down to her hands, the rope, and the lip of the crevasse. She knew the men were fixing additional anchors, looping ropes through a pair of pulleys, and then she could see Pemba, lying on his belly at the edge of the void, calling...something, to Ricky, and lowering the sling.

There was a sudden jolt on her belay line, and more shouts. From behind her, she knew the blasted anchor had come free. *Shit!* From where she stood, she knew Pemba and the others would be oblivious to her plight. They were focused on the crevasse rescue.

So.

It was all up to her. She dug her crampons in hard, imagining all the while what it would feel like to skid to the edge of the crevasse, and then over it. To lose herself in its murky depths. And lose Ricky, too, just when she'd found her.

No! She set herself firmly against the fear nipping at the heels of her resolve. *You can do this thing!* She flung her braking arm across the front of her body, keeping the rope from running through, and nearly cried out with relief when she felt the pressure ease. Quickly, she scrambled for a better foothold in the ice, and with a satisfying *crunch* felt her crampons dig in.

There was more movement on the rope. Ricky had to be on her way up now, and Allison began to guide her back to the rim, reeling her in like a prized fish on a line.

With the men steadily working the ropes of the pulley, the injured Sherpa's head soon bobbed to the edge of the crevasse, blood flowing freely from an ugly cut above his left eye.

Thank God. Ricky would be next, once she'd made sure the Sherpa was safely clear.

Pemba grabbed at the injured man's harness. He dragged him up and over the lip and then pulled him a safe distance away, speaking rapidly to the dazed man in his native tongue.

Allison returned her attention to the rim. Long seconds stretched out before her, taunting her. There was no movement of the suddenly slack rope, no sound from the crevasse, and still no sign of the mountaineer.

"Ricky!" Allison cried out, not caring whether the fear in her voice betrayed her.

And then a black cap appeared at the rim of the chasm, quickly followed by a hand digging an ice ax into its jagged edge. "Right here," she grunted, as Pemba returned to give her a hand.

Ricky heaved herself up and over the side, landing on the side of the crevasse like a fish tumbling into a boat.

It was only then that Allison allowed the exhaustion to take over. Choking back a sob, she collapsed back onto the ice, panting and spent, her limbs trembling uncontrollably after her supreme effort.

Ricky was saying something to her now, but she couldn't hear her, couldn't move. She simply lay there on the cold, ancient glacier, her eyes tracking up to the cloud-like pennant flying high above, while the summit itself seemed lost in the clouds. Her head was aching now, a painful drumbeat pounding out a shattering rhythm in her skull.

What the hell had just happened here? Her head swam at the thought of what might have been. Knowing that she had no right to have survived it at all. Dammit, nothing seemed to make sense.

Nothing.

Death...it had been so close, she could still feel the whisper of the chill its brief caress had left upon her heart. Marking her and Ricky both. Staking its claim.

Yes, death had been near. And the summit of Everest had never seemed so very far away.

Chapter
Ten

It's funny how it is when you survive a near-death experience. People either won't leave you alone—buzzing around you, tapping on you for good luck, telling you how scared they would have been—or else they won't go anywhere near you. They figure that if the grim reaper comes back, searching for the one who narrowly evaded him last time, they don't want to be anywhere near you. It reminded Allison Peabody of why her boss back at Johnson-Kitteridge-Johnson told her he feared air travel.

"It's not that I think I'm gonna die, Allie. But what about the guy sitting in the seat next to me? What if it's time for his number to come up? What the hell do I do—move to another part of the goddamned plane?"

Well, for what little difference it made in the end, Mike and Patsy Donaldson had moved to the back of the plane, as far away from the young stockbroker as they could get. Allison didn't blame them, really. They had their own problems to worry about.

Lou Silvers, however, had been his usual caring, concerned self, and Jim Harris was nothing if not the consummate expedition leader; he'd stood just a shout away from Sandra Ortiz outside the medical tent while the physician checked her out. But she hadn't seen Pemba at all once they'd threaded their way back through the Icefall, and the usually sociable Kevin MacBride and

Phil Christy had kept their distance, too.

"Jesus, Allison," Kevin had said inside the dining tent, "what a freakin' sound! I'll never forget it. And the Icefall—it was like it was exploding down on you. We thought you were a goner, for sure!" He'd grabbed a bottle of water and ambled back to his own tent, a curious, wondrous look on his face. That was yesterday, and she hadn't seen him or Phil since.

Good.

Let them avoid her. It was probably better anyway, given the way her head ached, her back was still sore, and—geez what an old woman she was! Sandy had given her a shot of an anti-inflammatory and admonished her to take it easy for the next day or two. It was all the physical stress she'd experienced at altitude that was causing her the problem, or so she'd been told. Here on the mountain it hit you harder, you felt it more, and it took longer to recover.

That was all well and good. As long as she was ready to head up to Camp II in a couple of days. And she would be, she swore to herself. Although yesterday, she might not have been so sure of it. She barely remembered the post-avalanche climb out of the Icefall, short-roped behind Pemba for added safety.

She was aware, however, that Ricky had stayed behind to help bring the injured Sherpa down. He would be okay, she'd heard later; and she knew that outcome was thanks only to the swift actions of Ricky Bouchard. It turned out the Sherpa was a support climber for the Spanish New Millennium climbing team, and its leader had made his way to the Peak Performance camp last night. In halting, stilted English, he'd expressed his gratitude to them all, his bloodshot eyes moist with tears.

Today, the sun shone brightly in the sky above Base Camp, and Allison welcomed the warmth of it through her fleece jacket. She carefully made her way back to her tent, after having spared Dr. Ortiz the effort of having to make a "house call" to check up on her. Her mind-numbing headache had receded somewhat, but her back and legs still complained of the thrashing to which they had recently been subjected.

She was lucky; they all were.

Allison sighed, remembering. Despite how close it had been, they'd all survived. Well, there was that.

And while she might have disagreed with Ricky's initial approach to helping the felled Sherpa, there had been no doubt in her mind that she and Ricky *would* help him, if they could. Allison had been called selfish in her day, and upon reflection she was sure that there were times when the charge had been an accurate one. Times she'd been too busy, too distracted to bother herself over the problems of others. However, if someone's life were in danger...she liked to think that no matter what the circumstances were, no matter the time or place, she would do what she could to help.

Rendering aid when needed.

That was not always the way of it, Allison knew, whether it be in the world she'd left behind, or here, in the shadow of Mount Everest. The best of intentions, the strongest tenets of character, those things had a way of breaking down, of eroding away, the longer one spent in Everest's "death zone."

Where you got so tired and so weak, that it was all you could do to be responsible for your own survival, to get yourself down the mountain alive.

Where it didn't matter about the quality of your team, the preparedness of your plan, or the amount of money you had in your bank account. When you got over 25,000 feet, you were on your own. And it was then you felt the stinging coldness of being alone, and struggled to control the fear that held your hand and dogged your steps.

She'd heard the horror stories.

Of climbers so focused on bagging the summit that they blithely passed by their fellow climbers, collapsed in the snow. And left them behind on the descent, as well.

Of the woman who took two nights to die on the North side, again while passing climbers could do little to help her. And of her distraught husband who, upon hearing she was impossibly alive after that first sub-zero night, took off alone to find her, never to be seen again.

Or of the expedition leader, stranded high on Everest, out of O's and out of luck. He had no power left to move, and the spent climbers below could not return to bring him down.

But his radio had power.

And as the dead of night descended on Everest, as the heat and the life slowly, painfully, leeched from his body, he was able to speak to his pregnant wife a world away and tell her that he loved her.

To let someone die? Or to attempt to save him or her, and maybe lose your own life in the process? She prayed to God she would never have to make that choice.

Although in a way, yesterday she already had, right? Maybe that's how it happened. You didn't think it through, not really. You just threw yourself into a situation out of instinct or fear, and suddenly, there you were. Sliding on your ass towards a bottomless crevasse because a stupid anchor wouldn't hold in brittle ice.

And that would have been it.

Her life. Ricky's. The Sherpa's. Snuffed out—not with the roar of an avalanche, but the whimper of a failed belay. For all her other risk-seeking activities, her extreme vacationing, this was as close as she'd ever come. And it was not at all what she'd expected. She never could have guessed, anticipated the anger that she'd felt at thinking she might die. How she'd summarily rejected what was happening. And the conviction she'd held, the insistence that no matter what, failure was not an option.

Surely, that kind of danger was something Ricky Bouchard had come in contact with many times during her career as one of the world's top alpinists. Dealing with it was simply part of what Ricky was trained to do. She'd been there, done that. This time was no different, save for the fact that the mountaineer had had a bit of help.

Ricky...

The tall woman was another one Allison hadn't seen much of over the past day. Although, unlike some of the others, she didn't get the sense that she was avoiding her.

"Take it easy, get some rest," Ricky had told her when she'd seen her on her way for some hot tea yesterday, and that was that.

They hadn't really had an opportunity to talk about what had happened up there. Allison was ready to move on, to put the fear behind her. She knew she had to do that, or else she would have no chance of moving higher on the mountain. It wasn't that. Rather...just what the hell had Ricky Bouchard been thinking, anyway?

Had she gotten angry, stubborn, too?

Or else...for a moment up there, when she'd thought that Ricky seemed likely to cast herself over the side of the crevasse on her own, it was as though...as though she just hadn't cared whether she made it or not.

Allison found her booted feet suddenly turning, taking her in the direction of Ricky's small yellow tent at the edge of the encampment. What was going on inside that dark head of the mountaineer? Seeing as how there were no other volunteers for the job, Allison Peabody decided that it was up to her to find out.

❄•❄•❄•❄

"Hello, Ricky?"

Ricky Bouchard put down the book she was reading, and glanced towards the vestibule of her tent. She had heard the approaching footsteps on the scree and half-heartedly hoped they would pass her by. She was off the clock, and it was a "down" day.

For most of the climbers at BC in-between forays up the mountain, the days were spent eating, sleeping, and resting; conserving their energy for the next push. Some climbers passed the time playing cards, reading, or engaged in small talk with the other expedition members.

As a guide, Ricky had duties of a more professional nature, and that was fine with her. She always was one who liked to keep herself busy, active. But even she knew that it was important to get the proper amount of rest on Everest, or else when you were working high and needed to call upon your deepest reserves of energy, you might find out your gas tank was empty. And that meant nothing but trouble. Both for herself, and the clients she was responsible for.

Still, her private time was her own, and there was precious little of that, as it was. Dammit, she hated to be disturbed! She'd set up her tent on the periphery of the compound for that very reason.

"Ricky?"

At the very least, she should have been bothered right now at the intrusion. And normally, she would have. Except...

"Are you in there?"

Unbidden, her mind flashed back to the sight yesterday that had nearly shattered her composure to pieces. Not to mention, strangely, what it had done to her heart.

The *crack!* and the rumbling roar of the avalanche.

A terrible sound that she knew all too well, for it had constantly resonated in her soul ever since Jean-Pierre had been killed. A thrumming, tortuous melody that had nightly haunted her dreams.

Not again!

She'd turned uphill and seen the stricken look on Allison's face as the younger woman started to fall, as powerless to do anything against the white wave that threatened to sweep her away as Ricky was to save her.

As helpless as she'd been to save Jean-Pierre.

And then, the wave had passed. Hit a natural ice wall just above Allison, and pitched over her, taking her for a bit of a tumble, but leaving her none the worse for wear. Ricky had been frantic as she'd clambered back over the unstable Icefall, foolishly crossing an untested ice bridge, desperate to get to Allison's side. It had seemed like hours had passed before a powder blue arm had lifted, and she'd heard a shaky voice insisting she was fine.

Relief had flooded through Ricky then, but it was short-lived. The real danger had only been just beginning, for the both of them.

Allison called for her again.

The mountaineer cleared her throat. "Right here." She snapped the book shut and crawled out of her tent.

"Sorry—am I disturbing you?"

"Not if you've got some tea." Ricky's blue eyes twinkled as she gazed up at the stockbroker.

"Gosh, no." Allison blushed. "But we...I could go get some if—"

"Take it easy." Ricky hoisted herself to her feet. "It was a joke."

Allison shifted nervously from one foot to the other. "Oh." Her face turned a deeper shade of crimson. "I get it. It's because all the other times—" Allison blanched as the mountaineer stood to face her. "Jesus, Ricky!" She lifted a hand out towards her face. "You've got a black eye!"

Sure enough, there was a deep purpling and bruising around the taller woman's left eye.

"It's nothing." Suddenly self-conscious, Ricky flinched her head away, avoiding Allison's touch. "It must have happened yesterday, when I was trying to secure the Sherpa onto the line. He was out of it. He didn't know what he was doing, or that I was trying to help him, and he hauled off and gave me a good elbow right there."

"He's lucky you didn't lose him off the ledge!" Allison said, chagrined.

"Didn't lose him," Ricky said simply, toeing at the rocky

ground. "But I almost lost me. I completely lost my hold on the wall."

"I felt it," Allison whispered, remembering the awful wrenching on the line. It was then that the anchor had given way.

"So...shouldn't you be resting?"

"You're one to talk," Allison responded. "I've had enough of that. Thought I'd take a walk. Doctor's orders." Well, it was true. Sort of. Sandy Ortiz had told her to listen to her body. And right now, her body was telling her that she wanted to spend some time with Ricky Bouchard. "Want to come?"

"Ah...yeah, why not." Ricky slid on her sunglasses. "I suppose I could keep an eye on you."

Feeling satisfied at her small victory, Allison led the way across the glacial scree towards a set of gunmetal gray boulders. It was another unbelievably clear day on the mountain, one she wished they could bottle for those days to come when the fortunes of weather turned, as they were bound to do.

The sun heated the rocks, and when they arrived they both took off their jackets and sat down, reveling in the warming rays. A view of Everest dominated the skyline, and their eyes were drawn to it, powerless to avoid its lure.

"I hear a couple of the teams are heading up the Icefall tomorrow," Ricky said, "gunning for Camp II. They want to get ahead of the other teams, in terms of acclimatization."

"Is that a good thing or bad?" Allison gazed at the mountaineer's profile, so sharply defined against the white backdrop of Pumori. .

Ricky chuckled. "A good thing, if they want to break trail and fix ropes for everybody else. And a bad thing," she continued, "for the same reason."

There was silence for a time, and they watched a small flock of birds in the distance, picking away at a scattering of garbage.

"Ricky, I—"

"Allison—"

The two women laughed nervously.

"Me first," Allison insisted. "It's about yesterday." She paused. "I've been asking myself, trying to figure it out...what were you trying to do?"

The mountaineer's posture stiffened. "What do you mean?"

"You *know* what I mean, Ricky. Trying to go into that crevasse like you were. It was suicide!"

"You've got it all wrong," Ricky replied, trying to keep the anger from her voice. Dammit, how did she manage to get herself into these sorts of conversations, anyway—and with Allison Peabody, in particular? It was one of the reasons why she loved mountain climbing so: the mountains didn't talk back.

"There was no time. I weighed the odds. I was willing to take the risk. And," she faced Allison, "you're a client. It wasn't your risk to take...like you did."

"I think I'm big enough to make those kinds of decisions for myself." Allison defiantly thrust out her chin, displaying the same stubbornness that had caught Ricky by surprise up in the Icefall. "Don't you?"

Ricky's mouth tensed, and she turned her attention back to the shrieking birds. What was she supposed to say? There was no way she would ever tolerate someone like Allison risking her life on her account.

Ever.

The only reason she had at last given in, was the nightmare thought of Allison following her into the crevasse if she refused her help. And she'd had no doubt that the younger woman would have done just that. With precious time bleeding away, Ricky had finally decided that Allison's chances were better above the fissure rather than inside of it. And so she'd relented.

"Well, don't you?"

Obviously, the woman by her side expected some sort of answer.

"I guess it's too late to say 'no,' huh?" Ricky expelled a sharp burst of air. "Considering you *did* make the decision for yourself yesterday, after all."

"And lucky for you I did," Allison sniffed, folding her arms.

"Yeah, I..." the mountaineer ran a hand through her ebony hair, "I did want to say—"

"Yeeess?"

"I—" *Keep it simple, Veronique. Keep it simple!* "Thanks," she blurted out. "Thanks. That's all."

Allison cocked her head. Well. "You're very welcome. Glad I could help."

"I—" Ricky's brow furrowed as she struggled with finding the right words. "I saw how the anchor came out. I know I felt it when it gave way." She hesitated. "How...how did you hang on—?"

"I don't know how," Allison answered slowly, softly. "I

really don't. All I remember thinking was that it was something I had to do. That there were no other choices but that...one thing."

"Another client might have just let go...saved themselves," Ricky heard herself saying, and it was true. Who was she, and the Sherpa too, for that matter, to Allison?

Or to anyone else on the expedition?

She was an employee, a guide—nothing more. Ricky had been stunned when she'd at last hoisted herself out of the crevasse, to find Allison collapsed near the lip, completely spent. Her sweeping gaze had quickly taken in the younger woman's position closer to the edge, the trail behind her in the snow, and the blown ice anchor.

Allison lowered her head, embarrassed. "I don't know about that."

"I do."

Wordlessly, they both lifted their eyes once again towards Everest, towards the great shark fin of its peak jutting out of an icy sea.

Silent.

Elusive.

Sitting there, Ricky somehow found herself so close to Allison that her arm was brushing up against the smaller woman's, and the mountaineer was surprised to find herself growing uncomfortably warm. And yet, she had no desire to move away, to end the moment. It was the sun at this altitude; that was all.

How brightly it burned in the thin air.

How intense.

❄ ◆ ❄ ◆ ❄

"Jim, howza 'bout another candy bar?" Paul Andersen flexed his hands like a wide receiver awaiting a pass from his quarterback.

"Can do." Jim Harris swiveled around to the table behind him laden with all sorts of high-calorie goodies, grabbed a Three Musketeers, and completed a throw to the young guide.

"Thanks, buddy."

Ricky Bouchard watched in amazement as the tall, lanky mountaineer tore into the candy bar. He peeled back the silver foil wrapper, and closed his eyes as he bit down into the rich chocolate. It was the third one he'd had since they'd gathered in the dining tent along with Sandra Ortiz and Jangbu Nuru, to plan for the next day's acclimatization climb.

No one on this expedition would starve to death, Ricky wryly considered. One thing had become readily apparent to her in the few weeks she'd been associated with the Peak Performance Adventure Company, and that was that their food was in "peak" condition, too.

Ricky was used to losing weight on every high altitude expedition she'd ever been on; it was the body's natural response to working high and hard on reduced oxygen. It was a struggle to keep the pounds from melting off of you, particularly when the shoestring teams she'd been on before had opted to pour their financial resources into permits and gear, rather than on good grub. She'd gotten used to eating the bland, over-salted freeze-dried food products from Eastern Europe, and the surplus Russian army rations that tasted as though they'd been around since the fall of Leningrad.

But here, with the Peak Performance people, she'd never had it so good. With full American-style breakfasts, fresh bread and green vegetables—green!—brought in daily via yak trains. And lunches and dinners to rival the best restaurant fare she'd ever had, not to mention the abundance of high carb snacks and drinks available 24 hours a day. She might just end up gaining weight on this trip, after all. That was, if Paul Andersen managed to leave some for everyone else. The young man had to have a hollow leg.

"Our clients will be here in a little bit," Jim said, pushing up the sleeves of his dark brown sweater to reveal a pair of well-muscled forearms. "But for now, I just want to make sure we're all on the same page, tomorrow." He paused, swinging his gaze around the table. "Gonna be a big day."

"How does the weather look?" Ricky asked. She trusted the weather forecasts as far as she could throw them. Instead, she preferred her own assessment of the clouds and conditions she saw in front of her...relying on what her gut told her, rather than on the opinion of some shirt and tie sitting behind a desk in London. Still, she knew the clients would ask, and she thought they might prefer a more formal response rather than the opinion of her own digestive system.

"Pretty as a picture," Jim answered, "for the next few days, at least." He rubbed at his beard. "There's a low pressure system forming to the west, but they think it's liable to fall apart before it gets here. So it looks like we've got a clear window to get up and down."

"You never get six straight days of good weather on this mountain," Ricky commented. She knew that on this sortie they would be spending two nights at Camp I, above the Icefall, and then move up the Western Cwm for another three nights of acclimatization at Camp II. "If the weather does get stormy, I think it would be a good thing."

"Why do you say that?" Paul Andersen finished his candy bar and wrapped the foil into a ball. "Bad weather makes for cranky clients."

"Better to have them exposed to crappy weather at lower altitudes," the mountaineer explained. "Let them get a good feel for it. How to adapt to it and handle it. Because it's sure as hell bound to be worse up high."

"Well, the weather says 'go,' our timetable says 'go,' so we're going," Jim firmly stated. "And with the great weather we've been having," he eyed Ricky, "maybe it'll hold through summit day, eh?"

"From your lips, to the Mountain Goddess' ears!" Paul chuckled, tossing the wrapped foil into a nearby trash bucket.

"Yeah, well, it would seem that the British team got the same forecast," Sandra Ortiz said. In between treating the aches and pains of the PPAC members, the Base Camp manager and team physician had been spending her spare time monitoring the local radio traffic. They're already at Camp I. And I hear the International Expedition is moving up tomorrow." Her brown eyes peered pointedly out of her wire framed glassed. "Early."

"Shit!" Jim Harris swore, and his cheeks flushed. "Just what we need. Those goddamned amateurs! I don't want to be looking up their slowpoke butts from here to the summit! Those guys are dangerous—they don't know what the hell they're doing!" His eyes flashed. "We're leaving at 4:45 a.m. then. At the latest."

"They shouldn't be allowed on the mountain," Paul Andersen added, frowning.

"Last time I checked, there wasn't a lock and key on the Namche Trail," Ricky said, her eyes narrowing. "Like it or not, if you can pay for the permit, you can climb."

"But they're idiots, Ricky," Paul protested. "You saw proof of that, the day you got here!"

Ricky knew the guide was referring to the Sherpa who'd

suffered the attack of HAPE, and died. His downfall had been in
pushing himself up the mountain, too high, too fast—more than
likely at the demand of the International team's leader. "I didn't
say I liked it," Ricky replied, her voice like ice. "I'm saying it's
not our right to deny someone else the chance, that's all, as long
as they stay out of our way. If they want to kill themselves, or
maybe even make the summit, it's their choice."

Since the dawn of time, since the beginnings of mankind's
self-awareness, Ricky knew that the spirit of wanderlust, of
searching, of the desire to see what was just over the next rise
until there was nowhere else to go, ran deep and true in many
men and women. She knew a thing or two about it, herself.

Whether it was a Viking crew clambering into a longboat
and fixing a westerly heading, or explorers like Lewis and Clark,
Amundsen, or Hillary, these men were remembered by history,
revered by it.

But there were others.

Nameless. Faceless. Forgotten.

Perhaps they'd been laughed at in their day, belittled for
their dreams, their desires. Misfits, drawn to the challenge of
the adventure like some sort of personal Holy Grail. A few were
prepared; knew what they were up against. Others were
equipped with little more than the boots on their feet and an aching yearning in their hearts, searching for something they were
hard-pressed to put a name to, that singular thing to call their
own.

Perhaps they had simply wanted to belong.

Or not.

And perhaps they had found that purpose, that significance,
somewhere within the fanciful journeys they had set themselves
upon. Blazing the trail for those more "notable" explorers to
follow.

There probably wasn't a climber among the International
Expedition members that had ever scaled an 8000-meter peak
before, or who had worked at high altitude on oxygen. But to a
man or woman among them, Ricky was sure that they had a
dream. And as surely as she knew that nothing in this life was
for certain, she knew that when your dreams died, you did, too.

Perhaps the Internationals had no business being on the hill.
Whether they did or not, they had to find that out on their own.
Live by the consequence of their choices.

The look of dismay that had passed over Jangbu's weathered

face at the mention of the Internationals had not escaped Ricky's notice. It was quite likely that the wiry Sherpa had friends on the team, family even, who were simply trying to earn a living while staying alive in the process. They all had the right. It was up to each person what he or she did with it.

Choices.

Doctor Ortiz cleared her throat, sensing the tension in the air. "There's a Japanese team also, that I hear is heading up sometime tomorrow." She turned to the team leader. "The point is, there'll be quite a few teams on the mountain, Jim. We all knew that coming into this. We just have to deal with it as best we can. See if we can't work with them."

"What time are the Japanese heading up?" Jim asked, calming down a fraction.

"I'm not sure."

"I can find out," Paul offered, grinning. "Do a little more of my Base Camp diplomacy."

"Good enough," Jim agreed, mollified. "Now," he riffled through a sheaf of papers and produced a checklist. "Tomorrow, I want us to make sure everybody is wearing their radios. I know that didn't happen on the first climb through the Icefall." He eyed the guides carefully.

Silence.

Ricky knew she had carried hers. Without it, she wouldn't have been able to call for help after the avalanche. And when she'd checked out Lou and Allison before heading up, she'd confirmed they had theirs.

"They're heavy, Jim." Paul Andersen blurted out. "The clients aren't gonna like it. I know that's why Mike and Patsy didn't bring theirs."

"I don't care. They've simply got to get used to it. If they can't handle it down here, how will they manage higher up the mountain?"

"Okaaay," the younger man sighed. "But they're not gonna be happy about it."

"If they've got a problem, have 'em see me." Jim's voice was insistent. "I'm not about to have any problems with this team because of a lack of communication."

Ricky remained silent. Although she hadn't used radio communication much in the past, she agreed with Jim now that it was a very good idea for the Peak Performance clients. With an expedition as big as theirs, with members whose experience lev-

els varied so widely, she saw it as an absolute necessity in terms
of avoiding problems.

For example, an experienced, fully acclimatized climber
could make it from Camp I to Camp II in the Cwm in under four
hours. For a climber who was laboring, it might take twice that.
Factor in variable weather conditions, equipment problems and
the like, and it was apparent to her that for safety's sake the
guides had to know who was still out there, and where.

"Which leads me to my next point," the big man continued.
"I'll be the one to run sweep on this climb. Which means you're
off the hook, Ricky." He smiled faintly. "If there's anyone who
needs to be turned around, then I'll be the one to do it."

"Uh...good idea," Paul said, gulping. "At 70K, I'd hate to
have to be the one to tell these nice people to take their balls and
go home."

Jim nodded, acknowledging the weight of the responsibility
he bore. "Another thing." He paused. "Let's give our people a
free rein on this one. Don't stick as close...we need to see what
they can do. I know Kevin and Phil shouldn't have a problem,
but keep a relaxed eye on them, Paul, just in case."

"You mean I take a pass on the Donaldsons?"

"Something tells me they'll be lagging," Jim responded,
sighing. "So that means I'll pick them up. Ricky," he swung his
dark brown eyes to the mountaineer, "you okay with continuing
on with Lou and Allison?"

"Sure," she told him, her face a study of indifference.
Climbing with Allison Peabody and Lou Silvers. There were
worse things she could think of.

"What's the word on Allison, anyway?" Jim addressed the
doctor. "That was some ride she took the other day. And how
about Patsy Donaldson...is she really ready for this?" The doubt
was plain in his voice.

"Well, without betraying doctor-patient confidentiality,"
Sandy Ortiz pushed her glasses higher up on her nose, "I can tell
you that Allison is fine. She was a bit shaken up, but she's one
tough lady. She should be okay up there, all things considered."

"You agree with that?" Jim regarded Ricky intently. "You
were there."

"I'm with Sandy," Ricky said, choosing her words carefully.
"Allison's not the most technical climber in the world, but as
long as she's feeling okay, she's got a shot. Lou, too, for that
matter," she continued. "He did okay up there, despite the prob-

lems he had acclimatizing at first. I'll keep an eye on him. On them both."

"That'll work." Jim made a note on his checklist.

"Patsy, I'm not so sure about," the doctor continued. "She's really had a rough go of it."

"And Mike, too," Paul added. "He hasn't been feeling that great, believe me. He's had a helluva time getting over that virus."

"Ultimately it's up to each individual whether they feel ready to climb," Sandy clarified. "All I can do is offer them a professional opinion."

Jim pursed his lips and nodded in agreement. "If a climber gears up and is ready to go, then all we can do is support them as best as we can. Their contracts say that, after all. But if there comes a time when, in my judgment, they're jeopardizing their own safety or the safety of the other members of the team—"

"Then they get turned around," Ricky finished for him.

"Yup. It's my call, and mine alone. I'd rather have a pissed off client with a lawsuit on my hands, instead of a dead client."

Ricky felt relieved to hear the team leader state his "turn-around" policy in such clear terms. It was one of the major concerns she'd had, wondering where that particular responsibility fell. Was she, the team's junior guide, authorized to send someone back? And even if she tried to, would they listen to her? Better to let Jim worry about it. It was just as much a business decision as a climbing one. And if she thought a climber was in trouble, she could always radio him to make the call.

"How's the stocking going up high, Jangbu?" Jim posed the question to the climbing sirdar.

"Good...good," the Sherpa replied, a smile creasing his face. "Ropes fixed to Camp III, tents, fuel. Bottles on the way," he said, referring to the oxygen canisters.

"Nice job," Jim told him. "So we're ready to receive clients through C2. Remember," he added, "that from Camp III onward, I want everyone breathing gas." He looked at Ricky. "No exceptions."

"Right," she said, already feeling her throat constrict at the mere thought of it. But she'd signed on under that condition and taken Jim's money. There was no way around it.

"It should be a good week, folks," Jim said, pushing back in his chair. "A nice solid climb... We'll start getting a good indication of how people will fare up high. Especially at Camp II.

At 21,000 feet, if you're gonna have a problem with altitude, it'll show up by then."

"Agreed," Ricky said.   Sometimes symptoms of altitude sickness stayed hidden at lower elevations on the mountain. But the physical effort of a multi-day acclimatization climb would begin to take its toll on an individual who was prone to such an ailment.   And this jibed with Ricky's belief that the lower you were when you found you had a problem, the better off you'd be.

"So, we'll have two nights at C1, climb through the Cwm, and then take three nights to acclimatize at C2...maybe poke around the *Bergschrund* a little," he added, referring to the ice wall that stood at the end of the box canyon that was the Khumbu Glacier.   "Then we'll descend in one day back here. Sound like a plan?"   He flashed his gleaming white teeth in a smile.

"Sounds like," Paul said, and they all agreed.

"Oh, we'll be using two and three-man tents above the Ice-fall, plus a bigger one for the Sherpas," Jim said as an after-thought, standing.   "I'll take the three-man, along with Kevin and Phil.   The rest are two-mans...or should I say, two persons," he bowed in deference to Ricky.   "We'll put the Donaldsons in one, you and Allison in one, and," he turned to Paul, "you and Lou Silvers in the last one."

The team leader headed for the entrance to the dining tent. "Everybody's okay with that, right?"

Ricky helplessly felt her mouth open and close as she watched Jim's broad back pass her by.   A thousand reasons screamed through her mind as to why she and Allison Peabody would not make the best of tent-mates.   She was used to being on her own...alone!   But dammit, for some reason, she simply couldn't find her voice.

"Good," Jim called back over his shoulder.   "Now if you'll excuse me, before the clients get here, I gotta take a leak."

So, Ricky thought with no small amount of despair, *now I've got a roommate.*

One who was petite, blonde, silly and annoying at times, and at others, earnest and selfless.   The mountaineer closed her eyes and breathed in deeply, trying to steady herself.   *Oh, Shit!* There was one thing she knew now, without a shadow of a doubt. She and Allison Peabody would either both get to the top of Everest...or kill each other, trying.

Chapter
Eleven

What a difference a few days and a little experience made.

She'd done it! Made her way up through the Icefall with nary a backward glance. Well, maybe there had been one glance or two, making sure that Ricky Bouchard was down there, somewhere. Allison was proud of herself, and she hadn't been scared at all, climbing past that point where the avalanche had occurred. What were the odds of it happening twice, right? Like getting struck by lightning. She'd already paid her dues on this trip.

She'd been a bit taken aback, however, at how the guides had let the clients strike out into the Icefall first, rather than leading the way. Kevin MacBride and Phil Christy had taken off immediately, totally psyched at leading the way. With a shake of his head and a grin in the early morning glow of dawn, Paul Andersen had clipped into the rope and gone after them.

Next went Lou Silvers, at Allison's insistence. It was the least she could do after he'd done the same for her last time. Besides, for some reason she was more comfortable being directly connected to Ricky on the ropes. And lastly, somewhere back there, had been Jim Harris and the Donaldsons.

Carefully threading her way between the popping and cracking seracs, she'd successfully swallowed her fear when she'd faced one particular crossing she remembered from the last trip. There had to have been at least three ladders lashed together

over a crevasse that had seemed to lengthen while she'd gazed
upon it. But she'd found her way across, and in a tad under three
and a half hours she'd made it topside.

Everyone had made it, eventually, including the beleaguered
Donaldsons, bent nearly double as they fell into camp, trying to
pull enough air into their abused lungs. With Jim Harris shep-
herding them towards some hot tea and a seat, they'd looked as
though they would need at least a week to recover. As it was, if
they had any hopes of keeping up on the summit pace, they'd
barely have two days.

Most of the group had spent the afternoon relaxing and
chatting with members of the other teams on the small landing
above the Icefall. The British had already been there a day, and
more teams had arrived hard on the boot heels of the Peak Performance team.

Like Base Camp, the neighborhood was getting crowded,
filled with climbers of varying levels of expertise, yet all with
the same goal: to claim Everest for their own.

Later on, they'd all eaten a hearty dinner of chicken and
rice, prepared by Dawa Sherpa, Lopsang's nephew. The Base
Camp sirdar had recommended his relation as just the man
needed to run the dining tent at Advance Base Camp, also known
as Camp II, and so the young, energetic Dawa had gotten the job.
The fact that he had fairly good climbing skills, enough to get
him through the Icefall, at least, had helped.

Tired, sated, and happy to have completed this first leg of
the climb, the Peak Performance team had straggled to their tents
for some well-deserved shut-eye. *And that's where the problem
had started,* Allison reflected.

"You're not going to leave your boots in the vestibule, are
you?" her tent-mate had demanded. "With the winds, snow
could blow in and get into them."

"But it's not snowing, and the winds are calm for once,
Ricky," she'd told her, noting with some surprise how quickly
her black eye had faded. "Besides, I want the extra room."

That had elicited a dark frown from the tall woman. And
then, tersely, "Are you going to be long?" She'd gestured to the
book Allison had been writing in and the lamp burning brightly
by her side.

"I plan to write in my journal every night, if I can," Allison
had told her. "It helps me calm down and get ready for the next
day. So yeah, I'll be a while. Maybe another 15 minutes. Is that

okay?"

"Great," the mountaineer had grumbled, unwilling to settle herself down.

Allison was comfortable now, warmly ensconced in her sleeping bag, propped up on one arm as she wrote. But as for Ricky, she could see that she still looked restless. Tense. She had to admit that she'd secretly been pleased when she'd heard she'd be rooming with the mountaineer, but now...Ricky was simply getting on her nerves. Why didn't the woman just relax? Out of the corner of her eye, Allison noticed the way she was crouched, as though she might need to make a break from the tent at any moment.

"Going somewhere?"

"What?"

Allison pointed her pen towards the tent flap. "Are you going or staying? I can't tell."

"Staying...I guess," Ricky said, settling reluctantly onto her backside and pulling her boots in after her. She placed them at the foot of her sleeping bag.

Allison returned to her writing, pretending not to notice the taller woman's defiant glare. Let the mountaineer have to scrunch herself into her sleeping bag. What did she care?

"You don't snore, I hope." Ricky was fumbling with her hair, pulling it out of the ponytail she wore it in.

"What if I did?" Allison muttered beneath her breath, growing more annoyed by the minute.

"Didn't catch that."

Allison could feel the heat of Ricky's blue gaze upon her. So blue.

"What did you say?"

"Not since I was a kid," Allison sharply replied, irritated with herself now for allowing something so silly to distract her. Who did this Ricky Bouchard think she was, anyway? Some tight-ass camp counselor? And here she'd thought she'd been making progress.

That she and Ricky might even become...friends.

No way.

Not if this was the result of it.

Snoring? Allison bit off a gloating laugh. Oh, yeah baby. Ricky Bouchard would find out first hand.

"Not that it matters when we get up high," Ricky told her, finally unzipping her sleeping bag. "The air is so thin you can't sleep, really. All you can do is lie there in a half-awake daze, panting, trying to get some rest."

"Sounds nice," Allison said in a tone that implied just the opposite. "Thanks for that picture."

Ricky continued to prepare herself for sleep, obviously engaging in practiced high-altitude rituals honed over a lifetime of experience. "You may overheat with what you've got on."

"Pardon me?" Allison gave up all pretense at writing now, shoving her pen down and slapping her journal closed. She watched, open mouthed, as Ricky stripped down to a T-shirt and her polypro pants.

"You're going to get hot. Look at you. Isn't that a climbing sweater?"

"I'm quite comfortable, thanks."

"I'm telling you, you're going to heat up."

"And I'm telling *you*," Allison said, her green eyes flashing, "that I think I should know how I feel. Some of us aren't as hot blooded as you, okay?"

"Don't complain to me in the middle of the night about it, then." Ricky shrugged and started to slide into her bag. "Speaking of which, do you have to get up much at night to...you know—"

"I plan to use my pee bottle, if you must know," she coldly enunciated. The anger was rising in Allison's voice, but dammit, she was powerless to stop it. "What—are you going to tell me now that I better not mix it up with my juice bottle?"

"I—"

"Save it, will you?" Allison reached for the light and violently switched it off. "Maybe you think the best thing for everybody would have been if I had stayed in Base Camp, right? Or maybe if I'd never gotten on a plane to Nepal in the first place."

Allison fell back in her sleeping bag, her heart pounding, wondering what it was about Ricky that got to her so. Even when she'd sworn to herself she would never give her the satisfaction; and with just a few innocuous comments, she'd lost that resolve and let her defenses crumble in the face of it. Why did she let this woman's...respect for her, or imagined lack thereof, matter so much?

A wetness.

With some distress, Allison was mortified to discover that hot tears were streaming down her cheeks. Oh, this was great.

Just great. Maybe now, if she noticed, Ricky would explain to her the high-altitude dangers of frozen tears.

The silence stretched out, long and unforgiving.

Allison was acutely aware of the mountaineer's presence so near to her; how could she not be? When Ricky Bouchard was around, you knew it. She fancied she could feel the heat of her; imagined that the feeling was real—the wonder of the dark haired woman's seeming imperviousness to cold—and she let it warm her, too. That warmth, together with the courage the darkness gave her, at last allowed her to speak.

"I'm surprised you're still here," she hiccuped. "It's got to be killing you, being with such a total rookie."

Ricky did not answer her at first. Allison heard her exhale, and then, "I was going to leave." A pause. "Until I realized I didn't have much on."

And in the darkness, Allison could hear the smile in her voice.

"With your metabolism, you'd hardly have noticed," she said, allowing herself a smile, too.

"Yeah, but anybody outside would have."

Allison laughed aloud, at that.

"I–I'm sorry, Allison."

The stockbroker could sense that the mountaineer had rolled over on her side, now, and was facing her.

"It's just...I'm used to being on my own."

"But you weren't always, were you?" Allison turned towards Ricky, feeling a slight breath of a chill as the tears dried on her face.

"No. Only since I lost my climbing partner."

Allison heard the pain in the low voice that rumbled in the darkness, and she knew of whom her tent-mate spoke. It was Jean-Pierre. It had to be. Of course! Why hadn't she realized that sooner? No wonder Ricky had been so uptight about the whole thing.

"I've never had a climbing partner," Allison said softly, not caring what the mountaineer thought at that lame admission. It probably fit in with how Ricky viewed her—as a novice. Well, in many ways, Ricky was probably right.

Suddenly, she felt a touch on her arm in the darkness, reaching out, finding her own hand.

"You do now." A firm grasp. Warm. "Partner."

❊ ◆ ❊ ◆ ❊ ◆ ❊

The Valley of Silence.

And it was that, Allison thought, as she trudged her way up the Western Cwm towards Camp II. Here in this great valley nearly a mile deep and four miles long, they were sheltered from the brunt of the Himalayan winds, with Everest on the left, Nuptse on the right, and Lhotse dead ahead. A stark contrast to the riot of noise she'd grown so accustomed to over the past few weeks: the incessant howling of the winds, the groaning Icefall, and the sounds of several hundred of people inhabiting too small a space.

Here in the Cwm, however, the air was calm and still, silent but for the crunch of her crampons biting into the ice, punctuated by the sounds of her own effort. A ribbon of colorfully garbed climbers stretched out before her and behind her, creeping their way along the silken whiteness of the valley. Some climbers, she could make out, were from Peak Performance; many more were not.

Of the thirty plus teams in Base Camp, it was apparent that quite a number were making their presence known in the higher elevations. Allison idly wondered if this traffic jam would last all the way to the summit. God, she hoped not.

Time for a drink.

Allison ground to a stop and gulped down several mouthfuls of water. Feeling the heat, she decided to peel off her sweater, leaving only a thin, polypropylene undergarment on her upper body. She'd considered wearing a T-shirt, but Ricky had warned her that the intensity of the sun's radiant heat in the bowl-shaped Cwm could potentially burn her. And then there was the chill she'd get if cloud cover and snow showers suddenly moved in.

She was moving well; all her teammates were, from what she could tell. But a lot could happen during the three hours plus it would take to get to Camp II, that distant blip at the head of the Khumbu where the jagged slopes of Everest met the ridges of Lhotse.

Replacing her water bottle in her rucksack, Allison turned and let her eyes track down the Cwm to the tall, distinctive figure of Ricky Bouchard. The mountaineer was climbing between her and Lou Silvers this time, trailing a bit closer to the attorney. Lou was keeping up, but the distance between them had widened slightly, and Allison knew that Ricky would be dropping back a bit to make sure he was okay, reminding him to stay hydrated. Capturing the red and black clad mountaineer in her gaze, Allison did not wave. Instead, she focused on conserving her energy at this altitude in such heat, where your every move had to be parceled out and planned for in advance. But she could tell by a subtle incline of Ricky's dark head that she'd seen her, and she allowed herself to feel the calmness, the encouragement of that connection.

Ricky Bouchard.

Her bunkmate and climbing partner.

Who would have thought it?

They had arrived at a truce of sorts after that first night in the tent. Ricky had her habits and routines, that was for sure, and although she rarely spoke, when she did there was plenty of good advice to be found in those words, if she were willing to listen. And as for Allison, well, she realized that she herself maybe wasn't the easiest person to live with. Perhaps she had some shaping up to do.

And so last night she'd made sure to check with Ricky that it was okay to keep the lamp burning while she'd made her final journal entry, and had decided to move her boots in from the vestibule, after all. Because they'd been pretty damn frozen the morning before, as Ricky had predicted.

So...they were still getting used to each other. It would take time and patience, but something told Allison it would be worth it. And then some.

Allison shoved off again, working her way carefully along the icy slope. It was amazing, she considered, how dramatic the difference in the weather was from when they'd started out. It had been another bitter cold dawn when they'd left Camp I, the objective being, Jim Harris had told them, to avoid the broiling heat of a bright late morning in the Cwm.

Quickly, once the sun had blinked an eye over Lhotse, the valley had turned from a freezer into an oven.

"Keep drinking and keep your glasses on," Ricky had warned them all before they'd departed. "The last thing you want in the heat of the Cwm is to feel dizzy or to come down with a high-altitude headache."

And so here she was, dressed more for a hike in the Green Mountains than for an Everest trek. There were the thick glacier glasses that could've passed for beachwear, not to mention the comfort she took in the familiar scent of the coconut-based sun-

screen that coated her face and gloveless hands, and the feel of
the perspiration gathering under the band of her Peak Performance cap. Her mind struggled to grasp the contrast between
those warm weather associations, and the crackling of her crampons digging into the surface of the Cwm; the wet, cool smell of
the ice. It reminded her of the spring skiing she'd done a few
years back in Telluride.

Allison smiled to herself, sparing a quick glance upward at
the jet stream ripping off the summit. All in all, she felt pretty
damn good. The trail was well marked, and she took care to
avoid the occasional "wanded" crevasse. Each season, the Sherpas posted bamboo wands at the sites of what might otherwise
appear to unsuspecting climbers as secure snow bridges. In fact,
many of the bridges were little more than a house of cards.
Without adequate warning, a climber might start across the
bridge, only to break through the unstable surface and plummet
into the fissure below. Roped or not, inside a crevasse was no
place where Allison Peabody intended to be. Her experience last
week in the Icefall was close enough for her.

Keeping her feet moving, Allison fell back into her step
breathing, pushing herself just hard enough to maintain a steady
pace upwards without blowing through her energy reserves.

Heat and ice.

In many ways, very much like Veronique Bouchard.

What? God, maybe I'm getting dizzy from the heat, Allison
thought, hearing herself draw in a startled gasp. She shoved the
unexpected thought of the mountaineer to the back of her mind,
muzzling it. Now was not the time. *Step. Breathe.* She had bigger things to worry about, like making it to Camp II before she
was broiled alive.

Instead, she let her mind trip to less confounding subjects.
Step. Breathe. Idly wondering what was going on back at the
office, before quickly deciding that she didn't much care.

And then there was Lionel.

Ugh. *Step. Breathe.*

Hoping that Lou Silvers could find the power somewhere
within himself to realize his dream, and return safely home to
the wife and two little girls whose picture he'd shown her about
four or five times already. *Step. Breathe.*

Would the good weather hold, and was Ricky Bouchard
involved with anyone?

Whoa. Dammit, Allie! Cut that out. Like it's any of your business anyway!

Okay... *Step. Breathe.* The heat...summer, summer, summer. Uh...how were her parents doing, anyway? Elizabeth and Richard. Or, "Liz and Dick," as she referred to them in her less charitable moments. She wondered if they had even realized she was gone. Or cared, if they had.

The scent of the sunscreen in the air catapulted her back in time, through a rushing blur of colors, of memories, of triumph, and of hurt.

Summers on the Cape, and the house they'd had there.

The "cottage," her parents had called it, although it was bigger than the year-round homes of most of her school friends. They'd been conceited enough to give the damn place a name, "Driftwood," and Allison supposed it was fitting enough. How adrift she'd felt there, how invisible, like the gnarled, weathered pieces of wood that the tide purged itself of one day, only to reclaim on the next; the wave action smoothing away the indentations of the driftwood upon the sand, as though it had never been there at all.

The pool at the Yacht Club where Allison had been sent, along with other children her age, to learn how to swim. Allison hated the swimming lessons. Some small part of her young mind couldn't stand being told what to do. But until she could learn to swim, her parents had said she wouldn't be allowed to go in the ocean past her ankles. So, pouting, she'd given in.

The club was all right. As an only child, it was an opportunity for her to meet some other kids, to make friends. But she missed the sandy beach at the rear of the cottage, where she would play for hours on her own, building sand castles and making up stories about the beautiful princesses and handsome princes who lived in them, never even minding how the sun burnished her pale skin.

She remembered that one mid-summer morning at the club. An overnight thunderstorm had pelted the grounds, leaving scattered branches loose on the lush, manicured lawn, and raising the level of the water in the pool until it nearly reached the tiled rim. The early morning air was warm and muggy, with a faint mist still rising from the drenched grounds.

She'd been taking the swimming lessons for what seemed like forever, although it had probably been no more than two or three weeks. Today was the day they would attempt to swim the length of the pool, earning those bands with the ducks on them that the big kids wore, signifying that they were indeed certified swimmers and allowed to venture into the big pool on their own.

She recalled the morning as though it were yesterday.

The yellow-flowered bathing suit she wore.

The scrape on her elbow from the day before when she'd slipped on the gravel drive of the cottage.

Walking reluctantly on the darkened, wet concrete to the edge of the pool; slipping into the rain-chilled water with the rest of the kids, her teeth chattering as the cold temperature chased her breath away.

One after another, they started up the lap lanes. There was Bobby, just "Bobby," who lived near them at the cottage, she knew, but he never played with her. He was off, flailing his way through the water, without a single backward glance.

More children went, until it was that little brown-haired girl's turn. She didn't want to go. She was afraid. She was crying so hard that she could barely speak, and Allison felt badly for her, although she'd never learned her name. After a few moments of low words from the instructor, the bawling girl was scooped out of the water, her chance lost.

And then, "C'mon, Allie! Your turn. All the way to the end. You can do it!"

"You can do it." The words of Miss Ingstrom, a woman she hadn't seen in more than 20 years, now. But the instructor had believed in her. Told her so. Made Allison believe it, herself.

Taking a deep breath, puffing her cheeks, she'd gingerly lowered her face in the water—the part that was so scary—and then pushed off with her feet from the side of the pool. Oh God, what if she sank like a stone? What if she forgot everything she'd learned? What if—?

It was like a movie that should be starring some other little girl, only she was in it. Like the pieces of a puzzle, suddenly, it all clicked. And there she was, swimming! Legs pumping, arms whirling, head swiveling to the side to take gasping breaths of air just as she'd been taught to do. Knowing she was moving into the deep end of the pool where the depth was well over her head, but not caring. Not caring at all, because she could swim!

Conscious of the blurred form of Miss Ingstrom walking alongside her on the pool deck, cheering her on, encouraging her. Her hand bumped the far wall and then, spluttering, she'd realized there was nowhere else to go. She'd done it! The rest of the kids were clapping and cheering, even Bobby. How proud she'd felt when she'd slipped the duck band over her foot, the first thing she ever remembered earning on her own.

The lesson was over.

All the kids had completed the swim, save for the red-eyed, little brown-haired girl. Allison had heard the instructor whispering to her that she could try it again tomorrow, if she wanted, and that made Allison feel better for her. She would have her chance, after all.

The crowd of wrinkled but victorious children was released and, heeding a silent siren, they began to scamper over to a cabana where the parents usually waited. There, the adults might have a morning juice or an eye-opener, conversing amongst themselves, waiting for the lessons to conclude.

Allison could feel the excitement in the air, hearing the peals of joyous laughter ringing from her classmates. Shoving limp strands of blonde hair behind her ears, she found herself running too, caught up in it all, racing with her friends towards the cabana. They fell into their parents' arms, chattering about their triumph and how they'd prevailed against all watery odds.

Even now, Allison could feel a sharp squeeze in her chest as she remembered raking the throng with her eyes, searching for a pant leg or a hem of a skirt that she could recognize.

She saw the little brown-haired girl getting a hug from her mommy. And Bobby, too, although he was trying to squirm his way out of it.

And then it hit her. Her mommy wasn't there. Her mommy never was there, or her daddy either, for that matter.

There was no one to tell.

She felt the smile leave her face, replaced by the blank "I don't care" look that she was already well on her way to perfecting. But her heart felt it, and the burst of joy that thrummed within her began to melt away, like a spilled ice cream cone on a hot summer's day.

"Allison?"

It would all be okay. Her mommy and daddy had good reasons for not being there. They'd told her so, right?

"Allison! C'mon, let's go!"

Allison lifted her head. It was the nanny. Cindy or Mindy— it didn't really matter, they came and went so fast, and they always seemed to be more interested in their yucky boyfriends and the big schools they went to in Boston, rather than in playing with her.

"Sorry I'm late. Where's your tote bag? C'mon, we've got to run to the grocery store!"

So she'd sullenly stuck a thumb in her mouth while her shorts and top were tugged on over a damp bathing suit, and off they had gone.

By the time her mother had deigned to motor over for the weekend, just in time for the Gibsons' annual cocktail party, her good news had dulled and soured. She'd told her and shown her the duck band, but only so her mother would let her go in the ocean. *"That's nice, Allison dear,"* she'd told her, giving her a pat on the head before picking up the phone to make a call.

She never did tell her father. A man she rarely saw from Memorial Day to Labor Day. He stayed away from the Cape, as a rule, content to let his wife and daughter enjoy the fruits of his labor.

"There's work to be done," he'd told her. *"You'll thank me someday, Allison. You're too young now to understand."*

No.

She hadn't understood. And when she finally did, when she was finally old enough, she'd found she didn't care, one way or the other. They were just people to her, by then.

Strangers who, sadly, happened to also be her parents.

But it had been a long, painful road, getting her to that point. For far too long, it had always been about struggling to find ways to get what she craved, what all her other friends seemed to receive so freely: her parents' attention, their acceptance, their love.

What she wouldn't have given, to be just like everybody else.

But she wasn't.

Hell, they'd driven that notion home into her head often enough. She was Allison Peabody, of the Boston Peabodys. A rare, exotic bird in a cage, with her wings kept clipped and her emotions held in check. Never to be liberated or to know what it was like to really fly. A thing to be trotted out and admired, only when it was convenient.

"You know our daughter Allison, don't you? She's a student at Smithfield Academy."

"You're special, different, better than everyone else," they'd told her. Even then, Allison had wondered how that could be, when they'd barely even noticed she was alive.

Well, she'd tried. Thought that maybe she could earn her

way into their good graces, pay her dues. So she'd obediently taken the music and dance lessons, performed in the recitals, and remembered searching the faces in the crowd during the applause, looking futilely for ones she might recognize. Received the top grades on all her report cards as expected, but never closely examined or questioned.

She'd tried her best, crying her heart out in the dark of night, smiling during the day, and excelling at everything she tried. After all, a Peabody would never fail, right?

But none of it worked. Perhaps if there had been a cross word or a raised hand, at least she would have felt...*something.* But it was their cool indifference that inflicted the cruelest cut of all.

It was during college, she knew, that she'd started to go in the other direction. Somehow, somewhere along the way, she'd decided that if being a good girl didn't work, she'd do the opposite. And so she'd started acting out, undertaking these crazy adventures: the white water rafting, the parachuting—everything, and then, most recently, the climbing. Taking those first uncertain steps that had finally brought her here, to this place.

One thing Allison knew for sure was that she wasn't the same woman who had first stepped on that plane in New York some weeks back. Things had changed. *She*...had changed. And it felt good.

Letting out a great gust of air, Allison thought about the mountaineer behind her, winding her way up the Western Cwm, watching her back.

Ricky Bouchard was right.

Something as big as Everest, you had to be doing it for the right reasons. The margin of error was so thin, that to give it anything less than it deserved, than you deserved for yourself, could prove to be disastrous.

Shifting her eyes skyward to regard the plume, she realized that now it wasn't about her parents. Or Lionel. Or her job.

It was about her—period.

About proving something to herself. Accomplishing something—*for* herself. Finding a peace in that, and letting that peace be enough.

When the ill-fated George Leigh Mallory had been asked why he desired to climb mighty Everest, he had answered with his typically dry, British aplomb: "Because it is there."

Allison had asked Ricky that same question last night in

their tent, after she'd extinguished their light. The mountaineer had been silent for a moment in the dark, considering that age-old question.

"Why do I want to climb Everest?" she'd finally repeated, in her low, slightly accented voice. "Because *I* am *here.*"

Well. Allison Peabody had to admit it; she kind of liked the sound of that.

❊ ◆ ❊ ◆ ❊ ◆ ❊

Even before she got to the spot where the climbers were huddled, pointing, Ricky Bouchard knew.

Knew by the twisting in her gut that they'd stumbled upon the first frozen evidence of the ultimate price Everest exacted from those who dared its icy slopes.

A body.

She'd seen the small crowd begin to form as they'd advanced up the Cwm. One by one, climbers had peeled off the main trail, attracted by a small splash of color that did not otherwise belong in this barren, glistening place.

Kevin MacBride, Phil Christy, and Paul Andersen were there, as well as several climbers from other expeditions. Directly in front of her, Ricky had watched Allison stop, and then move over to where the rest of the climbers had gathered, beckoned by their excited calls. She stood there now, on the periphery, a stricken look on her face.

Ricky quickened her pace, not an easy thing to do on the slick glacier, but she was fueled by the jolt of anger she felt coursing through her veins. Bodies were a fact of life on Everest, so common up high that they virtually became a part of the scenery. They were more rare at this lower elevation, but it was not unheard of for a climber's remains to tumble down from above, dislodged from the mountain's icy grip after a hard blow or a monsoon storm, months or sometimes years after they'd been killed.

It was next to impossible to transport the deceased back to Base Camp from a high altitude world where merely planting one foot in front of the other required supreme physical effort and mental discipline. As a result, the dead were mourned, true enough, but were mostly left where they'd fallen in a final, permanent joining with the mountain.

But Ricky Bouchard believed that didn't mean they

deserved any less respect.

As the mountaineer approached, her blood began to boil. She saw several of the climbers poking, prodding at the pathetic frozen bundle of tattered clothing, shrunken flesh, and blanched bones. They stared at the corpse with a perverse fascination, unwilling to really touch it, yet unable to look away.

All except Allison Peabody. The young woman had partially turned her back to the ghastly scene, her face ashen.

"Is it a westerner or a Sherpa?" Phil Christy asked, dubiously eyeing a boot that lay not far away from the figure crumpled face down in the snow. A translucent white foot jarringly poked out from the edges of torn blue gaiters and a down suit; this man had obviously been climbing up high.

"Can't tell," Kevin MacBride answered him. He worked his way around to the head of the figure, where tufts of dark hair ruffled in the light breeze. "Maybe if we can get a look at his face." He pushed at the head of the body with his boot. The figure remained immobile.

"What's going on, here?" Ricky breathlessly demanded, shooting an accusatory glare at Paul Andersen.

"We...ah, we're just checking out—"

Ricky shoved past him. The idiot. He should have known better. Some senior guide.

"He must've been here a while," Phil was saying. The young man had dropped to his knees now and had crouched over low to peer at the small, silent figure.

"Christ," Kevin swore, "he's frozen solid!" The burly climber gave the corpse another shove with his foot, and then another, harder. "Like a freakin' iceberg!"

"Back off," Ricky growled, pushing her way to the front of the onlookers.

"Hey, Ricky!" Kevin MacBride did not even lift his head. "Check this dead guy out!" So intent was he on his examination of the body, that he was blissfully ignorant of the danger signal flashing in the mountaineer's tone.

"I said," she stepped closer, "back off!" And with that, she gave him a shove, hard enough so that he slipped backwards to land on his rump in the snow. She grabbed at a ragged dark blue tarp that was half on, half off of the body. Probably placed there earlier by Sherpas fixing the ropes along the route, she guessed.

Kevin sat awkwardly on the glacier like a toppled snowman, indignation coloring his cheeks. "What the fuck is your problem?" he shouted angrily, his voice echoing hollowly in the Cwm.

"Leave this man be." Ricky slung off her backpack and fished out several ice pickets, intending to drive them through the tarp to secure it over the poor man.

"We were just checking it out," Kevin retorted, struggling to regain his feet. "It's not like we've ever seen anything like this before!"

Ricky started to cover the dead climber, gathering any loose fragments of his personal effects close.

The empty boot. A ragged, worn section of rope. Shorn pieces of clothing.

"Well, get used to it," she muttered, trying to calm herself, "because you're gonna see more." She shook her head, not really caring that here she was, picking a fight with a client. Kevin MacBride was a yahoo asshole, and that made him danger-ous while he was on the mountain.

"This man had friends," Ricky said tightly. She drove a picket through the tarp, securing it down deep into the snow and ice. "A family. For God's sake," her voice shook, "show a little respect."

"Well where were his friends up here, huh?" MacBride obstinately thrust his chin out as he dusted himself off, unwilling to let the subject drop. "They just left him."

"He's a Sherpa," Ricky said, gently pushing a tattered seg-ment of homespun cloth, the colors faded, back under the tarp. "He knew the risks. He probably died up high, and his body fell or got blown down here recently," she explained, her mouth set in a tense line. "He hasn't been here long. I would've heard about it. All it takes is a night out here to freeze to a particular spot. But..." she took in the poor condition of his remains, "he's been dead for a while. Years, I'd say."

"Don't you care who he is?" Phil Christy piped up, deter-mined to show his friend some support. Some of the other gawk-ers had already begun to continue the climb up the glacier to Camp II, uncomfortable with the scene they were witnessing. "You're just gonna leave him here, too? Nice."

"Have you got a better idea?" Ricky snapped her head up, her eyes boring through the darkness of her glasses into Christy. "Because I'd love to hear it."

"Can't we move him?" MacBride was nothing, if not per-sistent. Obviously, he was used to getting his way.

"Where to? Are you offering to dig him out and carry him down?" Ricky's voice was harsh. "The Sherpas know he's here. That's enough."

"Well..." MacBride looked suddenly lost as he considered this notion, like a child who'd misplaced his favorite toy.

"She's got a point, there, buddy," Phil said at last, giving his friend a nudge. "Like I'd ever be able to haul your fat ass outta here."

"Ricky's right," Paul Andersen said, feeling the time was right to step in and try to regain some control over the situation. "It's what happens on Everest. It's hard enough sometimes to get the living out, let alone the dead."

A sudden gust of wind blew down the Cwm, lifting a corner of the tarp. Ricky grabbed at it, weighing it down with her knee while she reached for another picket. This was as close to a burial as the poor man would ever get, and she wanted to do right by him, as she hoped one day others might do for her, if need be. He deserved to rest in peace.

Hell, they all did.

"C'mon, guys," Paul said, the anxiety plain in his voice. "Let's get going, huh? We've gotta get to C2."

Ricky ignored the mutterings as the men departed, though she did glance up as the climbers moved out. She was surprised to see that Allison was still there, looking directly at her, now. Lou Silvers had also arrived and stood solemnly behind her.

"You better get going," Ricky sighed, turning a practiced eye to the sky. The sun had disappeared behind fat, low-hanging gray clouds, and the air was starting to chill. "The weather's changing, and it's still another half-mile or so to Camp."

The wind picked up again, and Ricky returned her attention to the disorderly tarpaulin. She heard a crunching sound in the snow, and then there was a pair of small, chapped hands next to hers, holding the tarp down.

"I want to help."

"No."

"Please. I want to stay."

"No, I—" Ricky caught herself and removed the sharpness from her voice. This had nothing to do with Allison. Her new partner had done nothing wrong. "Thanks," she started again, softly. "But I won't be much longer here. I'd feel better if I knew you and Lou were on your way to camp, eh?" She tried a frozen smile. "Maybe you can make sure there's a cup of tea waiting for me."

Ricky held her breath, watching how Allison's delicate features ebbed and flowed as she considered this offer. She didn't
want the young stockbroker anywhere near this...this reminder
of what could happen to the best of them while they were on the
mountain. This was her own duty, and she would handle it alone.

"Okay." Allison pushed herself to her feet. "If you're
sure."

"I'm sure. I'll be right behind you. Just let me finish up
here. Lou," she leaned behind Allison to regard the attorney,
"you okay with that?"

"No prob, Ricky," he said, pulling on a pair of gloves. "I'm
getting colder by the second, just standing here."

"Get moving, both of you," Ricky said firmly. "See if you
can't beat the weather."

With a final look backward, Allison took off up the slope,
followed closely by Lou Silvers.

Thank God.

Ricky knew this whole...episode had rocked Allison, that
was plainly evident. And still she'd wanted to stay, to help.
That took guts, though by this time the mountaineer was not as
surprised as she might have been at that offer. She'd been finding out for some days now that there was a lot more to this Allison Peabody than she'd ever originally given her credit for.

Looking around the impromptu burial site, Ricky saw
another segment of cloth, about the size of a long handkerchief.
It was once white, although now it was yellowed and stained
with the weather and grit of the Cwm. But Ricky immediately
recognized it for what it was: a *khata*, the Sherpa's prayer scarf.

Whether it had served him well in life, or not, she would
never know. But in death, she was determined that he would
keep it with him. Reverently, she slipped her hands under the
tarp, and tied it securely around a frozen arm, silently reciting a
brief Buddhist prayer.

A final swing of her ice ax, and it was done; the tarp was
secure.

Ricky Bouchard sat back on her heels, catching her breath,
wondering about this man whose life had come to an end here,
trapped in the frozen embrace of a mountain in whose shadow
he'd probably lived his entire life.

Was it worth it?

The breeze picked up again; cold. The light was growing

flat, diffused. But the mountaineer had no desire to move, not yet. Thick, wet snowflakes began to fall, slowly at first, and then faster, spinning and whirling a path down to the earth, coming to rest on the battered tarp where the Sherpa lay.

Chapter
Twelve

Acclimatizing.

It was a "siege process," or so the experts called it. But Ricky Bouchard knew that for many climbers, it was a process that brought them to nothing but a frustrated end. Bodies screaming for air, dizzy, and nauseous, they would have to retreat down the mountain, their dreams for summitting Everest—over.

The idea was to gradually work your way towards increasingly higher altitudes, giving your body time to adjust. And so you hopscotched from camp to camp, spending several nights in each at a time, alternately descending to the lower altitudes for recovery. The final push, from Base Camp to Summit, took five days time, if the weather cooperated. The first day was a non-stop trek from Base Camp to Camp II. The following day was a last chance for would-be summitters to rest, and do one final check of their equipment.

The third day, the altitude weary climbers would make their way to Camp III, at 24,000 feet. The battered, exposed tents comprised a much smaller camp, defiantly chopped out of the wind-swept ice of the Lhotse Face. From Camp III onward, oxygen-starved men and women would change into full body down suits and breathe bottled gas, providing some measure of relief against a "death zone" environment that was incapable of sus-

taining life. At that altitude, your system would rebel and begin
to shut down, your organs clamoring for oxygen that simply
couldn't be found in the thin atmosphere. And so your body
would begin to consume itself for energy, a last, final step in the
process that has been slowly leeching you of sense and strength
from the moment you first stepped foot on the mountain.

Ricky had seen the altitude hit climbers more times than she
cared to count. It reached out its cold, indiscriminate hand to the
best of mountaineers and the worst of tentative novices, alike.
Those who valiantly fought against the pain, the confusion, the
dullness of body and spirit, those who struggled their way to
Camp III, oftentimes made it no further. For those able to go on,
they could look forward to an exhausting, dangerous six hour
hike to Camp IV at 26,000 feet, a camp situated on a godless,
rock and ice strewn mesa known as the South Col.

There would be no night's rest to be had at Camp IV. The
objective was to spend as little time in that inhospitable environment as possible. There might be a short, restless nap, or time
for one last "brewing up" on hot beverages and soup. The strongest climbers would have arrived at the South Col by mid-day.

By 10 p.m. or so, it would be time.

Time to gather what remained of your power and your wits
for the final push to the top of the world. If you were lucky, you
might make it in another 12 to 14 hours.

Or not.

And then there was the getting down.

Ricky Bouchard knew all about the science behind acclimatization. As a mountaineer, she made it her business to know.
She also understood that her own body was different, able to
handle the punishment of altitude much better than others. In
the thin air, her lungs were better able to draw in the O2 and process it, and her red blood cells were able to carry and store more
oxygen, directing it to vital muscles and tissues.

But those physiological benefits would never make her
completely impervious to the effects of altitude. Eventually, in
the wrong conditions, she knew it could hit her, too. Rather, she
was simply smart in how she went about it; gradually increasing
her altitude, monitoring her recovery time, making sure she kept
physically active the higher she went. That way, she felt she
gave her body's natural advantage an even better shot at going
the distance, without needing supplemental oxygen. It had
suited her well, until now.

Ricky hated the damned oxygen apparatus. Those masks that always fogged up, the lines that sometimes froze, and the way the bulky equipment reduced your field of vision. It was a wretched contraption; it made your throat run as dry as a sandy desert, and how disgusting it was the way the mucus built up inside the mask, freezing, with nowhere else for it to go.

It was all bad business, and there was a part of her, the traditional part, who believed that if you couldn't climb Everest unassisted, without bottled gas, then you shouldn't do it at all. Because the one thing she was certain of was that no matter how good a climber you were, if you disturbed your body's natural acclimatization process with the use of supplemental oxygen, and then you ran out, you immediately got into serious trouble. Like a toy that had wound down, or a tire with the air blown out, you just ground to a stop, unable to move, until you got to another O2 source.

And in the vagaries of an Everest climb, where nothing was a certainty, Ricky hated like hell to have to rely on something other than herself to get up and down. Something that might get her killed...like that Sherpa they'd found.

As she'd suspected, the other Sherpas had known he was there.

"Maybe it be Ang Sherpa, or Tashi Sherpa," Jangbu had told her, when at last she'd plodded into Camp II just as the snowfall had intensified and really begun to blanket the Cwm. "Ang lost five seasons ago, Tashi, seven."

Ricky had found the wiry sirdar in the small Camp II cook tent, where she'd wandered to scrounge a thermos of hot tea from Dawa. All of the Peak Performance team had made it in safely; Jim Harris and the Donaldsons, last but not least. After the hot, draining climb, completed in the beginnings of a snow squall, everyone was content to collapse in their tents to recover. The mountaineer hadn't seen Allison, but she was sure the tent was where she would find her.

"It's not going to be an easy climb," Ricky had told the Sherpa, tiredly thinking that a bit of a nap in her own tent sounded like a pretty fair idea.

"We have good power. Good Sherpa," he'd grinned, referring to the strength of the team of Sherpas working with Peak Performance. "We go all the way to top. Like always, right, Ricky?"

"Maybe." She'd turned to leave the cook tent, and then

stopped. "What's it look like up high. Any news?"

"Deep snow. Snow very deep. But no worry," Jangbu had assured her. "Sherpa fix ropes. No problem."

"I may help you out some, day after tomorrow," Ricky had told him, thinking the exercise would serve her well, in terms of acclimatization. "Bring a load of supplies up to Camp III, at least. I know I can make good time."

"You like Sherpani," her old friend had chuckled. The female Sherpas were just as capable as their male counterparts at handling high altitude climbing. "Jangbu use you next season, okay?"

"Depends on how many rupees you're offering," Ricky had laughed, giving the Sherpa a parting wave before ducking out into the blowing snow.

There was little activity in their camp, and she could see a few huddled forms moving about through the snow in the next camp over. It was the British team, she guessed. The snowfall was not entirely unexpected; the weather on the mountain could change in a heartbeat. The storm might last until evening, or it could last for three days, you never knew.

For Patsy Donaldson's sake, she hoped the snow eased off by morning. The plan was to spend a total of three nights at Camp II, but Patsy was showing symptoms of altitude sickness again. According to Jim Harris, the small woman had done her best to keep up with her husband on the trek up the Cwm, but a headache and nausea were hitting her hard. Jim had been in contact with Sandy Ortiz in Base Camp, and the doctor had advised that if Patsy wasn't feeling better by the next day, she should be brought down the mountain to recover. Oftentimes, just a quick descent was all it took to shake off the symptoms, but Ricky knew that Patsy had been laboring all along, and she seriously doubted the woman's chances to summit on her own.

The mountaineer didn't know Mike and Patsy Donaldson well; they weren't the sort of people whose company she would normally keep. With Mike's Fortune 200 bravado and Patsy's garden club mentality, she wondered at times just how well they understood the deadly seriousness of making an attempt on Everest, where sometimes if you got yourself stuck and let out a cry for help, there was no one there to answer. Mike was driven, determined to make it to the top, as though you could summit on demand; and he seemed hell bent on dragging Patsy along with him. Ricky got the sense that if she were left to her own devices, the bone-tired Patsy would've backed out long before now.

Ricky exhaled, feeling the bite of the cold air at the back of her throat.

Well, it was still a long way to the summit and plenty could happen before then. *Just do your job,* she told herself.

The tall woman crouched down and slipped into the vestibule of her and Allison's tent, taking care to remove her boots before crawling inside.

"Hey, I—" Ricky stopped short. Allison was in her sleeping bag, asleep. She lay on her side, facing the interior of the tent, her blond hair tousled, her right arm curled up under her head.

Just do your job, the mountaineer repeated; but it was more than a job, she knew that now, especially where Allison Peabody was concerned. The younger woman had reached out to her, God knew why, and though Ricky had tried to dissuade her, she had persisted. And now...she'd hated that Allison had had to see that Sherpa today, even though such things were a fact of life here on Everest. She worried even now how that had affected her, and what dark fears might haunt her dreams. Allison's brow was furrowed, her eyes were squeezed shut, and her free arm and legs twitched, as though warding off some unseen phantom. Ricky felt an overwhelming desire surge through her body to protect this woman, to keep her safe, no matter what.

"Allison?"

A low whimper escaped the blonde's lips, and her twitching became more pronounced.

"Allison!" Ricky put the thermos down and reached out to give Allison's arm a light shake.

"Wha—" Allison bolted up into a sitting position, her green eyes as wide as silver dollars. "What the—"

"Sorry." Ricky edged away, giving her space. "I thought I should wake you. You were having some sort of nightmare, I think."

"Jesus!" Allison rubbed at her face, still clearly disoriented. "I—I don't even remember falling asleep." She swallowed and took several deep breaths. "I was just lying here, thinking about things." She lifted her eyes to Ricky. "I was thinking about this afternoon, and that poor Sherpa, and then I was climbing and so were you, and—"

"Ssssh, don't worry about it." The mountaineer could not help herself. She scooted closer. "It was just a dream."

"Easy for you to say." Allison managed a shaky smile. "Pretty silly, huh?"

"Nah." Ricky paused. "I get nightmares, too."

"You do?"

"Uh-huh." Ricky grabbed for the nearly forgotten thermos, anxious to change the subject now. Dwelling on bad dreams certainly wouldn't be of any help to Allison. Best to forget about it and help clear her head, instead. "Look what I've got." She produced the thermos. "My turn for the hot tea."

"Hey, thanks!" Allison brightened, cheering at the sight of the steaming liquid.

Ricky poured two cups, and soon the women were silently drinking, oblivious to the snowy winds picking up outside, snapping at the tent.

The tea helped, but Ricky could see that there was still something on Allison's mind. Her face was quiet and still in the dimness of the tent, her lips set in a tense line.

"Ricky?"

Uh-oh, the mountaineer inwardly sighed. *Here it comes.*

"Yes?"

"Can I ask you a question?"

"Sure."

"Why do you climb? How did you get started?"

"Well, that's two questions, isn't it?"

Allison regarded her apprehensively, worried that the mountaineer had slipped into one of her sour moods. But Ricky didn't mind, not really, and she saw her tent-mate visibly relax when she curled the corner of her mouth into a wry grin.

"I don't remember actually starting," she told her. "It's just something we—me and Jean-Pierre, I mean—we've always done." She hesitated, lowering her eyes. "And I'm going to carry on. It's all I've ever wanted to do." She played with the handle of her cup. "It's all I know. And that's enough for me."

"But you can't climb forever," Allison blurted out. "Can you? What about the future? Your future."

Ricky felt the heat rise to her face. She wasn't angry, but here Allison was, pushing her again, prodding. Making her think about things in her life that she preferred to leave unexamined. After all, it was far simpler that way.

"I guess I never thought that far ahead," Ricky answered slowly. "Or...or thought that I'd ever have to deal with it. After all, Jean-Pierre didn't."

Before the words even finished leaving her mouth, Ricky already regretted uttering them. She could see Allison's jaw drop and her face pale, as she absorbed the full implication of the mountaineer's statement. Well, it was true.

Veronique Bouchard, sitting on a rocking chair, old and gray?

Not likely.

She knew that eventually the life she led would catch up to her. Even she could buck the odds for only so long.

No matter.

When death came, whenever it came, she would be ready.

"Geez, Ricky, you're scaring me." Allison's voice wavered in the deepening gloom. "You're not planning on going anywhere, are you?"

Ricky could sense the stockbroker's growing panic, and so she decided to reverse course for the time being. No need to get her so frightened. After all, once the expedition was over, Allison Peabody would leave, and that would be that. And Ricky's destiny, that silent companion who never left her side, would be there just the same.

"No," Ricky forced a faint smile to her face. "I'm not."

"Good." Allison leaned forward, keeping her eyes locked on Ricky's. "Because I need you. To get to the top, I mean. You promised me."

"That's right," Ricky answered, averting her eyes from the challenge of Allison's gaze. "I promised."

Chapter
Thirteen

It had been some stay at ABC—Advance Base Camp—Allison Peabody considered, as she listlessly poked at her beef stroganoff. The snow squall had turned into a snowstorm that persisted for two days, and it had not been until this morning, after two nights of high-altitude misery, that Jim Harris and another Sherpa had been able to escort a suffering Patsy Donaldson down to Base Camp.

Patsy had been nauseous, had a headache that wouldn't quit and, until Jim Harris had given her a hit of bottled oxygen, had been alarmingly disoriented. Allison thought for sure that the woman's Everest adventure had to be over. Mike Donaldson had not accompanied his wife back down, and a part of Allison was surprised at that. No matter what sort of personal aspirations she might have, she herself couldn't ever imagine not sticking close to a person she cared about if he or she were hurting.

But here Mike was, sitting across from her in the small dining tent, his jaw working as he chewed at a piece of bread. He'd stomped into the tent right after Patsy had left, telling them he fully intended to stay on and finish his acclimatization. Allison hadn't said a word, and neither had Lou Silvers, Paul Andersen, or Kevin MacBride. They all had their own problems, here at 21,300 feet. No time to play judge and jury on the state of the marital relationship between Mike and Patsy Donaldson.

For the past two days, Allison had felt that she was constantly panting, laboring to catch her breath. Ricky had told her that an increased respiration rate was her body's natural response to the reduced oxygen levels, but still, she had to wonder. If it was this bad at this altitude, how in the world would she ever be able to function higher up?

Between frequent sips of hot Sherpa tea, Lou Silvers let loose with harsh, ragged coughs. "Khumbu cough," they called it, yet another reaction to the dry, thin air. The attorney's face was gray in the flat light, and his eyes were bloodshot. Phil Christy had come down with an even worse case of the cough, and had barely moved from his tent since they'd arrived.

"How's Phil?" Paul Andersen wondered. "He seemed pretty bad yesterday."

"Ah, he'll shake it off," Kevin replied. "He'll be fine in a day or two. He wouldn't miss this for all the world. You know," he continued, "we've got a bet going, to see who touches the top first."

"You're joking," Paul retorted. The senior guide was also feeling the altitude somewhat. He sat huddled over his tea, bleakly nursing a runny nose.

"I am not," Kevin proudly declared.

"What are the bets?" Mike Donaldson wanted to know, using another piece of bread to mop up a section of his plate.

"Well, if I win, he's gotta marry my sister."

Paul Andersen nearly fell off his stool. "Say what?"

"Hell, he's been dating her for six years. Shit or get off the pot, ya know what I mean?"

"Sounds romantic," Allison muttered, pushing away her half-eaten plate of food. She had no appetite at this altitude, and having to watch Mike Donaldson heartily tuck into his food wasn't helping things any.

"And, as unlikely as the possibility may be," Kevin continued, grinning, "if Phil wins, I pick up his bar tab for the next year."

Allison cast a skeptical eye at the former collegiate football player and slowly shook her head. "Like I said, sounds romantic." She leaned to one side as Dawa, the cook, removed her plate.

"You finish, Miss Allison?"

"All done, Dawa, thanks," she replied.

In the cramped, enclosed space of the tent, Dawa had been

busily bustling in the background, constantly attending to their needs. Pemba would be proud of how his nephew was doing, Allison thought. She would be sure to tell him so.

"More tea, here," Mike Donaldson barked gruffly.

Dawa scurried to place Allison's plate down, and he grabbed the pot of tea from the burner. But the Sherpa did not move fast enough for the businessman.

"I said, more tea!" Mike shouted, shoving his cup in the direction of the cook just as Dawa started to tilt the teapot. The amber liquid began to pour out, right onto Donaldson's hand.

"Shit!" He leapt up from the small table and shoved his hand into a cooler of drinks. "You idiot!" he growled, his eyes blazing. "What's the matter with you? Why don't you watch the hell what you're doing!"

"Sorry! So sorry, sir!" Dawa scrambled to clean up the table, where very little of the tea had spilled, really, while he repeatedly bowed at the much larger man. "So sorry," he cried. He understood very little of what the westerner was saying, but the tone was unmistakable. Desperately searching for some way to appease his anger, Dawa handed him a towel.

Mike Donaldson swatted the limp towel away. "Get away from me! You've done enough damage. I'm gonna get your ass fired so fast, boy, your head will spin!"

"It was an accident, Mike," Allison said, an edge of anger creeping into her voice. "He said he was sorry." Dawa was clearly rattled by what had happened, and it was an accident after all. And partly Mike's fault, to boot. And heavens! The poor Sherpa didn't deserve to be treated in such a manner. It just wasn't right.

"Accident my ass!" Donaldson growled, examining a reddened patch of skin on the back of his hand.

"Chill out, Mike," Kevin MacBride laughed. "You're freaking the poor guy out." He pointed to Dawa, who stood trembling in the corner of the tent, unsure of just what to do next. "Should we call a med-evac for you, 9-1-1, or what?"

In the face of the younger man's laughter, Mike Donaldson sheepishly began to settle down. "Well, he should still be more careful, the little troll!" He returned to his seat, rubbing at his injured hand.

"Tch—watch it," Kevin said, still smirking, "or you're gonna end up with more than eggs in your quiche, my friend."

"I'll keep that in mind," Mike grumbled, waving the Sherpa

away.

Dawa gathered up a few dirtied plates and cups, and left the tent. "Back soon," he said, looking furtively over his shoulder.

"Take your time, buddy." The businessman returned his attention to his tea.

Allison was furious. Was that whole episode really necessary? The insensitive idiots. She couldn't believe she was stuck with the likes of these people for such an important climb. How different they'd all seemed back at the bar in Kathmandu.

So interesting. So decent.

And how had she appeared to them, she wondered? Perhaps, in a different way, she'd also changed, disappointed them. If that were the case, then good. Because Allison knew she hadn't much liked herself, back then.

Lou Silvers was the same man, and Allison thanked God for that. She found a certain steadiness and comfort in the older man's presence. And as for Ricky, well, what you saw was what you got. The mountaineer had no time for games or pretense. There was just a simple, caring honesty, character traits that were all too rare in the self-absorbed, selfish company so common in the circles where Allison Peabody moved.

Well, that would change. Soon.

"You can have Sandy take a look at that tomorrow," Paul began, finally commenting at last.

"It's fine," Mike said brusquely, cutting him off. "Kevin's right. This is no big deal. At least, not compared to what Patsy's going through."

"Yeah," Paul quickly added. It was clear that the young guide was anxious to change the subject. "It's a shame she had to descend."

"She's a gutsy lady," Mike's voice was firm. "That's why I married her. This isn't over for her, not yet." He paused, frowning. "I'm glad Jim was able to take her down. I'd hate to think of her with that woman, Bouchard."

"Ah, where is Ricky, today?" Lou Silvers asked innocently, his clogged head deafening him to the warning bells sounding in Mike Donaldson's voice.

"She's helping to carry a load of supplies up to Camp III," Allison said, weighing her words carefully. "Oxygen, rope and stuff."

By God, if this turned into a Ricky Bouchard bashing session, Allison would have none of it. They had all been sitting on their butts over the past two days, gasping for air in the snow, like fish out of water. But Ricky...even during the snowstorm, she'd had been doing everything possible to work towards a successful summit bid for the Peak Performance team: checking on equipment, supplies, and overseeing the plan for fixing the ropes. Now that the weather was clear, she was using the free day to further advance that cause. The sooner the camps were stocked, the sooner they could go for the top before the monsoons came.

"Nice," Mike said, though his tone of voice implied just the opposite. "Shouldn't she be here with us? Especially since Jim's gone? Besides," he looked darkly at Paul Andersen, "aren't we paying for service from you people, and it's for the Sherpas to do the grunt work?"

"Well...uh," the guide blushed, "it is a light couple of days here. It's just a case of getting acclimatized and poking around the *Bergshrund,* if you want. You do that at your own pace." He cleared his throat, clearly feeling the heat bristling from Mike Donaldson. "Besides, Jim gave her the okay."

"You can never have enough O2 at Camp III and above," Lou Silvers added, finally catching on to the tension in the air. "If that's what she's carrying, more power to her."

"I agree," Allison stated, grateful for the attorney's support. "She's been doing nothing but helping us all out, whether you're aware of it or not. And we're not supposed to be babied on this climb," she said, looking fiercely at the men. "If we can't handle ABC on our own, forget about making any summit attempt."

"Yeah, well that woman has got some serious attitude problems," Kevin retorted. "You know, she shoved me the other day. You all saw it!"

"What?" Mike Donaldson cried, the indignation plain on his face. "Unacceptable. Did you tell Jim? Christ, that woman's a loose cannon!"

"Why you—" Allison was outraged. She knew the likes of Mike Donaldson. He was a part of the life she'd left behind. A soft, spoiled man who prided himself on being hard of heart. A man whose arrogance was only exceeded by the size of his ego; accustomed to getting his way, whether it was in the boardroom, the bedroom, or a small tent high in the Himalayas.

Kevin waved a hand disparagingly. "I can fight my own battles."

"You've got it all wrong!" Allison swung a steely-eyed

glare from one man to the other. "You're damn right I saw what
happened. She warned you to stay back. She was trying to move
you away from a dead man you were disrespecting, and you fell.
I was there. I know what I saw."

"She should be reported to Jim," Mike Donaldson stubbornly repeated.

"Aw, c'mon, Allison," Kevin whined. "The guy was dead!
I wasn't hurting anything!"

Allison's lips set in a tense line. "It wasn't right. What you
did...wasn't right."

"Gimme a break!" Kevin slapped the palm of his hand
down on the table. "She's a freaking mental patient, if you ask
me. She never has anything to say, or when she does, she's
always pissed off. She's got some chip on her shoulder, Allison.
And if I were you, I wouldn't turn my back on her for one minute
in that tent of yours!"

"I trust Ricky to watch my back," Allison said in a near-
shout, not caring what the men thought of her emotional defense
of the tall, dark mountaineer. "More than any of you! Why, do
you even know what she's accomplished? She's the best climber
of all of us!"

"Probably the best female climber in the world," interjected
Lou helpfully.

"So she doesn't socialize with us too much," Allison continued, her voice shaking. "Last time I looked, this wasn't a cocktail party. And unlike the rest of us, she knows that without the
Sherpas' help, we'd have no chance—none—of getting to the top
of this mountain. If I were you, I'd keep that in mind!"

"She's right," Paul Andersen said, his lean face looking
rather thin and pale. "We need the Sherpas. They're good people."

"Yeah, well, if Miss Nut Case thinks so highly of 'em, I'd
have to wonder." Kevin crossed his arms in front of his chest,
his point made.

Allison felt a rage flood through her body. An anger with
herself, first and foremost, that she couldn't find the words to
make these people understand just what kind of a woman Ricky
Bouchard really was. And an anger at Kevin and Mike, and at
Paul too, for making themselves feel better about their own
shortcomings by conveniently tearing down someone else.

"Kevin," Allison stood, struggling to think of the hundreds
of different things she wished she could say to the smug-faced

idiot before her, "you are *such* an asshole." And with that, she stormed out of the tent.

Outside, she stood in the snow, her chest heaving, fighting to regain her equilibrium. She shouldn't let those jerks get to her, she knew that; but to hear them bad-mouth Ricky like that...it struck a chord deep within her. She could not...would not stand for it. Not while there was a fighting breath left in her body.

The sunlight was bright, playing off the fresh snow in flashes of diamonds and crystal. She'd forgotten her glacier glasses inside the dining tent, but damn if she would venture back inside to retrieve them now. Instead, she squinted at the Lhotse face, a wall of white ice rearing up in front of her. She let the frigid air roll over he body, cooling her off, calming her. Somewhere up there was Ricky Bouchard. Toiling away. Doing what she loved. Hell, Ricky would've known how to put those guys in their place. Why was it, that when it counted most, she always found herself coming up short? Somehow, she felt as though she'd let Ricky...her partner...down.

"Hey—don't let them get to you, Allie."

Allison heard a rasping cough and turned to find Lou Silvers crunching through the snow behind her.

"They're not worth it." With a crooked smile, he handed her the glasses she'd forgotten.

"Thanks." She slipped them on. "But you know...those guys...they just don't get it. What gives them the right?" she said angrily, wondering at the same time what suddenly made her such an authority on the matter. Perhaps it was what Ricky had taught her, in word and in deed.

About having respect for the mountain. Respect for others. Respect for yourself.

"You can't let it bother you," Lou persisted. "Ricky wouldn't."

"I know," Allison sighed. "But I just can't help it."

The attorney stepped closer and wrapped a reassuring arm around her shoulders. "It's because you care," he told her. His voice was rough as sandpaper, but Allison could hear the warmth behind his words. "Ricky's a special woman. You've taken the time to find that out." He paused, as if debating with himself. "And she's lucky. Lucky to have you for a friend."

Allison gazed at him wonderingly.

A friend?

Well.

She'd never considered that.

Lou gave her a final squeeze. "And you did fine, Allie." He grinned. "Remind me never to cross you!"

As she watched the older man plod back to his tent, she felt her spirits rise.

Ricky and she were friends. She kind of liked the sound of that.

Too bad Ricky had no idea.

Yet.

❈ ♦ ❈ ♦ ❈ ♦ ❈

It was late in the afternoon by the time Ricky, Jangbu, Pemba, and Sherpas from the other expeditions tramped back into Camp II. They'd spent all day higher on the mountain, working, and now the sun was beginning to set. The western sky was ablaze with color; rich fall hues of gold and red painted against a brilliant spring blue canvas.

It had been a good day, a productive day, as far as Ricky was concerned. Camp III was completely stocked; their supplies and tents were securely stowed under rocks and a tarp in an ice shelf they'd carved out of the unforgiving Lhotse face. The site was clearly marked with climbing poles and pickets flying marker flags bearing the Peak Performance Adventure Company logo, a warning to all comers that the precarious spit of ground so high on the mountain was already taken.

The ropes were also fixed all the way to Camp III, and in the next few days a co-operative group of Sherpas from most of the climbing teams on the mountain would be making their way even higher. Their objective would be to establish the final camp, Camp IV on the South Col, threading lines as they went.

Bright and early tomorrow morning, Ricky and Paul Andersen would lead the remaining PPAC clients back down to Base Camp. After a luxurious four-day rest there at lower altitude, it would be time to hike back up the mountain, all the way to Camp III that time, in their final acclimatization climb before the summit attempt.

Ricky was pleased. They were ahead of schedule, had already gotten a bit of a snowstorm out of the way and, with any luck, they'd be all the way up and down the mountain in another few weeks. Her job here, as a junior guide, would be finished.

She would pocket the money and not look back.

But what then?

Probably she'd bum her way around the world until the money ran out, doing whatever she wanted to do. Which was to climb, mostly.

Perhaps she'd take another run at K2. After all, the world's second highest peak was nearby; she could get to it by way of a precarious trek through Pakistan. She was quite familiar with the challenges it presented; she'd already summitted a few years back, with Jean-Pierre. But to do it now, solo, would be an accomplishment of a different sort. K2 was a harsh mountain, demanding near-technical perfection from the mountaineers who dared its heights.

To chance it on her own, well, she was one of the world's best free-climbers, right? Let others call her crazy, as long as she knew what she was doing. She had the physical skills, the sound judgment, and the necessary innate ability to protect herself. She was a pro at testing her own limits.

At pushing, always pushing.

Or she could go home, to Val-David.

Home. That's what she called the little town in Quebec. Even though, since she'd first taken off on her life's great adventure as a teenager with Jean-Pierre, she'd scarcely resided there for more than a few days at a time.

Her parents still lived there, Andre and Marie, so there was that.

Her reserved father, who'd never really tried to understand her. Perhaps he'd never really figured out how. And her mother, the country artist, who was torn between letting her free-spirited daughter live the life she'd chosen, and standing by her dour, dentist husband who had hoped for better, more practical things from young Veronique.

Ricky loved them both, very deeply, and they loved her in return. But whenever they all were together, there was always an undercurrent of tension present in the room, like a stick of dynamite ready to spark. Each one of them by turns fanning the flame, or else desperately trying to smother it.

Marie Bouchard's elegant, classically beautiful features, so like her Parisian grandmother's, would grow pale and cloudy, as she fretted over the dangerous hobby of her daughter. And just when was Veronique going to get around to marrying Jean-Pierre, anyway?

Andre Bouchard worried too, in his own way. Not only for the safety of his daughter, but also for the future that would be left to her once this mountain climbing nonsense was finished with. Of course that friend of his, the assistant dean of undergraduate studies at McGill in Montreal, would be happy to do what he could to gain Veronique admission. A solid education under her belt—that was the key. All his daughter had to do was say the word.

But Ricky never did say the word and, anxious not to make things worse, had never told them what really lived in her heart. Never a "Mama—Jean-Pierre and I...we're not that way!" Or a "Papa—don't you see, I plan to climb for as long as the mountains will have me. There is no other future than that!" She'd never quite figured out whether it was to spare them or to spare herself. Either way, keeping her silence hurt just the same.

The last time she'd been home, however, had been the worst. It was three years ago now, right after Jean-Pierre had died. Ricky had felt she'd owed it to her friend's parents to tell them face-to-face what had happened, to take ownership of the responsibility, the guilt she'd felt. But Jean-Pierre's parents, God, they'd let her have it, hadn't they? In a way she never could have anticipated.

She had wanted to be blamed, looked forward to their vengeful recriminations as a way of working through her own pain, but instead they'd left her on the hook. His mother had smiled sweetly at her through the tears, holding her hand and telling her how blessed Jean-Pierre had been to have her in his life. How she'd inspired him to do the things he might never have otherwise accomplished on his own. And his father, choking back his grief, with a face that was older, creased by nature and time as Jean-Pierre's would never be, telling her how his only son had died doing what he loved. And how that was so much more than any man had reason to expect in this world.

Ricky's own parents had been another story.

Andre and Marie Bouchard had expected her to stay home for good this time. To stop tempting the Fates, as her mother had said. Wasn't what happened to poor Jean-Pierre warning enough? But the one thing Ricky didn't want to do was to stay in one place for too long, and that included home.

It gave you too much time to think.

About things you might have done differently.

About how someone else was dead, someone you loved,

when it should have been you.

It was in the freedom of climbing that Ricky found her peace; she always had. And so that was what she'd turned to once more, informing her parents that she'd be leaving the next day for South America, and Aconcagua.

That was when her father had exploded.

How twisted his dark, handsome features had become as the bitter words spilled from his mouth. How dare she persist in this irresponsible lifestyle of hers! If she were determined to amount to nothing, well, he was through trying to help her. He was washing his hands of it. And how dare she continuously put her mother through such anguish, wondering as the long Canadian winters slowly blossomed into spring, whether her daughter was alive or dead? And how dare she walk out on him now, leaving him alone in Val-David to face Jean-Pierre's parents every day, knowing that their son was dead and her foolish dreams were the cause of it?

Ricky hadn't been back to Val-David since.

Fighting against a heaviness in her chest, the mountaineer had finished a solitary dinner in the dining tent. Jangbu and Pemba had tumbled straight into their sleeping bags after some tea, but Ricky was determined to keep her strength up. Dawa was quiet as he'd served her a large bowl of chicken noodle soup, tea, and some bread. She didn't press him into conversation; she didn't much feel like talking, either.

Not now. Just thinking of her parents and how she'd left things with them was like poking at an open wound, and Ricky was angry with herself for letting what had otherwise been a good day end on such a sour note.

She was alone now, and that was fine with her, really. All the other Peak Performance team members had eaten and returned to their tents, Dawa had told her, eagerly anticipating getting under way at dawn, and heading down.

There was no sign of Allison, and the mountaineer assumed that the younger woman had turned in as well. Ricky knew from experience that the longer you were on the mountain, the more exhausted you became, so it was not unusual that the clients were already tucked away in their sleeping bags. For many, sleep would be elusive, and instead the best they could hope for would be a few hours of dozing, punctuated with restless tossing and turning. At over 21,000 feet, there was no such thing as getting in a comfortable position.

Ricky had noticed how Allison had been a bit taken aback at how hard the altitude had hit her breathing rate. She'd sworn to the mountaineer that even standing still she felt as though she were running a 100 meter dash. That sort of a response wasn't unusual; Ricky had seen it often enough in other climbers. It took time to adjust; that was what the acclimatization process was all about. And so over the past couple of days, Ricky had been pleased to see that her tent-mate's comfort level had been improving.

Allison was doing well.

Ricky let her eyes track to the rising moon, so warm, so bright, and so low on the horizon she half thought she could pluck it from the sky, if she were of a mind to.

Allison.

Shaking her head, Ricky zipped up her jacket for the short hike back to their tent. It was cold, and her breath formed a great plume of moisture in the relatively still air. Darkness was falling fast now, as it did here in the mountains, and in the twi-light Ricky could see the warm glow of lamplight from within a half dozen tents, including her own, where the occupants were still reading, talking, or fiddling with equipment. Allison would be writing in her journal, as she had every night of this climb, and Ricky found herself smiling at the thought; felt some of her somber mood lift.

She'd found herself enjoying the blonde's company over the past week, more than she ever would have thought possible. Sure, the young woman talked too much and asked a lot of questions, but Ricky hadn't realized how being alone for as long as she'd been had taken its toll. She had thought she'd been fine with it, preferred it even, but now...she wasn't so sure. Slowly, reluctantly, she'd found herself getting used to having Allison around. Looking forward to it, to her, at the end of the day.

Hmnn.

A most unexpected turn of events.

Ricky knew that the end of the Peak Performance Adventure Company's expedition to Everest would mean the end of her association with the young stockbroker. Allison would simply pack up her gear and, with first class tickets in hand, jet her way back to New York.

To the bright future that awaited her there.

While she, Ricky, would resume her gypsy's existence, sinking back into the anonymity she so craved.

Right?

She'd move on to K2. A monster of a peak. One that only the best technical climbers in the world would take on. Not like, say, a Gasherbrum II. A smaller mountain at 26,361 feet, also straddling the Pakistan-China border, but one that a solid climber with some high altitude experience—an Allison Peabody, for instance—would find challenging but realistically attainable.

Jesus! Ricky zipped open the tent and crawled into the vestibule. *What the hell are you thinking? You're the one without the steady job, not her. Remember?*

No, Allison would leave, returning to her friends and family, a changed person, perhaps, but one who would gradually fall back into her comfortable, carefree lifestyle. She'd shift her focus once more towards making her millions on Wall Street, while her memories of Everest, and Ricky, would fade away like fleeting wisps of a half-remembered dream upon the dawn of a new day.

With a frustrated sigh, Ricky unstrapped her crampons and tugged off her boots, wondering why the thought of that, of Allison leaving and forgetting all about her, seemed to irk her so much. And dammit—there went her good mood again!

Grunting, Ricky worked her way on her hands and knees to the inner tent.

"Hi, honey! How was your day?"

Ricky heard the smile in Allison's voice, the playfulness in her tone, but she refused to give in to it all. She was in a bad mood now, and by God she was determined to stay that way.

"Fine."

Allison put her pen down and closed her journal. "How is Camp III shaping up?"

"Okay."

Ricky scooted out of her climbing pants, leaving only her polypro leggings, pointedly ignoring Allison's attempts to draw her into conversation.

"Are you feeling all right?"

"I'm *fine*." Ricky's voice sounded muffled as she struggled to pull her sweater over her head.

"Are you sure? Because I—"

"I said I was fine!" With an angry yank, the sweater was free. Ricky flung it to her corner of the tent and pushed errant strands of dark hair out of her face. She was simply not in the mood to play twenty questions with Allison Peabody. And what did it matter, anyway? Why was Allison even bothering? Soon she would be gone, and that would be that.

From the corner of her eye, Ricky saw Allison stiffen. "You didn't run into Kevin and Mike, did you?"

"Kevin and Mike?" Ricky said flatly, turning to face her tent-mate.

"Those jerks!" Allison's voice rose an octave. "I knew they wouldn't leave well enough alone!"

Before the surprised mountaineer could respond, Allison was off and running.

"I told them what I thought of them, or at least I tried to, Ricky, I swear it!" Allison's face grew stormy. "So you're not Miss Congeniality, so what? It's because they don't understand you, that's all. And the very idea of reporting you to Jim, just because that idiot Kevin fell on his fat ass in the snow," she sputtered, "why, if I'd realized the big deal he was going to make of it, I would have shoved him down myself!"

"Hey—hey!" Ricky was grinning now, in spite of herself.

"And that Mike Donaldson, he's just horrid, Ricky, horrid! I don't know how Patsy puts up with him. He doesn't understand," she continued, flushed, "how lucky they are to have you guiding us!"

"Hold on!" Ricky eased closer to the agitated stockbroker.

"Why, I have half a mind to—"

"Slow down," Ricky chuckled, feeling her mouth slide into a comfortable smile. "What the heck are you talking about?" she asked, although she already had a fairly good idea, thanks to Allison's impassioned speech.

Finally pausing to draw in a halting breath, the blonde's eyes locked onto Ricky's. "You didn't see them?"

"Who?"

"Mike and Kevin...or Paul?"

"Nope."

"So...they didn't tell you what happened at lunch?"

"No," Ricky cheerily responded, her tongue planted firmly in cheek. "But you just did."

Allison regarded the mountaineer for a long moment, and then she released a great gust of air. "Great. Just great. I must sound like a stark-raving idiot." She blinked twice at Ricky before turning her head away, her cheeks flaming like ripened apples. "Sorry," she muttered, clearly embarrassed, and Ricky took sympathy on her then.

"No," she told her, "it's okay Allison. Don't worry about it."

Allison still would not look her in the eye.

"I'm glad to know it," Ricky added. "Really. Stuff like that...it's typical on expeditions like this. And..." she pursed her lips thoughtfully, "I...I know I'm not the easiest person to get along with. You should know that by now, too!" Plan beta—try to make light of it, the mountaineer reasoned.

"But it's wrong!" Allison's voice was a near-shout, and she did lift her eyes to Ricky's then.

The mountaineer was stunned at the hurt, the feeling she saw in the moist green gaze, drawing her in. *God, this bullshit has really gotten to her!* "Let it go," she soothed, hating to see Allison so upset. "I'm used to it. It doesn't bother me."

"Well, it bothers *me*!"

"But why?" Ricky asked her, feeling at a total loss now. "I'm just not worth it."

"Why?" Allison's eyes flew open wide. Her mouth wordlessly opened and closed as, warring with her emotions, she considered for the very first time the implication of Ricky's question. "It's...it's because I care, that's why," she said at last, a slow comprehension spreading over her features. "And..." she lifted a hand to where Ricky's rested on her knee, and covered it with her own, "you *are* worth it." The hand continued to travel upward, to lightly brush against the mountaineer's cheek. "To me."

Allison fell silent. Shyly waiting for some sort of a response—for anything—from the mountaineer.

All of a sudden, Ricky felt warm. Uncomfortably so, and she knew it had less to do with the little stove in the tent and more to do with the heat of the probing stare that suddenly rendered her tongue-tied.

"Well...uh, thanks," Ricky croaked, hoping Allison had not detected the strain in her voice. "Ah...goodnight then." Quickly, she slid down into her sleeping bag and turned her back on Allison, praying that any expression on her face had not betrayed her, too.

Though she feigned sleep, Ricky's eyes were wide open, staring sightlessly at the wall of the tent as she fought to get her emotions under control. The light began to dim, and then was extinguished.

"Goodnight, Ricky."

The voice in the darkness was so soft, with a trace of sadness in it. Ricky felt a jolt of regret course through her. God, what a mess. This was all her fault! Allison was reaching out to her, literally, and what had she done? Turned her back on her.

Typical, Ricky, the mountaineer berated herself. *Just typical!*

Allison Peabody cared about...her. Just the mere possibility of that concept astounded Ricky, although there was no denying it, not now. It was a feeling she was so unused to, had turned away from it so many other times in the past, taking the easy way out. It was less complicated that way, or so she'd told herself.

Relationships, and the tangle of emotions that went along with them, were for other people, not her. Ricky had always taken care to deny herself such indulgences in the past, choosing instead to believe that there was a certain aesthetic nobility in that. In the light of day, she prided herself on the bravery of such a higher calling. But in the cold of the night, when she found herself alone and unloved by virtue of those same beliefs, she derided herself for the proud, ignorant fool she knew herself to be.

She, Veronique Bouchard, who had scaled the world's seven summits, who had stared down death time and time again and lived to tell about it, was...afraid.

Risking your life on a mountain was easy.

Risking your heart was another matter.

God, how Allison's innocent caress had rocked her! Such casual intimacy with another person Ricky had rarely allowed herself, and with anyone else—anyone—the mountaineer would never have let them touch her. She would have shied away, or stopped them. But she hadn't done that.

Not this time, not with Allison Peabody.

Was it the shock of it all? Maybe, Ricky considered. Not at Allison's touch, no, but at the way she'd found herself responding to it. Letting the power of it work its way down into the very core of her being, settling there, finding a home.

Her face had burned from where Allison's gentle fingertips had strayed, and Ricky had been overwhelmed. Had been completely at a loss as to what she should've done next.

If anything.

And so she'd done what had come naturally. She'd

retreated. And found a comforting, miserable familiarity in that.
God only knew what Allison must think of her now.
Good night. Hah!
Sleep was the last thing on Ricky Bouchard's mind.

Chapter
Fourteen

Allison Peabody was exhausted.

Funny how different the reality was from the fantasy.

It seemed as though all the picture books she'd ever read on mountain climbing always featured glossy, full color photographs of climbers moving higher and higher through the clouds, with vast dramatic vistas unfolding just over their shoulders. There would be a climbing pole in their hands or maybe a trusty ice ax, while their determined faces would be turned towards the summit. Looking up, always up.

They conveniently forgot to illustrate how much of a pain in the butt it was to climb back down. There was a lot less glamour in that to be sure, Allison considered, and she found herself mentally fashioning her own photo captions.

"Famous mountaineer cleans frozen snot from oxygen mask on Everest's Yellow Band."

Or how about: "Exhausted climber glissades on her ass from Camp II all the way down to Base Camp. Fellow expedition members point and snicker."

No, those pictures never made the books, Allison thought wryly.

After waking up this morning when the dawn was still only a glimmer in the eastern sky, she and her fellow climbers had descended from Camp II back to Base Camp, all in one shot.

Leaving Allison with a pair of legs so rubbery that she thought
she might soon simply collapse where she stood. Not forgetting
the wicked headache she had, to boot. But she had a mission to
complete before this day was over, and she was nothing if not
determined.

She wished she *could* have slid down the mountain on a
soft, forgiving blanket of snow, but of course that was impossible. Like everyone else, she'd had to descend back through the
bowl-shaped Western Cwm, and negotiate the always-dicey
Khumbu Icefall. This, after spending a night where she'd gotten
absolutely zero sleep.

Not that Ricky Bouchard had, either.

The mountaineer had been deathly still all night long. So
rigid and unmoving, unnaturally so, that Allison knew she had to
have been wide-awake.

And no wonder, Allison thought. *Considering the way I
basically threw myself at her.*

The Peak Performance climbers had crashed in their tents
soon after arriving back at BC, focused on recovering energy and
O's after their week up high. Later, after the sun had begun to
set, a number of them—Allison included—had ventured out,
enjoying the air that to their acclimatizing bodies now seemed
thick with oxygen. Many had gone to the dining tent for dinner,
and Allison had let them go, focused instead on making her way
to the expedition's sophisticated communications tent.

The climbers were happy to be down, that was apparent.
There was a boisterous, party atmosphere in Base Camp, and
energy crackled in the atmosphere like lightning before a thunderstorm. They had taken on the mountain, tested themselves,
and passed. Even Patsy Donaldson had appeared remarkably
well, in the brief sighting Allison had had of her, watching her
chase her husband's longer strides towards the dining tent.

Of Ricky Bouchard, Allison had seen little. The tall mountaineer had been silent when they'd awakened and prepped for
the descent, and Allison was privately grateful that the thin air,
the frigid cold, and a pressing timetable made the lack of conversation between them appear normal.

Almost.

Allison's stomach had twisted when she'd caught Ricky furtively eyeing her from time to time, only to turn away when their
eyes met. Once, she'd thought her quiet partner might even
speak, but then the wall had gone up and Ricky had closed down.

And there was no way Allison had been ready to broach the subject. Not then. Not while there were still so many questions swirling through her mind. So much that she'd still needed to think through. Decisions she'd needed to make. Not the sort of conversation one wanted to have in the dark, surrounded by below zero temperatures, at 21,300 feet.

But there was one thing she knew for sure, and that was that she'd never met anyone quite like Ricky Bouchard. Never met anyone else she'd felt this way about, either, and it was high time she admitted that to herself. Reaching out to her climbing partner as she had, well, maybe the timing could have been better, but she didn't regret it. As far as Allison was concerned, it had been a natural, physical thing to do, fueled by the feelings she had for the woman.

Did that mean she, Allison, was gay? Oh, that would be another good one she could spring on her parents, she wryly considered. In truth, she'd never given it much thought before. Frankly, she had little time for labels and didn't much care what the outside world saw, looking in. If she did care, she wouldn't have led the reckless, sometimes-irresponsible life she had to this point. And where she herself was concerned, she preferred to look at it in the simplest of terms, calling to mind a quotation she half-remembered from a collegiate philosophy class she'd taken a lifetime ago: "The heart has its reasons, which reason cannot know."

So, she was through trying to make sense of it all.

She was just going to go for it.

Especially now, after the time she'd spent in the communications tent this evening, making her $6.00 per minute satellite phone calls. Hell, it had been late morning their time when she'd phoned the States, so at least they couldn't bitch at her about that.

And sure, Ricky had avoided her since last night. It would be easy to think that meant that their relationship had taken a giant step backwards; that they were once again strangers, stuck at square one.

But Allison Peabody, of the Boston Peabodys, knew better. She'd seen the flicker of...of something, in Ricky's glacier-blue eyes when she'd reached out to her. Had watched her eyelids slip shut for a brief, telltale instant, as the mountaineer had leaned into her touch.

Perhaps living this close to the edge, this high on the highest of mountains, made one bolder. More willing to risk it all.

Whatever.

At this moment, with her head pounding out a wild tempo that matched the beating of her heart, Allison knew she had absolutely nothing else to lose.

❋ ✦ ❋ ✦ ❋ ✦ ❋

It wasn't easy to sneak up on Ricky Bouchard.

The mountaineer had very keen hearing, a sense of smell that would have served her well as a five-star sommelier, and eyesight that rivaled a golden eagle's. Yes, only the stealthiest of predators could catch Ricky by surprise. As for the likes of Allison Peabody, she hadn't a chance in hell.

It's gotta be her, Ricky sighed, detecting the approach of footsteps that to her sensitive ears sounded like an avalanche of rocks pouring over the scree. She knew Allison's step by now; it was heavy and loping, with a firm, set purpose, matching the determined look she'd come to know and admire on the younger woman's face.

Ricky had been sitting outside her tent despite the coldness of the night. She'd been trying to pull her thoughts together, to come to some sort of conclusion concerning what she should do about this latest...complication. She'd been avoiding dealing with it...with her, though she'd known it would be only a matter of time before the blonde tracked her down.

Now, the moment of truth was near. And it had a name.

"Allison."

A breathless response as the footsteps faltered. "How did you know it was me?"

Ricky slowly turned, easily making out the lighter form of the stockbroker against the encroaching darkness. "A lucky guess."

Allison was securely bundled up against the cold; she had on her powder-blue pile pants and jacket, as well as a woolen hat and over-mitts. She had her arms folded around her middle, holding herself stiffly as she approached.

"Aren't you cold out here?" Allison stomped her feet against the ground, and took a swipe at a stubbornly dribbling nose.

"No," Ricky replied, pushing herself to her feet. And it was true. The mountaineer enjoyed times like this; alone, reflecting on the day, thinking of the challenges that lay ahead, with the massif of Everest looming above in silent witness to it all. She needed this time for herself. Well, maybe sometimes it would have been nice to have had some company, but there wasn't anyone she could think of whose company she'd prefer at a time like this.

Except.

Except for... Dammit! This wasn't helping matters any. There was no way she was going to cross the line with Allison Peabody. She had her rules. She was above it all. She didn't need this. Didn't want it. Didn't crave it.

"Well," Allison's teeth chattered in the cold, "aren't you going to invite me in?"

"No," Ricky said, glancing down at the tips of her boots. "I—it's late."

She heard Allison's breath catch in her throat. "Listen, about last night—"

"You don't have to apologize," Ricky told her, feeling quite noble at that statement. They could get past this thing and move on, right?

"Oh, I'm not going to apologize, Ricky," Allison shot back. "I suppose I should say I'm sorry, but I'm not." She gulped in a breath. "You probably think I'm just some naïve little dilettante, don't you? Somebody who thinks they can climb Everest on a whim, or screw the good-looking guide on a bet, right?"

"Allison!" Ricky inwardly cringed at Allison's harsh words. "You know I don't think that; you don't know what you're saying!" She stepped closer to the younger woman and was surprised to see that she had squeezed her eyes shut, with her face uplifted to the mountain. She still held her arms closely, not for warmth, but against the pain.

"No...no, you just listen to me until I get this out," Allison demanded, even as the tears began to spill down her cheeks. "Maybe you think I don't understand what's going on...understand you, or even myself. But I do, Ricky, I do. You taught me that."

"You're just confused," Ricky offered, wishing Allison were gone. And hoping like hell that she would never leave.

"Don't you dare!" Allison's eyes snapped open. "Don't you dare belittle how I feel. Or what I know is between us!"

"I wasn't," Ricky replied miserably. "I just—"

"For the first time ever in my life, *ever*," Allison cut her off,

"I can see things clearly. Maybe it's the clear air at this altitude, I don't know." She laughed bitterly. "You know...I called my boss today. Told him I was taking an indefinite leave of absence."

"No!" Ricky's heart was thumping in her chest. Allison couldn't be doing this. She shouldn't!

"And then," the blonde continued, "I phoned my wanna-be fiancé. Told him I was breaking it off...because I'd found someone else. And do you know what?" A pained smile twitched at her lips. "For the first time since I've known him, he found himself a pair of balls. Wanted to know who the other guy was, so he could punch him out. Poor Lionel." She slowly shook her head. "I think I could take him with one hand tied behind my back."

"Allison," Ricky felt herself weakening, found herself falling under the spell of the green eyes desperately searching her own. "I don't know what to say...what to think."

"Think what you want." Allison wiped a mitten at her tears, and sniffled. "But I know that this past month has been the best one of my life. I feel like I *have* a life, for once. A value. A purpose." She took in a hitching breath of air. "So if you want to walk away from this...from how I feel, from how I *know* you feel too," she said, thrusting her chin out, readying herself for the emotional blow that was sure to follow, "that's okay. But I don't want to lose this feeling, Ricky." A pause. "I don't want to lose...you."

Ricky Bouchard felt it hit her, then.

Hard.

Below the belt.

And she was furious. How dare Allison not play fair? To just waltz into her life, now, when she'd least expected it. To touch her soul in such a raw, honest way, as no one else ever had. Ricky watched the tears streak Allison's face, absorbed the silent pleading in her features. She wanted to be numb to it all, to simply walk away, but she couldn't.

Not now.

Because worst of all, damn Allison Peabody to hell, she'd made her care for her, too.

"Ricky...*please!*" A soft cry.

"C'mere," Ricky said gruffly, pulling Allison close. "Those tears are gonna freeze, you know," she whispered into a cold ear, warming it. *You don't need this! You don't need this!* Her mind screamed to herself, even as the reaction her body was having to the presence of the smaller woman in her arms, told her she was a liar.

"I don't want to lose you, Ricky," Allison repeated, her words sounding mumbled through frozen lips. She pulled away slightly, lifting her eyes to the mountaineer's, awaiting an answer.

And in that moment, in the cold of the night, with the flicker of distant fires dancing across Allison's face, all Ricky wanted to do was to make her warm, to share with her the heat of the fire she'd kept banked within her heart for so long.

"You won't," she told her, barely recognizing the hoarse voice as her own. She tightened the embrace, and, powerless to stop herself, lowered her lips to Allison's. She boldly attacked the coldness she found there, challenging it, willing it all away. And when Allison eagerly responded, her own lips demanding that the fire melt the ice, Ricky felt the last of her resistance crumble, come tumbling down.

And then she was falling, falling. Releasing her safety tether, plummeting helplessly towards oblivion. And when she finally hit bottom, she discovered, much to her fuzzy surprise, that it didn't hurt at all.

❀◆❀◆❀◆❀

Keeping her eyes closed, Allison Peabody fought to hang on to a last few precious moments of sleep, to a wisp of a dream that was simply too good to awaken from. She'd never felt so warm, so safe, so...loved? But gradually, external sounds intruded upon her consciousness—demanding, insistent, intent upon drawing her from that special place.

The cries of the birds just awakening to the promise of a new day's dawn.

The clanking of pots and pans in a cook-tent.

A soft chiming of a distant prayer-bell, barely audible over the creaking of the glacier.

Any one of those noises could have been the one that originally roused her from her sleep. After all, anything was possible. Or...or perhaps it was something else. Perhaps it was another sound; more of a vibration, really. The deep, steady inhales and exhales of the woman whose arms were wrapped securely around her. Or the heartbeat drumming out its comforting rhythm beneath her ear.

Oh—my—God!

Allison's eyes snapped open, and she drew in a sharp breath. Oh, she was awake now, all right. And damn, it hadn't been a dream, after all. It was real, every bit of it, and it came flooding back over her in a cascade of conflicting emotions.

How she'd resolved to confront Ricky Bouchard, to confess to her how she felt. Telling herself that no matter what the mountaineer's response might be, she would abide by it. That regardless of whether Ricky was willing to let her be a part of her life, Allison knew that some major adjustments in her own life were in order. And so she hadn't regretted what she'd told Lionel. Or her boss at Johnson-Kitteridge-Johnson. She felt at peace, in a way, with all of it. Never in her life had she been so honest with herself—ever.

It felt good.

And with that honesty, came a responsibility.

To be true to herself.

To not hold anything back, no matter how much it hurt.

So that was how she'd found herself standing outside of the mountaineer's tent late last night.

Freezing.

With her head feeling as though someone were driving nails into it.

Planting her feet and taking a stand against the tall, dark haired woman who had so captivated her over these past weeks, wobbling on legs so rubbery she'd feared they might fail her at any moment.

She'd laid it all out there, all right. Had let Ricky have it with both barrels; had put her heart on the line. She'd seen how the mountaineer had recoiled at her words, and her heart had plummeted into her boots when Ricky at first had denied that there could ever be anything between them.

And then...then she'd somehow found herself in Ricky's arms. So warm. So strong. A place where she knew she belonged. Where she never wanted to leave.

Home.

Ricky had told her then, and shown her, too, that she felt the same way. It had felt like...heaven.

But the throbbing ache in her head had quickly brought her back down to earth. Exhausted, weak with relief, she'd allowed Ricky to guide her into the mountaineer's tent; forced herself to swallow the water pressed upon her. She'd been vaguely aware of her boots and jacket coming off, of the soothing massage at the base of her skull, of the quiet words telling her everything would be okay.

And after that...

Allison felt a burst of heat rise to her cheeks at the memory of what had happened next. A fire not of passion, but of embarrassment. She, who'd finally gotten Ricky Bouchard exactly where she wanted her...had promptly fallen asleep.

Well.

There was nothing she could do about it now. And what the heck—it had turned out to be the first sound night's sleep she'd had in more than a week. And she had no doubt of the role the mountaineer had played in that. Now, her headache was gone, and she felt simply...wonderful.

It was a brand new day, Allison thought, blinking her eyes at the tarpaulin roof of Ricky's tent. A day that was filled with possibilities. She'd told Ricky how she felt, and she hadn't been turned away. Quite the opposite, in fact. And so maybe, thanks to her headache, she had squandered a choice opportunity for getting to know her climbing partner on a more...intimate level, but there would be time enough for that.

Allison felt her face crease in a smile. God, and to think she'd been willing to put Lionel Kitteridge off for the most trivial of excuses.

"Not tonight, Lionel, please. I've got a meeting in the morning!"

And here she was, plotting how to get Ricky Bouchard to share her bed 17,600 feet high in the Himalayas. *God, you have no pride, girl!*

Allison groaned.

And the arms enfolding her squeezed back.

Startled, Allison lifted her head to find two blue eyes peering at her out of the early morning gloom.

"Good morning." Deep, rich tones. A music she would never tire of.

"Ah..." Allison knew her blush was deepening, but she was powerless to stop it. "Good—" She coughed, her voice rough with sleep. "Good morning."

"How do you feel?" Allison could see a trace of worry flit across Ricky's features.

"Better. Great, actually," Allison rushed to reassure her.

"Headache's all gone. Thanks."

"You're welcome," Ricky said, shifting her position slightly, so as to better regard the smaller woman. "I feel pretty 'great' myself."

"Good," Allison managed to get out, barely. All semblance of rational thought fled her mind under the onslaught of the mountaineer's gaze. God, did Ricky have any idea of the power she had over her?

All it took was a stolen glance.

An electrifying touch.

A word unspoken.

Get it together, Allison! She tried to focus. There was so much they had to talk about. So much more she wanted to—

"Lopsang should be coming around soon with tea."

"Oh, gosh, I'm sorry!" Allison blurted out. Immediately, she pushed herself up into a sitting position and began rooting around for her boots and outer clothing. What had she been thinking? "I—I didn't mean to fall asleep here. Could this get you into trouble?" She found her jacket and pulled it on, barely managing to avoid giving the mountaineer a left uppercut in the process.

"Take it easy." Ricky adroitly dodged Allison's flailing arm. "I don't know, and I don't care if it did. I was more worried...about you," she said simply, lowering her eyes.

"Oh." Allison paused in her struggles. "Thanks." Her brow furrowed. "I think. I mean, Ricky, I'm not sorry about this. About any of it." *Jesus, what are you doing? Just get out now, before you say something really stupid. You know you're not yourself anyway, until you've had some caffeine in the morning.* She rushed to leave, twisting towards the door of the tent, even as her body already was mourning the loss of the mountaineer's warmth.

An arm snaked around her waist, holding her back. "I'm not sorry, either."

And then suddenly she was gathered into a searing kiss. So hot, so intoxicating, that she lost herself in it. Lost track of who she was, and where she was, but never of the heady knowledge of who she was with. No, that was the one thing she needed to count on. Now, more than ever.

"Well," she gasped breathlessly when Ricky finally released her, "that was...um...nice." Allison's mind spun and whirled out of control as a pair of blue eyes sparkled at her.

Propped up on one elbow, her long dark hair spilling loose over her shoulders, the mountaineer smiled. "See you later, then?"

"Yeah," Allison squeaked. She knew she was grinning like an idiot, and there wasn't a damn thing she could do about it. "Until then." She offered Ricky an exaggerated wave as she began to crawl out of the tent. *We have a date! We have a date!*

"Allison?"

"Yes?" She swiveled around, her voice an octave higher than normal.

A familiar pair of boots dangled in front of her face.

"You won't get far without these."

❋ ◆ ❋ ◆ ❋ ◆ ❋

Ricky Bouchard was not normally a patient woman. She infinitely preferred action to inactivity, speaking out and moving on to debate and analysis. The ability to decide, to make a decision and take immediate action upon it, was a universal power she had long ago recognized for what it was, and at the same time she knew that she was in the minority, one of the few who dared to embrace that position. It was too easy, too comfortable, too familiar for the vast majority of people on this earth to stay right where they were, stuck, whether it was in a physical, emotional, or psychological place.

It hurt sometimes to act, but pain was something the mountaineer was not unfamiliar with. Taking that chance, throwing yourself into the unknown, could make all the difference between living your life, and merely marking time.

In the extreme, it was life itself.

Or death.

Climbers who'd waited too long before deciding to turn around on a summit attempt, their decision-making abilities sabotaged by too high an altitude and too little air. Teams where there was no clear leader, or where the leader was more worried about not hurting anyone's feelings rather than ordering someone down off the mountain who was not keeping up.

But in a few specific areas, Ricky knew herself to be capable of patience in great abundance. She'd been known to hold back at a lower camp for days, until her gut instincts told her the time was right for a summit bid. Or she would take her time and work with less experienced climbers, as long as they had a desire to improve their skills coupled with a deep, almost spiritual, respect for the mountain.

And then there were relationships.

Or a lack thereof, to be specific.

In the abstract, she believed they were fine—for other people. She'd been able to safely compartmentalize that part of her life, telling herself that having someone to love...to love her completely, was something she could put off until "someday." And in the meantime, there were the mountains, right?

It had been easy, early on, living in a small town in a remote area of Quebec. She'd been a loner, marching to her own beat, and her fellow townsfolk had known enough to give her a wide berth. Later, as inseparable as she and Jean-Pierre had been, most people had thought they were a couple anyway, and had left it at that. Hell, even her parents had assumed as much; Jean-Pierre's, too, for that matter.

Oh, she was not entirely without experience. There had been the time Jean-Pierre fixed her up with that buddy of his from Montreal. What was his name...Paul? So they'd had one too many beers, and the night had been just a bit too cold, too cold to spend it alone, or so Ricky had foggily determined.

She wasn't proud of it.

It wasn't what she'd thought it would be by far, what she remembered of that night, anyway. And Jean-Pierre had been angry with her afterwards, when she'd given his friend the cold-shoulder.

"Why don't you give him a chance, Veronique? He's a decent guy, and he likes you!"

"He's not for me, Jean-Pierre. It's...not for me. I don't need that sort of complication in my life."

"Complication?" Jean-Pierre had been baffled. *"Ricky, it IS life!"*

In time, Jean-Pierre had learned to let her go her own way, and she was grateful for that. He'd stopped questioning, pressing her, and had simply, cheerfully accepted her for who and what she was.

"As long as you're happy, Ricky."

"I am. Believe me."

"You think you are," he would laugh, *"but you don't know what you're talking about. Just wait. One day,"* he would wag a finger at her, *"the right person will come along, and leave you a stumbling, mumbling fool. And I will be there to say 'I told you*

so.'"

Ricky sighed and let her hand travel inside her sleeping bag to the spot so recently occupied by Allison Peabody.

It was still warm.

You were right, Jean-Pierre. And how I wish you were here to say so.

Last night, holding Allison in her arms, chasing away the loneliness she'd imposed upon herself, it had felt so good. So right. And left her desperately craving more. So she didn't have much experience with this stuff—so what? She was a woman who decided things. Who acted.

She knew what she wanted in life.

And what she didn't want. And that was a life without Allison Peabody in it.

Ricky heard the crunching steps of Lopsang drawing closer, as he moved from tent to tent with his morning tea. *Tea in bed, eh, Ricky?* God, what was becoming of her? She should be up and about by now!

Instead, Ricky's eyes flickered to her right.

There...on her bedroll.

She snared a thread of short blonde hair between her thumb and forefinger. The mountaineer held it aloft, watching the way it caught the dawning light, and then she drew it to her nose, breathing in, imagining that Allison was still near.

So, the stockbroker had been a bit nervous this morning. Well, that was certainly understandable. After all, it had been Allison who'd been brave enough to make a move. To risk it all.

With her career, her friends...and more.

If she hadn't, Ricky honestly didn't know if she would've had the guts to. Maybe she would have found another way to rationalize her inaction to its proper place in a back corner somewhere, convincing herself that her gut told her that the time wasn't right. That instead she had to be patient, one more time.

Ricky smiled, hearing Lopsang's noisy approach. She hadn't had her tea yet, but a warmth coursed through her such as she'd rarely felt, ever, this high on any mountain.

Deciding.

Sometimes, it was a life or death decision.

And maybe, just maybe, by having taken the first bold step, Allison Peabody had saved them both.

Chapter
Fifteen

Sandra Ortiz was a dedicated physician. One who knew her craft inside and out, despite her youth. More than once, when she'd been completing her internship and residency, she'd been mistaken for an earnest, over-zealous candy striper. It certainly didn't help matters any that her petite, smooth-skinned appearance made her look as though she were 32 going on 17. However, her medical colleagues who had chosen to judge her by her looks rather than her considerable abilities had soon found themselves left in her dust.

She was a serious practitioner, one completely focused on her craft, and she'd moved impressively through her rotations with top ratings. She'd decided on Internal Medicine as her discipline and accepted an offer to join a group practice in Denver with that specialty. It was there, four years ago now, that she'd first met Jim Harris.

Behind her wire-framed glasses, Sandy Ortiz had tried not to look surprised at the big man with the rakish smile and chiseled features who'd dwarfed her examining table. He'd had a stomach complaint that had turned out to be nothing major, just the stress of getting his nascent trekking business off the ground.

They'd gotten to talking, and later he'd been quick to notice the nature prints in her office—the photographs of the mountains around Denver—many of which she'd taken herself. She wasn't a mountaineer, not by a long shot, but the hiking she did, whether alone or with friends from med school, was a way of blowing off steam from the pressures of her career. High in the hills, with the sun shining on her back and a fresh trail beneath her feet, she re-charged her batteries.

Centered herself.

To Jim Harris, she was just the kind of person he needed on his expeditions: someone who knew the mountains, and who appreciated and understood what the climbers were up against. And who had medical training, besides. It had taken a few weeks of phone calls, a few dinners, and one or two unanticipated tumbles in bed, although Jim was very married, before she'd finally agreed.

And found herself in place as the official Peak Performance Adventure Company team physician, as well as ersatz camp manager.

Her partners were fine with it. Hell, she pulled more than her share of the patient load when she was in town. Her PPAC activities might amount to two or three expeditions per year, at most. And at the very least, the publicity would draw more patients to the practice.

This was her third trip with Jim Harris to the rocky, glacial slopes of Everest's Base Camp. And this was as high as she preferred to go, thank you very much. Content to occupy her time with medical and managerial duties, she left the high altitude climbing to Jim and the others. But when Jim had successfully summitted that first time, two years ago, she'd felt it through and through; it had been her success, too. Five clients and two guides had also tagged the top that day with Jim, and Sandy knew that he was determined to surpass that record this time around.

It had been a typical expedition so far, fraught with the usual trials that were part of the cost of doing business in this part of the world. Such as making sure the supply of oxygen would arrive in time. Maintaining the flow of fresh food by way of balky porters from the lower elevations. Keeping the peace with other expeditions in Base Camp's "shanty town," and trying to rise above the typical intrigues that occurred every season: who stole whose crampons from the base of the Ice Fall; which team was shirking its roping responsibilities; and who was sleeping with whom.

But she never lost sight of her primary mandate: to provide

top-shelf medical care in an extremely challenging environment. It was this factor which concerned Dr. Sandra Ortiz the most. Her patients—the employees and clients of the Peak Performance Adventure Company—were her top priority. It was her responsibility to care for them, to counsel them, and to pull the plug on them, if necessary.

It was a hard enough thing to do, to deny someone their life-long dream when they were so close, but too often the physician had seen the line become blurred beyond rational recognition between taking calculated risks to realize that dream and losing your life. She hadn't had to pull rank on anyone so far, although she'd come close two years ago with that climber from Britain.

Cyril Easton. He'd signed on with Jim's team and had met them all for the first time in Kathmandu, at the beginning of the climb. Although he'd had a nine to five job in an office as an accountant, he had balanced that occupation with considerable climbing experience at high altitude, and so Jim had taken him on.

Sandy had watched with some concern over the course of the expedition as Cyril grew increasingly weaker, as his system rebelled against the acclimatization process. Somehow, he'd heaved his body as high as the required overnight stay at Camp III prior to the final summit assault, and seemed intent on going for the top along with the rest of the team.

That last morning, the poor fellow couldn't keep any food down, his pulse oxygen levels were below 60%, and he had an infected sore on his heel caused by the new pair of climbing boots he'd foolishly purchased right before the trip. In other words, he was a statistic ready to happen.

She'd done her best to advise the Brit not to attempt the summit, and she and Jim had had words over it, too.

"If he wants to give it a shot, who are we to stop him? He's done okay so far. The guy's got guts!"

Sandy hadn't agreed, not by a long shot. Fortunately, the decision had been taken out of her hands when Cyril remained in his tent at dawn the next day, moaning and nearly incoherent. Within a few days, with treatment, he'd shown remarkable improvement, and by that time Jim and the rest of the team were standing atop the Mother Goddess.

Success all around, that was for sure, the physician considered. They'd made the summit, so there was that good PR, and no one had died. Even better.

This trip...this trip was presenting its own set of challenges. The various medical staff assembled in Base Camp had already taken turns, on and off, tending to members of the physician-less International Expedition. Not a safe way for those expedition members to take on the mountain, but she and her colleagues would never deny a needy person medical care, particularly in this barren place.

And within the PPAC group, she had several concerns as well.

Patsy Donaldson, first and foremost.

The woman had been presenting symptoms of HAPE to varying degrees since the day she'd arrived, and Sandy had serious doubts as to whether Patsy should even head back up the mountain at all. Unfortunately, this differed with her husband's opinion. And Lou Silvers, too, had a cough that he just couldn't seem to shake. It wasn't a serious problem yet, but it might easily turn into one, at a most inopportune time.

Other team members had had the usual aches and complaints typically associated with acclimatization and intense physical activity, and she'd been dispensing both her advice and her meds on a daily basis. Additionally, she'd taken to observing the team members on her own, listening in on their conversations, remaining attentive to the camp buzz. The sooner she was alerted to a potential problem, the better for the patient involved. What was an annoying discomfort at sea level could quickly become life threatening at altitude, and it was that point that she persisted in emphasizing with those who sought her assistance.

If only they would listen.

But here, in the shadow of Everest, the dream of every climber loomed large. Larger than life.

"Hi, Sandy! What's up?"

A pair of hands briefly draped around her shoulders. Even if he hadn't spoken, she would have known it was him. By the stomp of his walk. The scent of him. So earthy. So raw. But she pushed that out of her mind. They were simply friends now. Nothing more than that, right?

And she was a professional.

"The usual, Jim." She twisted around on her stool to face him. "Just doing an inventory of our medical supplies." She absently tapped a pen against her clipboard. "We seem to be going through them like crazy. More so than during our other trips."

"Oh, yeah?" He leaned his elbows against the table and picked up a box of sterile pads, examining it. "More meds out means less money in," he observed absently, before giving her his full attention. "How's everybody doing?"

"Not great," she sighed, leaning back, "but not lousy, either. It's the usual stuff," she explained. "They've just got to watch themselves...listen to their bodies." She paused, regarding him carefully. "And not push themselves to do what they shouldn't."

"You mean Patsy."

"C'mon, Jim. You know you were nearly carrying her on your back by the time you got her down the other day. She's not adapting well at all." Her dark brown eyes bored into his. "Don't tell me you can't see it."

"Did you tell her that?" He put the box of pads down and straightened up, his bearded face tensing.

"You know I can't discuss with you any conversations I've had with my patients." She stood, matching him in determination for what she lacked in height. "But we both know that Patsy can barely handle Base Camp, let alone a summit attempt." She pursed her lips. "I need you to be with me on this, Jim. Please. God knows that husband of hers isn't," she snorted.

The team leader ran a hand through his rumpled hair. "Everybody else doing okay?"

"Fine," Sandy told him, knowing she hadn't heard the last from him on the subject. And that worried her. "I'm taking everybody's pulse ox daily, along with a B/P check. We're hanging in there."

"Glad to hear it." Jim stepped closer, so close that she could feel the heat of his body. He rested a callused hand on her shoulder. How heavy it felt, even through the thickness of her sweater. "You know you're an important part of this expedition, Sandy," he said softly. "Whether we succeed or not...depends on you."

"I know that, Jim," she snapped. But she did not pull away from his touch, detesting herself for it. "Believe me, I don't ever forget that."

She allowed herself to be swept closer to him, powerless to reverse course, like a battered leaf swirling down a rainy sidewalk grate.

Suddenly, Doctor Sandra Ortiz felt tired. Very tired, indeed.

❀ ✦ ❀ ✦ ❀ ✦ ❀

"A Big Mac."

"Nah, Whoppers are better."

"Pizza. With anchovies."

"You guys are nuts." Kevin MacBride sat in the dining tent surrounded by his fellow team members. "You wouldn't know fine cuisine if it jumped up and bit you in the butt. When I get back, I'm going straight to Taco Bell for a Chalupa. About five of 'em, at least."

"Not before we've stopped off someplace where you can buy me the first of a year's worth of brews, my friend." Phil Christy lifted a warning finger. "We've got a little bet going, don't forget. One that I intend to win."

"Hah!" The curly haired former footballer took a deep draught of his *chang.* "You've got it wrong, buddy. You mean, we'll need to hit a jewelry store, so you can spring for an engagement ring for my sister."

"Fat chance," Phil grinned, rubbing at the unfamiliar bearded growth on his face. "You'll be watching my ass all the way up the summit ridge."

Kevin almost sprayed a mouthful of *chang* on the table. "Thanks for that visual," he choked. "One that inspires me to return the favor. You are gonna lose, bro. Big time."

"How about you, Allison?" Lou Silvers turned to the stockbroker sitting next to him. "What food do you miss from home?"

"Well...I hadn't really thought about it," she said, and it was the truth. She'd been so involved in other things—taking on this latest adventure both heart and soul, and learning so much about herself in the process—that she hadn't given much thought to missing anything from home. Not the pressures of her job, not the cold indifference that was her family and boyfriend, and, most of all, not the food.

"Come on, there's gotta be something, sweetie!" Patsy Donaldson circled an arm around her husband's elbow. "Why, just last night, Mike and I were talking about the delicious chateaubriand for two that we get at Maison Jacques."

"I'll have to think about it and get back to you later, okay?" Allison smiled tightly and pushed herself away from the table. "I'm gonna turn in, guys. G'night."

"Aw, leaving so soon?" Kevin MacBride lifted his mug of *chang,* and already Allison could see the fevered glaze shining from his eyes. "Can't I buy you a round, Allie?"

Amazing, Allison thought, *how with just a little alcohol, some people come down with amnesia. Not in a million years, asshole.* "Thanks, Kev," she slapped his shoulder as she headed towards the exit, "but it looks like you're doing okay without me."

Allison stepped outside into the brittle chill of another cold Everest evening, glad to be liberated from the stifling tent. The rest of the crew was just getting started on another night of drinking and story telling, and she'd found she had little taste for those pastimes, these days. Much like a certain tall, dark mountaineer who she'd seen entirely too little of, today.

Since waking up in Ricky's arms, they'd each gone their separate ways. Her climbing partner had spent much of the day going over plans for the team's next sortie up the mountain, while Allison had spent the time relaxing, writing in her journal, and reading.

Ricky hadn't been in the dining tent at dinner, but that was hardly unusual. Allison saw no reason why the private woman would break with her routine now, and stop eating with the Sherpas in the cook tent.

Still, she hadn't been able to get Ricky out of her mind all day. The mountaineer had kept intruding on her thoughts when she'd least expected it. She'd found herself losing her train of thought while she was writing, and realized more than once that she'd ended up reading the same paragraph in her paperback over and over.

Finally, she'd just given up and let her mind trip to thoughts of what a revelation last night had been, and the endless possibilities of what lay in store.

God, where are you, Ricky? Allison zipped up her jacket against the cold and stuffed her hands into her pockets. A good place to start would be the mountaineer's tent at the edge of the compound. It was a clear night, and the yellow tent was plainly visible in the pale moonlight, with the heights of Pumori shimmering in the background.

"Want to go for a walk?"

Allison's breath caught in her throat. She was surprised, certainly, at the shock of a voice sounding behind her, but it was a thrill of excitement, too, that stuttered her heart at the low, textured tone buzzing in her ear. She spun around to find Ricky Bouchard standing there, with a black and red Peak Performance cap pushed back on her head, a grin on her lips, and a thermos tucked under her arm. The light of the moon reflected off the planes of her face, the high arch of her cheekbones, the shadow of her throat. And her eyes... Allison gulped hard, trying to maintain her composure under the scrutiny of the two blue orbs twinkling at her like stars fallen straight down from the firmament above.

It was all she could do to bob her head in the affirmative.

"I'll take that as a yes." Ricky tilted her head away from the dining tent. "Let's get out of here, eh? I swiped some hot tea from Lopsang." She started to walk, and Allison followed closely beside her.

Allison fairly floated across the scree, oblivious to the night sounds of Base Camp: the groaning of the glacier, the laughter from distant dining tents. There was nothing but the pounding of her heart, the blood roaring through her ears, and the over-whelming nearness of the woman next to her.

It reminded her of the first time she'd parachute jumped. She'd been as scared as hell. But the excitement...the anticipation of what the experience would be like had propelled her past her fears with a vengeance, until suddenly she'd found herself at the front of the plane and out the door.

And then she was flying, falling into the unknown, and thrilling at every mind-blowing moment of it. It had all been so...incredible, and she was unable to keep a shiver from running through her body at the memory of it.

The tremor did not escape the mountaineer's notice.

"You cold?" Ricky cocked her head and studied Allison's smaller form.

"Yes. No. I mean...uh—"

They had arrived at the edge of Ricky's small encampment. There was a faint glow from within her tent, a delicate beacon of promise beckoning to Allison like a lighthouse in the darkness.

Ricky shuffled her feet, confused. This was not at all what she'd anticipated. She'd been looking forward all day to seeing Allison again, and had hoped—no, she knew—that the young blonde felt the same way.

Still, the last thing she wanted to do was pressure her.

Patience.

"Look. If you'd rather—"

In frustration, Allison did the first thing that came to mind. She reached out and placed a hand behind the taller woman's neck and pulled her down, silencing her with a kiss. At last Allison broke away, praying to God that her knees would not fail her now. "I'd rather."

Ricky's eyes widened, just like a child's on Christmas morning. "Really?"

"Oh yeah," Allison groaned. In an instant, her world was turned topsy-turvy and she next found herself inside Ricky's tent with little memory of exactly how she'd gotten there.

She kept her eyes open, wanting to see it all, to feel, to touch. Layers of clothing were hastily peeled back and discarded, and as the powerful body of the mountaineer at last came into view, it was Allison who felt as though she'd just unwrapped a gift of which she was undeserving.

They quickly came together—hard, fast, and furious. Every kiss robbed Allison of her breath; the silken feel of Ricky's skin sliding against her own was an exquisite torture from which she found herself begging for release.

"Allison, I—" Ricky's lips tore away from Allison's, and her mouth hung open, panting.

"What? What is it?"

The mountaineer turned her head away. "I–it's—"

Allison lifted a hand to Ricky's cheek, a sudden grip of fear clutching at her heart. What if Ricky was having second thoughts? Oh, God, not now. Not just when they'd found each other. "You can tell me anything. You know that, right?"

"It's just that..." Ricky turned pained blue eyes to her, "I want to please you so much, Allison. I want to show you how much I care, but I'm afraid I haven't really—" She tilted her head away again, taking care to rest her weight on her elbows. "I don't know—"

And then Allison knew. "Hey," she said softly, as both understanding and relief cascaded through her. "This is all new to me, too." She pulled the mountaineer tightly to her and was relieved beyond all measure when Ricky returned the embrace. Allison could not help but let her hands roam over the finely muscled back; allowed herself to revel in the sensation of being caged, cocooned by the tightly coiled power of the taller woman's arms and legs.

Allison was powerless to stop the fire stoking within her, one that only Ricky Bouchard could quench. She blew out a breath of air. "You know how to get to Carnegie Hall, don't you?"

Ricky lifted her head, her long dark hair tumbling down and raking against Allison's sensitive skin like a hot brand, claiming her. "No."

The puzzlement on Ricky's face was priceless, and it almost made Allison laugh aloud. God, she never knew it could be like this. With anyone, ever. What had taken her so long?

"Practice, baby. Practice."

Ricky grinned. Once more, with renewed confidence, she lowered herself down onto Allison's willing form. She nipped at the base of her throat, and then at a slow, leisurely pace, traced a hot, wet path up to her earlobe. "Let me see if I can play this one by ear."

Chapter
Sixteen

Summer in the Northern Hemisphere.

It meant a moderation in temperature from cold to warm for the more northerly landmasses, while other areas traded winter snows for a searing, dry heat or perhaps the torture of a hot, humid subtropical cauldron. For Mount Everest, whose heights in winter were subjected to a staggering, inhuman cold that bottomed out the most resilient thermometers that science had to offer, the irony was that the summer season was when the bulk of the region's annual snowfall accumulated.

It could fool you at first, starting out as a deceptive dusting of white talc. And then, before you had a chance to make it back to your tent or on to the next camp, a summer blow would set upon the mountain in all its fury, robbing you of your vision, turning you around and around until you were lost, its wind-driven ice-pellets lashing at you like a cat o' nine tails.

Climbers had learned early on, the hard way, that if they were to have any chance at all of summiting Everest, they would have to squeeze their expeditions in between the frigid cold of the winter, and those summer snowstorms. Not that a late spring snow during an expedition was an entirely unwelcome thing. It was preferred in small doses; it could cover the rocky scree up high, and provide firmer footing. Too much snow, however, could founder individual climbers, and derail entire expeditions.

At 26,000 feet in waist-deep snow, breaking trail, fixing rope, and moving up supplies soon exhausted even the fittest of mountaineers, and forced them to turn back.

If they still were able.

The weather patterns of the Himalayan region have long fascinated meteorologists, who find them to be as intense and unforgiving as they are unpredictable. In the summer, the Himalayan range is the mountainous battleground between the dry Tibetan climate to the north and the moisture-laden Indian monsoons to the south. Spring is that fragile time of transition when the line of combat is constantly shifting in the snowy sands, giving mountaineers the narrow window they need to make it safely up and down the mountain.

Each day in springtime, the hot, humid air to the south pushes farther north, rising up the Khumbu Valley in dark, blooming thunderheads. When the clouds finally punch through the layer of more stable, drier air above them, they do so with a violent force, and so the monsoons begin. In Nepal and India, it rains. But on Everest...it snows. A blinding white, unmerciful assault. And woe to the climber then, who has not retreated from the higher elevations.

All things on Everest are ruled by the Jet Stream winds, and it is these winds that help to paint the line of climatic demarcation. The roaring Jet Stream, which many climbers have likened to the sound of a freight train barreling its way high across the mountain, in the spring blows to the south. With the approach of the monsoon season, the winds weaken and shift to the north, actually passing directly over the summit in the process. Once the Jet Stream is beyond the mountain, the winds die down almost entirely. This is the window the climbers wait for, and it usually occurs each year within the first week or two of May.

The problems that can occur during this window, however, lie mostly in the capricious nature of the Jet Stream. Unstable, fickle, it can suddenly storm back across the summit, slamming the window shut, wiping clean the face of the mountain with its bitter cold winds. Or, worse, it can combine with the moisture boiling up from the south to trigger the deep snowfalls that are catastrophic at any altitude.

Weather services do their best to provide expeditions with state-of-the-art satellite forecasts. But even armed with this weapon, so much of a climber's success on Everest comes down to the luck of the draw, and pushing that luck to the limit. Sometimes, it gets pushed too far, as in the season of 1996, when twelve climbers lost their lives on the mountain; nine as the result of one horrific late afternoon storm. But even today's high-tech forecasts could not have helped George Mallory's expedition in 1922, two years before his final, ill-fated climb. Then, the experienced mountaineer's mistake had been tarrying too long in the shadows of Everest; and with June and the monsoon season came the storms and the heated air that caused an avalanche, wiping out seven of his Sherpa porters in a single cruel blow.

The weather.

It was the one thing Veronique Bouchard knew that could make or break an expedition. On Everest in particular, there were some years when the weather never cleared long enough for a successful siege of the mountain. Not that it ever stopped people from trying.

It had been snowing up high; Ricky could tell by the swirling mists of white that obscured the upper reaches of the mountain late each afternoon. Reports from the climbing Sherpas of snows heavier than usual at Camp III and on the Lhotse Face had confirmed her assessment. As a result, Jim Harris had decided to keep the Peak Performance team in Base Camp an additional day before shoving off on their last acclimatization climb. But the reports hadn't kept the International Expedition tethered to BC, or the British team, either. They had already started up.

Ricky had been surprised at Jim's willingness to postpone their departure until tomorrow, and she wondered now, as she made her way to the communications tent for a meeting with Jim and Paul, whether that decision hadn't been based on a desire to give Patsy Donaldson an additional day's rest. Not that the mountaineer disagreed with Jim's call, on either account. Heavy snow high on the mountain was not a good thing, particularly when there were still lines to be fixed, and God knew that Patsy could use the extra day.

In fact, most of the clients hadn't seemed at all bothered by the delay. The prospect of one more idle day in the thick air, sleeping well, and eating even better, was met with a mixture of quiet acceptance and relief.

One client in particular hadn't minded, and Ricky smiled to herself at that.

Allison.

And, truth be known, she herself had felt the same way.

It was a glorious late morning in Base Camp; the winds were fairly restrained, and the moderate temperature, coupled with the radiant heat from the brilliant sunlight above, was enough to send most climbers scurrying for their T-shirts and sun block. Streamers of prayer flags dangling from tent frames and *puja* altars fluttered on the rippling breezes, each snap of a flag sending a prayer off to the Mother Goddess. Ricky let her eyes travel over the various camps parked at the base of the glacier; she could see that a number of climbers and Sherpas alike were taking advantage of the good weather. Damp equipment was laid out to dry, batches of laundry were getting done, and many simply opted to enjoy the out-of-doors, soaking in the healing, restorative rays of the sun.

As for the climbers who'd departed early that morning for the upper camps, there was no sign of them in the Icefall. By this time, they would already have cleared the frozen river and been well on their way up the Cwm, moving towards Camp II.

Amazingly, Ricky felt no restlessness in her gut at the thought of other teams getting the jump on her. Once, in fairly recent times—last week, say—it might have mattered. Get on the mountain, do what you came to do, and get out. That had been her credo. But now, the thought of eking out an extra day in the relative comfort of Base Camp, immersed in all things Allison Peabody, did not seem too terrible a way to pass the time.

Ricky felt her pulse quicken as her searching gaze found the younger woman. There she was, lazily reclining on a couple of sun-heated rocks near the cook-tent, chattering away with Lou Silvers. She wore a simple white T-shirt, dark blue fleece stretch pants, and had a blue and white sweater tied off around her waist. She leaned back on one elbow against the rock, her booted feet kicked out in front of her, with a black and red Peak Performance cap perched jauntily on her blonde head. The tall mountaineer couldn't see her eyes through her glacier glasses, but whatever Lou was telling her had made her laugh; Ricky could just hear it as she idly noted how her own legs had begun inexplicably to detour towards the sound.

Hell, she was early for her meeting, anyway.

Lou Silvers saw her coming and must've said something to Allison, because suddenly the younger woman turned and waved, a beaming smile lighting her face. Easily, effortlessly, Ricky found herself grinning in return and quickening her pace.

God, Ricky, you are in it deep. If only Jean-Pierre could see you now!

It had been some few days, that was for certain, since the night she and Allison had gone for the walk that had never happened.

It had hit her like a fifteen-ton *serac*.

An explosion of senses, of thoughts, of feelings she'd told herself she was dead to, or else not capable of. Whatever she'd imagined it would be like, being with Allison, the true power of it had left her reeling, and helplessly yearning for more. The simple truth was, that getting so close to someone she actually cared about, in the most intimate of ways, had humbled her.

For Ricky Bouchard, she who had climbed the world's highest mountains, who had dared the icy reaches of the Eiger's *Norwand*, who for "fun" had executed an amazing one-day free ascent of El Capitan's "Nose"—and was able to bivouac in time for dinner—the connection she felt when she was with Allison was the most singularly sensual thing, in the physical sense, that she'd ever experienced.

And as for the person that Allison was inside, well, Ricky had to laugh. God knew, she'd made many acquaintances over the years throughout her travels, but she'd seldom permitted herself to make any friends. After all, it distracted you, and that was how you got hurt. Jean-Pierre Valmont had been the rare exception to that rule, and the silent curtain of grief that draped her heart was the price she was still paying for loving him.

It was different with Allison. It was a fever that burned within her, driving her onward, and she simply couldn't get close enough. She wanted to know it all: her hopes, her dreams. What her past had been like, and what brought her joy and sadness. Had she written in a journal all her life, and would she ever let Ricky read it? Would she ever consider climbing another peak together—Gasherbrum II, perhaps? And, the most important question of all: did she like butter-pecan ice cream?

At the same time, Ricky had been startled to find herself talking to Allison about her own past, about what had happened back home with her family after Jean-Pierre's death, and was startled at how easily the words came. She'd kept so much of it bottled up for so long, deeply stored in those compartments within herself that she'd let gather dust, but that she still toted around with her like a 120 pound pack. For once...no, for the second time in her life, she felt...safe, in sharing her own thoughts and fears with another person.

The rational, logical part of her mind told her she'd gone over the top, that she'd only known Allison for little more than a month. But when she listened to her soul, in the quiet of her heart, she heard and recognized the truth: that the sum of her whole life had led her to this barren spot at the roof of the world, and to this woman. They were meant to be...*had* to be. The thought of it not being real, of it being a fleeting, mountainside dalliance, was simply too shattering to contemplate.

She'd seen it happen often enough on other expeditions; the international community of elite alpinists was a small one. They were people who'd come together because of a love of life and a love of the mountains.

People in peak physical condition, camped in a challenging environment far away from home, well, nature took its course. Hell, just because she'd rarely taken part in the festivities herself, didn't mean she was blind to it all. God knew she'd had to endure enough lurid stories from Jean-Pierre. And when the climbs were over, more often than not, so were the romances.

But that wouldn't happen with Allison, Ricky just knew it. Already, they'd been talking about what their options were after the expedition was over. It wouldn't be easy for either of them, but Ricky had never shrunk from hard work. The best things in life, she'd found, were always worth her best effort.

All this, at 17,600 feet. Ricky pulled up to where Allison and Lou reclined. *Hell, at sea level, it'll probably kill me!*

"Hiya, Ricky!" Allison sat up and folded her hands around her knees.

"Ricky!" Lou Silvers stood, dusting off the seat of his pants. "What's up?"

"I'm on my way to meet with Jim and Paul," she told him. "Gotta review the plan for tomorrow. After all," she snuck a sideways look at Allison, catching her eye, "we can't hang around BC forever."

"Aw, I don't know about that." The compact attorney threw his arms open wide. Like Ricky and Allison, he also wore a T-shirt. "This day's been great. And I feel great, too." He took in a deep pull of a breath, so that his well-muscled chest puffed out like a bantam rooster's, then released the air with a loud whoosh. There was no sign of the raspiness that had marked his breathing earlier in the week. "See?" He placed a hand on the left side of his chest. "Today's the first day in a week and a half that I'm not worried about coughing up a lung."

Ricky flashed him a smile. "Well, you sound better." And he looked better too, Ricky noted privately, observing with some relief that he'd lost some of the ghostly, bluish-gray pallor that was so common among those having trouble getting the O's they needed in the thin air.

"And doesn't he look well?" Allison chimed in, echoing Ricky's thoughts.

"That's because I got to talk to my girls." He struck a thumb towards the communications tent. "I was just telling Allie about it. That satellite phone is something," he said, shaking his head in amazement. "I could hear them clear as a bell. You ever try it?"

"Uh, no." Ricky averted her eyes from the kindly attorney's gaze, finding a darkened weather stain on a nearby tarp suddenly of interest. *Me on the satellite phone. Right.* And whom exactly would she call, anyway? Her parents? Not likely. Ricky was not a phone person, or even a letter writer, for that matter. She believed that you saw people when you saw them, and hopefully you'd be able to pick up where you left off. And if you didn't, or couldn't, well, maybe you weren't missing out on that much after all. No, better to leave such high-tech gadgetry to the clients.

"Anyway, I got ahold of them just in time. They were getting ready to leave for school." Lou dug into an unzipped pants pocket and pulled out a thin wallet. "Have I shown you their picture?"

"No." Ricky nearly flinched as the attorney stepped closer and pulled a laminated photograph out of the billfold. Kids. Pictures. Family. It wasn't that she didn't care, it was just...aw, what the hell.

"I know I've already bored Allison with it a time or two," he blushed. "Sorry."

"Nonsense," the young stockbroker replied. "They're beautiful. You've got every reason to be proud of them, right, Ricky?"

Ricky gazed at the snapshot suddenly thrust into her hand. The setting appeared to be at a birthday party, as nearly as Ricky could surmise. A petite brunette woman was kneeling on a thick carpet of green grass, her arms hugging twin girls that were miniature versions of their mother: long dark hair, button noses, and large round eyes that gazed out of porcelain doll faces. In the background was a picnic table laden with cake, sodas, and paper cups and plates. Other small children sat at the table, their attention more occupied by the cake, pretzels and chips on their plates, than with the picture-taking going on.

"That's Lesley, my wife," Lou explained, "and our girls, Laura and Lisa."

The girls' sunny smiles fairly flew off the surface of the picture, and straight into Ricky's heart. Yeah, they were beautiful. Shielded from the harshness of reality by the constancy of their own innocence, guarded and protected by the love of two parents who obviously cared for them so very much.

"I took this at their last birthday party." Lou edged closer to Ricky, pointing. "That's my Lisa, on the left. She's missing her front tooth, she told me," he chuckled, "and now Laura said hers feels loose."

Ricky noticed how Lou never took his eyes off the picture as he spoke, as if by keeping his family in his field of vision, he could very nearly smell the sweet, earthy scent of freshly mown grass, hear the pealing of the children's laughter, feel the soft warmness of his twin daughters in his arms.

"Something tells me Laura's tooth is going to fall out soon, too," he continued, lost in his remembrances. "Especially since she doesn't want to miss out on a visit from the Tooth Fairy."

"They...they're gorgeous," Ricky said, and she meant it. She handed the picture back to Lou. "How old are they?"

"Seven." He slowly replaced the photo in his wallet, reluctant to let his family go. "We...we had a hard time, Lesley and I, having children. And what we had to go through, well, we waited a long time for these two," he said, his voice growing thick with emotion, "but it was worth it. They're my pride and joy."

Allison reached out and gave the attorney's hand a warm squeeze. "I can see why," she whispered.

"I–I just miss them, you know? The last time I was away on such an extended climb was before they were born."

"You'll be back to them soon," Allison reassured him. "And think of the stories you'll have to tell! Daddy on Mount Everest."

"Yeah." Lou rubbed nervously at the back of his neck. "And Lesley swears she's never going to let me do anything like this again." He grinned sheepishly. "You know, I think that's one I'm not going to fight her on." He paused. "Anyway," he squared his shoulders and lifted his nose towards the enticing scents drifting from the cook-tent, "let me see if I can't scrounge up a bit of whatever Lopsang has on the lunch menu. And then," he checked his watch, "nap time."

"No kidding," Allison agreed, stifling a yawn. "Better rest up while we can."

"Not a bad idea," Ricky said, turning her eyes towards a scattering of clouds beginning to converge in the valley to the south. "Looks like the afternoon squall is going to arrive right on schedule."

The climbers at Base Camp enjoyed the sunlight that warmed the valley in the late morning hours and provided welcome relief from the relentless cold of the upper camps. But, by warming up the rocks and causing convection winds, pulling the moisture up from lower elevations, that same heat created its own smaller version of monsoon-like weather.

Usually, only enough of the moisture would make it as high as Base Camp to cause small afternoon snow squalls. By sunset, both the snows and the winds would be gone, and the horizon would flame with a blaze of fiery reds, blues, and golds sparkling against a white canvas. At times, the squalls could be so localized that it might be snowing in one part of Base Camp, and clear in another. Once in a great while the mini-storms would intensify, and sock in climbers at the foot of the Khumbu for days.

"More snow coming?" Lou wanted to know.

Ricky sniffed at the freshening breeze. "Yes. It will be snowing within the hour. But not enough to push back our departure again," she said matter-of-factly. "I'm sure of it."

"We'll be leaving the same time as before?" Allison asked, facing the mountaineer.

"You'll hear more about it at the meeting tonight, but yes," Ricky told her. "We'll head up before dawn."

"Don't remind me," Lou groaned, and he offered them a wave. "I'm outta here. Catch ya later," and he moved off towards the dining tent, with a lightness in his step that Ricky had not seen since he'd arrived at the base of Everest. *And just in time,* Ricky thought. The greatest physical challenges lay just ahead.

"Well," Ricky leaned on the rocks next to Allison. A small smile flickered on her lips. "Looking forward to tomorrow?"

"Yeah. It'll be good to get back up the mountain. And at

least then," Allison lowered her voice, "I'll have an excuse to share a tent with you."

Ricky pursed her lips. They'd both decided to keep their newborn relationship low profile in the camp. It was nobody else's business anyway, and they'd agreed that the possible in-camp repercussions might create the sort of static that they would rather do without, especially when there was so much else at stake. "You don't need an excuse, Miss Peabody," Ricky told her, remembering warmly their last several secretive nights together, "but I can assure you that at 24,000 feet, you won't feel like doing much more than falling into your sleeping bag and passing out. Oh, while you try not to freeze to death," she added.

"With you around?" Allison flashed an impudent grin that quickened Ricky's pulse. "Not a chance."

"Allison, I—" Ricky suddenly felt at a loss for words, her eyes drinking in the young blonde who had changed her life so dramatically, in such a short time. There were a thousand things she wanted to tell her, if only her heart could speak.

How good it felt to stand here like this, just...talking.

How complete she felt now, after years of not even realizing how she'd studiously, deliberately, shut herself off from feeling. From being.

How, for the first time in her life, she felt a part of something far more significant than the next big adventure, the next great mountain to climb. The sensation was similar to gazing over a rocky precipice, and knowing that there was nothing but 15,000 feet of open air between her and a valley floor. It was terrifying and exhilarating at the same time, and she never wanted it to end.

"Hmnn?" Allison's face was tilted up to her in the late morning light. So beautiful. Waiting.

"I...uh—" So much to say. But not here. Not yet.

Ricky swallowed hard, pushing her emotions down before they swamped her. *Get a grip!* "I've got to go. See you later, then?"

Allison discreetly brushed against Ricky's forearm with the back of her hand. "You can count on it."

❉ ◆ ❉ ◆ ❉

"So based on the latest load of supplies Dorje and his team

took off with yesterday, we'll have nearly three-fourths of the gas we'll need for our summit attempt stocked at Camp III, ready to go." Jim Harris stood tall in the communications tent, which had become the Peak Performance Adventure Company's site for small, impromptu meetings. Larger, more boisterous gatherings, like tonight's team orientation for the following day's climb, were held in the bigger, more comfortable environment of the dining tent.

"Including the rigs?" Paul Andersen scratched at the new beard on his face, as though he were still getting used to the alien growth. "I know Mike Donaldson will want to know."

"Bottles, regulators, masks—the whole nine yards," Jim told him. He leaned forward with one foot placed on the seat of a low stool, and balanced a hand holding a steaming up of coffee on his bent knee. "They won't have to worry about carrying it up there."

"Exactly my point. Or rather, theirs." Paul's thin lips formed a pained smile.

"Yeah," Jim conceded, "I know he's fairly...demanding. You've been doing a good job working with them, Paul."

"He does have his moments." The head guide flashed a sidelong glance at Ricky Bouchard. The dark haired woman sat close to the tent's flaps, tugging at her cap, shifting her position, looking as though she might bolt for the exit at any minute. "But hey," he chuckled, "clients are people, too!"

"Are we about finished here?" She'd sat quietly while Jim had given out the assignments; once again she'd be shadowing Lou and Allison all the way to Camp III and back. And she hadn't said a word when Paul and Jim had gotten into a political debate over which teams would do the final roping and trail breaking from Camp IV to the summit; hell, she'd do it herself if she had to. And she'd listened for about the fifth time to Dr. Ortiz' "what symptoms to look out for high on the mountain" lecture, and although the advice was well given, Ricky had to wonder why someone like a Patsy Donaldson was still climbing when many of the very symptoms Sandra Ortiz had enumerated were so plainly visible on the petite woman.

Planning was a good thing, Ricky didn't quibble with that, but over-planning, well, it was a fact that on any mountain it was best to expect the unexpected. Things could and did go wrong, and no amount of planning could completely guard against it. Instead, over the years she'd found it better to learn how to adapt, to roll with the surprises, and not do the stupid things that got you into trouble in the first place. Like using those damn oxygen rigs. They were bad news, she just knew it; and she hated like hell the fact that her deal with Peak Performance required that she use one. But there was no backing out now.

"Got somewhere to go, Ricky?" Paul Andersen snickered. "You wouldn't be thinking about getting a head start on us, would you?"

"I don't *need* a head start," she drawled, unsmiling. She turned to Jim Harris. "What kind of oxygen are we using?"

"Well—" he began, but Sandra Ortiz cut him off with a silencing look.

"Our supplier has given us a blend of Poisk and Zvesda," she said, eyeing Ricky carefully. "Why do you ask?"

"The Poisk are 3 liter canisters, right? And the Zvesda are 4 liters?"

"Correct."

"Heavier and bulkier," Ricky noted, frowning. She didn't like the idea of using Zvesda at all, not that Poisk were much better. Both were Russian-made, and at high altitude in sub-zero temperatures, it was not unheard of for the regulators to freeze over and jam. "You're talking about adding on another 2-3 pounds of weight, and at 28,000 feet, that's one hell of a difference."

"We're going to use the Zvesda strictly for sleeping," Jim quickly assured her, knowing it had been a battle to get the mountaineer to agree to use gas for this climb in the first place. "It'll be available at Camp III and Camp IV during the summit push." He drained the remainder of his coffee. "But from Camp IV onward, we'll only carry the lighter Poisk."

"And remember, Ricky, that even though the Poisk have less capacity," Dr. Ortiz added, "the Sherpas will be sure to have laid in a cache of extra bottles at the South Summit, so you'll have no problem getting up and down with a continuous flow."

"Uh-huh." Ricky still didn't like the sound of it, but who was she to make a big stink about it? After all, she was just an employee, right? And plenty of climbers used O's, without any problem. Sure, it wasn't the pure, natural way for them to take on a mountain, but it got them where they wanted to go.

"You never know, Ricky." Jim Harris flexed his bent leg to the floor with a loud stomp, and grinned at her. "You might find out you like it."

"I doubt it," she grumbled.

"That's it, folks," Jim said, ignoring the low crackling exchange on the radio behind him. It was a routine report coming in from one of the other teams moving up—the British expedition, from the sound of it. When climbers were on the mountain, there was radio chatter all day long on various frequencies, with team members checking in at designated intervals.

"Hold on, Ricky," Jim called after her as she bolted for the exit. "I'd like a word."

Damn. The mountaineer pulled up, allowing Paul and Sandra to slip past her.

"Yes?" She turned to face the big team leader and could not help but notice the tightness around his eyes, the pinched set of his mouth—telltale signs of tension. Jim Harris was a good climber and a fair man, or at least that was what she'd understood over the years by virtue of his reputation. If she had thought otherwise, she never would have signed on with him. But there was a quantum difference between being a climber and being in the business of climbing.

So much had changed over the past few years; it was a very different sport from the time when she and Jean-Pierre had first started out. Back then, she'd been content with a used, three-season tent that she'd made do with year-round, and with a military surplus sleeping bag, opting instead to spend what little money she'd had on the best pair of boots she could afford.

Now, everything was so commercialized, so...impersonal.

She didn't know what it was like to run a business, to have those sorts of pressures weighing on you day and night—she had no desire to know. It had to change you, she guessed. It affected you in some deceptively subtle yet permanent way, in the way you related to the mountain, and how you perceived its relationship with you.

Instead of unparalleled freedom and a certainty about who and what you were, it was about balance sheets, designer gear, and corporate sponsors. It placed the mountain and the challenge of it all in the world of the abstract. It wasn't real anymore. And that was how you lost your way.

On the mountain, and in your life.

"How's it going?" he asked, his dark brown eyes probing her.

"Fine."

"I mean...how's it going with the clients?" He cleared his throat. "You know, this being your first time as a guide and all."

"Okay," Ricky said slowly, her posturing stiffening. Small talk was not Jim's forte. At least, not with her. And she had some idea of where this was going.

"Because I know that sometimes it can be tough. Different levels of skill, different backgrounds, different personalities..."

"What are you trying to say, Jim?" Ricky demanded, feeling the blood rush to her face. It was clear the team leader was uncomfortable trying to express himself in this situation. Maybe she could put both of them out of their misery.

Harris released a frustrated burst of air. "Look, Ricky. I would never question your climbing skills. You're one of the best in the world at what you do—that's why I wanted you on this expedition. I know," he continued, stating his case, "that if something goes wrong, if I need you to, you can rocket up that damn hill like a bullet."

"But?" Ricky said tersely, getting angrier by the second.

"But...can't you try to chill out? With some of the clients, I mean."

Ricky ground her teeth. "Chill out."

"C'mon, Ricky." Jim gazed helplessly at her. "You know what I'm talking about. You can come on pretty strong sometimes. It's like," he groped for the right words, "like you don't give a shit whether people like you or not."

"I don't," Ricky told him, her voice rising. "Jesus Christ, Jim! You hired me to be a guide, not a God-damned party hostess."

"And I'm trying to run a business," he countered, matching her in tone. "I don't want my clients coming to me with complaints about an employee."

An employee.

Of course. How silly of her to forget the fact that she'd signed away a big chunk of her free will when she'd swallowed her pride and inked the PPAC employment contract. She'd told herself then she'd do her best to do what she was told to do, to try and make it work.

But this...God! It had to be that idiot Kevin MacBride and his pal, or maybe Mike Donaldson. She hadn't been oblivious to the shadowed glares Mike had been casting her way lately, and yet she was hard-pressed to figure out a single thing she'd done or said to him. *Maybe that in and of itself,* she reflected, *is the problem. Guys with egos as big as his don't like to be ignored.*

"Just try to loosen up, Ricky," she heard Jim say, his voice softer now, pleading, trying a different tack.

"I'm as 'loose' as I'm going to get." Ricky sighed tiredly, feeling as though she'd lost a battle she'd never really been given a chance to fight. "But," she forced a smile, "I'll see what I can do."

❄ ♦ ❄ ♦ ❄

It was late.

Late enough that the rest of Base Camp had gone to sleep. The climbers who had stayed below that day due to the poor weather up high, had long since made their way to their dome-shaped tents, looking forward to an early start the next morning. That number included not only the Peak Performance team, but also the Spanish New Millennium Expedition, a Japanese team, and several other mixed groups.

It is never really quiet at the base of the Khumbu, no matter how late the hour. The glacier continues its onward march, groaning and creaking in the dark. Closer, there might be the crunching footsteps of a lone Sherpa making his way across the scree, or a climber, rousted in the night by the call of nature. There is always the flutter and snapping of the Buddhist prayer flags in the breeze, and the sounds of the stronger winds sweeping down from the upper mountain, their deep, throaty moans ebbing and flowing, so that at times, mixed in with a low hum, there is a nearly mystical, lyrical chorus of distant chimes. All of this under the ever-watchful eye of the Mother Goddess: deceptively benevolent in calm; cold and unforgiving in a sudden storm.

Allison Peabody was as warm as anyone could hope to be, lying in a tent at the foot of Mount Everest. Due, in no uncertain terms, to the fact that her primary heat source in this particular tent, situated at the periphery of the Peak Performance compound, was an extraordinary mountaineer from Quebec. There was a dim light in the interior, thanks to the mini-stove that Ricky had fired up earlier to heat water for tea. Shadows flickered off the canvas, bobbing and weaving as the winds blew outside. Inside, Allison burrowed deeper into the oversized black sleeping bag that covered her and Ricky, seeking out a more natural source of warmth, fueled by a need they both shared.

As constant as the mountain itself was, Allison considered, the landscape around it was always changing. The features of the Khumbu were never the same from day-to-day, season-to-season, year-to-year. And each time a bitter wind lighted upon Everest, it was sure to make its mark: sweeping clean the icy slopes, the loose snow, the rocky scree. Always carving a new face, shifting, evolving.

Look no further than yourself, Allison. How different *she* was, since that day when she'd caught her first distant glimpse of Everest as she'd flown into Kathmandu, and next being greeted at the airport by the most striking woman she had ever seen. Back then, she'd had a fast-track career, an almost-fiancé, and one hell of an attitude. And all that she'd cared about was the prospect of scratching another notch into her "extreme vacationing" bedpost, and moving on.

But now...none of those things mattered. Nothing did, save for the intoxicating woman by her side whose long limbs were tangled up with her own; skin against skin, the heat of two spent bodies radiating against the coolness of the air. Allison's heart had finally begun to resume its normal beat, difficult enough after such exertion at high altitude, and she'd been amazed at how swiftly the drumming in Ricky's chest had slowed, how rapidly her short, choppy breaths had lengthened and extended into a deep, even, drawing in and out. Another sign of how well the mountaineer adapted to high altitude. God, had she fallen asleep?

Movement, and then Allison felt a pair of lips press softly against her temple. "I'm going to miss this."

The buzz of Ricky's voice against her skin sent a fresh bolt of desire ripping through her. "What—are you planning on going somewhere?" She let her hand travel teasingly over the muscled flatness of the mountaineer's belly, and lifted her head so that she could see her face in the flickering light. Ricky had offered to meet Allison in her tent, but the younger woman had declined, preferring instead over these past nights to rendezvous in the privacy of Ricky's more secluded location. Still, it was hard each morning in the pre-dawn, tearing herself away from the warmth of the mountaineer's strong embrace to wobble half-awake back to her own tent. Well, after tomorrow morning, it wouldn't matter. Moving up the mountain as climbing partners, they'd be back to being tent mates. And that was just fine with Allison Peabody.

"*Non, Mademoiselle,* I wouldn't think of it." Ricky edged herself up into more of a sitting position, her blue eyes twinkling. "But we've got a mountain to climb tomorrow, or have you forgotten?"

"Nooooo." Allison scooted closer to Ricky and found herself gathered up into her arms. She rested her head on the mountaineer's shoulder, once again overtaken with emotion at her good fortune. God, to feel this wonderful, to have found such a special person in such a crazy, mixed-up world; if this were all a dream, she hoped never to awaken from it. "But we'll still be together, right?" She reached out and let her fingers play with the thin, braided protection cord the *Rimpoche* at the monastery in Tibet had given Ricky. It was knotted securely at the taller woman's neck. She never took it off, Allison had noticed, and why should she? It had obviously served her well.

"We'll be together, all right." A low, rumbling laugh sounded in Ricky's chest. "Stuck together like two frozen Popsicles, I think."

Allison gazed up at the mountaineer, smiling cheekily. "Not the way your motor runs."

Ricky lifted an eyebrow. "I think you overestimate my high altitude skills."

"I'll be the judge of that."

In the dim light from the cook stove, Allison could see a flash of the mountaineer's teeth. "So you will," Ricky said softly, dipping her head to capture Allison's lips with her own.

Oh, God! It took Allison's breath away. She found herself shifting her position slightly so she could deepen the kiss, probing with her tongue, reaching out, tasting, touching. The goosedown bedding fell away from her back, and a shiver skipped through her as the coolness of the air hit her skin.

Ricky gasped and pulled away, breaking the kiss at last. Allison felt one arm snake around her middle and pull her closer, if that were possible, while another adjusted the sleeping bag.

"Better?"

"That depends," Allison groaned, blowing fine strands of blonde hair from her forehead.

"We have *got* to get some sleep," Ricky chuckled, reaching out to turn off the stove. "You'll regret it, otherwise."

"No regrets, ever," Allison replied, her voice a fierce whisper. She rested her palm on the mountaineer's chest. And then, hesitantly, "What about you?" Beneath her fingertips, she could feel the tempo of Ricky's heartbeat increase.

Silence for a moment, and then, "No."

Inordinately relieved, Allison let herself sink into the mountaineer's warmth. They continued to lie there quietly, listening to the wind, the murmuring of the glacier, and the beating of each other's hearts. Allison tried to fall asleep, willed herself to feel tired; but sleep would not come. There were simply too many thoughts careening around her mind, poking her, prodding her, keeping her awake.

"Ricky?"

"Mnnn?"

"About tomorrow."

The mountaineer cleared the sleep from her throat. "Yes?"

"I mean, we're getting down to it now, aren't we?" Allison paused for a moment, before deciding to plunge ahead. "I've never felt as good as I do now, or as strong, and I wonder."

"Wonder what?"

"What...what if I'm not good enough?" She quietly released the words into the darkness, as though they were more of a plea than a question. "What if I don't have what it takes?" she rushed onwards. "Do you ever feel that way, Ricky?"

Allison could feel her partner take in several deep breaths; the seconds ticked by and for a time, she wondered whether the mountaineer would respond or not. Maybe she'd stepped over the line, pushed her too far.

Another deep breath. "About the mountain?" Ricky finally said, "No. The Mother Goddess doesn't care how good I am, or not," she continued, obviously weighing her words carefully. "She doesn't need to know how many 8,000 meter peaks I've climbed, or whether I can...somehow find the strength within myself to keep going in an 80 knot wind that's ripping off the summit, trying to blow me halfway back to Kathmandu. She welcomes me, regardless of who I am or what I've done. The rest is up to me."

The mountaineer fell silent for a moment, and Allison waited for her to go on. It was as though Ricky were talking to herself, rather than aloud, and allowing the young blonde a rare glimpse of her inner soul in the process.

"That's at the heart of it, I guess," Ricky told her. "It's not about you against the mountain. It's you against yourself." She swallowed in the darkness. "Jean-Pierre realized that, even before I did."

Allison reached out a hand to Ricky's cheek and felt the muscles of her face form a small smile.

"I'll be forever grateful to him for that. He helped me get the hell out of my own bad-ass way." She sighed. "So that's what it's about, Allison. What is...simply is. No triumphs. No regrets. Just the doing of it; of being totally, completely alive in the moment." She turned towards Allison. "Am I making any sense?"

Allison blinked away the pools of moisture forming at the corners of her eyes. "Yeah. It's how I feel when I'm with you, Ricky," she said hoarsely. "I've never felt so free, so alive. So...safe."

She could hear Ricky's breathing catch, and suddenly the mountaineer was hovering above her, her face barely discernible in the darkened interior of the tent. But she could see the wonder, the amazement flit across her features, and then Ricky was on her, speaking in the language of the physical world, the language she spoke best. Where deeds served as words, punctuated by a boundless passion and an unparalleled giving of self.

Allison allowed herself to be swept away by the rush, by the cascading emotions washing over her. Just when she thought it was impossible to climb any higher, Ricky took her to new heights that left her dizzy and gasping for breath. She'd never been here before in this rarified air. It was all so new to her, and so she simply held on as though her life depended on it.

Maybe it did.

She let herself be carried away by their union, felt all earthly bonds slip away, and she gave herself up to its power. For a fleeting moment she was disoriented in the clouds, and then she was home, enveloped by a warm, protective connection that knew no physical limit. And still she was giving, taking, reaching higher, ever higher; the flesh, striving to transcend to the spiritual. Lost, and found, her soul set aflame by the rapture of it all.

Chapter
Seventeen

Step, breathe. Step, breathe, slide.
Step, breathe. Step, breathe, slide.
Ricky Bouchard pushed forward, her crampons biting securely into the ice with each step she took. *A journey of 29,035 feet begins with a single step,* she wryly considered; truly that was how it was with Everest.

Where progress was measured inches and feet at a time. Where you pressed on in an inhospitable environment, with the cold, blowing winds reaching into your mouth to the back of your throat; raw, clawing, and dusting your jacket, wind pants, and gaiters with a fine covering of snow.

Ricky smiled through a pair of chapped lips. *Ah, this is mountaineering!*

Sure, it was cold, but deep in her gut she was warm. A furnace burned there, heating her limbs, processing the oxygen-rich blood that helped to make her the kind of climber who excelled at altitude. And what a beautiful day it was, perfect for making their move. Dazzling sunlight splashed down, sparkling on the blue ice and snow like fistfuls of stars thrown down to earth.

Ricky slid her jumar up the fixed rope and took another strong step. She looked ahead, following the snaking line up the steep slope of the Lhotse Face, and detected the tiny cluster of tents in the distance that was Camp III, at 24,000 feet. Still

about another hour away, at her current pace. She could easily
have made it in half the time, but was purposely moving slowly
in deference to her fellow climbers on the rope: Paul Andersen,
Kevin MacBride and Phil Christy in front of her, along with Jangbu Nuru. Directly behind her was Allison, followed by Lou Silvers. Farther back, bright slashes of color against the smooth
ice, were the Donaldsons, Jim Harris, and Pemba.

Two days ago they had moved up from Base Camp to Camp
II, to complete their final acclimatization climb. Everyone had
made it, including a panting and sluggish Patsy Donaldson and
her husband, who was not faring much better. Even Lou Silvers'
cough had returned, and it was clear that the attorney was disappointed by that negative turn of events. A cough at Base Camp
was one thing. A cough at 24,000 feet could break a rib or cause
agonizing chest and throat pain.

But there had been no rest for the weary at Camp II. After
just one day's stay, they'd left for Camp III this morning at 5
a.m. sharp. They would sleep at the high camp for just one
night, but it was a critical step in the overall acclimatization process. A climber who was unable to overnight at Camp III would
not be allowed on the summit push. That was an ironclad rule on
Everest.

The Camp III trek was a test of sorts for the climbers, and it
took its toll. Ricky had seen how slowly everyone had been
moving this morning when they'd broken camp, gasping for
breath in the meager air. She'd noticed the redness of Lou's eyes
before he'd put on his goggles, telltale signs of broken blood
vessels. They all were feeling it, the effects of the thin air: the
coughing and headaches, the cracked skin and bleeding fingers.

You forced yourself to eat and drink, although you had no
appetite, and then the food sat trapped in your stomach like a
leaden rock, your body unable to supply enough blood and oxygen to properly digest it at altitude.

And then there was the cold.

It had been zero degrees Fahrenheit when they'd departed
Camp II, and it would be even colder when they arrived at Camp
III.

Yes, it was a hard climb, and yet it was nothing when compared to what still lay in store. The idea was to give your body
and your mind a taste of what was to come. Because as difficult
as this climb was, the summit push would be the challenge of
their lives.

Ricky ran through a mini-inventory of how she felt: breathing well, hands and feet warm, eyesight fine, arms and legs pumping away with an economy of effort. *God, it felt good to be working up high again!* She'd missed that. More than she'd realized.

Step, breathe. Step, breathe, slide.

She spared a glance backwards down the steep slope, her eyes seeking out Allison Peabody's powder-blue form. A warm glow of pride filled Ricky at how well her partner was doing. Allison hadn't complained a bit at Camp II, although it had been apparent to the mountaineer how tired she'd been, thanks to the agitated, unsatisfying sleep that was so common to climbers at altitude. It had been all Ricky could do to hold her in the cold darkness of the tent, whispering quiet words to her, words she'd never said aloud to anyone before, soothing Allison's restlessness. Now, she could see that the younger woman was moving up well and had established a slow, steady pace that would get her to Camp III in a reasonable time.

The guides had taken the lead when they'd started out this morning, the idea being that they would direct the way through the ice and newly fallen snow. The clients would then, literally, be following in their footsteps. Deceptively, the first part of the climb was over a gentle snowy incline, reminding Ricky of the slopes where she'd first learned to ski, back home at Mont Tremblant.

But then they'd hit the *Bergschrund,* the wall-like divide that marked the Khumbu's upper end. She'd climbed over it a week earlier, when she'd helped Jangbu and the other Sherpas tote supplies up to Camp III. From the *Bergschrund* onwards, the slope rocketed upwards at a forty-degree angle, presenting an even more difficult challenge than before, thanks to the recent snow.

A rope had dangled down the face of the icy wall, inviting her to the next Camp, then still over 2 hours away. After a quick glance behind her to Allison and Lou, she'd returned her attention to the thin line. She'd simply reached out, grabbed it with a gloved hand, clipped her jumar to the line, and begun to climb.

Taking on the steep slope at altitude was hard work for the clients, and as Jim Harris had directed her and Paul, the idea was for the guides to stay in loose contact with them, without babying them. Advice Jim would do well to follow, Ricky thought, remembering how he'd barely gotten the Donaldsons to Camp II.

Now, even with her reduced pace, another backwards glance showed that Jim, Mike, and Patsy had drifted out of sight. Perhaps it was the angle of the slope that obscured them from view, but even so they had to be well back.

Allison was still all right, just below her, but Lou Silvers was clearly flagging, taking more and more time between deliberate steps.   Ahead of her, were the bulky forms of Kevin MacBride and Phil Christy. Since they'd hit the *Bergschrund,* Ricky had been watching the two men playing leapfrog on the rope, jockeying for position. Apparently, they were sparring over who would get to Camp III first.

Ricky was disgusted. It was a ridiculous thing to do, especially at altitude. Breathing had to have been difficult for them, so that each attempt by one to pass the other was like watching an underwater fistfight, with motions exaggerated, slowed. The foolishness of their efforts was compounded by the fact that each time, the "passer" had to unclip from the rope and step out of the trail to pass, before safely clipping back onto the line. The new snow had consolidated and glued itself to the hard blue ice at some points, but in other areas it was still loose and unstable. Either way, a slip and fall would mean a long way down, untethered. Or worse, could open a fracture line and—

Assholes!

They were at it again. MacBride this time, she could tell by his purple and white pile hat, trying to pass Phil Christy. Overstriding just outside the cut of the trail, intent on passing his friend. And he made it, too, oblivious to the chunks of ice his awkward footsteps had dislodged.

One chunk in particular, the largest, about the size of a backpack, came tumbling down the slope. Heading right for Ricky Bouchard.

Merde!

Alone, Ricky would have had no problem in dodging it. But instantly, she grasped the fact that it was following the fall line, gaining speed, and would be heading directly towards an unsuspecting Allison Peabody below.

There was no question, really, in her mind, of what she had to do. No time to call out a warning, even if there had been a way for Allison to get clear. And then it was simply a case of her own mental determination overriding the visceral mountaineering survival instincts she'd honed so well.

Plant your feet!

Brace yourself!

Ricky crouched down like a linebacker, turning her shoulder into the oncoming missile, hoping to deflect the blow as best she could, while still diverting it from its natural path.

Plummeting down the Lhotse Face with all the grace of a squared wheel, the ice chunk slammed into her, exploding, blasting the breath from her lungs and sending her spinning. Ricky felt her feet give way but she was ready, maintaining her spatial orientation despite her tumbling. She twisted her body so that she was face down, head uphill. She gouged the pick of her ice ax into the ice and snow, rolling towards its head, then pressed her chest and shoulder down on it, hard. In the same motion, she firmly pulled the end of the shaft up against her opposite hip. Then it was a matter of digging in her feet for all she was worth, and praying that she would able to self-arrest.

It was over before it had barely begun.

She was lying there, panting on the cold blue ice, while shattered, smaller pieces of the ice chunk skittered and chattered their way harmlessly down the slope.

Well, that was different.

Ricky allowed herself the luxury of staying were she was for a few precious seconds, sucking air and trying to figure out just where the hell she'd landed. Amazingly, it was only a few meters off the trail. She'd somehow managed to self-arrest almost instantly. Hell, the ice anchors on the line she'd been attached to hadn't even been tested.

With a heaving breath, she used her ax to push herself to her feet. Ahead of her, MacBride and Christy hadn't noticed a thing, the idiots. They were continuing on, with Kevin in the lead, this time. Despite the cold, Ricky's blood began to boil. Until—

Allison!

Twisting around, Ricky saw that the young blonde was standing stock still, her hand on her jumar, halfway through another move up. She was fine, although even from this distance Ricky could tell by Allison's posture, by the look on her face, that she'd seen it all.

I am in big trouble, now.

Ricky gave what she hoped passed for a cheerful, "I'm fine" wave, and made her way back to the trail and the fixed rope. She started up the slope once more, making sure that Allison had done the same. It took her a few moments but she did, carrying on in the same, steady pace that she had demonstrated before.

The last leg of the climb to Camp III passed in a blur for Ricky. She didn't give a damn about the snow that had gotten in her gaiters and down her neck, about the crack in her glacier glasses, or the dull, throbbing pain she felt in her left shoulder, a sensation that intensified each time she took a deep breath. No, all that she had on her mind, as the small collection of red Peak Performance tents grew closer, was getting her hands on Kevin MacBride and Phil Christy.

Clients or not.

It was bad enough that they might've killed themselves, but to risk the lives of others was totally unacceptable. If they wanted to act like rookies instead of the hard-core climbers they purported to be, then they could do it on somebody else's watch, not hers.

She pulled into camp hard on their heels and unclipped from the line. She let her fury build with every step she took as she crunched past the tents whose fragile platforms had been carved into the ice thanks to hours of backbreaking Sherpa labor.

There was MacBride, sipping from a thermos of tea, laughing with Paul Andersen, while Christy was nearby, removing his harness.

"You owe me, buddy—"

Ricky barreled up behind the ex-footballer, grabbing him by the shoulder and spinning him around.

"Next time you try to kill yourself, leave innocent people out of it!"

The thermos fell, spilling its hot contents onto the ice and snow with a soft *hiss.*

"What the *fuck* are you talking about?"

"Ricky!" Paul yelped, alarmed. "What's going on?"

"I'll tell you what's going on," she said, keeping her eyes locked on Kevin. "It's about these two jerks playing king of the hill all the way up the mountain." She shot a sideways glare at Paul. "Or did you pretend not to notice?"

"Well—" He lowered his gaze to the ground.

"Everest isn't going anywhere," Ricky continued, getting in MacBride's face. "You stay clipped to the line unless you've got a damn good reason not to be."

"What's the big deal?" Phil Christy said, his voice raised, and he nearly fell as he continued to fumble with his harness in the cold. No harm done."

"No harm? No *harm*—" Ricky took a step towards Christy.

"He could've unzipped an entire fracture line and caused an avalanche with all this new snow. As it was, he just let loose with a few ice boulders. They could've taken out any one of the climbers below."

"Well they didn't," Kevin petulantly stated, doing his best to edge away from the enraged mountaineer while still keeping his ego intact.

"Only because I got in the way," the mountaineer told him, her voice dropping to a dangerously low register.

"Gee, Ricky, I would've thought you were faster than that," Kevin told her, a sneer in his voice. "Better luck next time." He turned away and motioned to one of the Sherpas that had set up the Camp. "Hey, bro, howz about some more tea?" His boots crunched in the granular ice as he made his way past Paul, with Phil Christy sullenly following him. "Goddamn hot head," Kevin muttered to the young guide, purposely loud enough for Ricky to hear. "You gotta do something about her, man!"

That's it! Ricky followed after him, her gloved hand balled in a fist.

"C'mon, Ricky!" Paul got between the tall woman and the retreating climbers, looking nervously over his shoulder. "Let it go. It's not worth losing your job over, is it?"

Ricky's radio suddenly crackled to life.

"Harris to Bouchard, Harris to Bouchard, come in please."

Losing her job. How had she forgotten that little, annoying fact? That was what all this was about, wasn't it?

For her, it was about making money.

From the clients' perspectives, it was about spending it, and getting what they'd paid for, right? This wasn't "her" mountain, not anymore. This was real estate for sale, going, going, gone to the highest bidder.

Paul had gotten it right. After all, he certainly knew *his* place. And how kind of him to remind her. She *was* just a hired hand. And what was it Jim Harris had said?

"I don't want my clients coming to me with complaints about an employee."

"Ricky?" Paul's voice intruded on her thoughts. "That's Jim."

"Harris to Bouchard. Ricky?"

Jim Harris. Her boss. Ricky keyed in her mic. "Bouchard, here."

"Ricky, can you make your way back down...here and give

me and Pemba a hand...bringing in Mike...and Patsy?"

Ricky could hear the strain in his voice. God only knew the difficulty he and the Sherpa had been having in getting the Donaldsons up the steep Lhotse slope. She turned to look back down the mountain. There was Allison, still about 25 yards out, making her way in. Lou Silvers looked to be a good 10 minutes behind her, and there, much farther down the hill, were the struggling Donaldsons, along with Jim and Pemba.

Ricky took a step away from Paul, back towards the edge of the camp. Here on the Lhotse Face they were so exposed, both the Peak Performance tents and the clusters of tents belonging to the other expeditions. The wind swept down from the summit, still a vertical mile above, whipping against the tents in a constant airborne attack. Here, there was more sky above than earth below. The canyon from which they'd just emerged seemed so distant, as though it had somehow fallen away, been blown back by the winds when she hadn't been looking.

"Ricky?"

So Kevin MacBride and Phil Christy were arrogant fools of the highest order. So what? Perhaps this was not her fight, after all. *Just keep your mouth shut, Bouchard.* She had a job to do, and it was radioing her.

Ricky took in a deep, burning breath of air, shrugging off the nagging ache in her shoulder. She stole one last look at MacBride, filing away her anger. Another time, perhaps.

She tapped her mic. "I'm on my way."

❀◆❀◆❀◆❀

It was amazing, high on Everest, how much the extreme conditions changed you in ways you didn't even realize; how eventually even the most basic niceties of daily human interaction dwindled down to nil. The huddle of Peak Performance tents was barely eight feet from the tents of the British expedition on the left, and the Japanese encampment on the right. More tents were carved into the ice ledges a bit farther up the slope, but that location, being even more exposed to the wind and the weather, was considered less desirable. In spite of their proximity to one another, the various camps might as well have been miles apart. Barely a word passed from team to team, from tent to tent. At 24,000 feet, one's energy, air, and sense of neighborliness were all in short supply.

And this was some neighborhood, Allison Peabody had considered as she'd crawled into her tent to await the return of
Ricky Bouchard. They were all stacked on top of one another, as
though crammed into an icy high-rise tenement. Tatters from
tents of seasons past littered the ground, along with used oxygen
canisters and other unrecognizable debris. *Man vs. Nature,* Allison thought wryly. Why was it that the first step, too often, was
to trash it?

Thinking of trash... Allison held her hands over the small
pressurized gas stove where she was melting snow for tea. God
knew, Ricky would need it by the time she got back.

No thanks to that jerk Kevin MacBride, and Phil "me too"
Christy.

She'd seen what had happened out there on the slope, had
watched it all unfold, frozen in place, powerless. An instant
before, she'd been mentally castigating Kevin, and not for the
first time that day, when she'd seen him make his move on the
ropes. Had stood in horror as the ice boulder he'd dislodged
came pin-wheeling down the mountain, gaining speed, seemingly
heading right towards her.

Until Ricky had put herself in its way.

No!

There hadn't been time to think, to act; her mind had barely
been able to wrap itself around what was happening when the ice
chunk had crashed into her lover, disintegrating into a thousand
smaller pieces with the force of the impact. And then Ricky had
been falling, tumbling down the hill towards Tibet, until somehow, impossibly, she'd arrested her fall.

Even then, Allison hadn't been able to move, to shout, to
breathe. Instead, after an agonizingly long minute, the mountaineer had risen up from the steep slope, shaking the snow and
ice from her clothes like an oversized Labrador just returned
from a refreshing swim. And with a diffident wave, Ricky had
continued on as though nothing had happened. *Nothing.*

Finally, half numb with shock, she'd started back up the
mountain after Ricky, her worry over the dark haired woman's
condition escalating as they'd approached camp. But she'd had
no time to assuage her fears; one minute she'd seen Ricky pull
into Camp III, and the next, the mountaineer was barreling back
down the slope.

"On my way to help Jim," Ricky had said brusquely, not
meeting Allison's eyes, and the younger woman had neither the

breath nor the energy at that point to challenge her.

The wind rattled the tent, snapping at it; all the climbers were indoors now, marshalling their strength for the return trek tomorrow. The sweet scent of the tea filled the air, its aroma stubbornly standing fast against the outside elements that threatened to sweep it away. Allison sat half tucked into her sleeping bag, her arms wrapped around her middle, trying to stay warm.

Ricky, where are you?

As if answering her silent call, the tent shuddered as the vestibule was zipped open.

Grunts, as heavy climbing boots and crampons were removed and set aside.

And then there was a smaller gust of wind as the inner flap parted, and a dusting of spindrift wafted in, along with one very exhausted looking mountaineer.

Ricky collapsed on her back onto the floor of the tent, breathing harshly, pawing at the zipper of her jacket.

"Here, let me." Not waiting for a response, Allison crawled to Ricky's side and helped relieve the mountaineer of her outer layer. "You sure you wouldn't be warmer if—"

"I want it off." Ricky's voice was hoarse, her mouth set in a grim line.

"Okay." Allison eased it off the taller woman's shoulders, stealing a furtive glance at her partner's features.

Noting the weariness in her face, the cheeks burnished to a golden hue by the wind and sun; the raccoon-like whiteness tapering around the rim of her eyes where the glacier glasses had shielded them, framed the vivid blue chips of ice that stole her breath away every time they glanced her way.

Ricky lay back down, focusing her eyes on the roof of the tent.

"How are Patsy and Mike?" Allison began to pour a mug of steaming hot tea.

"They're in."

The tension was rolling off of Ricky in waves—dangerous, unpredictable. Once, that threat might have scared Allison off, sent her scurrying for cover, but not now. Now, she recognized the symptom for what it was: Ricky was hurting. And by God, she was going to help her, whether the mountaineer liked it or not. Allison reached out and gently placed the mug in her hand. Ricky accepted it, but made no move to drink.

"How are you?" Allison asked, her voice soft yet clear

above the moaning winds.

"Fine." Blue eyes continued to glare at the domed roof.

"Ricky, what you did today—"

"I'd do again." Ricky violently cut her off and pushed herself to a sitting position. "But it shouldn't have happened at all," she said, finally capturing Allison in a smoldering gaze. "If you had been hurt, Allison, I swear to you I would have killed him where he stood."

Uh-oh. There was no doubt in Allison's mind, by the look of fierce determination on her partner's face, that she'd meant every word of that vow. For a brief instant, she was afraid for Kevin MacBride. And then, "It's okay, Ricky," she soothed, knowing the last thing she should do right now was to match the mountaineer's negative intensity. Sure, MacBride and Christy were worthless losers. The fact that she happened to agree with Ricky in that regard would not help to calm her down right now.

"I–I was just more worried about you," Allison continued, slipping off a thin polypro glove so she could reach out and caress Ricky's cheek. "If anything had happened to you—" She felt her throat cinch shut, cutting off her words.

"Look," Ricky closed her eyes and sighed, leaning into Allison's touch, releasing some of her anger, "I'm probably going to be fired."

"No, you're not."

"It's okay," Ricky said tiredly, reaching for Allison's hand and chafing it with her own. "I gave MacBride a piece of my mind when I got into camp and, well," she lowered her eyes, "I think that's gonna be it."

"No, it *isn't*," Allison said more firmly, pulling her hand away and lifting Ricky's tea. "Here. Drink this. And I don't think you'll have anything to worry about from Mr. 'Asshole' MacBride."

"Allison..." Ricky's eyes narrowed, as a not-so subtle realization dawned upon her. "What have you done?"

"Drink."

"Allison!"

"Drink!" Allison shooed the mountaineer into taking a sip as she poured another mug of tea for herself.

Warily, Ricky swallowed a mouthful of the hot drink as instructed. "Now tell me."

"Kevin is a sorry excuse for a man, much less a climber," Allison began, her face growing flushed, "and his buddy isn't much better."

"You won't get any argument from me."

"Well, he was shooting his mouth off when I got into camp." Allison bit her lower lip. "About you."

"I figured as much." Ricky put her mug down and lightly rested her hand on the blonde's knee. "It's just a matter of time until he tells Jim and—"

"No, he won't," Allison blurted out, plunging into her story. "I took a hang gliding class at Lake Havasu last year. One of the guys in the group was Davis Mumford. Maybe you've head of him?"

"No. Should I have?"

"He writes an outdoors and adventure column for the Boulder Sentinel. Sometimes the national syndicates pick it up."

"MacBride and Christy are from Boulder," Ricky noted, her brow furrowed.

"Yeah, well, Davis and I got to be pretty good friends and...and anyway, I decided to hit those two jerks where it hurt." She paused for dramatic effect. "Right in their over-inflated egos."

"Allison!" Ricky's eyes flew open in alarm. "What did you—"

"The 'Ugly American,'" Allison intoned, her hands framing the words, "'Climbing Higher and Stooping Lower Than Ever Before. Starring Kevin MacBride and Phil Christy.'"

"You didn't," the mountaineer groaned.

"I most certainly did!" Allison was on a roll now. Just the memory of how arrogantly Kevin had assured her he would get Ricky fired, made her blood boil. "The way they've scattered their garbage over half the mountain. The lack of respect they have for the Sherpas. Their utter disregard for the traditions of Everest and what it represents."

Ricky began massaging her temples. "Allison..."

"I'm not done yet!" Allison shot back. "The cruel bets they have going—can you imagine—some poor girl having to marry Phil as a result?"

"It's Kevin's sister," Ricky said dryly. "Maybe they deserve each other."

"And then there's the danger they are to themselves and others," Allison continued on. "Not to mention the avalanche they caused."

"It wasn't an avalanche," the mountaineer muttered. "Not

really."

"Oh, and did I mention," the corner of Allison's mouth turned up in an withering smirk, "how especially...close...Kevin and Phil seem to have gotten during this climb?"

- "No..."

"*Yes!*" Allison crowed, feeling quite proud of herself.

"You shouldn't have," Ricky slowly shook her head, her face a mixture of irritation and gratitude. "I can fight my own battles."

"I know you can," Allison told her, her green eyes shining, "but this is my fight, too." She recalled with some satisfaction the look of abject fear on Kevin MacBride's face when she'd threatened to expose his personal shortcomings to his hard-core Boulder buddies, not to mention to the rest of the Colorado climbing community.

Unless he backed off of Ricky Bouchard.

Permanently.

"We need you on this climb, Ricky." She hesitated, and then spoke the words her heart knew to be true. "*I* need you."

Wordlessly, Allison patted her lap, beckoning the mountaineer to her. She could see a flicker of hesitation in her eyes, and then Ricky surrendered, leaning back into Allison's embrace with a bone-weary sigh. Small hands reached under the thick fleece of the tall woman's sweater, and began to gently massage the tightly corded muscles of her neck and back.

Allison watched Ricky fight a losing battle, saw how heavy lids gave in to exhaustion and promptly closed.

"I need you, too," Ricky murmured. "So very...very much."

Chapter
Eighteen

The next morning the Peak Performance team descended like sleepwalkers from Camp III to Camp II, torturing a whole new set of leg and back muscles on the downward trek along the steep Lhotse Face. The weather was fair, which helped, but even so it was all they could do to fall into their tents, eat and drink what they could, and wait for the next morning to arrive.

Allison doggedly continued to make entries into her journal, and Ricky marveled at that. After a hard day's climb, one that required hair-trigger instincts of action and reaction together with a single-minded sense of focus, she herself preferred to let her mind go blank and wander...to recharge. But not Allison. The younger woman loved to read, to write, and to talk; and Ricky had been pleasantly surprised that the most minimal of responses on her part, the occasional grunt "yes" or "no," seemed to infinitely satisfy her partner.

The descent from Camp II to Base Camp the following day had been uneventful, save for the usual gut-churning thrill of the passage through the Icefall. To Ricky's trained eye it was plainly evident how the terrain of the Khumbu changed from day-to-day: an extra ladder lashed on for stability here; a fragment of a rope dangling limp next to a new line there, replaced where a *serac* had come crashing through.

All indications that in this high altitude world, any sign of stability at all was illusory, a trick of the mind one played on one's self just to be able to make it sanely through the day.

Ricky Bouchard thought differently. She welcomed the changes. Counted on them, in fact. It was the uncertainty itself in her life that had become the constant that she needed, craved.

And then along had come Allison Peabody. Holding out a hand to her like a lifeline, drawing her in from the stormy seas. Ricky had reached out and taken hold, had taken that chance; and now she had no intention of ever letting go.

The team had immediately collapsed into their tents at Base Camp, exhausted beyond all measure, but infinitely relieved to be back down in the thicker air. The plan called for five days of much needed recovery at BC before that final summit push. *Hell, twice that amount of time wouldn't be enough for the Donaldsons to get back on track,* Ricky worried, *but it would have to do.* Jim looked spent, too, she'd noticed, but that wasn't surprising, considering all the extra work he'd had climbing with Mike and Patsy.

On the Camp III trek, it had finally been at Jim's insistence that she'd been summoned back down the hill to assist him and Pemba with the couple; Mike had been adamant beforehand, she'd later heard, that they didn't need or want the extra help.

As it turned out, it had taken several hours just to travel that last 700 feet or so into camp, with Patsy barely taking a step or two every half minute. There was no way—no way that she could make the summit in that condition; Mike either, for that matter. But it was ultimately Jim Harris' call, Ricky knew, his responsibility. At $70,000 dollars per client, it was up to him to turn them back.

Lou Silvers hadn't moved from his Base Camp tent since they'd returned, hoping to shake his "Khumbu cough" once and for all. Of Kevin MacBride and Phil Christy, Ricky had seen very little and that was just fine by her. They'd kept their distance, including the time earlier this morning when the mountaineer had watched MacBride actually turn around and head in a different direction when he'd seen her coming, a stricken look marring his face.

Good.

It still bothered her that Allison had taken him on, threatening him. After all she was a big girl and used to standing on her own two feet. But privately, well, she had to admit that she was touched by Allison's gesture. No one had ever done that before

for her, stood up for her, and it felt pretty damn good. The prospect of Kevin MacBride and Phil Christy being exposed in the
Boulder media as loutish climbers with nebulous sexual prefer-
ences was simply an added bonus.

Ricky's boots crunched across the moraine as she made her
way towards the supply tent. These next few days at Base Camp
would be a recovery game, a roll of the dice to see if your body
still had what it took to get you to the top of the mountain. And
it would be a waiting game, too, with climbers keeping one eye
lifted towards the summit plume, and another locked on the
weather reports, biding time until the weather window made an
appearance.

Now, during the down time, was when you checked on your
supplies, making sure you had everything in place for the final
push; when you tested and re-tested equipment, knowing that all
it took was a snapped strap on your crampon or a balky seat harness to stop your summit attempt dead in its tracks.

During that same time, Sherpas up high would be fixing the
final ropes to Camp IV and above, all the way to the Hillary
Step. The lines were an unnecessary convenience for Ricky; she
believed a true mountaineer should do without, however she also
knew there was no way the majority of the clients on any of the
commercial expeditions could make the summit without the
fixed ropes.

"Halloo, Ricky!"

It was Jangbu Nuru, gliding confidently over the scree as
though he were a lithe ballet dancer moving on a snow-white
stage.

"You hungry?" His weathered face creased into a smile as
he gestured towards the Sherpa dining tent. "Lopsang make big
promise—ramen soup!"

"Maybe later," Ricky told him, knowing Allison was still
napping in her tent. "I've got some things I want to check out
over in the climbing supplies." She turned and studied the great
icy massif rearing up behind them. "You gotta be ready. You
never know when the mountain's gonna give us a break, eh?"

"When the time is right, she let us know," the sirdar chuckled, pushing back on the floppy black and red pile hat perched on
his head.

"You sure about that, my friend?" Ricky teased him, knowing how seriously the Sherpas took the relationship they had
with the Mother Goddess. No Sherpa climber worth his yak but-

ter would make a move up the mountain unless the signs were
most auspicious.

"Listen to your mother, Ricky," the wiry little man chided
her as he continued along his way, giving her achy shoulder a
firm clasp as he went. "Listen to your mother."

My mother.

Ricky stepped into the supply tent, her thoughts spinning.
Here, in this land of rock and snow and ice, it had been weeks
since she'd last seen anything green, caught the scent of honey-
suckle on the wind, felt the thickness of lush, verdant grass
pushing up beneath her bare feet. Her hands found a loose
length of rope, and she idly began to coil it up, looping it around
her bent elbow and hand, even as her mind drifted thousands of
miles away.

It was May in Val-David. And she knew what her mother
would be doing now, as she had done every May ever since
Ricky was a little girl: planting flowers in the small garden she
kept at their home.

Ricky had paid it no mind, had never taken the time to
appreciate it; it was simply something mothers, her mother,
always did. Perhaps in Marie Bouchard's case, it was a visual
extension of her artist's eye—the colors, the shapes, the variety
of the flowers.

Every year Marie would carefully order a selection of seeds,
cultivating the flowers first as small seedlings indoors, a conces-
sion to the abbreviated Canadian growing season. By the time
May arrived, and the worst threat of a late frost had passed,
Marie was ready to transplant them to the nutrient-rich bed she'd
carefully prepared close to the house and a safe distance from
the pond behind their home.

Not that Ricky had ever cared a whit. She was always too
busy to pay much attention, hieing off to the mountains with
Jean-Pierre every chance she could get. Sure, the flowers were
nice to look at when they bloomed, if you went for that sort of
thing, but she never could understand why each year her mother
insisted on planting only annual flowers, doomed to die at the
end of each flowering season. And so every following year her
mother had to start from scratch, an inefficiency Ricky never
would have tolerated for herself.

Long after she had left home to seek her destiny among the
highest peaks of the world, her mother continued her solitary
pursuit, her husband, Andre, knowing well enough to keep his

distance. Alone, she patiently toiled, breathing buds to life, nurturing them, and sending them to the compost bin when their all-too-brief moment in the sun was gone.

Until that one spring, a few years back now, when Ricky and Jean-Pierre had stopped over in Val-David before heading west to the Canadian Rockies. This, after wintering in Argentina, when it had been the best time of year to do some climbing there.

In spite of the usual tensions with her father, it had been good to be home. To allow her mother to cook her favorite meals for her. To take long walks into the hills near her home where she'd first honed her craft. To sleep, warm, in a child's bed in her childhood room, capturing, if only for a moment, fleeting remembrances of the hopes and dreams that child had once had.

Ricky had always been an early riser, but she supposed that was something she'd learned from both her parents. And so, when she arose on this particular morning, her father was already gone, off to his dentist office in town, and her mother was nowhere to be found. Not in the kitchen, the den, or in the sunny loft she'd appropriated as her artist's studio.

Puzzled, Ricky had stood by the kitchen counter nibbling on a brioche, when she'd heard the schrrrpt! *of a trowel slicing into rich loam, turning it over.*

"Bonjour, Mama!"

"Bonjour, Veronique!"

Marie Bouchard was on her knees, protected from the dew-covered grass by a small quilted pad. Lined up beside her were at least two score seedlings, sitting pertly at attention in their tiny pots. Ready at last to take that final, permanent leap into the great outdoors, after a week of hardening off for a few hours each day on the rear patio.

"Papa is gone, eh?"

"Yes." Marie rubbed at her forehead with the back of a gloved hand. "He went in even earlier today than usual. The Tocchet boy...he had a toothache that worried your papa."

"Ah."

Marie returned her attention to her flowerbed, alternating between the trowel, a hand fork, and a small spade as she began to transplant the flowers to the garden bed. Each year, the flowers and design were different, Ricky was aware enough to at least notice that. She wasn't quite sure how her mother did it; like clockwork the flowers would rise up from the earth each spring, a boisterous, sweet smelling display of color and life.

"Where is Jean-Pierre this fine day?" Marie reached for another potted seedling.

Ricky restlessly shuffled her feet and leaned against the porch railing. "He went with his father to Montreal for the day."

"Ah," Marie intoned, sounding very much like her daughter had just a moment ago.

Her mother returned to her digging, her classic, patrician features somehow looking right at home amongst the wild mountains of the Laurentians; here with a smudge of dirt on her cheek and a tight chignon that was fighting a losing battle against the gentle breeze that slipped down from the hills.

Ricky lifted an eye towards the sun in the eastern sky, and regarded it carefully. It was still early, and a long day stretched out ahead of her where she had nothing planned and nothing much to do. Jean-Pierre had abandoned her, and over the past week she'd tramped her way along every trail to be had within a 20-mile radius of her home.

Maybe today was the day to simply relax. To take it easy. And yet, inactivity to Ricky Bouchard was anathema. If she had to stay here all day, cooped up with her mother, doing nothing, she was certain it would drive her mad.

Her eyes traveled back to the flowerbed. "There are a few weeds over there, you know," she pointed to the far corner.

"So there are," Marie calmly replied.

"I suppose I could get them for you, while you're doing that...stuff." She gestured at the air dismissively.

Marie lifted her blue eyes to her daughter's and studied her carefully, the expression behind those eyes, unreadable. Finally, she nodded. "There's an extra pair of gloves inside—"

"I don't need them," Ricky said quickly, pushing away from the porch and striding over to the garden. She made quick work of the weeds, tossing them in a small pile to be discarded. Then she sat back on her heels and rested her dirtied hands on her thighs, casting a glance towards the potted seedlings.

"So, what do you have there?"

A look of faint surprise crossed Marie's features as she regarded her daughter curiously. "Well," she cleared her throat, "these taller ones are snapdragons. They'll be pink, yellow, and wine-colored." She then pointed with her trowel to another grouping of seedlings, smaller than the first. "These are pan-

sies." Some of the tiny flowers had already started to bloom in yellow and white, scarlet and blue; their petaled heads waving lightly in the breeze like society matrons in their bonnets.

"And over here," she directed Ricky past the pansies, "are my zinnias. They won't bloom until later, after the rest of this lot, and they don't tolerate frost well, but," her mother sighed wistfully, "they're so beautiful. I've simply got to have them."

"You were going to put those zinnias...where?" Ricky wanted to know, not quite allowing herself to catch her mother's eye.

"I'm going with the rose, a bit of yellow, and the white variety this year," Marie said, with just a hint of nervousness in her voice. "So...because of that, and their height you see—I thought I'd use some in the back, and here," she held her arms out to the sides, "as a border."

"Sounds good to me." Ricky shrugged, grabbed a hand spade, and began to stab it into the earth.

"Non, non, non!" Marie cried out, the horror plain in her voice.

Ricky froze. So, she'd done something wrong.

Again.

Well, that was what she got for even trying.

And she let herself feel the hurt, the pain, as the child she would always be in her mother's eyes.

"What I mean is," her mother said haltingly, reaching out to place her gloved hands on Ricky's own dirtied fingers, "...let me show you."

Ricky beamed, the hurt kissed away.

"You want to dig a hole, yes, big enough for the plant roots to be below the surface level of the soil, but not too big," Marie told her, reaching for a potted zinnia. "And we'll water the flats of the baby flowers and let them sit a little bit before we plant them, eh?"

"Okay," Ricky said, reaching for the watering can behind her mother.

"Here, look at this snapdragon," Marie explained, lifting a seedling that was ready to be planted. "You must gently loosen the root ball, here, like this." She took Ricky's hand, guiding it towards the seedling. She let her hold it, cupping her fingers around it and delicately working them into the small globe of dirt and new growth. "This lets the roots spread into the soil as the flower grows. You see?"

"Yes," Ricky said softly. *"I see."*

And then they had been off, the minutes quickly turning into hours, digging, planting, and watering.

And talking.

About everything...and nothing.

Simply enjoying one another's company; two grown women who happened to be mother and daughter.

Not until the sun started to slip towards the west, and the last potted flower was safely put to bed in its new home, did Ricky and her mother stop their work.

"Well, that was something!" Marie Bouchard said, pushing herself up to her feet with a groan. *"I'd say we've earned a break, wouldn't you?"*

"I'll make the iced tea," Ricky said, grinning through the splotches of dirt on her face.

"Wash your hands first!" her mother warned her, a sparkle in her sky blue eyes.

"Yes, Mama." Ricky laughed easily and ambled back towards the house.

Later, sitting on the porch overlooking the garden, Ricky turned to her mother, the woman who had given her life and yet still, in so many ways, remained a mystery to her. *"Mama, why do you do this?"*

Marie Bouchard knew very well what her daughter meant. She took a sip of her tea and thought about the question, wiping her lips with a napkin before finally answering.

"I suppose I first did it as a way to tame this...wild place," she said. *"And the growing season here is so short as it is, what with the frosts lingering in the spring and coming so early in the fall. I suppose I wanted...needed, for that brief period of time, something to look at, a thing of beauty, that was mine."*

"You don't get that from your painting?" Ricky was confused, thinking of all the beautiful works her mother had created over the years: landscapes of Val-David, scenes of the country life, of country people.

"No, you're right, I do," the older woman said, gazing thoughtfully at the seedlings. *"But that's more of a certainty. What becomes the final product is all up to me. I have the control. But out here,"* she lifted her tea towards the garden, *"there is uncertainty, in terms of the work. Will it survive? Will the frost come too soon? And then there are the insects and disease to worry about, and maybe even with all that, a storm will come*

up and destroy everything in the end." She paused, her classical profile backlit by the late afternoon sun. "Being able to create, to accomplish...in spite of all that..." She shook her head. "I have to have it. For myself." She turned to Ricky, probing her with her eyes. "Can you ever understand what this old woman is trying to say?"

"Yes, Mama," Ricky answered, understanding only too well that need which drove her mother. "I can. But why," she wanted to know, "why plant only annuals? They're just going to die anyway, and the next year you've got to start all over again— from scratch."

"You've answered your own question, Veronique." Marie reached out and awkwardly patted her daughter's hand. "A fresh canvas, n'est-ce pas? Another chance to start anew."

They sat there on the porch drinking their tea, watching the sun sink lower and lower, breathing in the sweet scent of freshly turned earth that lingered in the air.

Before the magical interlude ended, before they each retreated back into the comfortable emotional distance that time, hurt, and misunderstanding had stretched between them, Marie Bouchard allowed her heart to speak.

"Thank you...for today, Veronique."

Ricky swallowed hard, but did not respond. I will not cry, *she told herself, even as a tear sprang to her eye.*

"Wherever you go...every time I look out there, I'll think of you...and this day and...and how much I love you, mon petite fille."

"I'm not little," Ricky retorted, feeling a bit embarrassed now, a fisted hand wiping the tear from her eye.

"You'll always be my little girl..."

Blinking, Ricky found herself back in the supply tent, a half-coiled length of rope around her arm. It couldn't be that she missed her mother, could it? How was that possible, especially after the way she'd left things with her, and her father, too? And yet, how else to explain the sudden pang of heartache? Maybe it was just that she felt the loss of a relationship with Marie that she'd experienced only snatches of over the years, and now was wishing had been something more.

Or maybe...maybe being with Allison had helped to shine a light on other parts of her life, as well. Maybe with Allison, she saw that there could be more, and that she was deserving of it.

And maybe...maybe there was a way she could go home again
one day to Val-David, with Allison Peabody by her side, and
make things right.

Maybe.

But first things first. She had a mountain to climb.

Oh, Mama, Ricky thought, as she grabbed at another length
of rope, *if you could see your little girl now!*

❈ ◆ ❈ ◆ ❈ ◆ ❈

"I don't know about this, Jim." Sandra Ortiz said dubiously, as she continued her examination. Her eyes went sightless
as she lifted her stethoscope and listened intently. An uncomfortable looking Jim Harris sat on the exam table in the medical
tent, his flannel shirt unbuttoned. Without comment, Sandra
moved the chest-piece of her stethoscope to the upper left quad-
rant of the team leader's back. "Deep breath."

The big man complied, sucking in a deep breath of air and
then releasing it.

"Another." The physician moved the stethoscope to the
right.

Jim Harris drew in another breath of air, coughing this time
as he exhaled, the skin beneath this tan and beard noticeably pal-
ing.

Frowning, she removed the headset from her ears and let it
drape loosely around her neck. "Push up your left sleeve for
me."

Dr. Ortiz wrapped a blood pressure cuff around his arm,
pumped it up, and released the valve with a *hisss.*

"It's high." She removed the cuff.

"Hey—high altitude, high B.P. What can I say?" Jim
grinned, rolling down his sleeve.

"You can button your shirt now." Her mouth set in a tense
line, the young doctor made several notes in her chart, her pen
scratching noisily across the paper.

Finally, she lifted her eyes to the waiting team leader. "I'm
telling you, Jim, I don't like this at all. You've just been pushing it too hard."

"Sandy," Jim sighed, barely containing his annoyance,
"we've been over this before. I'm trying to climb Mount Everest
here, or hadn't you noticed. We've *all* been pushing it too hard."

"But you've got to be extra careful, especially with

your...condition," she reminded him, moving closer to where he sat on the examining table. "And it doesn't help that your pulse-ox has been dropping through the floor, too."

"Dammit, Sandy!" The veins in Jim's neck stood out as he pushed off of the table and hopped to his feet. "I've got a business to run here! And it's *your* job to make sure that I can continue to do that."

"I'm doing what I can," the doctor insisted, trying to calm him down. Losing his temper was the last thing he needed right now. "You know that, Jim."

"Yeah, well, once the word of this expedition gets out," Jim grabbed for his jacket, "and we hit our 'summit numbers,' I won't have to worry about this anymore. The reputation of the Peak Performance Adventure Company will speak for itself." A sudden cough cut him off and left him choking and gasping. His brown eyes burned into Sandra, daring her to come back at him.

Swallowing her pride and her better judgment, she did not.

"And then," the team leader sputtered, recovering, "I'll be able to hire the top guides in the world to do this babysitting shit for me. People like Paul Andersen again, or maybe Rolf Knowle, or even that guy the Brits are using. And I won't have to put up with a boatload of attitude from people like Ricky Bouchard again, either!"

"Easy, Jim," Sandra Ortiz said, her voice low. She moved next to her agitated employer and began a one-handed massage of his back. *Distract him.* "It'll happen. I know it will. But in the meantime you've got to take care of yourself. Let other people shoulder some of the workload for you."

"You're right," Jim sighed, leaning into her, allowing some of the tension to leave his body. "As usual." He smiled faintly at the smaller woman, with just a hint of a sparkle in his eye.

Sandra blushed. "Okay, then." Her mouth quirked in a half-grin. "Dismissed." She started to turn away, and then stopped. "Oh, Jim, about the Donaldsons—"

"Don't worry about it, Sandy," he temporized. "I won't let them overdo it. I'll give 'em enough rope so they feel like they've made a good run at it, gotten their money's worth, so to speak, and then I'll turn them back."

"It could be too late by then," the doctor said evenly, gazing up at him, wondering how the hell she'd ever allowed herself to fall so far, so deep. "And for you, too."

"Not a chance." He grinned, slipping his arms possessively

about her waist. "That's why I've got the best Base Camp doc in the biz, sweetheart."

❀ ◆ ❀ ◆ ❀ ◆ ❀

"So, do you think you'd ever like to go back home, some-time?" Allison Peabody had finally roused herself from her slumber and made her way to the dining tent, where she'd joined Ricky Bouchard for a very late lunch.

Thinking, Ricky stirred at a bowl of the promised ramen soup sitting in front of her. "No. Yes." Another stir. "I don't know." She looked up helplessly at her blonde friend. Some-how, over lunch she'd found herself talking to Allison about her home, about her parents. *Must be the day for it.* "I mean...the way we left things with each other." She pursed her lips. "It was bad."

"Because of what happened to Jean-Pierre," Allison sup-plied, tearing off a piece of brown bread and dipping it in her soup.

"I didn't really blame them," Ricky said, placing her spoon down and fixing her eyes on the colorful tablecloth. "How could I? After all, I blamed myself just as much."

"Ricky."

The mountaineer heard her partner's voice, but did not respond.

"*Ricky!*" The sharpness in Allison's tone forced Ricky to look at her. "Listen," she earnestly continued. "You've got to move past this...this guilt. It was an accident, for God's sake!"

"Maybe if I'd been there..." The mountaineer shook her head, feeling the blooming ache in her chest that was so familiar to her now.

"You would have done—what?" Allison demanded. "Out-run an avalanche moving downhill at 100 miles per hour? I don't think so, Ricky. You'd have died too, and you know it!"

The truth of the younger woman's words resonated in the tent, empty at this hour save for the two of them. The rest of the team had long since retreated to their sleeping bags for the usual afternoon's nap.

A pot of tea simmered on a burner, hissing faintly.

The winds outside were picking up; the standard afternoon squall was on the way, ready to lay down a new thin carpet of white.

And in the distance, the ever-constant crackles and groans of the Icefall punctuated the silence, giving notice of its powerful presence.

"You're right," Ricky said at last, simply, quietly. "I would have been dead, too." She paused, gathering her strength for what had to come next. For what she needed to say, and Allison needed to hear. "For a while there, I thought that wouldn't have been such a bad idea."

A sharp intake of breath. "Ricky, no!"

"He wasn't supposed to leave me alone," Ricky said, struggling to maintain her composure. "I was supposed to go first, you see. Or else, we'd be together." A choking laugh escaped her throat. "He messed up the plan."

"I'm so sorry," Allison said, reaching out to lightly stroke the back of Ricky's hand.

"Afterwards," Ricky continued, biting back the tears, "I thought about what it would feel like to just...let go. Who would care? Who would notice? I thought it might be freeing, in a way, you know? Leaving it all behind: the bullshit, the guilt, the pain."

Allison pushed Ricky's mug of tea closer to her, urging her to drink. "Here."

The mountaineer took a long, steadying draught. And then, "I found myself taking risks." She set the mug down. "Unnecessary risks. Almost begging the Fates for something to happen. Until one day, there I was, halfway up the North Face of the Matterhorn. It was late in the afternoon and I was losing the light, and to make matters worse a storm had set in. It was snowing, and the wind was blowing so hard, so cold...I knew I shouldn't go on and yet a part of me...the bigger part, refused to turn back.

"And I was furious. Believe me when I say, Allison," she regarded a pair of compassionate green eyes intently, "you've never seen me really angry, and I hope you never do. Anyway," she swallowed, "I just started...screaming. Yelling at Jean-Pierre at the top of my lungs. More pissed off at him in death than I'd ever been in life. I just screamed and screamed...forever, it seemed like. And the winds were blowing so hard, so loud, they just ripped the words away. I couldn't even hear myself. The only way I could tell I was even still yelling, was by the vibration and the pain I felt in my throat." She paused, fingering the tablecloth. "I was just so...so tired." Her voice broke.

Allison leaned forward on the table, her eyes locked on Ricky; supporting her, encouraging her. "What stopped you?"

"Jean-Pierre," Ricky laughed softly, shaking her head in amazement. "In a way. All I could think of was how he would've told me what bullshit it was. Taking the easy way out, when I never had before." Now, Ricky found Allison's hand and took it in her own. "And maybe...maybe there was a part of me, too, that hoped to make some...sense of my life. Of what had become of it. And hoping that maybe there was a little bit of...something, that was worth sticking around for."

"So you turned around and made it back down."

"Yeah." Ricky chuckled, remembering. "What a complete idiot I was. I had no business being up there that day, solo, in the first place." Her eyes sobered. "A couple of days later," she said, "I got the fax from Jim. Asking me to come aboard with Peak Performance."

"You made the right decision," Allison softly told her. "In more ways than one. You believe that, Ricky," her firm words could not mask a gentle plea, "don't you?"

"At the time, I wasn't so sure." Ricky fixed her eyes on Allison's and found herself gazing into the other half of her heart, the reflection of her own soul. "But, I am now."

Chapter
Nineteen

Perfection.

Such a rare, extraordinary thing. A thing to be prized, to be coveted.

Days, weeks, years, even a lifetime might go by without you ever having experienced it; not once.

Unless you knew where such a thing might be found. Or, through the grace of that higher power above, had the good sense to know it when it found you, instead.

In the brilliance of a highly polished diamond gemstone.

In the tinkling sound of a child's laughter.

In a sunset off Key West.

Or in the promise of a lover's smile.

On Mount Everest, there was perfection, too, of a different sort. Visible in abundance, to the discerning eye.

In the shimmering never-never land that was the distant summit.

In the chorus of the elements: the soprano and alto of the howling winds, the tenor and bass of the grumbling glacier.

In the morning sunrise over the plains of Tibet.

Or in the promise of a weather window, sitting fat and wide open on the horizon, just begging to be climbed through; a portal to the mist-shrouded other-world.

Perfection.

Sought by many, attained by few.

"So, tomorrow's a go!" Jim Harris lifted his cup of *chang* in a toast.

"All right!" Kevin MacBride cried out, as the rest of the Peak Performance team gathered in the dining tent joined in, cheering. All the clients were there, and the guides too, as well as Dr. Sandra Ortiz, Jangbu Nuru, Pemba, and Dorje.

At this final group meeting, Jim had once more gone over the details. Who had what roles to play. How they would climb through to Camp II tomorrow, recover for a day, and carry on to Camp III.

Then, would come the final push. A pre-dawn departure through the Yellow Band, a circlet of shale-like, sulfur-colored limestone that rimmed the summit, and then on to Camp IV. But there would be no overnight stay there, not in the "death zone" of 26,000 feet and above. The longer you remained there, the weaker you became, with your body, literally, breaking down. And so, at Camp IV they would breathe oxygen, resting as best they could throughout the afternoon and evening, gearing up for a 10 p.m. departure for the summit of Mount Everest.

Sometime in the late morning or early afternoon of the following day, if they were lucky, they would be standing at 29,035 feet, the highest point on earth.

And then, they'd have to get back down.

They would need six days of good weather, minimum, to make it happen; seven, to play it safe.

It had been a loud, raucous meeting, with the *chang* flowing freely, and Ricky Bouchard, as usual, had opted to stand off to the side in a corner, her arms folded. Allison had joined the rest of the clients at the main table, sitting next to a bright-eyed Lou Silvers. "We're finally gonna do it, aren't we, Allie?" he said, fighting back a cough.

"You bet," Allison replied, smiling, catching Ricky's eye and feeling herself growing pleasantly warm under the taller woman's stare.

"Whoa—" Jim held up a beefy hand, laughing. "Before things get too out of control here tonight," a rumbling laugh sounded in his chest, "I need you good people to remember something. Up there," he pointed in the general direction of the summit, "my word is law. And if we all stick together, we'll make it together."

Kevin MacBride frowned. "But that doesn't mean the faster

climbers have to hold up for the slower ones, right?"

"We stick *together.*" Jim regarded him levelly. "There are gonna be a bunch of teams like us, all trying to squeeze through the same damn window. We do this as a team, unless special circumstances warrant something different."

"And what would such a 'special circumstance' be?" Phil Christy asked, casting a sideways look at his buddy, Kevin, unaware of the hooded blue eyes of the mountaineer boring into his back.

"Team leader's discretion," Jim said, a smile playing at the corner of his bearded mouth.

"And we'll have to carry *two* canisters of oxygen each on the final push?" Mike Donaldson had a sour look on his face. "That seems like a lot, considering everything else we'll be carrying."

"There's no other way, Mikey," Paul Andersen told him, grinning broadly. Thanks to the *chang* he'd been consuming, the young man was perhaps a bit more pleased than he should have been to deliver that piece of news. "You need three bottles of g-gas," he burped, "to get up and down."

"As it is," Dr. Ortiz quickly cut him off, shooting him a warning glare, "the Sherpas will be carrying their own O's, plus your third. There will be total of nine liters available per client. More than enough."

"And those extras will be kept for us at the South Summit, right?" Patsy Donaldson asked, her fingers fluttering nervously in her red hair.

"Ready and waiting," Jim said confidently, "for all you conquering heroes. Okay, people!" He clapped his hands twice, sharply. "Tomorrow morning. 5 a.m. sharp. Be there!"

"I'm outta here," Lou Silvers said tiredly, waving good-bye. "Catch you in the mornin'."

"Good night, Lou," Allison said, and she moved to follow him.

"Aw, sleep is for wusses!" Kevin MacBride took another sloppy drink of his *chang*. "Why, I may not go to sleep at all. Next round's on me," he bellowed, slapping Phil on the back.

"One more, bro," Phil Christy smiled weakly, running a hand through his thin dark hair, "and that's it."

Ricky looked at the men distastefully. She'd seen it before—climbers who'd had too much to drink the night before a big push, and who ended up paying for it the next day. A hangover at sea level was one thing. But to tie one on at 17,000 feet, well, the results could be exquisitely excruciating. A wicked grin crept across her face. *Drink up, "bro."*

"You coming?" Allison whispered ventriloquist-style as she passed by the mountaineer.

"Uh-huh," Ricky whispered back. "Just let me grab us some more waters and...Snickers or Milky Ways?"

"Both," the smaller woman muttered back through clenched teeth, not breaking her stride as she exited the tent into the cold night.

Ricky moved over to the snacks table and began to gather their supplies.

"How 'bout you, Paul, my man!" MacBride was trying to convince Paul Andersen to stay for one more drink. The young guide had already had his share of *chang* for the night, Ricky had observed, and then some.

The tall, lean Midwesterner wavered, and then, "Aw, what the hell. One more," he laughed, his pale blue eyes taking on a glassy hue. "But first I gotta take a leak." He pushed away from the table and got unsteadily to his feet, just as Ricky was making her way by. He followed her out.

"Need some help there, Ricky?" he asked, acknowledging the load in her arms.

"No." She gave him an arch stare. "Do you?"

"Wha— Oh, I'm *fine*," he replied, stumbling after her over the loose stones.

"Riiight. Look, Paul, why don't you just go back to your tent and sleep it off? We've got a big day tomorrow." The mountaineer had serious doubts as to whether the guide was capable of making it to the latrine in his condition, let alone getting back to the dining tent for another round. And God knew, she had no intention of escorting him to either.

"Aw, c'mon, Ricky!" he pouted, his breath pluming in the frigid air. "Why don't you stay and have a drink with us?"

"Because I'm going to *sleep*," she said tightly, continuing on her way. *What the hell. Let him freeze his nuts off if he wants to.*

"Sleep." A sniggering laugh sounded behind her. "That's not what I heard."

Ricky stopped dead in her tracks and slowly spun around. "Pardon me?"

The young guide laughed again, oblivious to the danger.

"You *know* what I mean!"

"Why don't you tell me." Ricky stepped closer, the blood pounding in her ears, her eyes two narrow chips of stone.

"You and Alllieee," Paul sang in a stage whisper, smirking. "Making the sauce!" He stirred a finger into a circle he'd formed with his index finger and thumb, using a vulgar Sherpa expression and gesture.

Water bottles and candy bars tumbled forgotten onto the rocky scree. Ricky grabbed the unsuspecting guide by the scruff of the collar and slammed him into the side of the British team's *puja* altar, sending smaller stones and prayer flags flying.

"Where did you hear that?" Ricky demanded, her voice colder than the night.

"Whuh...whuh—" Paul was blubbering now, his lassitude and inebriation replaced with sudden uncertainty and abject terror by a blur of furious mountaineer.

"*Tell* me." She shook him bodily, her head buzzing, unsure of whether her violent reaction was because of what he'd said, or how he'd said it. And thinking that either way, it didn't much matter. Because it was none of his goddamned business anyway. She would not allow Allison to be hurt by this. Not here, not now, not in this place.

Ricky tightened her grip.

"I-I don't know!" came a high-pitched squeak. "M-m-maybe it was the Sherpa who-who works with Lopsang. He s-sssaid Allison was n-never in her tent in the morning. Hell, Ricky," he wheezed, "I'm s-sorry. I never meant anything..."

Ricky took several deep breaths, reining in her galloping temper. Paul Andersen was not the enemy here, she thought. The blood-red lens covering her eyes drained away, and she was able to take in his trembling form. *Get a grip!*

"What you heard, or think you heard?" she growled, "You forget all about it, you got me?"

The senior guide bobbed his head up and down in the affirmative.

"You forget you heard it," she released him, smoothing out the collar of his jacket, "and I'll forget you ever said it. Do we have an understanding?"

"Uh-huh."

"Good." A flash of teeth in the dark. "I'll hold you to that."

Ricky turned, scooped up her water and snacks, and struck

out towards her tent.

Ignoring the splattering sounds of Paul Andersen regurgitating—and God knew what else—behind the *puja* altar.

Frozen puke and piss, Ricky considered wryly, as the pounding in her chest slowed. She let her eyes track up the Icefall, over the Cwm, and up, up towards the hidden summit. *Mother Goddess, can you ever forgive us?*

❄ ♦ ❄ ♦ ❄

Allison Peabody had already tucked herself into Ricky Bouchard's oversized goose-down sleeping bag, kicking at the bottom of it with her feet to generate warmth. *Hurry up, Ricky!* she thought grumpily, waiting for her human furnace to arrive. Trying to keep her teeth from chattering, Allison lay in her cocoon, reflecting on the day...on the weeks that had brought her here to this point.

Tomorrow was it. And she was ready, she was sure of it; never more so than she was right now, with Ricky Bouchard as her partner. Both in life, and on the rope.

Ricky...

Allison burrowed deeper into the sleeping bag, breathing in hints of the mountaineer's distinctive, heady scent. The stockbroker smiled. Ricky was such a complicated woman, on the one hand, and so difficult to get to know. Yet on the other hand, there was not a trace of guile to be found in her at all, no posturing. What you saw was what you got.

Very different from the people Allison had known back home in her world, and only now was she coming to understand that she was the lesser person for it. *Been* a lesser person, living in that same orbit among them. She could never go back to that, never. She understood that now.

No, it was high time to unclutter her life. To return to the simple things. The simple values. The simple pleasures. And to strive to become the best person she could be in the midst of all that.

With Ricky Bouchard by her side, she had no doubt she could get there.

They'd grown up so differently, and to hear Ricky tell it, hers had not been an entirely idyllic upbringing. But at least she'd had parents who loved her, and who had managed to tell her so once in a while. She'd felt the mountaineer's pain today

when she'd explained about her family and how she—and they—
had dealt with Jean-Pierre's death. Allison knew from experience that to feel that kind of hurt—still so raw—meant that on
some level you still cared a damn.

And that meant that there was still hope.

For Allison, it had been a long time since she'd felt *anything* for her parents. Confronted by their chilling indifference
day after day, year after year, coupled with the side-show aspect
of the cultured, doting family that was their public face, it had
made her blood run cold...and then finally run dry.

She was immune to it all now. Nothing her parents could
ever do or say would ever hurt her again. She'd been closed up
and closed off for so long that she'd fairly forgotten how to feel
at all, until Ricky Bouchard had stomped into her life in the airport at Kathmandu. The first emotions the mountaineer had trig-
gered in her were the ones with which she was more familiar:
arrogance, anger, dismay. But how quickly all that had changed,
and she'd been powerless to stem the tide—the grudging respect,
the growing appreciation, the love...say *what?*

Allison pushed herself up onto her elbows, startled.

No! How could it be?

Was it possible to love someone after only a matter of
weeks? That happened only in storybooks, right? Shouldn't
there be more of a "getting to know each other" period? Allison
lifted up the top of the sleeping bag and gazed down at her naked
form. *Well, I suppose we know each other well enough,* she
rationalized.

The young blonde fell back into her goose-down nest and
stared at the tent ceiling, baffled. Her analytical mind, the one
that had made her one of the best traders on the Street, began to
take inventory. *You get all tongue tied every time you see her.
And you can't think of anyone else when she's not there.*

Okay. Maybe.

*No one has ever made you feel the way she does, and there's
no one on this earth you'd rather please more.*

Sounds like.

A life without her is no life at all.

Well... An exasperated breath blew fine strands of hair off
her forehead.

*Allison, you fraud! Admit it—you fell for her the minute you
first saw her at the airport. When she played pack-mule with all
your baggage while you took off hell-bent-for-leather for the*

hotel.

At that moment, the tent vestibule unzipped, and after a moment Ricky Bouchard flopped inside, laden with water and candy bars sprinkled with tiny pellets of ice.

"Ricky!" Allison sat up, clutching the sleeping bag to her chest, grinning broadly. "I've got something to tell you." News this good, that a girl only discovered once in a lifetime or so, was simply too wonderful to keep to yourself.

"I've got something to tell you, too." Ricky set down the supplies and began tugging off her fleece jacket.

"Me first!"

"Paul knows about us," Ricky said darkly. "Or at least...he thinks he does."

"I love you, Ricky."

"Don't worry, I straightened him out." Ricky folded the jacket carefully behind her, and started to shrug out of her thick red sweater. "He's not a bad guy." Her mind was clearly back at the Britishers' *puja* altar, with Paul Andersen. "He'd just had too much to drink, I think."

Allison sighed. Boy, for such a smart person, Ricky could be a little thick sometimes. "Ricky, I *love* you."

"Plus, he's out of his league when it comes to swimming with some of the sharks around here." Ricky pulled her dark hair free and raked a hand through it, thinking. "Anyway, I told him to drop it and forget the whole thing."

"Ricky..." Allison began to look around the tent for something heavy to throw at the mountaineer.

"Boy, will he ever be a hurtin' pup tomorrow."

"Ricky!"

The mountaineer finally swung in her direction. *"What?"*

"Did you even hear a word I said?" Allison demanded, idly wondering what the signs were that someone was falling *out* of love.

"You?" Ricky cocked her head to one side, studying Allison intently. "You said..."

A twitch, and then a flicker of understanding skipped across her face. The muscles in her jaw began to work, her eyes started to blink uncontrollably, and she swallowed, hard. "You said..." Her voice was a hoarse whisper, and then the words would not come.

"I'm trying to tell you I love you, you big idiot!"

Allison instantly found herself thrown flat on her back,

completely blanketed by one joyous mountaineer. Kisses rained down on her face and neck like the unbounded affections of an over-eager puppy dog.

Not necessarily a bad position to be in.

"I love you, Ricky," Allison said again, running her hands through Ricky's silken hair. "I never knew there could be anything out there like this...for me." She felt the warmth of the taller woman enveloping her, claiming her, a beacon of light shining in the emptiness of her world. "I couldn't wait," she said, feeling the tempo of Ricky's breathing increase. "I just had to tell you. If you don't feel the same way...that's okay."

A tightness formed in Allison's chest.

She'd said what she wanted to say. If Ricky wasn't ready, well, she was willing to wait. She groaned inwardly. No matter how much it killed her. "After all, we haven't known each other long, and there's usually a 'getting to know each other' period, and—"

Fingers pressed against Allison's lips, silencing her.

"Sssh!"

Blue eyes gazed down at her, sparking with fire. "I don't know what I ever did in my sorry life to deserve you. You're everything that I'm not." She dipped her head low. "But I do know that no matter where you go or what you do, you're not getting rid of me, Allison Peabody. You're stuck with me...forever."

"Forever?" Allison croaked, scarcely believing her ears.

Ricky tightened her hold and kissed Allison lightly on the nose. "Forever. That's how it is, when you love someone."

Allison closed her eyes then, feeling the tears of joy leaking down her face, and not caring a whit about it. She loved Ricky Bouchard! And she didn't care who knew it. And by some blessed act of a higher power, Ricky Bouchard loved her back. God, she'd never felt so good in her whole life! It was simply impossible to feel any better than she did right now...she never wanted it to end.

And then she felt Ricky's hands begin to roam, running up and down her body, stroking, caressing, seeking out and finding the heat within herself that she hadn't known she possessed. Skin sliding against skin; contact.

Feeling herself helplessly responding to that touch.

Once more she was being transported, carried away, and she let herself go, every nerve in her body standing on end, begging, pleading for the release that only one woman could give her. And when it came, and she cried out with the sheer joy of it, it was only then that she realized what words had guided her there, hotly repeated in her ear over and over again, echoing down into her very soul, searing it forever.

"*I love you, Allison. I love you.*"

❋ ◆ ❋ ◆ ❋ ◆ ❋

The moonrise was only a few hours old when Ricky and Allison arrived at the official Peak Performance Adventure Company *puja* altar. No expedition with Sherpas along was without one. As for the western climbers, they viewed it benevolently as a quaint local tradition. For the Sherpas themselves, they would not go up the mountain unless a *puja* altar was properly in place. And as for Ricky Bouchard, she intensely valued the Sherpa customs, respected them, and looked forward to demonstrating that respect by witnessing to the *puja*.

Weeks ago, when the Base Camp altars had first been constructed, a lama from a monastery down the Khumbu valley had officiated at the opening *puja*; a morning-long affair where the holy man's thick maroon robes had billowed in the wind as he chanted and blessed their altar over and over, lighting a juniper fire in the hearth, and throwing rice and *tsampa* on the flames while the *chang* flowed.

The *puja* altars were very distinctive, visible from a distance—piled high with stones that were flattened by travel along the glacial moraine, and framed by tall posts festooned with many-colored Sherpa prayer flags. As long as an expedition had members climbing high on the mountain, the Sherpas kept scented juniper branches burning on the altar; an offering designed to invoke the good will and blessing of the mountain gods.

This morning it was still early, a little after 4 a.m., and most of the Peak Performance members were still trying to shake life into their cold-stiffened limbs, grab a last hot meal before heading out into the dark, or else frantically trying to cure a hangover.

A canopy of stars sparkled above, a testament to the promised weather window. The moon reflected off of the mountain and the glacier, casting a dim, unearthly glow where people moved about in shadows and half-light. Gathered at the altar were Ricky, Allison, and a barely awake Lou Silvers. Lopsang's nephew Dawa Sherpa was there; once more he would be heading up with the team as the Advance Base Camp cook. The climbing sirdar Jangbu stood at the altar, surrounded by Pemba, Dorje, and the rest of the climbing Sherpas.

There was a light wind in the air, and it was cold, but inside, Allison Peabody felt warm.

Loved.

Protected.

For the first time, not caring what anyone thought, she hadn't left Ricky's tent in the pre-dawn as was her habit. It was her life to live as she pleased with whomever she wished, and that was exactly what she planned to do.

She'd been pleasantly awakened by a soft kiss on her shoulder, and Ricky's request: "Do something for me?"

"God, name it," she'd groaned, wrapping her arms around the mountaineer's neck; immediately, she'd noticed something was missing.

And there it was, dangling in the air in front of her. Her eyes had adjusted to the dark; she was easily able to make it out—a knotted red braid.

Ricky's protection cord.

"Wear this for me."

"Ricky, no!" Allison had pushed her hand away, alarmed at seeing the protection cord off the mountaineer's neck for the first time in since they'd met.

"Please."

"Ricky, I can't! It's yours!" she'd protested. "It's supposed to keep you safe—"

"And it has. Now it's your turn." Allison had felt warm hands brush lightly against her throat as Ricky secured the braided cord.

"But what about you?" she'd said weakly, after Ricky had sealed the transfer with a kiss.

"I'll be fine. I've got this." The mountaineer had reached for her white silken *khata* and draped the prayer scarf around her own neck. "You've got one, too. Don't forget it."

And Allison hadn't. She was wearing it now, along with the protection cord, as she watched Jangbu chant and place juniper branches in the fire. An offering for good luck. The flames crackled and popped, throwing sparks up into the night sky on a plume of white smoke.

The wind lightly played with the colorful string of prayer flags, sending them fluttering. In the darkness, Allison felt Ricky's gloved hand reach for her own.

She took it.

"The Sherpas believe," Ricky whispered quietly, "that each snap of a prayer flag in the wind sends a wish for a blessing to the Mother Goddess."

"That's beautiful," Allison softly replied, overwhelmed with the simplicity, the sacredness of the ceremony before her.

Jangbu bowed and rang a small copper bell. The *puja* was completed. The Sherpas filed past the altar and Lou Silvers followed them, each one leaving a small offering or tapping the altar for good luck. Ricky and Allison fell in behind, and when the mountaineer arrived at the altar, she lifted her ice ax and lightly tapped it against a facing stone. She stepped aside and let Allison do the same.

The younger woman was mesmerized by the flames. She watched them burn skyward, imagining in the sweetly scented smoke the restless ghosts of climbers past.

Blurred images of a future unknown.

She felt in a way as though she stood on the brink of some great discovery, a testing of the mountain, and of herself.

Allison felt a firm hand on her elbow. She looked up to find Ricky intently regarding her. Her partner's eyes glinted glacier blue in the firelight, the planes of her face, half hidden in shadow.

"You're ready for this. You know that."

Allison slowly returned her gaze to the flames. "I'm ready."

Chapter
Twenty

For climbers threading their way up the arms and shoulders of Everest on the final push for the summit, the climb is over familiar territory.

They hurry along the jagged twists and dips of the Icefall like faint-hearted children taking a shortcut through a graveyard on a moonless night. And they pass once again through the vast, silken smoothness that is the glacial Western Cwm, feeling the withering heat and the effort required now, more than ever, to reach Camp II.

The Peak Performance team had been forced to stay three nights at Camp II, rather than the scheduled two, when high winds and bitter cold had kept them huddled in their tents. But this morning had dawned calm and clear, and so they, like the other teams that had been delayed on the mountain, continued over the *Bergschrund* and on to Camp III at 24,000 feet. Moving a final time up the hard blue ice of the Lhotse Face.

Each climber was a smear of color against a brilliant white backdrop: planting crampons into the ice with a strong toe-pick, sliding their ascenders up the fixed rope, stabbing the spike of an ice ax a little higher, hauling their bodies closer to the summit one rest-step at a time.

Ricky Bouchard had been more than a little concerned over the delay at Camp II, on several fronts. First, she knew that the longer you spent at altitude, the more it leached the strength from your body. Fingers and lips cracked and bled. Cuts and blisters refused to heal. It simply wore you down. After five weeks on Everest, it was not unheard of for climbers to lose up to 20% of their overall body mass.

And then there was the frightful cold.

Up high, your body refuses to do your bidding, engaged as it is in its own desperate attempt to survive. With your heart, lungs, and other primary organs clamoring for oxygen, your body reaches out to your bloodstream, but there is precious little oxygen to be found there. And so, beyond your control, the body shuts down the capillaries in your hands and feet, diverting what oxygen there is to where it is needed most. And if you haven't stayed hydrated, your thickened blood only exacerbates the circulation problem.

As a mountaineer, Ricky knew that it was infinitely better to put up with the cold...to feel it. Because that moment when you stopped feeling, when your blood pumped as sluggishly and uselessly through your system as though it were more solid than liquid...that was when frostbite set in. She'd seen more than a few climbers in her day who'd lost fingers, toes and more, to the dreaded black plague.

For herself, with her superior ability to adapt to the vertical life, she didn't worry as much, although that didn't stop her from constantly remaining on her guard. But for others, the Peak Performance clients for instance, it was a concern. Even on a beautiful climbing day such as today had turned out to be, all it took was some extra moisture inside your boot liner, and quickly a cold foot could turn into a very dangerous, crippling case of frostbite.

This day, the Mother Goddess had smiled upon them and given them good weather. But the high winds—a "snapback" of the Jet Stream over the summit—had compressed the schedules of a number of teams making their summit bids. The British team was there now, right alongside them on the icy ledges of Camp III. The Spanish New Millennium team was there too, squeezed next to the International Expedition.

And so there was a very strong possibility that there could be a traffic jam up high come summit day—thus Ricky's second cause for concern. Because the "death zone" was no place to stand about cooling your heels, the mountaineer knew well enough.

The winds were picking up again, rattling the walls of their tent, releasing the pixie-dust hoarfrost that had formed there, a result of the condensation of their breath. They'd arrived at Camp III in the early afternoon, and it had been all the climbers could do to shove their packs inside their tents and dive for the sleeping bags.

Ricky reached out and brushed off some of the frost that had fallen in Allison's hair, and let her hand linger there. The small blonde was asleep. She'd been out as soon as the mountaineer had produced the orange steel and Kevlar oxygen canisters that Jim Harris now required of all climbers henceforward. She'd patiently helped Allison adjust the rubber hose, regulator, and mask attached to the heavier Zvesda four-liter bottle. Once the flow had started and Allison had been able to breathe more freely, she'd been out like a light.

As for Ricky herself, she hadn't yet put on the hated rig. Her breathing was still fine, as she knew it would be at this altitude—no headache, no nausea. She would abide by Jim's requirement that she not climb above Camp III without supplemental oxygen. But hell, they were still *in* Camp III and, well, maybe it was a technicality but...there was no way she'd be able to sleep with the damn thing on—no way. As far as she was concerned, it took away from her strength, rather than added to it. The less time she spent on the bottle, the better.

Instead, she'd busied herself melting water for tea, and preparing a packet of freeze-dried shrimp on the small stove. It was important at this critical juncture to keep drinking, to keep eating as much as you could—no matter how much your body rebelled against it.

They'd all made it safely into Camp III, with the Donaldsons, Jim, and Pemba bringing up the rear once again. Lou Silvers' cough was raging full force, and his bloodshot eyes gave testament to the physical stress his body was under. Even Kevin MacBride and Phil Christy had moved more slowly, been more subdued, and Ricky suspected that the mountain's humbling ways were finally being brought home to the young engineers.

Tomorrow was the day.

When they moved out of Camp III, past all that was comfortable and familiar, into the realm of *Terre Incognito*—the unknown land. Oh sure, she had two summits of Everest already in the bag. But you never knew what you were going to face in the death zone. It was a journey that was different every time.

From her first ascent by the Northern Route, when she hadn't known any better—that it simply wasn't *done*, not by rugged, world-famous alpinists, much less a young rookie from Quebec. To her last ascent a few seasons back with Jean-Pierre, when they'd tagged along on a scientific expedition as expert porters, more or less, just to get another shot at the summit for the sheer joy of it.

And now...now she had a job to do. To make sure the people on her team got safely up and down the mountain. But there was more than that. Something she hadn't planned on.

Having everything to do with Allison Peabody.

In a cold, inhospitable landscape where nothing was for certain, where your life hung on the end of a tether stretching along a knife-sharp ridge, she was committed that the blonde dozing next to her would see the world, however briefly, as she had seen it: from the summit of Mount Everest. To feel what it was like to have that accomplishment under your belt, knowing that you'd done it for the best of reasons, relying on the best within yourself to make it happen.

Ricky stirred at the heating shrimp soup, her gaze still on Allison. With her bulky oxygen mask on, the woman looked like a sleeping fighter pilot.

Ricky sighed. The summit remained a vertical mile above them, wreathed in a smoky plume of condensation. There was no guarantee that any of them would make it to the top, but, if conditions were right and climbers were in good health, then anything was possible.

But health and weather weren't the only factors determining one's success on the hill.

As they'd gone higher and higher up the mountain, Ricky had kept her eyes on all the climbers, Sherpas included, gauging their *samochuvstvie*. It was a Russian term, one she'd learned years ago from a climbing friend, Yuri.

A strong Russian bear of a man, who disdained the use of supplemental oxygen as she had.

Yuri was quick with a gap-toothed smile, and sported a taste for rotgut vodka nearly as strong as his desire to bag all 8000-meter peaks.

The big Russian found kindred spirits in herself and Jean-Pierre; people who climbed for the love of it. Who were compelled to push their physical limits higher and farther...because for themselves, there was nothing else, other than that.

Yuri was long gone, swept away by an avalanche on Cho Oyu, but the idea of *samochuvstvie* had stuck with Ricky. There was no direct English translation for it, or French either, for that matter. The concept was an impression of a climber's state of being, considered along with the observable aspects of their mental, physical, and emotional state.

Blustery words of confidence and a good pulse-ox level were one thing. But a climber setting out on the challenge of a lifetime without good *samochuvstvie*, well, as Yuri had claimed, that climber was asking for trouble. Over and over again, Ricky had seen this borne out. Maybe it came down to the fact that if your head wasn't in the game, then it was impossible for your body to run the plays that got you the win.

Doing a quick personal inventory, Ricky found her own power, her *samochuvstvie*, to be in good order. The same held true for Allison, Paul Andersen and, even Kevin MacBride and Phil Christy. But she could not say the same for Lou Silvers, the Donaldsons, or even Jim Harris, who Ricky noted had been moving as slowly as she'd ever seen him.

Perhaps that had to do with the extra physical burden he'd had working with Mike and Patsy Donaldson. Ricky had seen the way Patsy in particular had been hanging on the rope, relying almost entirely on her jumar—her mechanical ascender—to bear her weight.

A jumar was a handheld, metallic device with a self-braking mechanism. Attached to your harness, the fixed rope feeds through the jumar as you hold it in your hand and push it ahead of you. If you pull the jumar back towards your body or accidentally fall, a cam grips the rope and holds you in position. In a push-pull motion called "jugging," you can make your way up the ropes, one step at a time.

In Ricky's opinion, Patsy's version of jugging today, climbing her way up the steep Lhotse Face, had only been slightly better than her attempt of a week and a half earlier. With a pace like that, higher up the mountain, she would never make it. The mountaineer hoped like hell that Jim would put a stop to it before it came to that.

"Whatcha doing?" A tired, muffled voice.

"How does a little shrimp soup sound?" Ricky watched as Allison yawned and removed her oxygen mask.

"Good." She scooted closer to Ricky, her tired green eyes taking in the cramped tent interior. "Where's your O2 rig?"

"Ah, I'll use it later," Ricky replied. *Much.* No sense in getting Allison worried over her own bias against the balky things.

"I feel so...so uncomfortable, wearing it," Allison said a bit sheepishly. "But I have to say that the gas helps. I was feeling headachy when I got into camp, and now it's gone." She yawned again, ruffling her short hair.

"Then the oxygen has done its job." Ricky knew that to be true. When climbers were flagging up high, feeling the affects of altitude, a hit of oxygen nearly always revived them. The problem was, in her opinion, that if and when that oxygen stopped flowing, they crashed physically even lower than they were before.

"So..." Allison rubbed her hands together. "About that soup."

"Coming right up," Ricky told her, carefully pouring the steaming soup into a rounded cup and handing it to Allison. "And I think I can even guarantee a Snickers bar for dessert. But first—the hot stuff."

Allison grinned. "Thanks." She took a tentative swallow of soup, shivering. "Mnnn...that's better." Another sip. "This is good, Ricky. Really good!"

The mountaineer chuckled. "It's not like I had much to do with it. Just add water and—*voila.* Plus..." she poured herself some of the soup, "we used to say that boiled boot leather would taste good up high, if it was hot enough and you were cold enough."

"Ugh." Allison's face scrunched up distastefully. "I hope we never get to that point."

"Not this trip," Ricky grinned.

"Well, if it comes to that, you can do the cooking. God knows, I'd probably even mess that up. There was a reason why I decided to live in Manhattan, you know."

Ricky took a gulp of soup. "I thought your job—"

"Nope. It was the restaurants." Allison paused, remembering. "And the take-out. Thank God for bagels and deli."

The mountaineer studied her, confused.

"I can't cook to save my life, Ricky," Allison explained, grimacing. "I hope that doesn't disappoint you."

"Nothing about you," Ricky took her hand and lightly kissed it, "could ever disappoint me." The mountaineer had no idea where the words and gesture came from. They'd simply bubbled up from a warm reservoir deep within her chest, moving easily, tenderly, to her tongue and lips.

Allison's jaw clenched, and she turned away as though the words had stung.

"Hey, what is it?" Ricky placed a hand on a slumped shoulder and was surprised to feel it trembling. "Allison?" She was worried now. God, what had she done? "Allison...I'm sorry, I—"

"It's okay." The younger woman bit her lip. "It's just that...all my life, I've tried not to disappoint." She spoke slowly, choosing her words carefully, struggling to maintain her composure. "But whatever I did...whatever I said...it was never enough."

"Oh, Allison." Ricky quickly put her soup aside and gathered the smaller woman into her arms. Awkwardly at first, and then with more self-assurance, as she felt Allison collapse into her, sniffling. "Sssh...it's okay." She felt the silken hair against her cheek, stroked the back of her head with her hand. "You don't have to 'do' or 'say' anything with me—just be you. That's...what I...love about you."

A soft, relieved sigh. "Really?"

"Really." Ricky let Allison stay there for a moment, content to hold her, to share their warmth. Then, reluctantly, she gently extracted herself. "Now c'mon." She lifted Allison's chin. "Eat up, before this gets cold." She handed her cup to her.

"Okay," came the obedient response.

"You know," Ricky drained her own cup, and reached for more of the soup, "I...I would like to cook for you, sometime." There. It was out. Blue eyes lowered, and Ricky felt the heat rise to her face. It wasn't like she was presuming too much, right? After all, the climb would be over soon. So talking about the future was fair game, wasn't it?

Allison's jaw dropped. "You cook?"

"Well, yeah." Ricky slowly responded. This was not the response she'd expected.

"Really!" Allison shook her head in amazement. "I never would have guessed it."

"Why not? A person's gotta eat, you know!" Did her partner think she was a complete domestic washout? Okay, so maybe she wasn't a Martha Stewart acolyte with a fat budget to indulge her cooking and decorating whims. But during her summer vacations in Montreal as a child, visiting Grand-mère Bouchard, she'd known enough to keep her mouth shut as she'd stood at the knee of the stern but kindly older woman.

And there she'd watched. And learned.

Even to this day, the mere taste of anything with apples in it, reminded her of warm summer afternoons spent elbow-deep in baking flour, her small child's hands rolling out the dough for her grand-mère's apple cinnamon tarts.

"It's just that you've always been on the move so much," Allison hurriedly explained, sensing the mountaineer's rising distress. "It's not like you've had a fully equipped kitchen at your disposal all the time—"

"It's not what you've got," Ricky told her, a hint of mock-indignance in her voice. "It's what you do with it."

"In that case," Allison told her smoothly, "I can hardly wait."

"You sure you want to take the chance?" Ricky lifted an eyebrow, challenging her.

"When it comes to you and taking chances," green eyes fell on her, sparkling, "I know I can't lose."

❊ ✦ ❊ ✦ ❊ ✦ ❊

One didn't conquer Everest, Allison Peabody thought, *so much as survive it.* Wearily, she pushed her ascender up the fixed roped and heaved her body forward another step. They'd been at it for hours now, hours since they'd left Camp III in the frigid dawn. Hours, too, since Jim Harris and Jangbu had turned back to that very same camp, escorting a nearly incapacitated Patsy Donaldson.

The woman had broken down shortly after they'd set out for Camp IV. The climb had started easily enough, with a short traverse for a few hundred yards over a shallow slope. But then they'd slammed right into the 50-degree ice face of the mountain, and Patsy had quickly expended what little energy reserves she'd had left.

It was probably for the best, Allison considered, despite Mike Donaldson's vociferous protests to the contrary. God knew what kind of trouble the poor woman might've run into higher up. From the occasional squawking on her radio, she understood that Jim and Jangbu had deposited Patsy safely back at Camp III, and turned around to continue up to the South Col.

Where the hell did they get that kind of energy?

And the Sherpas...all the Peak Performance team members had been climbing at measured distances from one another, as Jim's plan dictated. But it was the Sherpas who still moved easily over the ice and snow, their small, powerful bodies born to the thin air and tempered for the high-altitude world.

Allison knew she was in the best shape she'd ever been in her life, and yet this climb to Camp IV was much harder than she'd expected. She'd been on autopilot for some time now, with her eyes simply tracking from one foot placement to the next.

Step. Breathe.

Occasionally, when she rested against the ropes, she chanced a glance in front of her where the red and black form of Ricky Bouchard toiled effortlessly along the icy slope. The fixed rope played out in front of the mountaineer, leading off into the whiteness above, a Jack's beanstalk disappearing into the clouds.

Higher they moved, and Allison struggled to fight down the aching discomfort of the bulky cylinder of oxygen jammed into her backpack—just a hint of what the weight would feel like closer to the summit after a 12 hour climb. She was cold—and hot at the same time, with the brilliant sunlight shining down from above.

As she'd hit the more technical portions of the climb, through the Yellow Band and the near-vertical portion of the Geneva Spur, her problems with the oxygen mask had started. The rig had begun to fog up her glasses, and at times Allison had felt as though she were viewing the world through a foggy mist. She'd spent time and energy pulling up frequently, trying to clean them. Worse, the condensation was constantly building up within the mask to such an extent that the moisture dripped down, gathering in a cold pool that sloshed around her chin.

Ugh.

Step. Breathe. Step, breathe, slide.

The rocky, shale-like surface of the Yellow Band had been the worst; scrabbling for miniscule toe-holds with inflexible, uncooperative crampons over steep broken rock. It had been an arduous, exhausting process, trying to keep from backsliding on the loose surface, with her ice ax rendered useless on the windswept limestone.

They were supposed to arrive at the South Col around 2 p.m., and Allison knew it had to be close to that time now. But

she'd stopped peering ahead, tired of the teasing destination that
with every glance had seemed no closer. To the contrary, as her
breath came in rapid, labored bursts and her arms and legs began
to tremble with the exertion, her goal seemed to pull further and
further away.

She almost ran into Ricky before she saw her.

"Hey there!"

A strong, familiar arm pulled her up and over the last few
steps. Immediately, a fresh gust of wind hit her in the face,
stronger and more powerful than any she'd felt on the climb.

"Good job!"

Allison almost sank to her knees in relief. She'd made it.
Traveled one more step along the tortuous road to the summit.

The South Col is a cold, brutal place, about 400 yards long
and 200 yards across. Its eastern edge drops 7000 feet straight
down the Kangshung face into Tibet; the other side is a 4000 feet
plummet into the Western Cwm. Not a place where you wanted
to be wandering around if there were a whiteout, or if it were
growing dark.

Directly ahead, peering through the fog of her glasses, Allison could see some activity centered around a tiny cluster of
tents: the winds pressed in upon them, distorting their shapes;
the windward sides of them already half-buried by the blowing
spindrift. She was reminded of broken, battered kites, shredded
by the elements.

She could feel the cold now, even through the full-body
down suit she'd been wearing since she'd arrived at Camp III.
God, it was hard to imagine that in just a few hours, she was supposed to strike out for the summit. Was she insane?

"Are you okay?"

She glanced up at Ricky. The high winds and the bulky
oxygen rig could not mask the concern in the mountaineer's
voice, and Allison realized that she hadn't yet said a word. She
wondered whether she were even capable of it at this point. But
she knew Ricky was waiting...could sense her worry. And so she
forced her chapped lips together and pushed a hoarse response
through her parched throat. "Fine."

"Okay." A breath. "Get into the tent as quickly...as you
can." Ricky was unclipping her from the line, and gently propel-
ling her in the proper direction. "I'll be there...as soon as I
can...all right?"

Allison mutely nodded, wondering whether Ricky could

possibly hear her teeth chattering. She stumbled towards the tents over the rock and ice, past the discarded oxygen bottles and litter of previous expeditions, feeling like a lunar explorer in all her unwieldy gear. Through her mist-shrouded glasses, she could see Dorje waving at her, and that had to be either Kevin or Phil crawling into an orange tent.

Sleep. That was what she needed now.

And Ricky Bouchard by her side, telling her she could do this thing, that everything was going to be okay. She had to believe in that.

She had to.

Chapter
Twenty-one

Time.

Ricky Bouchard gazed at the glowing dials of her watch, and turned off the alarm before it even sounded. 9 p.m. It was Jim Harris' plan to be away by 10 p.m., at the latest, on this final push for the summit.

The mountaineer had once again foregone sleeping on oxygen; she'd passed a few restless hours dozing since she'd crawled into the tiny two-man tent on the South Col, after having helped Paul and the Sherpas make sure everyone on the Peak Performance team had made it in. Allison had barely stirred when she'd arrived; the smaller woman was that exhausted. Ricky had gotten her to drink some hot tea and down an energy bar, before she had drifted back to sleep.

And so Ricky had bundled down next to her, an arm slung across her middle, pulling her close. The *hiss* of her oxygen flowing at about a 2 liter per minute rate was barely audible above the winds rattling the sides of the tent, and the mountaineer worried—not for the first time—whether people were ever meant to climb to these farthest reaches of the earth, not completely under their own power.

But it was not her decision to make.

In just an hour or two, there would be at least thirty people clambering up the mountain towards the summit. There was at least one climber on the British team, Ricky had heard, who intended to make his attempt without the use of supplemental oxygen. But everyone else—herself included—would be on the bottle.

Ah well. If that was what it took, in theory, to keep everyone strong and functioning, she supposed she could go along with it, just this once. And if the extra gas was what it took to get Allison Peabody up and down safely, then she'd decided she would go along with it with a goddamned smile on her face, besides.

Allison.

Even at 26,000 feet, with the outside temperature about 20 below, Ricky's senses reeled at having her near, the feel of her, the smell of her. To think...that this brilliant, beautiful young woman had given herself up to her, freely, purposefully, without fear. It had rocked Ricky back on her boot-heels and thrown her completely off her game, for the first time ever in her life.

And for the last time, too.

Quickly, Ricky unzipped the tent and scooped some snow into a pot to melt for water, and fired up the stove.

Then, "Allison!" She gently shook her shoulder.

"Unnngh..." A muffled protest.

"C'mon. Time to get moving."

"Oh..." Allison slowly pushed herself to a sitting position, lifting the bulky oxygen mask from her face. "I've had better wake up calls," she grumbled.

"Does this help?" Ricky leaned forward on her knees and placed a light kiss on a pair of startled lips that had just begun to open in a yawn.

"Well..." Allison considered, pulling off her knit cap and running a hand through her tousled blonde hair. "I'm not sure." She cocked her head at Ricky. Waiting.

"How about this, then?" Another kiss, deeper this time, more intense. Ricky could feel her pulse quicken and the breath begin to leave her body, and it had nothing to do with the altitude. She reached out a hand to caress the cool skin of Allison's cheek, warming it, and felt her partner lean into her, sighing.

The mountaineer allowed herself to feel the heat of their connection, the depth, the power of this thing they'd both decided to put a name to, and let that love wash over her, knowing that in this singular, aching moment, Allison could feel it, too.

At last the taller woman pulled away, leaving them both

gasping for air.

"Ricky?" Cloudy green eyes pinned her, taking her in, and the mountaineer found herself willingly held prisoner by the force of the gaze.

"Yes?" Her voice cracked. Damn. The altitude, no doubt.

"Don't ever leave me." There was a gentle pleading in Allison's words, a wish, a prayer.

The mountaineer's heart skipped a beat. Leave? She was a part of Allison, and Allison was a part of her. She'd found a new life in that conjoining of their souls, an inner peace in that unity of being. Blurring the lines forever between where one began and the other ended. A separation between the two was impossible. And so she intended to stay right where she was, happy to no longer have a choice in the matter. She gave the expectant blonde a crooked smile and dipped her head down for a last kiss. "Never."

❈ ◆ ❈ ◆ ❈ ◆ ❈

Ricky Bouchard hating waiting. When it was time to go, you went. It was as simple as that. She had that tight feeling of nervous anticipation in her gut; she got it before every summit push, right on time. Only taking action, clipping onto a rope and digging her crampons into the ice, would put it to rest. And it didn't seem as though moving out would be happening any time soon. *Damn.* Like a racehorse at the starting gate, she hated being fenced in, restrained. At high altitude, you had to get moving and stay moving. Your very survival might depend on it.

Instead, she'd watched through the misty darkness as the other teams had set out from Camp IV, first the British, and then, surprisingly, members of the International Expedition. Only climbers from the Spanish New Millennium Expedition remained in addition to the Peak Performance team, and now even they looked ready to depart.

Once more, Ricky checked her watch. Just past 11 p.m.

Over an hour behind their scheduled departure.

The winds had died down to a soft blow, but even with that the mountaineer had insisted that Allison stay in the tent until they were ready to move out. Boot-steps crunched on the ice, and there was a soft chattering among the climbers who remained, anxious faces drawn tight with the solemn knowledge of what they were about to undertake. They nervously fumbled with their headlamps, checking and rechecking their oxygen gauges.

Jangbu Nuru, the Peak Performance climbing sirdar, along with Dorje Sherpa and Pemba, had set out earlier with the extra oxygen canisters that would be cached at the South Summit, so named for the fact that from below, it appeared deceptively to climbers to be the true summit, which was in fact still a good 300 feet beyond. Once that stowing task was completed, they would drop back and pick up with the other climbers heading towards the summit, if the Sherpas still had the *samochuvstvie* to make a summit attempt.

Being a climbing Sherpa was one thing. A climbing Sherpa who had summitted, however, could command top wages among his peers, in addition to enjoying a more prestigious standing for himself and his family in the local Sherpa villages. A sirdar like Jangbu, who had a number of summits to his credit, was one of the best of his kind, Ricky knew. They were lucky to have him.

Pemba had already summitted once a few years before, but would be anxious to add another success to his tally. Dorje was a rookie. He came from a family of fine high-altitude climbers, and would be looking to carry on that reputation with a summit of his own. In a way, Ricky envied the Sherpas their early start. Climbing behind the slower International climbers was not what any of them had planned, but they had no choice now but to live with it.

Ricky made her way towards the cluster of tents where Lou Silvers and Paul Andersen had bivouacked, along with Kevin MacBride and Phil Christy. Jim had chosen to leave behind the three-man tent he'd shared with Kevin and Phil, and instead bunk with the now solo Mike Donaldson.

"We got Mike's oxygen rig squared away yet?" As Ricky spoke, her breath plumed in the cold air. She still hadn't donned her own mask, preferring to put that torture off until the last possible moment before heading out.

"Just about," Paul Andersen told her, his mask dangling beneath his chin. He nodded towards the tent Jim shared with the executive. "Jim poked his head out a minute ago and said they were about ready."

"We gotta get going," Ricky ground out under her breath. Everyone had been moving slowly to begin with, which hadn't helped. Mike Donaldson had not had a comfortable rest, nor had Lou Silvers. Then, while they were gearing up, they'd run into a problem with some of the headlamps, finding that several of the batteries had lost some of their charge in the cold. Next it was the oxygen, taking care that everyone had the two bottles in their backpacks that they would need to get to the summit. Not to mention the radios, the toothbrush cases containing shots of dexamethasone, and the bota bags of water, carried inside their jackets so they wouldn't freeze.

Ricky adjusted the guide's rucksack she had on her back, containing the required oxygen as well as an extra length of rope, a first aid kit, extra clothing, energy bars, and spare climbing equipment. God, at this rate they'd never make it to the summit by the 2 p.m. turnaround time Jim had pegged. Lou Silvers was nowhere in sight, and even MacBride and Christy appeared weary of cooling their heels and were greedily eyeing the relative warmth of their domed tent.

"Call me when we're ready," Phil Christy muttered, his eyes dull and lifeless in the partial moonlight. With that, he crawled back into the tent.

"Yeah—me too." MacBride shrugged off his pack and pushed it into the vestibule ahead of him. And then he was gone.

For a moment, Paul and Ricky stood there, silently, listening to Jim and Mike's muffled voices. The wind slapped lightly at the tents; equipment jangled as climbers clipped carabiners onto harnesses and moved out, kicking steps into the frozen crusts of snow.

The half moon skipped in and out of the clouds; when it was shrouded, the mountaineer could see a thin line of climbers snaking up the slope, discernible only by their headlamps, their individual lights bobbing in the dark like distant ships on an endless ocean. And then the moon would emerge, casting ghostly beams of light on the summit of Everest, a siren luring the high-altitude mariners to their fate. How Ricky yearned to be among them.

"Look, Ricky...about the other night—" Paul Andersen shifted uncomfortably on his feet, turning his gaze down the mountain towards the distant valley below.

"I said to forget about it, remember?" Ricky answered stiffly. She had no desire to open up this can of worms now, not at 26,000 feet.

"I know it's just—" He lifted pale blue eyes towards her. "I owe you...an apology. And Allison too, for that matter."

"You don't owe us...me," Ricky faltered, "anything."

"But I do," the senior guide countered. "I've been something of an asshole on this trip," he smiled thinly, "and don't think I don't know it."

"Ah hell," Ricky sighed, "let's just chalk it up to too much *chang* and hanging out with the wrong people, eh?"

"Yeah, but..." The young man swallowed and then shook his head, his eyes finding his booted feet. "It's more than that. When I heard you were going to be on the team, do you know how excited I was? The great Ricky Bouchard?"

Ricky snorted. "That's debatable."

"C'mon, Ricky—you're one of the best. And we all know I haven't even made it to the top of this baby." He gestured towards the summit. "Not yet. And then when I found out I was going to be senior guide instead of you—"

"Jim knows you better," Ricky said evenly, keeping an eye on Jim and Mike's tent flap, willing it to open. "He's more comfortable with you. Believe me, I can live with that."

"Well, I couldn't," Paul said hoarsely. "And so I acted like I didn't give a damn, like I knew what the hell I was doing," he paused, "like...I was better than you. And everybody bought my act, too."

"Not everybody." Ricky flashed the discomfited climber a small smile. Not people whose opinion mattered to her, like Allison's, Lou Silver's, or Jangbu's. "Look—no hard feelings, eh?" She removed her over-mitt and offered the guide her gloved hand.

Like a drowning man, Paul grabbed at it, shaking it hard. "Thanks Ricky...thanks. It's been great watching you work. I know I've learned a lot. But even so, I'm gonna need your help today, fer sure, you know?"

"We're going to need each other," Ricky softly reminded him.

"Hey!" The tent in front of them zipped open, and Jim Harris' head-lamped, hat covered head popped out like a gopher emerging from its burrow. He took a quick look around the huddle of tents. "Where the hell is everybody?" he growled. "Let's get moving!"

❀ ♦ ❀ ♦ ❀ ♦ ❀

Two polypro underlayers. A Thinsulate sweater, and pile pants. A powder-blue down climbing suit, with matching thick pile hat. A pair of thin Capilene gloves, mittens, plus Gore Tex over-mitts.   Two pair of socks: one, a light synthetic, and another pair of heavy wool. Plastic climbing boots, heavy neo-prene overboots, and gaiters. Harness, ice ax, crampons, back-pack, plus all the other equipment the Peak Performance climbers were required to carry with them upon leaving Camp IV: an oxygen rig and 16 pounds worth of canisters. Radio. Headlamp. Water. Energy snacks.

Not too much of a burden at sea level. But at 27,000 feet plus, Allison felt as though she were carrying the weight of the world along with her as she slowly but steadily made her way towards the first landmark on the final push: the base of the Southeast Ridge.

The oxygen certainly helped her in her burdensome effort, but it by no means made the experience feel anything close to a hike on the beach. The supplemental oxygen rigs relied on a lean mix of ambient air and compressed O2, so that 27,000 feet with the apparatus on actually felt like a thick, luxurious 24,000 feet, without it. Still, it was better than nothing. So she huffed and puffed along, following the easily marked trail broken by the climbers ahead of her, tying to ignore the rub of her heavy pack as it settled against her back.

For as long as she'd anticipated this moment, as often as she'd considered what it would be like, as much as Ricky had told her what to expect, she had to admit now that she'd simply had no idea.

She was cold, tired, and each breath through the damned oxygen rig scorched the back of her dry, raw throat. Whenever the moon cleared the clouds, she didn't even bother to look up. Instead, her world was confined to the immediate space around her: digging her crampons in on the broken wind slab, the thick, coiled consistency of the rope, the shadows lurking just outside the stark beam of her headlamp.

If she did look up, she knew what she would see. The sum-mit of Everest, teasing them, moving in and out of the clouds. Bouncing splashes of light; other climbers, moving up. And, closest to her, the broad back of Ricky Bouchard, climbing with a sureness and grace that Allison envied.

This was all new territory for her, in more ways than one. She'd never climbed with oxygen before, and now between the weight of the bottles in her pack and the moisture pooling at her chin, she could feel a thin carapace of ice forming on the exte-rior of the mask.

Ugh.

God, as long as the gas kept pumping, she figured she'd probably be okay. After all, others had gone before her this way, right? And then there was the length of the climb. This was the longest final push she'd ever been on; the summit trek was a grueling night and day-long marathon.

Mountaineers had learned through experience to head for the summit at night, knowing that the winds tended to be calmer then. The objective was to reach the top by late morning or early afternoon of the following day, and then descend while there was still daylight left.

Daylight.

And just where the hell was that sun, anyway?

The sky had begun to pale against the rim of mountains to the northeast, not that Allison had much cared to notice. It was one step after the other, punctuated by gasping breaths, feeling as though there were not enough air in all the world to satisfy her need.

She kept moving because she had to.

Because she needed to.

Because she intended to prove to herself that she could climb this mountain.

And because Ricky Bouchard believed that she could.

So in spite of all the physical hardships, in her dark, private other-world, Allison had managed to find a climbing pace that she could live with. She wasn't traveling as quickly as she might have liked, but in her loosely-gaited rhythm, she'd reached a level of "status quo" with her body: she wasn't feeling any better, but she wasn't feeling any worse, either. Sure, she felt like hell, but she'd found that hell in this place was at least tolerable.

When they'd left the South Col, they'd moved up along the Triangular Face, a 40-degree snow slope that led to the Southeast Ridge. The Face was a series of gullies; lines of thin, snow-filled grooves that led up to the long ridge that stretched across the mountain to the summit.

Allison had been tentative at first, and she'd stumbled more than once in the dark, her heart jolting into her throat each time. Falling was one thing; avalanches were another. Even at this altitude, they were a threat. She would freeze in place waiting for her harsh breathing to steady, whenever chips of snow and ice, dislodged by climbers above, scuttled down the slope.

It helped simply knowing that Ricky was in front of her,

leading the way; and Allison found herself willingly plodding along. Focusing on nothing but her steps, her breathing—and that was it. It required too much energy to think or do much of anything else. She was dimly aware of the other climbers on the path: Paul, Kevin, and Phil up ahead; then Ricky, herself, and Lou Silvers next, trailed by Mike Donaldson and Jim Harris. They were only separated by ten or twenty yards each—as dictated by Jim's plan, but it may as well have been an ocean apart, for all the contact she felt with them, save for one.

The only one.

God, when all this was over...

"Where's the fire?" A voice, a half-shout, sounding through an oxygen mask. But she recognized the blue eyes sparking at her in the smear of light beginning to color the sky.

"Wha—" A strangled gurgle.

When had she traversed that last gully? Was it a half an hour, or a lifetime ago? And now here she was, at the Balcony, she guessed. The base of the Southeast Ridge. Somehow, she'd lost all track of time. No matter. With a sense of calm, peaceful disengagement, she understood that her climbing partner would keep track of it for her.

"Take a break," Ricky said to her, peering at her intently. "We've got to wait...for the others."

It was only then that Allison noticed they were not alone on the Balcony. Paul, Kevin, and Phil were there, sitting on their packs. Several other climbers were shuffling about as well, people she didn't recognize. Some were taking pictures, or stowing their headlamps. Others were gobbling down chocolate bars, or awkwardly fishing for their water bottles.

"Here." Ricky propelled her towards the side of the rocky cleft, to an area more sheltered from the wind. "Sit down. Get something...to drink," the mountaineer commanded. "You better get your glasses out now too, okay?"

"Okay," Allison croaked. A bit of a rest was just what she needed right now. "This is...the Balcony...right?" Her eyes blearily tracked around the hotel room-sized space.

"Yeah." Ricky turned around to watch the climbers inching up the slope behind her. "We're making...good time."

Allison's eyes tracked past the mountaineer's shoulder. The tip of the sun was visible now, spilling rich, vibrant colors of red and gold over the dusty plains of Tibet, highlighting the ebony hues of Ricky's hair.

So beautiful.

She just wanted to freeze, well, maybe that wasn't the right word—to hold the memory of this moment in her mind's eye forever. Ricky Bouchard, at 27,600 feet, bathed in the glow of the rising sun, a mountain goddess impervious to the earthly elements that plagued other mere mortals such as herself.

"You...okay here?"

With a start, Allison realized that Ricky was talking to her.

"Yeah," she shouted, fumbling for her bota bag.

"You're doing fine, Allison...just fine."

Allison simply nodded. She watched as Ricky turned her attention to the other climbers straggling up onto the Balcony, feeling those few words from the mountaineer warm her more than any thermos of hot tea ever could. They were just 1400 feet away now. A little under five football fields in length. Probably another six hours or so of climbing. Little by little, one step at a time, she was getting there!

A fresh burst of energy sang through the young blonde. Maybe it was the rest break, the water, or the Snickers bar she'd scrounged, but Allison was ready to give it another go. And the sky lightening around her certainly helped, too, chasing the shadows and the doubt away. She pushed herself gingerly to her feet, pleased to find that her legs felt good and strong.

At the lip of the Balcony, Ricky and Paul Andersen were helping a climber in who wore a bulky black down suit: Lou Silvers. The attorney stumbled onto the Balcony, with Paul and Ricky at each elbow, bearing his weight. But Lou shook his head, pushed them away, and fell to his knees, tearing off his oxygen mask.

"Lou!" Allison moved towards him, alarmed. Just as she arrived he vomited onto the snow, choking and coughing.

"Easy...easy now...." From out of nowhere, Ricky Bouchard produced a thermos of hot tea.

"Jesus Christ!" the attorney gasped, taking a swallow of the tea before he began hacking again. Allison could not help but notice that there were splotches of blood mixed in with the mucous now spattering the snow.

"Lou. Are you okay?"

The compact attorney sat back on the snow, placed his hands on his thighs, lifted his watery, bloodshot eyes to Allison. "Never better," he grimaced.

"Right," Ricky said, placing a steadying hand on his back as her eyes tracked to the bloody snow.

"It's just...from my throat," he huffed, "or my nasal passages, Ricky. This damned bottled...air...is so dry."

"How's your chest?" Ricky asked as quietly as she could and still be heard. Allison knew what the mountaineer was thinking. Nausea, cough, a tightness in the chest—all were symptoms of HAPE—high altitude pulmonary edema. If that were the case, Lou Silvers would have to get down the mountain as quickly as possible.

"It's okay, Ricky." The attorney took another swallow of tea, and in fact Allison had to admit that his color had improved from the pale, washed out gray he'd had when he first stumbled onto the Balcony. "I...I'd like to still give it a shot. I...I think I can do it."

"It's not my call," the mountaineer replied, glancing to where Paul was now assisting Mike Donaldson and Jim Harris. She sighed, her eyes flashing to Allison before returning to Lou. "Remember, you gotta get down." And with that, she headed over to where Jim Harris was weaving his way onto the flattened portion of ice and snow.

Allison awkwardly knelt down next to the beleaguered attorney. "Lou, are you sure—"

"Listen, Allie," he stopped her. "I want this. But I'm not...crazy. It's not worth...my life." He slowly replaced his oxygen mask on his face. "I'll be careful."

"Okay," she nodded.

Other climbers were moving out from the Balcony now, and Allison could see a string of them winding up the Southeast Ridge, towards the summit. Muffled shouts drew her attention back to where she could now see Ricky in an animated conversation with Jim Harris, Kevin MacBride, and Phil Christy. Mike Donaldson simply sat on the periphery, gazing blankly off into space as he sucked at a bottle of water. A few more loud words, and Ricky suddenly turned on her heel and came stalking back.

"Let's get your gas changed now," the mountaineer said. She ripped her own mask from her face, revealing a mouth set in a tense line.

"Ricky?"

The dark woman remained silent, instead reaching for Allison's backpack. "Let me." She began to disconnect the bottle from the gauge, and dug down deeper to produce the fresh canister.

"Uh...what was that all about?" Lou asked, choking back a cough as he moved to switch to his own fresh supply of oxygen.

"Kevin and Phil want to...to pick up the pace," Ricky said tightly, refusing to lift her head. "Take off. Jim's gonna let them."

"What?" Allison cried out, astounded, her eyes flashing angrily to where the team leader stood next to Mike Donaldson. The big man had a hand on the executive's shoulder and was speaking intently to him. Donaldson, for his part, looked completely spent. Separating...splitting up...it was completely counter to the summit plan Jim had been preaching since the day she'd landed in Kathmandu. She turned to Ricky. "Are we going...that slow?"

"No, we're not." The mountaineer finished with Allison's rig, taking deliberate care to make sure the flow on her gauge indicated the appropriate rate. "But some of the other climbers out there...higher up...are. And..." she hesitated, "Jim and Mike have been having some trouble." She cast a glance over her shoulder at the two men. "So the plan's changed."

Allison felt an icy hand reach into her chest, squeezing her heart. She wanted to get moving again. The winds were really blowing now, cutting into her like a knife. "But we three are sticking together, aren't we?" She swallowed hard, fearing the answer.

Ricky snapped Allison's backpack closed, tugging on it once for good measure. Then, slowly, she lifted her eyes to Allison's, a look of fierce determination set in her face. "Yeah. No matter what."

❈ ◆ ❈ ◆ ❈ ◆ ❈

Kevin MacBride and Phil Christy had already been moving well up the Southeast Ridge by the time Ricky, Allison, and Lou left the Balcony. A somewhat rattled Paul Andersen had been hard-pressed to keep up after the two men. "Just try to keep 'em out of trouble, eh?" Ricky had warned the young guide before he'd clipped into the fixed rope and set off up the ridge for the South Summit.

"Are you guys okay here?" Ricky had asked Jim Harris and Mike Donaldson before heading out, doubting very much that they were by the woeful state of their *samochuvstvie*.

"Yeah, get...get going, Ricky," Jim had waved her off. "See

you topside."

The mountaineer wasn't so sure about that. Mike Donaldson had been fishing in his backpack for something for the last ten minutes, and showed no inclination of wanting to get moving again any time soon. And Jim Harris, for his part, had been doing very little to urge him on. Strange, Ricky knew, considering the timetable they were all on.

"Don't tell me Patsy kept the goddamned camera," the business executive had grumbled at last, shoving his pack aside.

"I'm sure someone can take your picture up there," Ricky had offered, putting forth her best "guide" effort.

"That's not...the *point*," Mike had cried out in an almost child-like voice. "We were supposed to be the *first*...the first married couple to make it to the summit...and now...now it's all ruined!" He'd wiped at his eyes in frustration, and in a surprising lurch of emotions within her, Ricky found herself feeling simply...sorry for the man.

Mike Donaldson's objective had been clear: to haul him and his wife to the top of Mount Everest, no matter what the cost. Looking no further than what good P.R. it would be for his business. What dramatic, spellbinding conversation it would make on the cocktail party circuit. He and Patsy would have become the toast of the town and then some, no doubt about it. But when the chances of that dream were dashed, when Patsy's poor body had finally reached its limit, so too had shattered the identity Mike had shaped for himself. He was set adrift now on the jagged white sea of Everest, without a clue as to what was expected of him next. He simply hadn't planned for this.

"You wouldn't have been the first," Ricky had told him evenly. "Two other couples...made it. The last just a few years ago." She'd shouldered her backpack and motioned Allison and Lou towards the fixed ropes. "Both times...the wife never made it down."

She'd turned away and left him there, not sure whether her words had even registered. That had been a couple of hours ago. Since then, as her strong legs had thrust her steadily up the slope, she'd stopped and turned around periodically to check on the two men's progress but a snowy cornice now hid the Balcony from view.

But she could see Allison Peabody behind her, and Lou Silvers, too, as well as several climbers from the Spanish New Millennium team. Above her there were a string of bundled forms

moving along the ropes, passing one another, jockeying for position, before they got to the difficult pitches like the Hillary Step
where they might be forced to cool their heels while slower
climbers made their ascents.

The sun had continued to rise as she'd moved along the
ridge, following its gentle arc north, and now, glancing southwest into Nepal, she could see the pyramid shadow of Everest
outlined on the earth below. She'd seen it before, of course, but
never so clearly, and it simply took her breath away—the raw,
natural beauty of it all. It was for sights like this that she
climbed. They stirred her heart, gladdened her soul. She hoped
Allison had seen it; she'd make sure at their next rest stop to
point it out to her.

The mountaineer squinted above, towards the summit. The
Jet Stream winds were blowing, and the plume had lengthened
from what she'd observed at dawn, but the weather appeared to
be holding. There were a few high cirrus clouds wisping about,
a certain sign of bad weather to come in the next few days, but
they'd be long gone from the summit by then.

Step. Breathe. Step, breathe, breathe, slide.

They were about 400 feet below the South Summit now, and
still making good time. But fast approaching in front of them,
were a series of massive rock steps about 100 feet high. The
choice here was to either climb up the rocks on the fixed rope,
which required a challenging bit of technical skill, or to track
around the rock band, and risk floundering in waist-deep snow.
Ricky saw three climbers slogging through the snow even now,
and she suspected they were from the more inexperienced International team.

It was apparent that the majority of climbers were taking the
ropes, and the mountaineer silently agreed that was the right
play. In the end, sticking to your course with less ice and snow
was a lot more attractive than taking your chances in deep snow,
which at first blush might look deceptively easier. But the avalanche danger was greater, and with one false step you might
find yourself on the express train to Tibet.

Ricky held up, waiting for Allison. "Can you handle…this?"
She stuck a thumb out to where a Sherpa for the British team was
jugging his way up the rope.

"No…no problem," Allison replied, tilting open her oxygen
mask to blow out a stream of condensed water. Her eyes shone
through her glacier glasses; she gave Ricky a brilliant, frozen

smile. "That was some sunrise, huh?"

"Yeah." Ricky grinned back, glad that Allison had seen it. It was all part of the experience, and she wanted her partner to see it all, to feel it all, as she did.

A groan alerted them to the approaching Lou Silvers. The attorney was about ten feet below them, and leaning heavily on his ice ax. "I suppose..." he coughed, "that son-of-a-bitch is...next, huh?"

"If you want to get...to the summit, it is." The mountaineer held out a gloved hand to him. "Tell you what." She nodded towards the vertical steps. "You guys first, eh?" This way, she figured that if they ran into any trouble, she'd be better able to talk them down, rather than up.

"Age before beauty...I guess." The attorney slogged his way past her, and Allison followed. "Thanks." He coughed again, an extended spell, this time, before digging in and beginning his climb.

Ricky stepped in close behind Allison as they approached the pitch. She lowered her masked face down to the smaller woman's ear, so she didn't have to shout above the winds. "I'm right behind you."

Allison briefly squeezed her arm. "I'm counting...on it."

Ricky waited at the bottom of the rock steps while Lou laboriously inched his way up, and then it was Allison's turn. The mountaineer was surprised at the feelings that suddenly assailed her as she watched her partner climb. Allison's movements were cautious but true, and Ricky had to admit that it was a sense of pride she felt welling in her chest, as the young blonde ascended in the morning light.

And there was something else, too. Not fear, exactly, but rather a sense of guardianship, perhaps. She found herself mentally directing Allison's every step, willing that she take the proper placements, fully prepared to stand between her and any danger that might arise. Hell, she already had, hadn't she? Ricky thought, remembering the ice fracture MacBride had caused.

Strange.

She'd never felt this way before, not really, even with Jean-Pierre. Oh, she would have done anything for him, and he for her, but at the end of the day they were still two individual, distinct people, each content to go their own way. But with Allison, it was different. She felt...responsible for her, in every good sense of the word.

It's about time, Bouchard. The mountaineer shook her head in wonder. *Maybe, you're finally growing up.*

"Good job!" Ricky called out, seeing Allison reach the top of the steps. Another climber was coming up the slope behind her, and Ricky could see two more in the distance. Neither appeared to be Jim Harris or Mike Donaldson. Oh well. She'd radio them once she got to the South Summit. "I won't...be a minute," she joked to the startled climber approaching. With a quick snap of her carabiner, she was on the move, easily handling everything the rock face had to offer.

Halfway up, about 25 yards to her left, she saw it.

A body.

The corpse was snagged in a cleft in the rocks, a frayed length of climbing rope still attached to its harness. It was face down against the rock, but the head of hair was full and dark, blowing in the wind. It was what had attracted Ricky's attention to it in the first place. Because of atmospheric conditions at 28,000 feet, bodies didn't decompose. By Ricky's reckoning, the climber, still wearing a blue and black down suit, could've been hanging there for a week or ten years; it was that hard to tell.

It wasn't the first body they'd passed on this final push; Ricky knew they'd gone by several others in the dark, knew from prior experience and from stories the Sherpas told, of where some ill-fated climbers of Everest lay. She continued on, silently grieving for the man, wondering whether Lou or Allison had seen him, too. It came down to the fact that the climber had made a choice.

As they all had.

Knowing they each must live or die as a consequence of that choice.

It was important to keep that in mind, up here. There would be no more *chang* and poker games as there had been at Base Camp. In the death zone above the South Col, it was a serious business. A deadly business. The deceased climber hadn't intended to remain here, dangling at 28,000 feet forever. But something had clearly gone wrong. Something he hadn't counted on. Or maybe he had, but in the end had been powerless to stop it.

Climbing...climbing was about life. About playing full out, and never looking back. About knowing that you were only as good after all as the strength of the rope you hung from, and the faith you had in your partner to back you up.

If one...or the other failed...well.

Ricky Bouchard had no intention of becoming a photo op on the Everest Body Count tour.

With a final boost she was over the final ledge, and on the last of the snowy ridges leading to the South Summit. The view was clear now of the remaining obstacles ahead of them: the snowy trek to the South Summit, the Cornice Traverse to the Hillary Step, and the last bit of knife-edged real estate leading to the true summit.

Allison was leaning on her ice ax, catching her wind, but Lou Silvers was sitting down in the snow. He'd once more removed his oxygen mask and was coughing and gagging. His face had taken on a bluish hue, and again the mountaineer noticed splotches of blood in the snow. The summit was still another three to four hours away, with the most difficult pitch—the dreaded Hillary Step—still to come.

Unclipping from the rope, Ricky stepped to his side.

"Lou—"

"I know, dammit, Ricky...I know."

"Maybe if you rested...for a while?" Allison suggested, looking to Ricky for confirmation.

"We could," the mountaineer said slowly, frowning. The sun was brightly shining where they stood, but far below in the valley, she could see a bit of a cloud layer moving up. Not particularly threatening, but the longer they delayed, the more uncertainty was thrown into the equation. And Ricky Bouchard preferred to deal in facts.

"No," Lou protested. "It's no good." He fumbled for his water bottle. "I feel like I could keep going...I...I really do." He took a swallow and grimaced. "Hell, I might even make it. But, it's like you say, Ricky." He shook his head, and a hoarse bark of a laugh escaped his throat. "It don't mean a damn...if you don't...make it down." He paused, straining for breath in the thin air. "So I'm heading down."

"Oh, Lou!" Allison knelt next to the exhausted attorney, wrapping an arm around his shoulders.

Lou removed his glacier glasses to wipe tears of frustration from his bloodshot eyes. "It's...it's okay," he assured her. "Really. I've got two...beautiful little girls...who want to see their daddy...again."

"And you'll see them," Allison assured him. "Soon."

Ricky could see Allison's distress at the thought of leaving Lou behind. After all, they'd come so far together. But again, it came down to choice. And Lou Silvers was making his. As far as Ricky Bouchard was concerned, it was the right one.

In the distance, fast approaching them on the downward slope, Ricky could see the colorful forms of Jangbu Nuru and Pemba Sherpa, returning from caching the spare oxygen at the South Summit. She'd have Pemba see Lou back to camp. Jangbu, no doubt, would be catching up with Jim and Mike.

Ricky turned a critical eye towards the sun, noting its height in the sky. The morning was fast getting away from them. She stomped her boots against the side of her ice ax, clearing clots of snow from her crampons, and waved at the Sherpas as they drew close.

"Okay," she announced to Allison, gently pulling her up by the elbow. "We've got...to get going."

Chapter
Twenty-two

Well, the top of the world certainly wasn't a lonely place, not this day anyway, Allison Peabody thought as she gazed ahead through foggy glasses at the Hillary Step. The icy vertical cliff, yawing nearly 50 feet high, presented the last bit of difficult technical climbing before the summit. There were at least half a dozen climbers at the base, one on the ropes moving up, and a cluster more perched at the top, waiting.

In addition, several climbers had passed her and Ricky as they'd taken an earlier break, back at the South Summit. Ricky had gotten on the radio then, letting the support people in Base Camp know that Lou and Pemba were heading down. The mountaineer had also gotten a weather update from Sandra Ortiz. It was squalling down below, but the doctor had maintained that the latest forecasts still showed the window as being open.

Other chatter on the radio had told her that Paul, Kevin, and Phil, along with Dorje Sherpa, had tagged the summit. Well, good for them, Allison had wryly thought, knowing especially how pleased the young Dorje would be, earning his first summit credit. As for herself, with the Hillary Step still between her and the top, Allison held her emotions back. Still would not allow herself to belief that Everest might be hers, too.

After checking to confirm that their cache of reserve O2 was where it was supposed to be, Ricky had led the way down the rocky, false peak of the South Summit, into the saddle-like ridge that wound its way up to the Step. Now, as Allison approached the climbers gathered at its base, she could see that Ricky was once again on the radio.

"Where are you, exactly, Jim?" Ricky shouted into the handset.

"Movin' up...we're movin' up... I think...South Summit...yeah. Approaching...South Summit."

"How's your power?"

"See you...up top...Ricky. Harris...out."

"Jim?" Ricky pressed down on the handset again. "Jim?"

Sighing, she clipped the radio handset back onto her pack strap.

"Everything...okay?" Allison gasped, nearly stumbling into the mountaineer thanks to a loose rock that had caught under her crampon.

"Yeah," Ricky replied, quickly steadying her. "The guys have just left...the summit. And Jim says he and Mike are right behind us...but..." Ricky's eyes flashed to the Southeast Ridge, "I don't see them."

"Well...they're down there...somewhere," Allison said breathlessly, following Ricky's gaze. She could see one more climber picking his way up the ridge. Farther below, moving towards the valley, her vision was cut off by clouds that were filling the lower reaches of the mountain.

"Is that...some weather...moving in?" Allison wanted to know. The winds were picking up, but the sky was still clear and startlingly blue where they stood. In fact, here it was a gorgeous, sun-splashed day.

"Sure looks like it...doesn't it?" Ricky told her. "But they say it's just a squall down in BC." The mountaineer turned to regard the climbers gathered at the base of the steps. Another climber had just clipped onto the rope that threaded down through the rocks, and several more waited their turn. Other climbers were snacking or taking pictures, and some merely sat in the snow, not moving at all, showing no inclination to tackle the Step any time soon.

"Let's take a number here," Ricky said, guiding Allison to the base. "You're ready for this, right?"

Allison could feel the intensity of the mountaineer's gaze upon her, even through her goggles. "Oh, yeah," she told her, and it was true. Since their stop at the Balcony, Allison had

found herself inexplicably getting stronger and stronger the
higher she climbed. Chalk it up to adrenaline. Or maybe it was
just that she'd stopped noticing the cold and the wind, the
damned oxygen rig and the numbing ache in her back and legs.

"I'll head up first," Ricky said, stepping up as another
climber began to slowly, cautiously work his way up the rope.
"You take your time...and I'll be waiting for you...up there."

"Okay." Allison's eyes drifted to the other climbers around
her. Those who'd seemed to have stalled. "What...what are all
these people doing?"

"Maybe...resting. Maybe...stopping." Ricky said, clench-
ing her jaw. And then, as though she'd read Allison's mind,
"They're responsible for...themselves, Allison. They all took
that on...the moment they left high camp. They make their own
choices...just as we make...ours."

Allison swallowed hard and said nothing. She simply stood
quietly next to Ricky, waiting her turn, feeling the winds begin
to swirl around her. The mountaineer was right. Again. Nothing worth anything ever came without some sacrifice...a price
that had to be paid. And only she could be the ultimate arbiter as
to whether that price was worth it...for herself. No one else
could make that call for her. No one.

Motion. Ricky's turn. The mountaineer moved up, and
clipped on. "Okay?"

Allison nodded. "Okay"

❋ ♦ ❋ ♦ ❋ ♦ ❋

When the black and red form of Ricky Bouchard had disappeared over the crest of the Step, Allison knew it was her turn.
She stepped to the base, trying to ignore the churning in her gut.
Looking up, she could see the winds blowing loose snow off the
lip of the Step, sending a sideways shower of sparkling spindrift
off into space. She was so high now, higher than she'd ever
been, and now, looking at the vertical wall in front of her, it
occurred to her that there was very little ground left around
them...anywhere, and a helluva lot of open sky.

No roof. No walls. This was why she'd taken up climbing,
right? To feel that freedom?

Ricky was waiting for her. There was nothing to fear.
Ricky had shown her the way, right?

"You going, me'm?"

Jolted from her reverie, Allison turned to see the ice-encrusted, sun-burnished face of a Sherpa behind her, obviously anxious to get moving up the ropes.

Fighting down her panic, Allison bobbed her head in the affirmative. She carefully clipped on, and then swung her ice ax into the wall and began to hoist herself up. *Just another wall...just another wall...* Allison chanted to herself as she planted one foot, one hand after the other. *Remember when you first learned to do this...back in the Tetons. Piece of cake.* Okay, so maybe that experience hadn't been at nearly 29,000 feet, but the technical principles were the same.

It was exhaustion more than anything that got to people at the Hillary Step. The pitch would be easy enough at sea level, easily accomplished even without a fixed rope. But at altitude, facing such a physical challenge after a nearly 12-hour climb, well, for many would-be summitters, the Hillary Step was one they simply could not overcome.

Concentrating, Allison continued to propel herself up the chimney-like prow of rock and ice. *Just another wall...just another—* A last dig with her ice ax, and then strong arms were pulling her over the lip.

"Good job!" Ricky's muffled voice sounded.

Allison was stunned. Surmounting the infamous Hillary Step had taken her all of five minutes. She found herself floundering on her belly in the snow, like a fish out of water, before Ricky got her away from the edge and helped her to her feet.

"Wow," Allison gasped, swiveling her head to take in the view. All around her was sky, blue sky. Dead ahead, was a thin, knife-edged ridge, a narrowing ribbon of white, trailing up to the summit about 200 yards away. The summit ridge sloped upwards from the left at about a 35-degree angle, peaking to the right in a series of formidable cornices—finger-like ridges of overhanging ice and snow. The trick was to stay to the left of the stress fractures in the snow, indicating where the cornices from time to time decided to detach and take an 8000-foot joy-ride into Tibet. But trailing too far to the left was no safe bet either; Nepal lay on that side, far, far below.

"This way." The mountaineer moved out onto the ridge, and Allison promptly fell into step behind her. The wind was blowing hard now, shrieking, its moan so loud that the young blonde could barely hear herself think. Which was probably a good thing, she considered, because she might not like what her mind was telling her. *You're so exposed up here...the wind is gonna blow you back to Kathmandu! What if you fall now? Your mother always said you were such a klutz! Just don't take Ricky with you, okay?*

Allison startled as a parade of climbers suddenly came streaking towards them from the summit: Kevin, Phil, Paul, and Dorje.

"Next!" She heard Kevin MacBride call out as he barreled past her. Phil scrambled close behind, crowing, "Free brew for me...next year!" indicating he'd won their bet. Paul Andersen stopped to speak to Ricky, and Allison watched the mountaineer offer the young guide her congratulations. "You're gonna have a wait...at the Step," she warned as he continued down, and he waved his acknowledgement of that fact.

"Good luck Allie!" he shouted to her as he passed by, and it was all Allison could do to nod her thanks as the traffic passed.

Finally, save for a group of figures huddled at the far summit, they were alone.

Taking her by the arm, Ricky planted the top of her ice ax and stepped around her. "Why don't you take the lead from here?"

Oh God!

Keep moving, just keep moving, Allison told herself. *Do what you know.*

Step. Breathe. Step, breathe, slide.

Closer. Closer.

She could see the climbers standing on the summit now; one of the British men she recognized from Base Camp, and there were others whose hooded shapes were unknown to her. A climber started down when she was still about 25 feet away, and she waited for him to pass.

Now!

The path was clear.

Plant the ice ax. Get a good toe pick. Don't make a mistake now.

God, the sky was so blue, and how the snow sparkled like a bed of crystal, unfolding out in front of her, so warm, inviting.

Closer.

But she wasn't there...not quite. And so she refused to let herself feel it. She didn't deserve to. Not yet. After all, she had no business being here in the first place, right? That's what her parents had said. And that asshole, Lionel Kitteridge, too.

Allison could spy a small metallic tripod, draped in colorful
prayer flags, the cloths snapping and standing at attention in the
blowing winds. The climbers were gathered around it, taking
pictures, chattering on radios, and then one of them turned to
clap her on the back, greeting her with a smile. "Welcome."
Keep going. Keep going.
Allison was confused. She stopped, and looked cautiously
around.
There was nowhere else to go.
She'd made it.
She, Allison Peabody, of the Boston Peabodys, was standing
on the top of Mount freakin' Everest.
And with that realization, the burden she'd been carrying on
her back since Kathmandu, since her childhood, since...forever,
simply shriveled up and blew away, taking that person she'd
once been, with it.
"Oh, God...oh...God!" she gasped, falling to her knees as
though she'd been stricken. She searched for Ricky but could
not find her. Everything was blurred. She pulled down her oxygen mask and took off her goggles, but still she couldn't see.
And then, "You did it! You did it, Allison!" She felt the
arms around her, heard the voice calling to her above the wind.
"I'm so proud of you!" She blinked, and only then understood
that it was tears that were blinding her, stinging her eyes.
"Oh, Ricky...thank you. Thank you!" she sobbed, not caring what anyone else thought. Dammit—this was her moment,
and she wanted to spend it with the woman she loved.
"Thank me—for what?" The arms squeezed her tighter.
"You did this...all on your own."
Allison thought about that for a moment. She had, hadn't
she? It had been her own two legs that had gotten her to the
highest point in the world—here, at 29,035 feet. That, and a
belief she'd had in herself—that Ricky Bouchard had instilled
within her—that an impossible dream could become reality.
"Here." Ricky was reaching in her backpack. "Let's get
some pictures."
"Oh...right," Allison replied, sniffling, wiping at her face.
She put her glasses back on to shield her eyes from the bright
light, and pulled herself to her feet. What an amazing sight, she
thought, gazing out onto the distant plains of Tibet. She was
looking down on it all, down on the world below, feeling its
powerful energy pulsing up through the earth and rock, thrusting

through the clouds to where it terminated beneath her very feet. She was a part of it all, and it of her.

"Hey!" she shouted, realizing that Ricky had been snapping away at her. "Let me...get some of you."

"How about I try one...of you both?" the British climber volunteered, and Ricky quickly passed him the camera.

The mountaineer moved next to Allison. It was close quarters. The summit of Everest was only about the size of a pool table or two—that was it. But with a 360-degree panorama to choose from: the Tibetan Plateau to the north, the magnificent Himalayan peaks of Kanchenjunga to the east, Makalu to the southeast, and Cho Oyu to the west—no shot was a bad one. The Brit took up a position facing northwest, so that the brightly colored prayer flags would be fluttering behind them in the picture. Allison felt an arm snake around her waist, and then heard in her ear: "I love you."

A broad smile split her face, just as the British climber snapped the picture.

"Ah...that'll be lovely!" he yodeled, his formal accent sounding somehow appropriate in this hallowed, ethereal sky-world.

"Thanks," Ricky said, taking the camera back. The climber started back down the slope, leaving them—for the moment—alone. She turned to Allison. "We should go."

"Just...just a minute," the younger woman replied. She began searching in her backpack. It was traditional to leave something at the summit of Everest. The prayer flags of course were in plain view. Others planted national flags, or left personal mementos and photos of loved ones. It was a very personal thing, and a tradition that Allison hadn't wanted to miss out on. God, even now it was hard to believe she would actually make good on that wish.

"Whatcha got there?" Ricky wanted to know, as Allison produced a shiny coin.

"It's my...I don't know...my good luck charm, I guess." She held the coin out to Ricky. It was a U.S. silver dollar, from the year of her birth. "I always took it with me on all my..." she shook her head, "'adventures.' From my first...parachute jump...to my first climb." She lifted moist green eyes to the mountaineer. "I never...realized I was searching for something...until I found it." She turned, and burrowed the coin deeply into the snow. "I don't need it anymore."

And it was true, Allison knew. She had been lost...adrift. But in loving Ricky Bouchard, she'd been found.

"Okay," Allison squared her shoulders. "What about you?"

"I—I've left things here before," the dark woman began.

Of course she has, you idiot! Allison chastised herself. *This has got to be old hat for her, by now.*

And then she realized that Ricky was shyly smiling at her. "But, this time," the mountaineer lifted the back of a gloved hand to lightly grace Allison's cheek, "I'm bringing something back."

❀ ♦ ❀ ♦ ❀ ♦ ❀

Every true mountaineer knew that reaching the summit was merely the halfway point of any climb. This was particularly true on Everest, where until you descended below Camp IV, out of the death zone, you couldn't afford to let your guard down for even a second. It was a difficult thing to do, especially when the summit rush had left your body, and the cold, the pain, and the lethargy began to seep its way back in.

Some climbers reached deep down into the bottom of their gas tanks, and called up enough fuel to get them all the way back to Camp II by dusk. Others were held up by bottlenecks on the trail or else decided to take their time, arriving back at the huddle of tents at Camp IV within two to four hours. Once there, they would collapse in their sleeping bags until the next dawn, sleeping on oxygen, recovering, before heading down the mountain.

If we can just get to Camp IV before this squall hits, I'll take this as a day well spent, Ricky Bouchard considered, leading the way back down the Summit Ridge. They were nearly to the top of the Hillary Step, and had caught up to several other climbers who either had already summitted, or else had decided to turn back.

The turning back was a tough call, Ricky knew, especially when your goal was in plain sight. But the extra half hour to an hour it might take to get up and down might be exactly the amount of time you needed at the back end of your climb to, say, get to the South Col before a hard blow hit.

And with each passing moment, the sinking feeling in the mountaineer's gut grew. They weren't going to make it in time. Ricky had been alarmed when they'd turned back from the summit to head down the way they had come. The "squall" clouds, as Dr. Ortiz had called them, clouds that had been filling up the valley like water tumbling over rocks, had not dissipated. Instead, they had risen closer, much closer. Boiling skywards from the Khumbu in angry, roiling thunderheads.

This was not a Jet Stream snap-back, Ricky knew. Rather, this was a localized weather disturbance, born and bred in the moisture-laden, summertime heat of Nepal. It might not last for days like some of the snap-back storms they'd experienced while on the mountain, but brother, could these local monsters pack a punch. Already, Pumori to the west was completely invisible, and the sky was taking on a flat, grayish hue.

Trouble.

"Andersen to Bouchard...Andersen to...Bouchard...Come in, Ricky!" Her radio crackled to life.

The mountaineer arrived at the top of the Step. The first significant hurdle on the descent. Quickly, she turned around to make sure Allison was in good shape behind her.

She was.

Peering over the lip of the Step to view the progress of a climber rappelling down the ropes, Ricky keyed in her handset. "Bouchard here."

"Ricky! We've got...a problem here!" The young guide's voice sounded strained over the airwaves. *"I'm at the South Summit. Jim...and Mike are here...and...and they're not in good shape."*

So.

Jim and Mike had never gotten past the South Summit after all.

"Is Jangbu with you?" Ricky demanded, her senses ratcheting up to full alert. This was not good.

"Yeah..."

Ricky turned her back into the wind, raising her voice in order to be heard. "Okay, then," she shouted, trying to convey a sense of calm to the younger man. "Have him stay there with them. You, too," she added. "We're on our way... Should be there in about..." she looked at her watch, "15 minutes or so."

"Ricky! There's more!"

The mountaineer could feel Allison come up behind her. "What?" she keyed her response into the handset, even as she felt her stomach plummet into her boots.

"It's the oxygen bottles." His voice was a near-sob now. *"I can't fuckin' find them...I can't. I think...they're gone."*

Chapter
Twenty-three

In a reality where the balance between life and death is precarious at best, where the thin white line marking the division between success and disaster is in constant motion, even the most innocent of actions, the most mundane of events, can result in the most dire of consequences.

A late start out of Camp IV.

Trailing through bottlenecks behind slower moving teams.

A good weather forecast turned suddenly bad.

Forgetting that in this, arguably the harshest environment in all the world, the brutal elements brought out the best in people, and the worst.

Ricky Bouchard squatted in the snow at the South Summit, next to the sheltered rock where, not three hours before, she'd checked on their cache of O2.

The bottles were gone now, all save for a couple of half-filled discarded canisters. The mountaineer rocked back on her heels. It was hard to tell what had happened. The canvas bag that had held them was gone, and scattered all around were empty bottles. The South Summit was the usual spot to swap oxygen on the descent. Evidence of that—the candy bar wrappers, the abandoned canisters—surrounded her. Perhaps an altitude-impaired climber had mistaken the Peak Performance cache for his own, and other climbers, following him or her, had simply compounded that error.

No one breathing supplemental oxygen would ever dare to make the attempt without knowing they had enough gas to get up and down, right? Unless you misjudged what you needed...or...unless you were a hodge-podge group of international climbers, low on resources and even lower on mountain savvy.

Whatever had happened, none of that mattered a damn, now.

Jim Harris and Mike Donaldson sat in the snow, side by side. Jim's head hung down low, and Mike had nearly pitched over onto his side. Paul Andersen was with Mike, trying to rouse him. Jangbu Nuru was on his knees next to Jim Harris. The sirdar was talking fervently in his boss' ear, but the team leader showed no signs of being responsive. Allison had removed her bota bag and was trying to get the men to drink, but both were ignoring her vigorous efforts.

There were no other climbers at the South Summit now, save for the Peak Performance people and Harry Owens, the British climber they'd encountered on the summit. Everyone else had descended from the spot, intent on beating the approaching weather. That grouping had included a distinctly rattled Kevin MacBride and Phil Christy.

"I don't know what the hell...they swapped their tanks with," Paul had told her. "They had to be discards...half full, if that. But...they wouldn't wait. So I told Dorje...to stick with them."

Ricky had simply nodded. There'd been no way the young guide could have forcibly kept them here, not with Jim Harris out of commission. And maybe it was for the best, anyway. If they escaped the brunt of the storm, well, good for them.

"You've got problems, then?" Ricky looked up into the shadowed figure of Harry Owens. His face was barely visible from the parka hood that enveloped his head, and small icicles dangled down from the bottom of what must've been a beard under his oxygen mask.

"Yeah." She groaned, pushing herself to her feet. "Too many climbers and not enough gas."

"I gathered," the Brit said quietly. "Look. I've just switched tanks but...I've got about a half left in this one." He held up the used bottle. "It's yours, if you want it."

"I—thanks," the mountaineer said, gratefully accepting his offer. *Think. Think!* She did a quick inventory of their oxygen supply. There were the two half-filled bottles that had been left at the site of their cache, plus the half from Harry. Ricky knew she had a full bottle still in her pack. She'd never bothered to make the switch earlier at the Balcony; hadn't needed to. From the moment they'd set out the night before, she'd purposely regulated her flow to a ridiculously low level.

She'd been required by contract to use the supplemental oxygen while climbing above Camp IV, and so she had. But Jim had never specified how much. Fearing the crash she might experience if the gas were somehow cut off—a frozen valve, a faulty rig—and hating like hell to have to use it in the first place, she'd simply taken liberty with the rules of the game. And now, knowing her own first bottle was at last nearly drained, she wasn't overly concerned. But as for everyone else? That was a helluva problem.

Ricky unclipped her radio handset. "Bouchard to base. Bouchard to base. Over."

"Go...-head, Ricky."

The voice of Dr. Sandra Ortiz crackled and popped through the radio, sounding relatively calm in the face of a mounting storm.

"We've got a storm coming, right?"

A pause. *"I don't know...to say, Ricky. All the fore...said—"*

"Look, you're breaking up," the mountaineer cut her off. "And...I've got a problem here. We're at the South Summit— repeat—the South Summit. The oxygen cache is gone. We've got very little...gas left, and Jim and Mike are...down. Repeat...Jim and Mike are not able to move under their own power. Over."

Another pause, and then Ricky could hear the panic in Sandra's voice.

"No...no...ygen? You've got...get them down. Give...shots of dex. ...ver"

Ricky squeezed her eyes shut in frustration. "I'll give them both shots," the mountaineer confirmed. "And I'll get them down. MacBride, Christy, and Dorje are already...on their way. Everyone else is here...over."

There was more static, more interference from the clouds and then, *"...heart condition. There should be meds...pack. Dose...now."*

"Repeat?" Ricky was astounded. Surely, the altitude was playing tricks on her hearing.

"Jim has a heart...dition. Medication in...backpack."

No. It couldn't be. "Sandra!" Ricky barked into the handset. "Bouchard to base. Bouchard to base. Over."

But the crackle and hissing of static was her only response.

Ricky Bouchard stared at the offensive handset, stunned.
Taking on Everest was hard enough with a strong heart, let alone
with one that could not perform up to capacity. A flash of anger
coursed through the mountaineer, but quickly she wrestled it
under control, determined to channel that negative energy in a
more positive, useful direction—like getting the hell down.

And, first things first: they had to get Jim and Mike up.

"Okay—" Ricky joined the huddled group, wondering if
they'd heard the radio chatter over the high winds. Not likely.
And as she drew closer, it was obvious to her that somewhere
along the trail, Mike Donaldson had lost or discarded his handset. "We're gonna give...both these guys a shot of dex," she
explained, pulling her first aid kit out of her rucksack. Paul—"
she checked Jim's oxygen gauge. As she'd suspected, it was
empty. The flow had been turned up to nearly 5 liters per
minute. At that rate, he had to have blown through his second
bottle of air before he'd even reached the South Summit.
"There's a spare bottle in my pack," she nodded towards it, not
bothering to explain. "Get it on him."

"Gotcha," the young man replied, clearly relieved to be
doing *something*. With trembling hands, he reached for Ricky's
bag.

Just a jab and a press, and she was finished with Jim Harris.
The shot elicited a moan from the man, and she was at least
grateful for that response. Quickly, she turned her attention to
the now nearly-prone Mike Donaldson. She checked his oxygen
gauge. Inexplicably, it registered as nearly full.

"What the—" Ricky swiftly dispensed with the injection,
and returned her attention to the gauge.

She tapped on it. Nothing. The needle refused to move.

Another tap, and then she looked at the valve. "Jesus
Christ!" she swore, roughly twisting the valve. It had been
notched in the "off" position. "He'll never get any air if it's not
turned on!"

"What?" Paul drew up behind her. "I checked it Ricky...I
swear to God, I...I checked it!" he exclaimed.

Ricky frowned. Maybe he had, maybe he hadn't. The altitude affected everyone differently. Hell, in a moment of waning

lucidity, maybe even Donaldson himself had reached back and switched the damn thing off.

"Forget it," she told the senior guide, instead turning her attention to Harris' pack. A brief search turned up no medication. If he'd even brought it along with him, he didn't have it now.

"We...topside, yet?" Jim Harris mumbled, shaking his head.

"Not this trip, boss," Jangbu told him, helping him to a more upright position.

Ah, the wonders of a fresh bottle of O2 and a shot of dex. Like a pair of toy soldiers with new batteries, Jim and Mike were reviving before her eyes. All right.

Next.

"We've got 3 canisters of...oxygen left," Ricky explained to them, glad in a way that the mistake with Mike's flow had just improved their position. "One is courtesy of...Mr. Harry Owens." She nodded towards the young man who still lingered with them on the wind-swept shelf. "They're only about half full. I...I want you three to take them now," she told them, sweeping her eyes over Jangbu, Allison, and Paul Andersen. "Try to keep the flow...as low as you can stand...it'll have to last."

"What about you?" Allison demanded.

"I've kept my flow way down...all along. I've got enough left," Ricky lied. Studiously avoiding Allison's gaze, she moved to collect the remaining bottles of O2.

Harry Owens handed them to her as she approached. "Thanks." She spared a glance down the mountain, at the swirling clouds that were nearly upon them. "You...should get going."

"Well, that's just it," the young man laughed nervously, stabbing his ice ax into the ground. "I seem to have lost my escort, you see. If it's all the same to you—"

"You're welcome to stick with us," she told him, smiling tiredly at the relief that visibly washed over him. She didn't blame the man. It would be impossible to beat the storm by this point. The inevitability of it all was upon them. So, better to face a whiteout in a group, rather than alone.

"Appreciate that, thanks!" Harry called after her, as she returned to the huddle with the bottles. Mike Donaldson was sitting up now too, groggily returning to life.

"Let's get these switched." She handed a bottle each to Jan-gbu and Paul, and then reached for Allison's backpack.

"I can do it."

"No, let me—"

"I said...I can do it," came the stiff reply.

Ricky flinched as though she'd been struck.

"Okay," she said meekly. She handed Allison the canister, and turned away.

"Ricky—wait." A hand on her arm.

"I-I'm sorry," the young blonde said, stepping in front of her. "But...I'm not a...complete idiot, you know."

"What?" Ricky kept her eyes on the darkening valley below. She knew what Allison was talking about; just as Allison knew she did.

Ricky sighed. The lower peaks were all but obliterated now, and closer, the South Summit was nearly consumed by the threatening clouds.

"I know you've got no oxygen left."

"That's not true..." Ricky protested. "I've still got...some." But she knew tank was nearly tapped. With every dry breath she took in, she had to pull harder.

"Ricky." The tone of Allison's voice, firm, and yet pained, forced the mountaineer to look at her. "What...are you doing?"

"What I have to do." She paused. "It's my job, Allison. I've got to make sure...these people...*you*...get down."

"But how can you do that...without gas?" Even in the bit-ing cold, the younger woman's face was growing flushed.

"Because I've done it before. I'm used to going...without. These people..." she gestured to the frightened, disoriented group, "aren't."

"But—"

"Trust me," Ricky hushed her. "I...know what I'm doing." She pursed her lips, debating whether to continue. But then she gazed into the face of the woman who had become her every-thing, and decided she deserved to know. "It's...it's gonna get ugly, Allison. When the oxygen runs out...and it will..." she slowly shook her head, "these people...will go into a physical nosedive."

"Me, too?" A small voice.

"Maybe." Ricky bit her lip. "Probably."

Allison remained silent, considering that information for a moment. And then, "Well, until that happens...*if* that happens, whatever I can do to help, Ricky. Just let me know. We're in this together, okay?"

The feeling flowed over Ricky like warm water—the love— calming her, a well of added strength from a source where she'd least expected to draw it from. "Okay," she nodded, her voice a hoarse rasp.

And then she looked to a fly-away wisp of Allison's golden hair, noting with some despair the thick, fat snowflake that had drifted down from the sky above to nestle there.

❄ ◆ ❄ ◆ ❄ ◆ ❄

"Left! Left! Stay left!" Ricky shouted into the winds, call- ing out to Jangbu Nuru.

Descending in a whiteout.

It was like swimming in giant bowl of milk, and there was no down or up, no right or left, just moving, keep moving, and don't stop, or else you'll die.

In a matter of minutes it had begun to snow heavily, and they had just about made it down the Southeast Ridge to the Rock Steps above the Balcony, before the winds had really kicked in, turning the squall into a full-blown gale. Negotiating the Steps had been difficult, and it had taken the collective efforts of Ricky, Jangbu, and Paul, to safely rappel Jim Harris and Mike Donaldson down them.

Then it was a question of sorting themselves out at the bot- tom, of re-attaching the short-ropes between Jangbu and Jim, Paul Andersen and Mike, and then clipping onto the fixed rope again once Ricky had been able to dig it out of the snow. Then they'd reformed in a single line, spaced closely together, with Allison and Harry Owens bringing up the rear.

The descent down the narrow Ridge and the technical climbing at the Steps, all in the midst of a snowstorm, had cost them precious time, the mountaineer knew. It was a double- edged sword: they had not a minute to spare, yet one false step taken in haste could cost one of them their life. After no sleep in nearly two days, they were walking dead on their feet, plodding blindly through the whiteness shell-shocked, bewildered.

Faster! Faster! Ricky's mind silently screamed, knowing that if she were of a mind to, she could be safely in her tent at the South Col within the hour. Or she could stay, moving down the mountain at an agonizingly slow speed, her progress only as fast as the slowest climber in the group. Stumbling over the rock and ice until they finally ran out of oxygen, and out of time.

But leaving was never an option for the mountaineer. She knew that these people were depending on her—one person, most of all. And so she alternated between breaking trail in front of Jangbu and Jim, and dropping back to help Paul with Mike Donaldson. The oxygen and the dexamethasone had revived him to the extent that he was mobile, but the executive was helpless beyond a basic stepping motion. He had virtually no strength left, and on the steeper sections of the slope where the snow and ice were hard, he weakly pawed at the surface with his crampons, unable to stomp his boot down hard enough to get a good foot placement. With Paul holding onto Mike's harness from behind, Ricky had ended up may times setting his boots by hand.

Jim Harris, on the other hand, seemed to have gotten a small amount of power back, but his oxygen-starved brain was constantly producing strings of nonsensical sentences and fragments of conversations with people who weren't there. Whenever he was aware enough to notice his surroundings, he peppered Jangbu and Ricky with child-like questions in a lost, slurred voice, not even seeming to recognize them.

"I want this *off*!"

Ricky moved to intercept the team leader, when for the fifth time in the last ten minutes, he grabbed at the carabiner on his harness that hooked him to Jangbu. Like a petulant child, he tried to remove it, but fortunately in his addled state he appeared to have no clue as to how to work the mechanism.

"Oh, no you don't!" Sweeping next to him she batted his hand away and continued guiding him down, that simple motion enough to distract him from his objective—for the moment.

Ricky could barely see ten yards in front of her, but she knew they had to be close to the Balcony. She could just about see where she was putting her feet, moving more by memory and feel than by anything else. She knew this mountain, she told herself. Knew it by heart. Had memorized there the majestic sweep of its buttresses, the dizzying promontory of its summit, the simple beauty of its glacial melt-water. She could get them all down blind, if she had to.

And it might just come to that, she considered. The winds were ripping off the Ridge; it had to be blowing at 50 knots by now, firing the snow sideways. Camera flashes of lighting, not unusual for this type of summer storm, occasionally flickered in

the whiteness, immediately followed by avalanche-like booms of
thunder; the sound quickly muffled by the heavy snow. It was an
other-worldly scene, and it was easy to let your mind drift if you
let it...to imagine things.

No! She squeezed her eyes shut, not that it made that much
of a difference. She was still feeling okay, and she had a job to
do. Her oxygen was long gone and in a way, she was relieved at
that. No more worrying...guessing when it might run out, and
the effect that would have on her. She'd felt the expected dip in
her energy level, that was inevitable, but she'd fought her way
back through it, and though the cold was settling into her bones
now, she still had confidence in her *samochuvstvie*.

"Ricky!"

Fear struck at the tall woman's gut at the alarm in Allison's
hoarse shout.

"Keep bearing left," she told Jangbu, handing him the
length of fixed rope she'd fished out of the snow. Then she
backtracked as hastily as she dared to Allison's position on the
line.

"What...what is it?"

"I can't...breathe," she said, the eyes beneath her goggles
widened in panic. "I keep pulling but I'm not...getting...any-
thing."

Already Ricky had turned Allison slightly, brushing the
snow off her oxygen gauge.

"It can't be...gone...already?"

The faint hopefulness in Allison's voice tugged at her heart,
but a quick glance told her what she'd already suspected she'd
see. The bottle was empty.

"All gone," Ricky said tightly. Quickly, she snapped open
the younger woman's backpack and removed the depleted canister, discarding it. "There. That should lighten your load a little
bit. But hang onto your mask, okay? You never know."

"Okay." A trusting whimper.

"You've got to...keep moving, now...okay?" Ricky dipped
her head down as she spoke, to keep the icy pellets of snow from
flying into her mouth.

"Ricky..." Allison's voice was barely audible, and the
mountaineer could see her eyelids fluttering behind her glasses.
"I'm...so tired."

"No!" The mountaineer's voice was fierce, and she shook
her partner by the arms, snapping her to attention. "You *promise*

me...you will keep...walking down this mountain. You don't...stop, okay?"

Slightly dazed eyes looked at her, searching for a moment and then flickering in understanding.

"I...promise."

❄ ◆ ❄ ◆ ❄ ◆ ❄

They'd been resting at the Balcony for several spare minutes they really couldn't afford, while Ricky gave Mike Donaldson another shot of dex. She was beyond caring what the additional dose of the steroid might do to the man's system; she figured living with the potential after-effect was better than dying without it. She suspected he was suffering from some frostbite in his hands and feet; his feeble attempts at any effective downward movement had been growing increasingly weaker.

Just before they'd arrived at the Balcony, Jangbu's oxygen had quit. The sirdar had made little of it, and Ricky knew her friend was used to doing without. But he'd been breathing bottled gas for days now while stocking the higher camps as well as the ill-fated cache at the South Summit, and she knew the sudden drop-off had to be hitting him hard.

Paul Andersen tossed his now-empty bottle aside just as they were getting ready to push off from the Balcony. "Well...that's that," he said dully, his lips thin and blue beneath his frost-coated beard.

"Can you take the lead this pitch?" Ricky asked him, watching as the discarded bottle tumbled away into the void. "I'll take Mike for a while," she said, figuring to give the guide a break while his reeling body adjusted. Also, that position on the ropes would place her next to Allison. The younger woman had been diligently keeping up her end of the bargain, plodding on, head down into the wind, and it had not escaped the mountaineer's notice that from time to time Harry Owens had offered her a few precious puffs of oxygen through his mask.

For that, she was inordinately grateful. She'd have to remember to thank him properly for his help once this was all over.

They pushed off from the Balcony, threading their way in a ponderously slow fashion down into the gullies of the Triangular Face. Roller-coaster rises and dips, where they would find themselves suddenly shielded from the biting winds, only to be hit full force once they'd struggled over the opposite side.

It was in one such protected gully at the bottom of the band, with Ricky once again leading the way, where she saw an object that didn't seem to fit in with the surrounding terrain. Not a rock...not an icy chunk of a cornice, fallen from above, but—a body.

"Hang on!" She held up a hand to Jangbu, who was still hauling an ominously quiet Jim Harris. Unclipping from the line, she swam through about five yards of deep snow. The body was mostly snow covered, lying in a fetal position, but glimpses of a blue and gold climbing suit could be seen—colors that had caught Ricky's eye.

Bracing herself, she turned the body over.

Oh, God.

The climber was Phil Christy.

Ricky dropped to her knees, frantically brushing the snow from his face and chest. *Damn, damn, damn!* She pulled off her over-mitt and glove and desperately felt for a pulse.

Nothing.

His goggles were gone, as was his facemask, and somewhere along the line he'd lost his gloves, too. His jacket was partially unzipped, and snow had begun to collect inside.

"Phil! Phil!" she shouted desperately, scrabbling for a shot of dex. She dug one out of her pack and stuck him with it. No response.

"C'mon...c'mon! Phil!" She slapped at his face, and tiny slivers of ice broke loose and tumbled to the ground. She pulled him up into a semi-sitting position, fighting back a twinge of nausea at how cold and stiffened his body felt to her touch. She leaned in close to his mouth and nose, listening for breath sounds, but again, detected nothing.

Swallowing hard, she gave her radio another try. She'd had no luck with it since her last abbreviated conversation with Sandra Ortiz at the South Summit. The interference from the storm might be too much, or perhaps by now her batteries had quit—it was hard to tell, but she had to give it a shot.

"Bouchard to base. Bouchard to...base. Over."

The wind gave up a lonely howl in response, as the mountaineer's gaze focused on Phil Christy's unmoving chest.

"Bouchard to C4. Bouchard..." she gasped, "...to anyone. Over."

Boot-steps slogged up behind her; it was Jangbu Nuru, wading through the snow to stand by her side.

"Is Mr. Phil," he said solemnly, mournfully.

"Yeah." She snapped the useless handset back onto her pack strap, and leaned forward. Gently, she lifted up one frosted eyelid, then the other. His pupils were fixed and dilated in widened surprise at the moment of his death, as they'd never been in life.

Bodies were a part of life on Everest, on any high mountain that challenged a climber's mettle. You got used to it. But she had to admit that it was just a bit more jarring when that body happened to be someone you knew. Someone who, jerk or not, you'd sat across from over breakfast, or who you'd heard joke about getting married if he didn't win a silly bet.

Well, Phil Christy had pushed himself and won the bet.

And lost everything else.

"We got to keep going...Ricky," Jangbu told her. "No help...Mr. Phil." The sirdar was anxious to get moving again, and for more reason than the weather. Sherpas were notoriously superstitious about dead bodies. It was bad luck to see one, even worse luck to be near one. The sirdar turned and began to tramp back to the huddle of climbers.

Ricky reached around the dead man and pulled off his rucksack, which through it all he'd somehow managed to retain. She eased him back down into the snow, and, offering him some small shred of dignity where he lay, secured the pack over his face. There was nothing else she could do, and she knew it. Not for him, and not for Kevin and Dorje, wherever they might be.

What the hell had happened, here? To have made it down the mountain so far, only to die here, alone, within an hour or so of Camp? Maybe he'd gotten tired once his air ran out, and he'd sat down to rest. Or maybe his glasses had fogged up, and he'd removed his glove to clean them.

So close.

Everest played no favorites, Ricky Bouchard knew that. She'd heard tales of climbers who'd died within scant feet of reaching their tents on the South Col.

On the mountain, the last laugh was on you.

Okay.

The only thing for it now was to get her people back to Camp IV, before darkness hit. That, she did have something to say about. Lifting her booted feet high against the thigh-deep snow, she made her way back to the fixed rope.

Uh-oh. The mountaineer drew in a sharp breath of air. Everyone was sitting down in the snow, everyone but Allison, who stood like a stone, frozen into position on the ropes.

The beleaguered climbers let the snow fall upon them, heads bowed, uncaring, like cars pulled to the side of a back-country road, stuck in a snowdrift.

Ricky made her way to a small, powder blue form. "How...are you holding up?"

"I—I," Allison choked out through frozen lips, "was afraid...that if I sat down...I wouldn't get up."

Ricky Bouchard was weary. She could admit that to herself, now. She wasn't exactly sure when the situation had begun to spin out of control. Maybe it had been at the South Summit, maybe at the Balcony, when Paul Andersen had begun to lead them off in the wrong direction, nearly taking the non-stop direct route to Tibet; or maybe it was now, with a dead body behind them and the mouth of a storm in front of them.

They'd fought the good fight, but finally, in the end, they'd arrived at the "give up" moment. She knew that if she didn't say a word, they'd all continue to sit right where they were, letting a lethargic, false warmth override what their dulled senses told them, until sleep seemed like the most wonderful, logical option in all the world.

Or.

Maybe this damned shipwreck was still salvageable. For Allison's sake, and for her own, for the life they deserved to have together, she had to try.

"You're doing great," Ricky assured the frozen woman by her side, feeling the cold tears spring to her eyes, unbidden. "I'm...so proud of you." She gave her a gentle hug, and though Allison's arms remained stiffly at her sides, clinging to the rope, the mountaineer was relieved to feel some of the tension leave the smaller woman's body as she relaxed and responded to the embrace.

"We're going to get moving now, okay?"

"Okay." A voice tired, emotionally drained, but determined.

Ricky summoned up a reserve of energy she did not know she possessed, and turned to the rest of the group. "Listen to me!" She worked her way around the huddle, grabbing at shoulders, pulling people to their feet. Doing anything she could to help them ward off the deadly inertia. "We can't stay here.

We're close. Real close." She paused to help Jangbu work his numb fingers to re-attach his short-rope to a hypoxia-dazed Jim Harris. "You've...got...to keep trying!" She shouted to be heard above the wind. "One step...just give me...one step at a time, and we'll make it...okay?"

"Hot toddies...on me...when we get there," Harry Owens weakly joked, and he pushed himself to his feet.

Offering him a frozen grin, Ricky moved to the front of the ropes. "Do whatever...you've got to do. Forget everything else...and focus. One...step at a time. And...don't stop, okay?" she pleaded. "Don't stop."

She turned and faced downhill. Maybe it was her mind playing tricks on her, but it seemed that the visibility had begun to improve somewhat. She thought she could see a good 30 to 40 yards in front of her now, so there was that. Camp IV was down there somewhere, and by God, she would find it.

Step. Breathe. Breathe. Breathe.

Okay. That worked. Time to try another.

Step.

❄ ◆ ❄ ◆ ❄

Pemba Sherpa had a good reputation among his peers. He worked hard, toted more than his share of the load, and had aspirations one day to become a sirdar like his idol, Jangbu Nuru. Pemba had to admit that he also enjoyed the prestige that came with working high on the mountains, just as his father had; and the money he received in a season's work was enough to keep his growing family fed and clothed for the whole year. Not too shabby.

Unlike some of his brethren, he didn't mind working with the western climbers. Mostly, the job was to stay out of their way, while at the same time to make sure you were at the right place at the right time, whenever they needed you. A delicate balance, and young Pemba had watched Jangbu Nuru carefully, imitating him, perfecting his craft.

It was Jangbu who had recommended him to Jim Harris and the Peak Performance Adventure Company, and he was grateful for that. Not all expeditions were the same; he'd found that out over the years. With Jim Harris, he ate well, was well clothed and kept, and there would be a bonus at the end of it all if they were successful.

Harris seemed an okay fellow, and Mr. Paul, too, but from what Pemba had seen, he had to say that he preferred the company of Miss Ricky, Jangbu's friend. She was a fine climber, one who he'd be willing to match against the best of the *Sherpani* and, unlike some of the other westerners, he'd never heard her complain. Like him, she loved the Mother Goddess, the best and the worst of her; he could tell.

No, she was not like the others. He's known that from their very first climb through the Icefall, when he'd seen her risk her life to save his friend Pasang Sherpa, who'd been working for the Spanish team this season.

And then there was that day several weeks ago, after he'd descended from one of the storms up high, when she'd sought him out in the Sherpa tent. Somehow, she'd heard that he'd lost one of his over-mitts in the hard blow, as he'd been attempting to dig out tent platforms. She'd given him a pair of her own, against his vehement protest. "Gore Tex" the logo had said, and Pemba had worn them proudly, instantly becoming the envy of the junior Sherpas on the team.

Yes, he would certainly become a sirdar one day, just like Jangbu. He was disappointed that he didn't have a chance at the summit today after all, as that would certainly have enhanced his reputation. But he'd been there before, and he would be there again one day.

He was patient.

And when Ricky had asked him to help Mr. Lou back to camp, he'd been happy to do it. Mr. Lou was a nice man, and he'd obviously been in some distress. Better to retreat and live to see another day; that was the Sherpa motto. When they'd arrived back at camp, it had been all Pemba could do to have the poor fellow swallow a few gulps of hot tea, before he'd keeled over in his sleeping bag and fallen into a deep, exhausted slumber.

He'd been safely in the Sherpa tent, drinking hot tea and dozing, when he'd heard the fragmented distress call from Miss Ricky to the doctor. He'd tried calling her on his radio, but this was not the first time he'd seen the contraptions fail. Instead, tired as he was, he'd instantly sprung into action.

Leaving his tent, he'd been shocked at the way the storm had blown up, and had been a little scared, too, but he knew what Jangbu would do in a situation like this. So he poked his head in the rest of tents, gathering up what oxygen bottles he could find—some filled, some partially empty. Then he'd grabbed a full thermos of hot tea, and had been steeling himself to start over the icy scree towards the ropes, when a dark figure had materialized out of the whiteout.

It was Mr. Kevin, who wasted no time staggering towards his tent, mumbling incoherently. Pemba tried to talk to him, but Kevin ignored him; it wasn't the first time that had ever happened. Regardless, Pemba knew he could expect no help from him.

Squaring his shoulders, he'd headed for the ropes. And then another form swirled into view, dressed in a blue and red climbing suit.

"Need a little help there, boy?"

It was one of the men from the English tents. He'd heard the Peak Performance transmission. And it seemed one of their climbers was still out there, too. He was the only one in their group, after the arduous day on the mountain they'd all had, with enough power to make a rescue attempt. Pemba had been glad to share his load of oxygen—it was certainly heavy—and he'd been glad for the company as well.

They'd decided to head up the slope towards the fixed rope at the base of the gullies, to see what they could find. To go any farther in this mess, with night approaching, would be ill-advised. And with any luck they'd meet Jangbu, Miss Ricky and the rest of the team before they got half way.

Well, they'd gone more than half way by now, and Pemba Sherpa was worried, very worried. Dark would be upon them soon, and the storm had only teased at letting up. Pemba kept turning around, checking to make sure the English was still with him, and also mentally marking his trail. He knew this mountain pretty well, but Jangbu knew it better, and he'd feel much more comfortable if they would just find him right now, thank you, so the sirdar could take the lead on the way down.

"I—I don't know how much...farther...we should keep going," the English shouted up to Pemba. "This is...no good."

"Little more...little more," Pemba replied, not breaking his stride. They were almost to the gullies now. Let them get there, and then see what they could see. Then, he'd make his decision. If only the Mother Goddess would smile upon him, the decision would be taken from him.

Pemba Sherpa kept plodding forward, pulling the fixed roped out of the snow with every step, with every slide. He'd been breathing the bottled oxygen for so long now that every swallow in his dry throat meant pain, but he knew that was nothing compared to what the climbers up the mountain were feeling. *Just a little more...little more.*

And then Pemba realized there was tension on the rope, tension from above. He pulled himself forward, through the swirling snow, and gulped hard as a tall figure clad in red and black suddenly loomed above him. For a moment, Pemba was frightened, thinking the apparition a mountain ghost, emerging from the mist to claim him for its own.

Until he heard a low, rasping voice greet him.

"Hi, Pemba. Nice gloves."

Chapter
Twenty-four

Allison Peabody was above it all.

Floating.

Detached.

A part of what was happening to the body she saw struggling beneath her in the snow, and yet not. Comfortably adrift, connected to her corporeal self by the most slender of tethers.

Suspended as she was, indifferent to it all, she didn't need to think, didn't need to feel, didn't need to breathe. Why go to all that effort when it was so unnecessary? Why bother...with anything?

And then suddenly she could breathe again, or at least she was getting more air than she had before. Perhaps they had arrived all the way back at Base Camp by now? But no, for there was walking, always more walking, punctuated by confusing moments where she had to rejoin her body and execute baffling maneuvers with an awkward, cold rope that someone kept pressing into her frozen hands.

Ricky.

The voice always in her ear, yelling at her, making her do things she didn't want to do, driving her on, and always the walking, more walking. Or was she being carried? Sometimes, it was difficult to tell the difference.

And then there was no more down. And she found herself staring through blurred, stinging eyes, toward smudges of color in the encroaching darkness; tents, sagging under the weight of ice and snow.

"C'mon. You can do it! Another step, Allison. For me. Please."

Next, her eyes were closed, and she understood that they were, but she saw no reason to open them at the moment. She was tired, so tired, more physically drained than she'd ever been in her entire life. Unable to lift a frozen arm or a numb foot that seemed to not belong to her in the first place.

She could detect through her closed eyes the glow of a dim light, and then her goggles were gone...her boots, too, and there was a calm, soothing voice, urging her to swallow some hot tea. A voice whose requests she had not refused of late, and she had no intention of starting to do so now.

And so she drank.

Felt the hot liquid coursing down her throat, warming her chest, thawing her belly. It felt...so damn good. Then the voice was in her ear again, gently murmuring now, no more yells, telling her that she'd made it, and that everything would be okay.

She couldn't help herself then, couldn't stop it if she'd wanted to. She was so relieved, so emotionally released, that she finally let her guard down. She let it go, let it all go, and it was a good thing her eyes were closed so she wouldn't have to remember any of this later. Have to remember what she'd been up against, and how so many times she'd wanted to simply give up.

Just like Phil Christy had given up.

It would have been so easy.

But she hadn't.

She'd focused and done exactly what Ricky Bouchard had asked of her, more than in her heart she knew she'd been capable of. And by God, they'd made it! She'd been so damn scared. Even now, the "what ifs" attempted to flood her muzzy consciousness, but fortunately, she was able to turn them away. Because Ricky was here with her, and she didn't have to think about anything else just now, if she didn't want to.

"This will make you feel better."

A prick of a needle against gradually warming skin.

And then Allison was drifting again, but it was a good thing this time, she considered, as her sense of detachment increased. It was all a dream. And she was so warm. So safe. She and Ricky, together.

She felt fingers brush matted strands of hair from her forehead, and then the hand was replaced by a brush of lips.

"Rest."

Whatever Ricky Bouchard asked of her, she would do.

❀ ♦ ❀ ♦ ❀ ♦ ❀

Ricky pulled back from Allison, a look of quiet grief on her face. Once more she checked the regulator attached to a bulky Zvesda bottle next to the blonde, making sure the oxygen flow was turned up to a luxurious 3.5 liters per minute.

The mountaineer was still having trouble wrapping her thawing mind around what had just happened, the cold, white hell they'd descended through. At the South Summit she'd told Sandra Ortiz that she would get everyone down, but...it had been close.

Too damn close.

If Pemba and Harry Owens' teammate, David Lowe, hadn't shown up when they did...the mountaineer squeezed her eyes shut, refusing to give in to the torture of what nearly had been.

She was feeling better herself; the hot tea and an energy bar had worked wonders, and she wanted nothing more than to stay by Allison's side, holding her, feeling the heat warming between them that told her the smaller woman was alive, and well, and real.

It had been chaos when they'd gotten back to camp; Paul Andersen had been close to a state of total collapse, and Jangbu, too. The hardy little Sherpa had pushed himself to the limit this day and had barely managed to survive it. David Lowe and another climber from the Spanish team had immediately begun to attend to an insensate Jim Harris and Mike Donaldson, forcing hot, sugar-laden brews into them. The sooner they and everyone else got out of the death zone and back down to Camp II—hopefully tomorrow morning, if the weather cleared—the better.

Ricky had been content to care for Allison herself, warding off those who sought to attend to her own needs, people like Lou Silvers, who'd been rousted from his slumber by the excitement. The attorney was feeling better, and though his cough was still in full flower, his color was healthier than when Ricky had last seen him. Clearly, he'd made a wise decision in turning back.

The mountaineer had turned the little stove in their tent on high, chasing away the frost that coated the floor and walls.

She'd gotten Allison comfortable, rubbing at her frozen limbs, taking care to examine her hands and feet for any signs of frostbite. Although the younger woman had a bad windburn on her face, and it looked as if her eyes might give her some trouble, it appeared as though she'd escaped relatively unscathed. Ricky had sagged back in relief, thanking any god who might have been listening.

She hated the thought of leaving Allison, even for a minute, but her work this day was not yet done. A client was dead, and she needed to determine what a certain Kevin MacBride, or perhaps Dorje, knew about it. Did MacBride know his friend was dead? Did he even care?

That's not entirely fair, the mountaineer thought, reaching for her boots. Silencing a groan, she tugged them on. She spared a last look at Allison. She was sleeping peacefully, as bundled up in sleeping bags, clothes, and blankets as Ricky had been able to manage without smothering her. Her breathing was good, and her color was too.

Sighing, Ricky mentally had to nudge herself back through the vestibule of the tent and out into the storm once more. It was almost full dark, and the winds were still blowing hard, maybe about 40 knots. She started tracking towards the central huddle of tents, and was nearly upon the commotion before she noticed it.

Lou Silvers was there, tired but alert. Pemba was there too, standing next to Jangbu, listening. The sirdar was chattering into a radio handset, tears of exhaustion and frustration rolling down his face.

"What's happening?" she wanted to know.

"This is shit. This is all...such *shit*," the attorney muttered.

"Lou," Ricky demanded more forcefully. "What's going on?"

"It's Dorje," he said, the despair plain in his voice. "He never made it back."

"What the—" A bolt of anger shot through her. Instantly, she spun on her heel towards Kevin MacBride's tent. To leave not one but two of your teammates on the hill—inexcusable.

"Forget it, Ricky." Lou stepped in front of her, holding her back. "The guy can't think straight worth a damn—I already tried it. He can't remember a thing. He's out of it."

Ricky released a sharp burst of air. "Who's he talking to?" she nodded towards the radio.

"Pemba's handset is only partially working. It can receive, but it can't transmit. We...we can hear Dorje...out there." He looked glumly at the two agitated Sherpas. "They can hear him, but they can't answer. Can't figure out where he is."

Jangbu collapsed into the snow, weeping. "I bad luck, Ricky. I tell Dorje's mother...I look out for him."

The mountaineer's heart nearly broke. She had never seen the sirdar so distraught, and yet she wondered what condition she would have been in if the situation were reversed, and it were Allison out there, all alone in the dark...in the cold.

Faint words sounded over the handset; Dorje, speaking in Nepalese.

She turned to Pemba. "What's he saying?"

The young Sherpa's eyes tracked down to his feet. He was obviously exhausted to the bone, he'd had made two runs up the mountain already. "He say," he wrung his hands, looking slightly ashamed, "won't someone please come help me?"

❄ ◆ ❄ ◆ ❄ ◆ ❄

There was one good thing to be said about being in a camp surrounded by a bunch of physically and mentally drained climbers, Ricky Bouchard considered, screwing the top down tight on a hot thermos of tea. Everyone pretty much had no fight left in them to stop her from doing what she intended to do.

There was no way she could leave Dorje out there. Not while she knew he was still alive. He was the youngster on the team of climbing Sherpas, and this was his first time working the high camps. How proud his family had been of him, Jangbu had told her, when they'd first sat down to review the strength of the Sherpa team.

God only knew what the hell had happened up there with the young Sherpa, MacBride, and Christy. They'd pushed themselves from the start, bursting out of Camp IV like racehorses pining for the lead. Then there had been the storm, the problem with the gas, and who knew what else, leading to hypoxia, or worse. They'd probably been just confused at first, then disoriented, and then...well, the one thing she did know was that a man was lying dead in the gullies, while another was lying warm in his tent.

And as for the third man...she was going to bring him back.

Oh, they'd tried to talk her out of it. Jangbu, Pemba, even a

half-frozen Paul Andersen. "Wait 'til morning," they'd said, but
the mountaineer knew that was time wasted that Dorje simply
didn't have.

A teammate was lost.

She planned to find him.

Quickly, she'd gathered up a few supplies, not trusting herself to return to her tent. Seeing Allison might weaken her
resolve, and she did not fully trust herself to resist that selfish
pull. The desire to just curl up next to her, close her eyes, and
let someone else worry about everybody else's problems. She
knew that Allison would forgive her, would understand if she did
exactly that.

But Ricky Bouchard knew she would never be able to forgive herself.

"Okay," she said, stowing two three-fourth's full Poisk bottles into her rucksack, along with the tea, some chocolate, and,
of course, more syringes of dexamethasone. "That should do it."

They were gathered at the opening of Lou and Paul's tent.
Pemba had grounded several lanterns just outside, throwing feeble splashes of light a few yards into the snow—beacons, to
guide her home.

"You're sure you don't want...any gas for yourself, Ricky?"
Lou's weathered face was clouded with concern.

"I'm sure," the mountaineer quietly replied, knowing her
body could not withstand another "dip" if she had to do without
again.

"And you've got Pemba's radio."

"Yeah," she told him, figuring a half-working radio was better than none. Maybe Dorje would sign on again and be better
able to describe his position. But she doubted it.

"Mebbe Dorje straight up...above," Jangbu offered helplessly. "You no have to go far, Ricky."

"Maybe." She smiled faintly at her old friend and shouldered her pack. "You'll make sure these people get out of here
tomorrow, if the weather clears?"

"Yes," the sirdar replied, lowering his head.

"Ricky!" Lou Silvers said, suddenly alarmed.
"Don't...don't leave me with a helluva lot of explaining to do to
Allison, you hear me?"

The mountaineer faced the compact attorney, fighting back
the emotion that suddenly assailed her from some unknown place
within. Lou Silvers was a decent man and had become a good

friend to herself and Allison over these past weeks.

She could see by the silent pleading in his eyes that he knew.

He knew the young blonde sleeping peacefully several tents away was more than just a client to her. More than just a friend.

Ricky swallowed hard, wondering how in the world she could be such a fool as to even think of attempting this thing. "Stay with her Lou, will you?" She took a deep, steadying breath. "Keep her safe," she added, and her voice nearly broke at that.

"I will," the attorney replied, locking his pale eyes on hers. "I promise."

Without another word, the mountaineer unzipped the opening and shoved herself out into the storm, into the dark void.

Nighttime on Everest—on any mountain for that matter—changes the rules. Landmarks that are in plain sight during the day, become invisible; terrain, more difficult to negotiate. Let alone if a blinding storm is blowing. This time, Ricky Bouchard would have to depend on her senses, on her instincts, moving by feel and by touch, relying on what the mountain told her.

She moved across the snow-covered scree, clipped onto the fixed rope, and began to push upward. The wind howled, icy pellets bit into her cheeks, and the thick snow swirled around her.

Her mind flashed back over the miles and the years, taking her once again to the thawing, ice covered pond behind her home in Val-David. Stepping out onto its blue-white surface, feeling it creak and groan under her weight, hearing Jean-Pierre's young voice calling out encouragement to her in the early spring air.

Knowing how Jean-Pierre thought she was so incredibly brave.

Knowing herself, that her solitary mission was incredibly foolish.

Wondering...would she ever make it across?

Ricky put her head down against the wind lashing against her, and continued to climb. Then, as now, there would be no turning back.

❈ ◆ ❈ ◆ ❈

Allison Peabody slowly drifted towards consciousness, her mind a complete blank; too tired to dream, too overstressed to think clearly. All she knew was that a chill had woken her. She was cold again, and now that she thought about it, it seemed like every bone, every muscle in her body ached, too.

Why, it was if she'd just climbed Mount Everest or something!

"Nnnngh."

She rolled onto her back, detecting the encumbrance of the oxygen mask, and it was then that the bits and pieces began to flutter together. And with those shards of memory tumbling into place, her pulse quickened.

Okay.

She knew she was back in her tent; she remembered that much, recalled the bitingly hot tea Ricky had made her swallow...*Ricky*! She could feel her presence near, even now. She forced open a swollen eyelid. There she was, right next to her, watching over her, with salt and pepper hair, and—

"Lou?" Allison blinked. And blinked again. The figure next to her was blurred, but she could see enough to know who it was—and who it wasn't.

The figure moved closer. "Right here, Allie."

"Wha—where's Ricky?" She slowly levered herself onto her elbows, groaning. God, it felt as though she'd been hit by a truck.

"C'mon. Let's try to get some more tea into you." Gently, he helped her remove her oxygen mask.

"Aah!" she cried out, reaching for her eyes as unforced tears began to stream from them. "I—my eyes...they hurt! Feels like...I've got sandpaper in them or something."

"Just a touch of snow-blindness, I think," Lou explained, tugging her hands away. "Easy there. Leave 'em alone, if you can. Just rest them. It'll go away," he soothed. "Really."

"Okay," she said, gasping against the painful stinging.

"Here." The attorney offered her some hot tea. "Drink this. It'll help to warm you up."

Gratefully, Allison accepted the tea, trying not spill it onto her trembling hand. She felt so cold now, deep down to the very core of her being. A part of her understood that this was a good thing; it meant that she was warming up, as opposed to the non-sensation of freezing to death. If it hadn't been for Ricky...

"Lou," she peered at the attorney through puffy, slitted eyes, "where's Ricky?"

"Well," he shaped his words carefully, "she's not here."

Allison was sure she hadn't heard right. "But...she was

here. She *was.*"

"Dorje never made it back, Allie," he told her, visibly bracing himself. "She went out there, after him."

"No."

"Allison—" he reached out for her.

"NO!" She shook him away, spilling her tea onto the sleeping pad.

"She wouldn't do that." A faint whisper. "She wouldn't." There had to be some other rational explanation. She turned to Lou, a pained, half-hopeful smile on her face. "Where is she? Really."

"Dorje was calling in on his radio," he continued with the devastating truth, "but we couldn't return the transmission. We're not sure where he is, but Ricky thinks she can find him—"

"No!" Allison lurched for the door of the tent. "Ricky, no!"

Lou sprang forward, grabbing for her arms. "Allison!"

"Let me go!" she cried out, fighting him. "Don't you see? I have to go. I have to help her!"

"You can't!"

"She needs our *help*, Lou!" Allison was weeping now. "Why would she do that? Why would she go alone? I have to—" With renewed effort, she pushed him away. Moving quickly on her hands and knees, she was through the vestibule and had unzipped the opening. Ricky Bouchard was out there, somewhere, all alone. It wasn't supposed to be like this. It wasn't.

"Allison!"

She ignored Lou's pained shout. But she felt the strong arms that wrapped around her middle, tackling her so that she lay half in and half out of the tent, pinned in place. "Please!" A hoarse whisper in her ear. "Ricky knows what she's doing. You have to trust her!"

"Noooo!" she cried out, the gut-wrenching howl of a wounded animal. She strained desperately at the force holding her down, tried to fight it, but it was all too much. And then the hardships of the last two days and the sudden shock of the cold finally reared up and took their toll, and she felt the strength draining from her body. She lay on the ground, empty, as the storm shrieked around her. "You promised you wouldn't leave me," she sobbed, the tears slipping off her face, dotting the snow beneath her. "You promised."

Chapter
Twenty-five

Allison Peabody sat quietly in her tent, half-propped up in her sleeping bag, her mind dulled thanks to the constant, mesmerizing hiss of her oxygen regulator. Lou Silvers sat next to her, an extra jacket wrapped around his legs, busying himself melting more snow for tea.

Through the night she'd waited in a lonely vigil, staring at the silent, useless radio by her side, letting her fingers from time to time trail up to the protection cord she wore around her neck. Ricky never should have given it to her, and she never should have accepted it, but it was too late to do anything about that now. The fates of Ricky Bouchard and Dorje Sherpa rested in the hands of the Mother Goddess.

Allison had begun to think that the storm might never end, but around 3 a.m., it finally began to ease; the tent walls stopped billowing in upon them, and by the time Pemba checked on them at dawn, delicate colors of rosette and gold were streaking through a clearing eastern sky.

But still no Ricky Bouchard.

If anyone could survive a night exposed on Mount Everest, Allison fervently believed that Ricky could. People had done it before, mostly unintentionally, but she recalled hearing a tale several years before of a daredevil Sherpa who'd pulled the stunt of staying out all night—on the summit, no less.

But of the others, those inadvertent victims, many had suffered the horrible, crippling injuries of hypothermia, hypoxia, and frostbite. The frostbite had to be the worst, she figured, not because it killed you, which it sometimes did, but because more often than not, it let you live.

Disfigured.

Handicapped.

She'd seen a case of it once, when she'd gone to climb Denali. They'd just arrived at the muddy, smelly Base Camp, when a young man was brought down. He'd been a solo climber, a bit of an eccentric loner, and had gotten caught in a storm he'd been ill equipped to handle. By the time rescuers found him, his limbs had been frozen solid. Which had actually helped, in a way. Frozen, he'd still been able to walk until they were able to get him to a med-evac zone.

Back at Base Camp, a physician had begun the thawing process: soaking his arms and legs in lukewarm water. But the way he'd looked...Allison had nearly been sick to her stomach. The skin of his face, his hands and feet, was a dark, charcoal color. And the swelling...his nose had appeared nearly flush to his face.

She could still remember his screams, as the dying tissue in his body tried to revive, only to give up its last. She'd heard later he'd lost both feet, and all the fingers on one hand.

No! Don't think about that. It will not happen. It won't!

All she could do was wait. And hope. She'd been afraid to fall asleep, afraid she might miss Ricky's call, but she was ashamed to admit that she had fallen into a dazed, hypoxic slumber more than once during the night. She superstitiously chided herself, fretting that by having done so, she might have somehow lessened the mountaineer's chances.

As time passed with still no word, a sense of detachment began to envelop her, deadening her senses. Idly, she began to wonder if she were going into shock. Or maybe it was just her system reacting, withdrawing the way it always had, before she'd met Ricky.

Because it was easier not to feel, not to hurt.

She could turn the pain off anytime she wanted to, right? After all, she'd spent her lifetime perfecting the self-defense technique.

She was at peace in her numbness, her isolation.

Preferred it, in fact—being alone.

And so she stayed that way when they came to get her,

insisting that she descend immediately, telling her that staying any longer in the death zone might mean she'd never get down at all. She supposed that fine point should matter to her, but it didn't really. How could they ever understand? And in the end, she hadn't the strength to fight them. So she let herself be short-roped half-blind down the Lhotse Face, all the way to Camp II. Told herself that she wasn't dying a little bit inside, with every step that took her farther away from Ricky.

At Camp II she blankly passed through the makeshift field hospital that had been the Peak Performance dining tent, letting the doctor from the British expedition poke and prod her, telling her how very lucky she was.

It wasn't until the next morning, after some perfectly kind, considerate strangers had guided her down through the Cwm and the Icefall into Base Camp, that she dispassionately took in the news that by the evening before, reports indicated there were two climbers with severe injuries in at Camp IV. The information had been hopscotched along an international chain of climbers and radios, since afternoon weather patterns and the altitude were still wreaking havoc with communications.

The injured climbers were to be brought down to Camp II possibly today, and from there, thanks to a rare, perilous helicopter landing in the Cwm, would be evacuated to Pheriche.

Two climbers, alive.

Barely.

Even then, Allison refused to let herself believe it. To hold out any hope. Because if she did...

No.

It simply hurt too damn much.

❀✦❀✦❀✦❀

The atmosphere in Base Camp changes distinctly after the summit attempts have been made. The energy, the excitement, the anticipation that pervaded in early April gives way as May draws to a close with a joyous exhaustion, or bitter disappointment, or grief.

The little town of Base Camp mourns if its community has been diminished by the loss of one or more of its members; the only thing that travels faster than news of a summit success is the word of a summit death. All the expeditions feel it, are moved by it; knowing, but for the whim of the Mother Goddess, it could have been one of their own.

Some swear to never come back, shaken to the core by the rawness of the experience, the brute-force game of survival that they have played out against the mountain. Others resolve to return again one day, stronger, perhaps better equipped, and with better luck. To finally seize the prize that has thus far eluded their grasp.

There is a distinct end-of-season feel to the whole scene. Some climbers, who for one reason or another never even made a summit attempt, are long gone. Others, who have returned from the higher camps, simply keep descending, anxious to return to the green, thicker air below. Expeditions are leaving; the sounds of equipment and tents being broken down and packed up echo through the valley. Sounds punctuated by the ever-present cracks and grumbles from the Khumbu, as though it were urging them along, hastening their departure.

Slowly, almost imperceptibly, the mighty glacier has begun to reclaim its territory. Temporary structures: tent foundations, latrines, cooking facilities, begin to tilt and pitch in opposing directions, a tinker-toy town after a small earthquake. The glacier movement can also generate great lakes of melt water in the most inconvenient of places—the makeshift volleyball court, or a sleeping climber's tent. By the time winter arrived, nearly all signs of any man-made structures would have been obliterated.

Leaving behind nothing but that sweep of rock and ice, thrusting impossibly high, touching the rich texture of billowing clouds above, standing out in brilliant relief against a sharply blue sky. Leaving behind memories, too, of what might have been.

Of what very nearly was.

Allison Peabody slowly picked her way across the rocky scree, her head bowed against the bright mid-morning sunshine. Powerless to withstand the exhaustion that had overwhe!med her body, she'd collapsed into her sleeping bag yesterday afternoon and slept straight through—the first real sleep she'd had in days. The rest had certainly helped her eyesight. The doctors had told her that the skin on your cornea would be replaced every 24 hours, if you rested your eyes.

They'd been right.

The swelling was down, and the crusty pain she'd endured had gradually dissipated.

Better still, the disconcerting feeling of not being able to fully see, was gone.

So now she could see, so what?

Would Ricky be able to see? Would Ricky be able to walk? Was Ricky even alive? Communications on the mountain were still terrible, Lou had informed her, when he'd stopped by Ricky's tent earlier this morning. Allison had chosen to sleep there, feeling closer to the mountaineer somehow, imagining, in the ebb and flow of her dreams that Ricky had merely stepped away momentarily, and that she would soon return. Laughing, smiling, and bearing a thermos of hot tea.

Lou had told her that a Nepalese army helicopter was going to chance the dicey landing above the Icefall shortly, and that hopefully, despite tired batteries and poor reception, that same information had gotten through to the people caring for the injured climbers at Camp II.

Multiple expeditions had pitched in to help out in the rescue, and Jangbu Nuru was still up there, Lou had added. As sirdar, he'd refused to come down until all under his charge were accounted for.

Jangbu. A better man by far than the majority she'd known in her lifetime.

The attorney had urged her to join him in the dining tent, and at first Allison had refused, her mind already on where they were taking Ricky, and how she could get to her.

"Please, Allison," Lou had pleaded. "You've got to keep your strength up. And..." he'd paused, "I—I promised her I'd take care of you."

That had nearly fractured her, punched through the wall of nothingness she'd carefully built around herself.

It was all she'd been able to do to wave Lou off, nodding that she'd join him shortly after all.

Cautiously, Allison chanced a glance up the mountain. It was hard to believe, here in the peaceful calm of Base Camp, that somewhere up there, the drama still continued. It felt strange to her, being down here in the deep valley, drinking in the thick air. Like she didn't belong here anymore...was separate from it all, somehow.

And indeed, that was true, she considered, crossing her arms in front of her chest at the chill she still felt, at the coldness that permeated her being like a guest who refused to leave. Her place was with Ricky, no matter what.

No matter...where.

On that, she'd already quietly made up her mind. There was nothing left for her in her old life, nothing that she even remotely cared to return to. If Ricky were gone...well, that would simply be that.

She stepped into the dining tent. Lou Silvers was there, gingerly sipping on a hot cup of coffee, a plate of pancakes sat in front of him, barely touched. "Hey!" His pale eyes crinkled in greeting. "Glad you made it, Allie."

She offered him what she hoped passed for a smile and sat down across from him.

Lopsang quickly presented her with a cup of hot tea. "What I get for you today, Miss Allison?" The Sherpa cook was distinctly subdued, the normal merriment gone from his dark eyes, his weathered face.

Guiltily, Allison's thoughts flickered to the young Dorje. Remembered that there were other people out there who, like her, worried, feared for a loved one on the mountain.

"Miss Allison? Pancake? Omelet?"

"Uh..." she caught Lou's warning eye, "maybe some toast, to start?"

The attorney frowned, but said nothing.

Allison fiddled with her cup and drew in a tentative breath. "I—I suppose I should talk to Sandra about how I can get down to Pheriche," she said stiffly, keeping her eyes on the steam rising from her tea.

"I think they're planning something for tomorrow. Jim and Kevin should be ready to travel by then."

"What about Mike and Patsy?" Allison asked as a matter of course. Two people she would likely as not never see again.

"They hauled off out of here early this morning. They couldn't get away fast enough. Left a lot of expensive stuff behind, too," he clucked. "Paid some Sherpa porters up from Lobuje to get 'em down. Last thing I heard was him mouthing off about having his lawyers look at the 'assumption of risk' clause in the Peak Performance contract." He shook his head, grimacing. "The guy still doesn't get it."

Risk, Allison thought. *And the choices you make.*

Just like Ricky had told her, you had to live with them. Trying, somehow, to factor in with them the vagaries of life.

A snowstorm that wasn't supposed to happen, and an oxygen cache that went missing.

A team leader who turned out to be unfit, both physically

and ethically.

And a mountaineer who had already performed above and beyond what was humanly possible, only to tempt the Fates once more.

Why had she done that? Why?

"You know," the attorney continued, picking idly at his pancakes, "I've been thinking. She saved me, up there." He looked to Allison for a reaction, but the younger woman kept her eyes lowered. "I can be so pig-headed sometimes...like when I'm doing a cross-examination in court. I just get so focused...I go for it. Risk it all, no matter what. But, if she had encouraged me to keep going...like Jim did with Mike," he paused, remembering, "I might have."

Allison lifted her eyes to Lou, saw the pain on the man's face, and the understanding, too. He knew what she was going through. Knew that his kind words were a poor substitute for that which she truly desired. Her heart stuttered as she allowed herself to feel that, to let herself go, allowing the ice that had built up protectively around her spirit begin to melt.

Ricky had done only what she'd had to do, what she was *compelled* to do, by being the kind of woman she was. The same quiet, noble woman of strength and character who Allison had fallen in love with.

"She saved me," Lou repeated, shaking his head in wonder.

The *whump-whump* of helicopter blades began to sound in the distance, drawing closer, heading for the Cwm.

"She saved us all," Allison hoarsely whispered, knowing it was true of herself, most of all.

❋ ◆ ❋ ◆ ❋

The helicopter passing overhead, a rare enough experience at altitude, drew the curious attention of those still remaining in Base Camp. Climbers stood in small clusters gazing up, solemnly aware of the unfortunate purpose of the unusual flight.

Paul Andersen had crawled out of his tent and was watching; he offered Allison and Lou a tired wave. The guide was in fairly good shape after all he'd been through, and he would be able to help guide the hike down the valley the following morning.

With its big engine whining, the chopper circled once, then disappeared from view.

"He's down," Lou said softly.

They stood there quietly, boring their eyes into the sky above the lip of the Icefall. The thin air at that altitude dangerously tested the helicopter's capabilities; takeoff would be critical.

Allison listened to the distant thumping of the spinning rotors, imagining that every beat matched the pounding of her heart. What was going on up there? How were Ricky and Dorje? When were they going to tell her *something*? Allison felt as through she were hanging on to the remnants of her sanity by only the thinnest of threads.

Just then a man approached. Tall and lanky, with curly black hair, a full dark beard, and a friendly, wind-burned face. "Thought I'd see how you were doing, love."

"Oh, Harry!" she cried, the recognition dawning. She threw herself into the Englishman's arms. "Thank you. Thank you for all your help up there. If it hadn't been for you—"

"Don't thank me," he said chuckling, patting her back. "That's some guide you people had. Shame about what happened, though," he added.

The emotion drained from her face. Wordlessly, Allison pulled away, returning her attention to the mountain.

Noticing her sudden withdrawal, Harry cleared his throat. "Well...ah, any news? That's what the whirlybird's about, right?"

Allison didn't answer him. Couldn't if she'd tried.

"Yes," Lou told him, speaking for the younger woman. "They brought Ricky and Dorje down from Camp IV yesterday, or at least that's what we've been able to gather."

"And?"

"And...it doesn't look good," Lou said tightly, his eyes fastened on the stiffened back of Allison Peabody.

The whine of the chopper's engine suddenly intensified. Rising slowly above the Khumbu, a black insect against the white vastness of the massif, was the army helicopter. It seemed to hover for a moment at the edge of the Icefall, laboring, and then it began to zip away towards the southwest, towards Pheriche.

"There it goes," Harry said, shielding his eyes as he followed it.

Allison watched it too, watched it take what was left of her battered heart off of the mountain.

"Okay." Dr. Sandra Ortiz emerged from the communication tent with one of the short-wave radios in her hand. "I was able to get that they've got the two patients on board and are heading to Pheriche."

"I've got to get there," Allison blurted out, feeling a panic begin to bloom in her chest at the thought of Ricky leaving her behind.

"We'll be having a group start down the mountain tomorrow, Allison," the doctor began. "You can—"

"No," she cut her off. "I have to go now. Today. To Pheriche."

"What?" The petite physician was plainly confused. "There's nothing you can—they're only getting stabilized at the clinic there, while the chopper loads more fuel. They'll be off to Kathmandu by the time—"

"I don't care!" Allison insisted, feeling flushed, angry, feeling *something*, for the first time in two days. Her hands clenched in two tight fists. "I have to go today."

"But—"

"Today!" she cried out, realizing she was on the verge of losing it. Desperately, she fought for control of her teetering emotions, worrying that if she gave way to all of them, right at this minute, she'd never be able to pull herself back together again. And she had to stay strong.

For Ricky's sake.

"Look," Harry Owens stepped in, looking warily back and forth between Sandra Ortiz and Allison. "We've got a yak train heading down this afternoon with some of our equipment and things. I—I'm sure you can go with them, if you feel you need to."

"I do," Allison said, willing herself to calm. "Thanks."

"It's the least I can do," the young Englishman said, tapping the bill of his cap. "I'll just see about it, then." He headed back towards the British camp.

Allison sighed heavily, weak with relief. Okay. She had a plan.

"You all right?" Pale gray eyes gazed at her in concern.

"Yeah," she told him, watching Sandra Ortiz retreat back to the communications tent. And was reminded of the conversation she'd overheard on the radio up top. Only days ago, though it seemed like years. "Excuse me."

She left Lou there, trailing instead after the physician.

"Is there something else I can do for you, Allison?" The doctor had stopped at the entrance to the tent and turned, detecting her presence.

"Why did you do it?" she asked, proud that she was able to keep her voice so firm, so even.

"I'm sorry. I don't know what—"

"Why did you let him go up there, knowing he had a problem?"

The doctor's face became an unreadable mask. "I'm sorry. I can't discuss any patient's medical history with—"

"Your *patient*," Allison ground out, her anger building, "was our team leader. He almost got himself killed. And he jeopardized the lives of the rest of us, too."

"I'm sure I don't know what you're talking about," Sandra said stiffly, but Allison could see her dark brown eyes begin to dart nervously from side to side.

"Don't worry about any lawsuit, lady. Not from me, anyway." Allison laughed bitterly. "That's not my style." She put her hands on her hips. "I just wanted to see if I could understand what kind of a doctor was willing to risk sending a man to his death." She shook her head. "And from where I stand," she let her eyes travel up and down the other woman's form, apprising her, "there's not much to see." She spun on her heel to leave.

"Wait."

Allison turned slowly back around, taking in the pained, stricken expression on the physician's face.

"You wouldn't understand."

Allison folded her arms. "Try me."

"I had to. You see..." she hesitated, "we have a history, Jim and I." Just mentioning the team leader's name seemed to lend her a sense of confidence, and she was actually able to relax her face into a small, shy smile. "I—I love him." Her hands fluttered self-consciously. "And...he loves me, too."

Oh, God. So that was what it all came down to in the end? To two people allowing themselves to be used by each other, telling lies and believing them, all? For what?

"That's not love," Allison said, gazing at the sad, misguided woman before her. "That's sick."

And she turned and walked away. The sooner she could get the hell out of here and get to Ricky Bouchard's side, the better.

❊ ◆ ❊ ◆ ❊ ◆ ❊

It felt good to be busy, to have something to do. Folding sweaters. Stowing gear. Cleaning up her campsite. It helped to keep her mind off...things.

Until she found her journal in her hands.

She didn't open it. Instead, with her breath catching in her throat, she quickly stowed it in her duffel, glad to have it out of sight.

She hadn't written in it in days. Wondered if she would ever write in it again. And, if she did, what sort of a story would the words she put to paper tell?

Allison finished packing up her own belongings, placed the duffle in the vestibule of her tent, and then made her way with heavy boot steps towards Ricky's tent at the far edge of the encampment.

Pemba had assured her he'd take care of her climbing gear, including dismantling her tent and Ricky's too, so all she had to worry about were the smaller, personal items. At some point, miraculously, all the gear was supposed to show up at the airport in Kathmandu, ready to go—wherever.

Taking a deep breath, Allison ducked inside Ricky's tent. Lou had offered to help her, wondering if this might be too hard on her, but she'd declined his assistance. She preferred to be alone for this solitary task, considered it as an elegy of a sort to Ricky, keeping her in her thoughts, keeping her memories alive, along with her oh-so-tentative hopes.

Gazing around the dim interior, it dawned on Allison for the first time how there wasn't much there, other than the small camp stove, and the odd bit of extra climbing gear. Not much of a personal nature, anyway. It appeared that Veronique Bouchard liked to travel light.

Allison threw what she could into a rucksack. Some clothes, including one of Ricky's thick, red sweaters. She could not help but nuzzle it, breathing in a faint trace of the mountaineer's scent.

Letting her heart feel the ache, the need.

After a time she gathered herself. Slowly, reluctantly, she folded it away. She moved to the head of the tent where Ricky had kept her lantern. Next to it she found a few other items: a Buddhist prayer book and a worn pocketknife bearing the faint initials *JPV.*

Jean-Pierre Valmont.

A small leather portfolio containing several folders was jammed behind the sleeping pad. Allison reached for it and saw that it was unzipped. Idly, she flipped it open, figuring it contained business papers. She saw at a glance that it did: paperwork and contracts concerning the climb, including profiles of all the Peak Performance clients.

With the profile of one "Allison Peabody" placed on top. A faint smile played across Allison's lips as she took note of a bold script across the bottom of the page: "Has possibilities, but will need to keep an eye on her."

Thank God she had.

Allison's eyes traveled to the photo of a pinch-faced, bored looking young woman, whose green eyes drilled into the camera as though she had much better places to be than in some two-bit photo shop, getting her picture taken. She barely recognized the sullen stranger staring out at her.

A woman who simply didn't exist anymore.

Allison carefully closed the portfolio and packed it away. The tent seemed so quiet now, so empty, without the powerful, natural force of the mountaineer's presence. But if she tried hard... The young blonde closed her eyes, sending her soul out among the cathedral spires of white, searching for Ricky. For her spirit.

She just *had* to make it. *Had* to be okay.

And then the tears began to fall, unbidden, because she knew things wouldn't be all right, not ever again. Ricky was only human. If she somehow survived this trial, their lives would be changed forever. The reports said the climbers were badly injured. How did you come back from that?

Well, she and Ricky would find a way. Together. *After all, Allison,* she crawled towards the door, *you're in this for the long haul.*

Just let that cantankerous mountaineer try to get rid of her!

Outside, she perched on the flat rock at the entrance to Ricky's tent, where they'd both sat together so many times, enjoying the sun, the stars, and each other.

The kindly Harry Owens had confirmed that the yak train would be leaving within the hour or so; and that was just fine with her. She definitely would be ready to say goodbye to this place.

She stared up at the mountain, thinking of all that had happened, of what she'd discovered about other people...and about herself. She was proud of what she'd accomplished, but at the same time, she knew a man had died up there.

Poor Phil Christy.

And as for his friend...a return to the lower elevations had helped in his recovery, but a stunned, devastated Kevin MacBride still was unable to recall exactly what had happened. They'd panicked when their oxygen had run out in the storm during the descent; he'd remembered that much. Confusion and lethargy had soon followed. They'd kept having to stop and rest until—until suddenly Kevin was alone.

On his own.

He didn't even remember stumbling back into camp or hearing Pemba's frantic visit to his tent. A typical reaction to hypoxia, Allison knew.

Was it all worth it, she wondered?

Worth the price?

If all that she'd been through had been necessary to bring her to this place, to Ricky—then yes, it most certainly was. Sighing, she allowed herself to find a certain peace in that.

She lifted her eyes towards the hidden summit; she could see the flag of its plume flying, misty white against the azure blue sky. Had she ever climbed that high? It seemed as though it were all a fanciful dream. She let her gaze track down...down along the Southwest Face into the Cwm, along 29,035 icy cold feet of hope and hell that finally terminated in the frozen river of the Khumbu.

She saw a blur of movement in the jumble of smaller seracs at the base of the Icefall, at the point where it widened out into the rock and ice delta of the lower moraine. She blinked and was pleased to find that her healing eyesight had not deceived her. It was a climber—no—two climbers, just finishing the traverse. Allison was mildly surprised. It was a bit late in the morning— just before noon—to be mucking about up there, although such a thing wasn't entirely unheard of.

They were probably just as anxious to get the hell out of there as everyone else was, Allison considered, and she slowly pushed herself to her feet. They had to be coming from Camp II. Her stomach fluttered at the thought of what news they might have on Ricky, but she had to know.

The climbers were moving slowly, probably not taking any chances now that they were nearly down, and Allison had to squint against the sun that was now nearly directly in her eyes.

She turned slightly to her right, still heading for the base of the Icefall, and now she could see the climbers again, closer. The first climber, wearing the floppy multi-colored hat of a Sherpa, had turned to help the second climber down; helped him awkwardly unclip from the rope as he stood half bent over, catching his breath.

Hmnn, Allison thought. *That second guy must've had a tough time getting—*

Allison's heart caught in her throat. The second climber had turned and was looking towards her. A climber wearing black pile pants and a red and black jacket.

No. It couldn't be.

She willed her feet to move.

Impossible.

The climber straightened and stood tall, impossibly tall, eyes fastened upon her now. She could feel the heat of the gaze, even through the glacier glasses the figure wore.

Could it be?

A gloved hand slowly lifted in greeting.

"Ricky?" Allison cried out, breaking into a shambling run across the scree. "Ricky!"

The figure started to lurch towards her, assisted by the Sherpa's hand at its elbow.

"Oh, God, Ricky!" Allison's voice was a choked gasp as she flung herself into Ricky's arms, nearly bowling her over. "Is it really you?"

It couldn't be, could it?

But there was no mistaking the embrace, the feel, the touch, the soothing words her hearing could not process, and the way her body and her soul reacted to it all.

And so her senses confirmed to her what her stunned mind refused to register: that somehow, someway, Ricky Bouchard had just walked out of the Icefall.

"Nice to see you, too," the mountaineer replied, her voice a thin rasp.

"I—I can't believe it..." Allison kept her head buried against Ricky's chest, afraid to let go lest this ghost holding her somehow disappear. "What are you doing here? I thought you were—"

"I climbed up this damn mountain," Ricky said, holding her tightly. "There was no way in hell I wasn't going to climb down."

"But...how?"   Allison lifted her head, her eyes brimming
with tears.   "We heard there were two climbers that—"

"There were," Ricky explained, coughing.   "It was a regular
party up there."   She released Allison and started to walk slowly
towards the tents.   She draped her arm over the smaller woman's
shoulder, allowing her to take some of her weight.   "It took me a
while to find Dorje, but I did, about 50 yards into the gullies.   He
was in bad shape.   Hypoxic.   I knew there was no way to get him
moving anytime soon.   Not in that weather.   So I started to dig
out a snow cave."

"A snow cave?"   Allison gazed at the mountaineer in wonder.

"Yeah," the tall woman croaked.   "It wasn't much but...it at
least protected us from the brunt of the weather.   I'd just about
had it finished, too, when this...this guy comes barreling out of
the dark...from above."

"What?"   Allison stopped, allowing Ricky to catch her
breath.

"Yeah.   From the International Expedition.   Wearing one of
our empty Poisk bottles, I might add," she said dryly.   "Poor guy
was frozen solid," Ricky shook her head, remembering.   "By that
time I was feeling pretty knackered, too."   The mountaineer
started to move again, with Allison carefully supporting her.
"So we hunkered down until the next morning."

"Until they found you?"

"Nah."   A rough laugh.   "We found them.   It took a couple
of shots of dex each to get 'em moving, that and a few...strong
words."   The corner of her mouth turned up in a grin.   We started
down the slope—you know the drill—one step at a time.   Didn't
catch up to Jangbu and a couple guys from that British expedition, until mid-afternoon."

"Thank God."   Allison almost wept in relief.   She angled
her head to take in the quiet form of the Peak Performance
climbing sirdar, Jangbu Nuru.

"And how are you doing, Jangbu?" she asked, realizing with
some small sense of embarrassment that she hadn't addressed
him up until now.   The wiry little Sherpa had been walking close
to Ricky on her other side, discreetly busying himself with a
balky carabiner.

"I fine, Miss Allison, just fine," he beamed, teeth flashing
from his dark skin.

"Hell, he's better than fine," Ricky chuckled hoarsely.   "I had to talk him out of having another go at the top."

They were approaching the tents now. Several Sherpas had noticed Jangbu's approach and were excitedly calling to him.

"I good luck again, okay, Ricky?" The sirdar peered carefully at the mountaineer, awaiting her response.

"Yeah," she told him, grinning. "You are, my friend."

And with another burst of a smile, the Sherpa left them, heading towards the growing crowd of his brethren. They welcomed him with shouts and laughter, slaps on the back, and an overflowing mug of *chang*.

"C'mon." Allison urged the mountaineer on. "Let's get you looked at."

"I'm fine," Ricky insisted. "It's...Dorje, I think, will be okay." She gazed in the direction the helicopter had flown. "But that other guy..." She pursed her lips. "Frostbite. Bad. Plus...he was bleeding from the nose and—" Ricky had to stop again. She pulled off her glasses and rubbed at her eyes. "I don't know."

It was then that Allison was able to fully take in the mountaineer's gaunt, haggard condition. The windburn had turned her face especially dark, her sunken eyes were two blue orbs set adrift in an angry bloodshot sea, and her lips were swollen and cracked.

"I—I hope he makes it," Ricky finished, wearily replacing her glacier glasses.

Allison could feel the mountaineer's pain. Ricky knew she'd tried her best, and yet she felt that her supreme effort still might not have been enough. But that was Ricky Bouchard. Always putting the welfare of others above her own.

No matter the cost.

It took a moment before Allison trusted herself to speak.

"When you didn't come back...I thought you were dead," she said quietly, struggling to keep her voice from faltering. "And then they said they'd found two climbers...badly injured...and I—" her composure finally broke, and she let the feelings flow at last... All of them.

Felt the hurt and the pain, the despair and the relief.

And the love.

She needed to feel that, most of all. Had been so afraid she never would, ever again.

She was unaware of precisely when Ricky took her in her arms again; she only knew that she was where she belonged—

wrapped inside those strong arms, safe.

Home.

And when her rockslide of pent-up emotions had given way at last to a few loose, skittering pebbles, she heard the mountaineer's husky voice buzzing in her ear.

"And how are you doing? Really."

Allison could feel her partner's body tense, awaiting her answer.

"I'm fine," she said. "Now."

And with those words, though she'd thought she hadn't any tears left to cry, she was wrong; they came spilling down just the same. She felt Ricky stroking her hair, trying to comfort her with small, gentle motions.

"I could never leave you, Allison," she swore to her. "Ever."

Chapter
Twenty-six

Ricky Bouchard and Allison Peabody sat at a small table in the secluded rear corner of an otherwise noisy, crowded, smoke-filled bar and would-be restaurant. Allison tugged at the hem of her short blue canvas skirt, which contrasted nicely with her red and white flowered cotton top. The mountaineer featured khaki shorts, a white T-shirt, and hiking boots. She laughed at something Allison said, the brilliance of her smile highlighting the deep tan of her skin.

The casual observer would've been hard-pressed to argue the point that both women, the taller one in particular, had not just come back from, say, an extended sojourn in the South Pacific. Were it not for the fact that said bar and ersatz dining emporium were in the shadow of the Himalayas, in Kathmandu.

"I don't care what you say," Allison said, shooting Ricky a look of feigned injury. "It's definitely quieter in these seats. We're not as close to the music."

"Quiet," the mountaineer replied, tongue firmly in cheek, "is not usually a word I would associate with this place."

"This place" happened to be "The Rum Doodle." The Rummer, as alpinists referred to it, was *the* hot spot in Kathmandu for the *après*-Everest climber crowd. With its dark spruce and oak interior, its somewhat sticky wooden floor, and a jukebox locked in a 1960's rock 'n roll repertoire, occasionally interspersed with dashes of Motown, it was as likely a place as any for high-altitude astronauts to re-enter the earth's atmosphere.

To "acclimatize" as it were, to the relatively lower reaches of the planet after long weeks away, breathing in the thick, luxurious, albeit smoke-filled air.

Upon returning to so-called civilization, a stopover at the Rum Doodle was a definite must. Founded and operated by British ex-patriots, the Rummer owed its name to a work of fiction, *Ascent of the Rum Doodle,* a satirical account of an old-time mountaineering expedition's ascent of the 40,000 foot make-believe Rum Doodle.

Although the food was mediocre, the drinks were better, but it was not exclusively the hospitality of the place that had for years attracted an overflow of patrons. Behind a long, deeply pitted bar, whose wooden edges had been worn smooth by decades of chaffing elbows and arms, hung four locked glass cases. The area was guarded hawkishly by the Rummer's management.

The cases did not hold prized liqueurs or elixirs from the Orient. Rather, each case protected the big boards that contained the Mount Everest summit register. Ricky had shown Allison the register as soon as they'd come in, and the younger woman had marveled at the scribbled inventory of history's climbing greats: Sir Edmund Hillary, Reinhold Messner, Ed Viesturs, and more. Drawing as close as she could to the register without eliciting the attendant's ire, she'd found on her own a "Veronique Bouchard"—more than one, in fact, with the most recent entry immediately followed by the flourished signature of Jean-Pierre Valmont.

"Can I have another burger?" Allison blotted the corner of her mouth with a paper napkin. "That was so good—I've been dreaming about them for weeks!"

"Only if you promise to share." The mountaineer casually lifted her hand, immediately getting the attention of a rather harried waiter passing by.

"Oh, no you don't." Allison circled her arms protectively around her depleted plate. "I saw what you did to my French fries." She offered her scowling companion a cheeky smile. "You're on your own, sweetheart."

After Ricky's stunning return to Base Camp, they'd taken their time making their way back down the trail. They'd nearly ended up leaving that afternoon anyway with the yak train, once Ricky had found out that Allison had already packed and was prepared to leave. It had taken all of the younger woman's considerable persuasive skills to finally get the mountaineer to relent, to take a couple of days and get some of her strength back, before they departed.

Once they'd begun their descent, however, it had gradually unfurled into a leisurely, intoxicating experience of re-acquainting themselves with the earthly things they'd nearly forgotten.

A juniper tree, swaying in a warm, afternoon breeze.

The sweet scent of a farmer's tiny field, freshly plowed.

And not waking up in the middle of the night, breathless, desperately gasping for oxygen that simply wasn't there.

They'd even stopped once more at the monastery in Thyanboche. There, Allison had been only too happy to again endure cup upon cup of the salted, yak-butter tea pressed upon her by the beatific, well-meaning monks. Knowing that by doing so it meant they would be granted another audience with the *Rimpoche.* Allison would have sipped their tea for a week if she'd had to, smiling and nodding all the while, for the opportunity of being able to offer thanks to the Mother Goddess for having granted them both safe passage.

Ricky would have been content to trek all the way back to Kathmandu, but when they'd arrived in Lukla yesterday, at the entrance to the Sagarmatha National Park, Allison had convinced her to board a small plane for the last 100 miles of the journey. Once back in the capital city, safely ensconced in the relative comfort of the Hotel Garuda, they'd taken the remainder of the day to just laze about, resting, relaxing, and rediscovering one another.

It was amazing, Allison had thought last night, lying contentedly in the mountaineer's arms, how quickly things could change. One week, you're on the upper reaches of Everest, fighting for your life while trying to keep from freezing to death, and the next you're in a near-tropical zone, fighting off the heat while you try to re-adapt to the smog, the growl of traffic, the sound of babies crying in the night. It was a dissonant, confusing clash of images, of sensations, of realities.

The only thing that had even remotely allowed her to begin to reconcile it all, to make sense of it, was the woman who'd slumbered so deeply beside her. She'd been unable to take her eyes off her, watching her as she slept; the mountaineer's face looked so relaxed, so at peace in the faint shafts of moonlight that skipped across their bed. She'd remained vigilant long into

the night, secure in Ricky's arms, aware of every rise and fall of
her chest, treasuring the mountaineer's survival for the precious
miracle that it was.

This morning Ricky had announced they were going to visit
the local hospital, where the authorities had taken Dorje as well
as the other climber she had rescued. Anatoli Rimskov was his
name, they'd found out, a climber who'd joined the International
Expedition from his home base in Uzbeckistan.

Dorje was improving slowly but steadily, they'd been
pleased to see. He'd lost a few toes, and several fingers on his
puffy, swollen hands were still in doubt, but the little Sherpa
remained optimistic about it all, shyly telling them how he
planned for another summit next season, even as he'd thanked
Ricky profusely.

They hadn't really been able to talk to Anatoli.

The high altitude cerebral edema, or HACE, had hit him
hard. He'd just come out of a coma but was still drifting in and
out of any real state of awareness. It would be a long haul back
for the man, the doctors had told them as they'd stood in the
doorway of his room, gazing in on him. In time, the medical
experts were cautiously hopeful he'd return to full cerebral function.

But he would never climb again.

Ricky had been quiet when they'd left the hospital, and
Allison had respected that, letting the tall woman take the time
she needed to work through that information, to come to terms
with it. All she could do was be there for her, supporting her,
reassuring her that the only reason either of those men had a
chance now was because of her, and no one else.

Gazing at the mountaineer now, Allison wondered not for
the first time at how quickly she'd recovered from her experience and regained her strength, showing very little signs of the
harrowing experience she'd been through. Ricky was still putting weight back on, they both were, and there were still a few
drawn lines in the white circles about her eyes where her goggles
had been, but other than that, her recovery had been nothing
short of amazing.

The waiter reappeared with Allison's burger and fries.

"Please?" Blue puppy dog eyes captured her, vanquished
her.

"Oh, go ahead," Allison relented, smiling. She pushed her
plate towards the center of the table. As if she could deny Ricky

Bouchard anything.

"Gee, thanks!" With childlike delight, the mountaineer tucked in, spearing a hot French fry.

Allison watched her partner enjoying herself. She could not help but notice how Ricky's rich dark hair seemed to shimmer in the glow of their tableside candle, how the planes of her face were highlighted, her features so noble, so beautiful in the amber half-light.

Ricky's survival, along with Dorje's and Anatoli's, would go down as one of the great stories of mountaineering. How could she, Allison Peabody, hope to ever measure up to such a legend?

The one-time stockbroker's eyes flickered to the register cases.

To the names that history would remember, even as it inevitably forgot those whose signatures were missing—those who'd made the summit, only to perish on the descent.

People like Phil Christy.

"Pretty impressive, huh?" the mountaineer said, following Allison's gaze.

"Yeah." She forced a smile. "All those names... So many famous people. People I've only read about. It's hard to think that somebody like me belongs up there."

"But you do belong," Ricky told her. She regarded her closely, sensing the subtle change in her mood. "You do."

From the corner of her eye, Allison noticed a tall, thin blonde approaching their table. "You ready, Veronique?" The woman, about 40 years of age and standing nearly to Ricky's height, handed the mountaineer a Sharpie.

Ricky stood, motioning to Allison to do the same. "Yeah, Gilly, thanks."

With a friendly, open smile on her face, Gillian Whitby, the Rum Doodle's manager, led the way to the bar. "What is this— three times now for you?"

"Yes," the mountaineer replied, winking at Allison. "But who's counting?"

To Allison's great consternation, as they approached the register the bar's lights began to blink. And a drum roll and rim-shot sounded from out of nowhere.

"What's going on?" Allison turned to Ricky, alarmed.

"We are," the mountaineer rumbled, placing steadying hands on her shoulders. "Don't worry. It'll be quick."

"Just us?" Allison's squeezed out hoarsely as she felt the
eyes of the bar patrons upon her.

The mountaineer flashed her a rakish grin. "Yep!"

"You knew this—you knew!" Allison cried, even as Gillian
Whitby's amplified voice began to announce them both, including a brief account of their recent exploits.

"Well, I *do* have some prior experience with this, you
know."

Allison took in a deep breath of air, trying to calm her rattled nerves, letting the warmth of Ricky's smile soothe her, the
touch of her hand on her shoulder, anchor her.

And suddenly the crowd was cheering, with loud, bawdy
wolf whistles scattered amongst the applause.

"Okay." Ricky handed Allison the Sharpie. "You first."

Ricky gently spun her around to face the open register. And
once again the stark reality of it all smacked her full in the face.

No. No way! A ripple of panic swept through her. To have
her name added to such an illustrious group—to this exclusive
club who in decades past would never have willingly accepted an
amateur such as herself as a member—it didn't feel right. And
to have her name be forever linked this way to the famous Veronique Bouchard—it was simply absurd.

Ricky saw her hesitation.

And knew.

She stepped closer to the smaller woman, dropping her
mouth to her ear so as to be heard over the raucous yells of the
crowd. "You earned this, Allison," she said firmly. "You made
it every step of the way, on your own." A pause. "If you don't
sign it, I won't."

"Ricky!" Allison snapped her head up, only to find herself
trapped by a pair of piercing blue eyes. "Your name's got to go
up there. It's only right!"

"I'm not going anywhere," she said slowly, evenly, "without
my climbing partner. You got that?"

Allison swallowed, hard. She got it.

She turned and signed the register, and quickly Ricky did
the same, adding her bold script beneath Allison's signature.
Amidst more cheers and applause, they made their way back to
their table, accepting congratulations along the way. The register case was carefully locked up, and the music started up
again—the Rolling Stones' *I Can't Get No Satisfaction* for about
the third time that night.

Their chairs scraped against the wooden floor as they slowly sat down. Allison could feel the heat of the mountaineer's gaze on her, regarding her carefully. She decided to bluff her way out of it and took a bite of her hamburger. But it was cold, and she could detect the blandness of its taste now, and it was all she could do to swallow it down.

"I couldn't have done it without you, Allison. You know that, don't you?"

A round of quart-sized beers suddenly showed up at their table.

"Compliments of the house," the bartender said, before diving back into the crowd.

Ricky nodded and gave Gillian Whitby a "thank you" wave.

"Oh, c'mon," Allison groaned. She took a gulp of the beer, hoping to kill the taste of the burger. "You could climb that thing blindfolded."

"No."

The tone of Ricky's voice, the serious set to her face, immediately got Allison's attention.

"That...night, in that snow cave." She hesitated, glancing out over the crowded bar, gathering herself, before returning her attention to Allison. "Dorje and Anatoli were fading in and out of it...and it was all I could do, to just try and keep it together, you know?"

"Oh, Ricky—" Allison felt her heart constrict at obvious pain her partner was in, remembering.

"All...all I could think of," the mountaineer lowered her eyes to the table and took Allison's hand in her own, "was that no matter what, I had to get back to you." She looked up and blinked through thick dark lashes. "That's what kept me going. Knowing you were down there, waiting for me."

Allison gave Ricky's hand a reassuring squeeze. "I would have waited for you forever, you know."

The mountaineer dipped her head, blinking away a tear. "I know."

They stayed that way for some moments, oblivious to the noise, the celebration, the smoke drifting around them. Two hearts, connected. Feeling that connection and treasuring it for the thing of wonder that it was.

"So," Allison sighed at last, pushing her plate away, "what's next?"

"Well," Ricky drawled, a smile playing at the corner of her

lips, "I thought maybe another drink or two...maybe a dance if things get crazy enough. Then," she leered suggestively at her companion, "who knows?"

"I *meant*," Allison said primly, knowing very well that the mountaineer had understood her original question, "what *next*? You know. The big picture. We've got a load of gear sitting at the airport, with no forwarding address."

"We could just be a couple of climbing bums for a while," Ricky grinned. "Nothing wrong with that, eh? I thought we could maybe do Gasherbrum II."

"Someday. After a nice, warm break," Allison warned, giving her an arch look.

"A break—oh yeah," Ricky quickly agreed, although it was clear the thought had never occurred to her.

"Okay." Allison steepled her hands together. A plan. It was good to have a plan. "That's one thing. Anything else on your mind?"

"Well," the mountaineer shifted uncomfortably, "as a matter of fact—"

"What?" The blonde leaned forward, interested.

"Ah, I got a fax back at the hotel. From a buddy of mine, Ty Halsey." She rubbed nervously at the back of her neck. "He's an editor for some magazine down in the States. It's crazy!" She skeptically shook her head. "He wanted me to do an article for him before I took this job. Now, he's all over it, of course. Looking for a woman's account—'battling for survival on Everest,' or some such fluff. I've told him 'no' a dozen times, but he keeps after me."

"Who's he work for?" Allison wanted to know, drinking from her beer.

"Uh..." The mountaineer's tan brow furrowed. "*Intrepid Magazine*?"

Allison nearly choked.

"Do you know it?" Ricky's face showed only mild interest.

"*Know* it, I'm a freaking subscriber! Ricky, that's wonderful!" the younger woman enthused.

"Yeah, well, I'm no writer." She pushed back in her chair and began to intently regard the ceiling.

"And I'm no mountaineer," Allison countered. "But that didn't stop me from getting to the top of the world's highest mountain...with a little help." She paused, gauging her partner's level of interest. Her slouched indifference could not hide from her the fact that, knowing Ricky as she did, if she truly hadn't been interested in the opportunity, she wouldn't have raised the subject in the first place. "Look," she said, "if you want—I'd be happy to help you with it."

An eyebrow lifted. "Yeah?"

"Yeah. That is, only if you wanted me to, of course."

"You know," Ricky sighed, thinking, "I've always wished there was a way to let people see what I see when I climb, you know? To feel what I feel, as though they were right there, themselves."

"You can. You *have,* Ricky," Allison said. "With me. You were an amazing guide."

The mountaineer waggled her hand. "Ah, beginner's luck."

"Luck had nothing to do with it, Ricky Bouchard, and you know it!" Allison's eyes sparked. "You could have done a hundred times better than Jim did at running that operation. In fact," she continued, warming to the idea, "that's something else you could do. Start your own company!"

Ricky looked at her sternly. "That takes money, Allison."

"And I say, we're in this together, okay? If I can help, I can help. So shut up and deal."

The mountaineer matched her gaze in fiery intensity for a moment, before she suddenly relaxed. "Gee—is this our first fight?

Allison felt the tension immediately drain from her body. "How quickly they forget." The corner of her mouth turned up in a wry smile. "Try about our 100th."

"Oh, yeah," Ricky said ruefully, slowly grinning, recognizing the truth in that statement.

"The point is," Allison continued more calmly, "that there are a lot of options open to you." She fell silent for a moment, and then a crimson blush lit her cheeks. "God, listen to me. We've only been together a month, and here I am already trying to run your life."

"I dunno," the mountaineer's face split into an open smile. "I kind of like the sound of that, actually." But the smile faded as she focused her eyes on Allison. Searching. Concerned. "But what about your plans? Your big career, the life you have back in New York—"

"The life I *had.*" Allison corrected her. "It was a sham, Ricky," she said, letting her heart speak for her. "It meant nothing—I can see that now. And it wasn't a life—at least not for me." She bit her lip. "Being with you...wherever you are...now *that's* what I call living."

"Really?"

Allison could see the barely shielded hopefulness in Ricky's eyes, see the tense set to her lithely muscled form. All she wanted to do was throw herself into her arms and tell her how much she loved her, that she would never hurt her, and that she was hers, forever.

"Really."

"Okay?" Still a touch of veiled anxiety.

"Okay."

Ricky grinned broadly then and visibly relaxed. "In that case," she leaned forward, her blue eyes sparkling with excitement, "let me tell you more about G-II."

"Oh, no you don't," Allison groaned.

"C'mon!" The mountaineer smirked. "If we leave tomorrow, we can be there in a week."

"No!"

"The trek to Base Camp is a little rough, but—"

"Wait—wait, wait, *wait* just a minute!" Allison threw up her hands in a "stop" sign.

"What?" Ricky cried out, as though she'd received the most grievous of injuries.

"If you think you can talk me into climbing Gasherbrum II—"

The mountaineer folded her arms. "Yeah?"

"Without first buying me another drink," Allison's green eyes danced, "then I think you've got frostbite on the brain," she finished, feeling quite triumphant.

Without removing her eyes from Allison, the mountaineer reached out and grabbed at a passing waiter. "Two more," she barked, sending him scurrying away to fill the order.

And suddenly Ricky's hand was on Allison's again, and she could feel the heat, feel the intensity radiating from the tall woman, burning her, scorching her skin.

"Just watch me thaw, baby." In the flickering glow of the candlelight Ricky's voice was low—a thrilling, seductive promise in the dark. "Watch me."

Be sure to read these other books by

Belle Reilly

Darkness Before the Dawn

A troubled Captain Catherine Phillips plans for this flight to Rome to be her last in the employ of Orbis Airlines. Unfulfilled by her job and adrift in her personal life, the only solution she sees is to quit—to run away—as she's done in the past. But a band of terrorist hijackers, as well as a gutsy young flight attendant Rebecca Hanson, throw a wrench into Catherine's plans. The pilot is forced to come to terms with the demons of her past even as she struggles to save her crippled aircraft and the lives of all aboard.

ISBN 1-930928-06-8

Roman Holiday

Orbis Airline pilot Catherine Phillips grudgingly decides to spend a lay over in Rome with Rebecca Hanson, keeping a protective eye on the recovering flight attendant. The two women are soon caught up in the magical splendor of the eternal City, seeing the sights and drawing ever closer to one another in the process.

ISBN 0-9674196-3-8

Storm Front

From the moment she receives a middle of the night phone call notifying her of a downed passenger jet, Captain Catherine Phillips, director of Orbis Airlines' new strategic operations unit, finds herself drawn deeper and deeper into the dark, dangerous world of international terrorism. Aided by a reliable investigative team including flight attendant Rebecca Hanson, Catherine quickly realizes the evidence from the terrible crash points to one terrorist in particular, a zealot who will stop at nothing to achieve his fundamentalist ends. In a cat and mouse game that spans the globe, Kate and Becky soon find themselves caught up in a desperate race against time, and the odds, where they must fight to hang onto one another, as well as their very lives.

ISBN: 1-930928-19-X

These and other great titles are available from the publisher at www.rapbooks.biz, or from booksellers everywhere.

Other titles from
Quest Books

Vendetta
By Talaran
ISBN 1-930928-56-4

Blue Holes to Terror
By Trish Kocialski
ISBN 1-930928-61-0

Staying in the Game
By Nann Dunne
ISBN 1-930928-60-2

Gun Shy
By Lori L. Lake
ISBN 1-930928-59-9

Murder Mystery Series: Book One
By Anne Azel
ISBN 1-930928-72-6

Available at booksellers everywhere.

Coming soon from
Quest Books

October Echoes
By Roselle Graskey

Under the Gun
By Lori L. Lake

Shield of Justice
By Radclyffe

Deadly Challenge
By Trish Kocialski

A lover of travel and adventure all her life, Belle Reilly currently lives in southeastern Pennsylvania, where she enjoys a somewhat less perilous existence than the exciting characters she creates. "The most excitement I have on some days," Belle says, "is keeping Ginger-the-cat at paw's length from my pair of lovebirds." Readers will remember Belle Reilly from her thrilling Catherine Phillips and Rebecca Hanson series: three novels full of action and romance, whose stories, at times, sadly presaged current world events. In her latest novel, *High Intensity*, Belle Reilly introduces us to a pair of new characters: stoic mountaineer Ricky Bouchard and adrenaline-junkie stockbroker Allison Peabody. Before we can strap on our crampons or clip into a rope, Belle sweeps us up onto a wild ride that takes romance and adventure to dizzying, impossible heights.

Printed in the United States
4624